W9-BAF-794

Mail-Order Mishaps

The Bride's Dilemma ©2019 by Susan Page Davis
Romancing the Rancher ©2019 by Linda Ford
The Marriage Sham ©2019 by Vickie McDonough
The Galway Girl ©2019 by Erica Vetsch

Print ISBN 978-1-64352-000-1

eBook Editions:
Adobe Digital Edition (.epub) 978-1-64352-002-5
Kindle and MobiPocket Edition (.prc) 978-1-64352-001-8

All rights reserved. No part of this publication may be reproduced or transmitted for commercial purposes, except for brief quotations in printed reviews, without written permission of the publisher.

All scripture quotations are taken from the King James Version of the Bible.

This book is a work of fiction. Names, characters, places, and incidents are either products of the author's imagination or used fictitiously. Any similarity to actual people, organizations, and/or events is purely coincidental.

Cover Image: Ildiko Neer / Trevillion Images

Published by Barbour Books, an imprint of Barbour Publishing, Inc., 1810 Barbour Drive, Uhrichsville, Ohio 44683, www.barbourbooks.com

Our mission is to inspire the world with the life-changing message of the Bible.

 Member of the
Evangelical Christian
Publishers Association

Printed in Canada.

Mail-Order Mishaps

4 Brides Adapt When Marriage Plans Go Awry

Susan Page Davis
Linda Ford
Vickie McDonough
Erica Vetsch

BARBOUR BOOKS
An Imprint of Barbour Publishing, Inc.

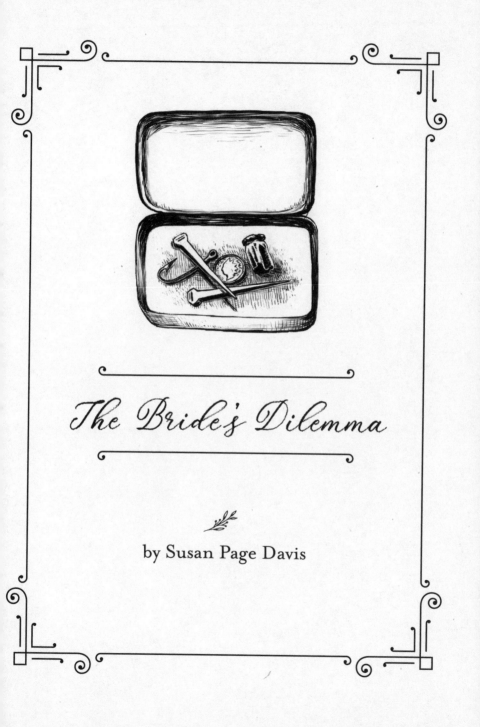

The Bride's Dilemma

by Susan Page Davis

Chapter 1

Cheyenne, Wyoming, 1883

With his mail-order bride arriving tomorrow, Caleb didn't need any distractions, least of all a fight. But as he passed the open stable door, a yelp jerked him out of his reverie.

"You lazy whelp!"

Crack, followed by another yelp. It sounded like a woman—or a kid. That was it, the boy who worked for the stable owner was crying out, and from the sounds of things, Buck Tinan was thrashing him.

Without stopping to consider the consequences, Caleb dashed inside. Sure enough, the big stable owner loomed over the cowering boy. Willy, his name was. An orphan, unless Caleb was mistaken, about twelve years old.

"I oughta strip your hide off," Buck roared. He raised his hand with a whip in it, but when he flicked the lash back over his shoulder in preparation for another blow, Caleb caught the end and jerked it. Buck stumbled backward.

"Wha—" He whirled to face Caleb. "Blair! What's the meaning of this?"

"You're whipping that boy," Caleb said. "What's the meaning of *that*?"

Buck glared at him. "Yon Willy needs a lesson in hard work."

"Well, that's no way to teach him. If your help doesn't know how to do the job right, it's because you didn't teach him. He doesn't deserve a whipping."

"That's up to me," Buck said. "You've got no right coming in here and telling me what to do." He lunged forward, raising the whip.

Before Buck could use the lash on him, Caleb dove forward, butting his head into Buck's midsection. They both sprawled on the floor. Buck gasped in a breath, and Caleb seized the whip and tossed it across the dirt floor between the stalls. Several horses snorted and shifted. Caleb balled his fist and shook it in Buck's face.

"You want more?"

"Get off me!"

Caleb stood. Buck fumbled until he grasped the edge of a stall divider and pulled himself up.

"You can't do that, Blair."

"I just did." Caleb shook his head. "Tinan, you bought three horses off me last month. If I came by and saw you lighting into one of them like you were that boy, I'd wallop you just as hard. You're supposed to train that kid to be a decent citizen, able to support himself and not be a burden on society. You're not supposed to abuse him."

"Why, you—"

The train whistle cut through the warm afternoon air, reminding Caleb that Miss Martin would be on tomorrow's train, and he hadn't done his shopping yet.

"I got to go," Caleb said. "You keep your hands off that kid and treat him right, or I'll report you to the sheriff."

Buck's lip curled. "Just do that. I'm sure the sheriff will tell you the same thing I am. *Mind your own business.*"

The whistle wailed again. Caleb hesitated. The boy had crept into an empty stall, but Caleb could see him crouching behind the divider. He was wearing a scarlet plaid shirt, and bits of color showed in the cracks between the boards of the dividing wall.

"You all right, Willy?" he called.

Buck stiffened, clenching his fists, but the boy replied softly, "Yes, sir."

"All right, then." Caleb nodded at Buck. "You'd best explain to him what you want done, and I mean with words, not with that whip."

"Get out of here," Buck yelled, stepping toward him.

Caleb didn't like to leave, but where did he draw the line? He turned on his heel and walked out. Maybe he ought to pause long enough to alert the sheriff to Tinan's behavior before going to the store. Or maybe he should have brought the boy along with him. He could take Willy to his ranch and give him chores there in exchange for his bed and board. Yes, that might be best. After he settled his bill at the store, he could stop back by the stable and ask Willy if he wanted to work on the Blair ranch instead of at the stable in town. The boy would probably jump at the chance, though Buck wouldn't be happy.

He squared his shoulders and focused on thoughts of the woman he was to meet. Eve Martin, soon to be Mrs. Blair. How would she feel about finding he'd taken on a boy? No, he told himself. His mission today was to stock up on staples for the kitchen and maybe a few new incidentals—new dish towels, for instance. What would she like to find in her new kitchen? That was today's question.

He stopped outside the store and swiveled his head to the left. The sheriff's office was only a couple of doors down. With a sigh, he turned toward it.

Sheriff Nichols, a fiftyish, no-nonsense man who carried about forty pounds more than Caleb did, looked up as he opened the door.

"Help you, Blair?"

"Yeah." Caleb walked in and shut the door behind him. "I was wondering about that boy, Willy, over at the stable."

The sheriff grunted. "What about him?"

"I was thinking he might be better off with somebody else."

"What do you mean?"

"Well, when I come by there just now, Buck Tinan was going at him with a whip."

Nichols pushed his chair back, got up, and walked over to the small woodstove in the corner. He picked up the coffeepot, shook it gently, then poured himself a cup. When he turned around, he arched his eyebrows.

"And?"

"Well, he can't just beat the boy like that."

"What did you do?"

"Stopped him."

Nichols took a sip of his coffee then walked slowly over to his desk and sat down. He may have experience and some respect in town, Caleb thought, but he was getting too old and too slow for this job.

"Is the boy all right?" Nichols asked at last.

"He said he was."

"And how's Buck taking it?"

"He's mad."

"You realize you may have caused the boy more trouble in the future?"

Caleb squared his shoulders. "Which is why I'd like to take him out to my ranch. I wouldn't hit him, Sheriff. I'd treat him good, and I'd look out for him."

"Not happening."

"Why not?"

Nichols sipped his coffee again and made a face, then set down the mug. "Tinan signed papers on that boy."

"He's adopted him?"

"He's his legal guardian. I can't change that, and neither can you."

Caleb frowned and stepped closer to the desk. "Even if we make a complaint saying he mistreats the boy? Can't you remove the kid from Tinan's care?"

Nichols shook his head. "That's only done in extreme cases. And I've got no proof."

"I'll bet you would have if you checked that boy over for bruises and scars. He's no doubt got fresh welts under his shirt right now, and maybe cuts."

"Do you want to sign a formal complaint, accusing Tinan of assaulting the boy?"

Caleb thought about that for only a second. "Sure. I'll do that."

"And then he'll press charges on you for assaulting *him*."

"I was protecting the boy."

"Your word against his."

Caleb brought his fist down on the desk. "You've got to do something. You gonna wait until he kills that kid?"

"Easy," Nichols said. "Looks like your temper's a bit jumpy too. Why should I put a child in your care, out on a ranch three miles from town? It would be harder to check on him there than it is at Tinan's."

Caleb's head whirled. Was Nichols checking on the boy here in town? He sincerely doubted it. He got the impression the sheriff was protecting Buck Tinan. A thought occurred to him, and he raised his chin. "Sheriff, I'm getting married. My fiancée is arriving on the westbound train tomorrow, and we expect to tie the knot right quick. We'd make a good home for the boy, a real family."

Nichols studied him through slits of eyes. "Does the future Mrs. Blair agree to that?"

"Well, I. . .truth is, I haven't had a chance to discuss it with her yet. This just happened, and she's traveling. . ."

"That's what I thought." Nichols stood, signaling their chat was over. "Look, about all I can do is talk to Buck Tinan. If I see marks on the boy, I'll tell Judge Curtis I have a complaint that the boy is being overly disciplined."

"Whipped," Caleb said. "Tinan was flogging him with a horsewhip."

Nichols nodded. "All right, fair enough. You write that down and sign it. Bring it to me tomorrow, and I'll see the judge gets it. He's off on his circuit right now, but he should be back next week."

"Next week?" That was far too long for Willy to stay in his situation.

"You heard me," Nichols said. "Now go on. And congratulations. Bring Mrs. Blair by after the nuptials if she's agreeable, and we'll look into you taking the boy. Otherwise, I don't see any point in pursuing it."

Caleb wanted to tear out his hair, but that would be pointless too.

"Fine." He turned on his heel and went out, shutting the door none too softly. He walked toward the general store, trying to stop thinking about Willy. He needed to concentrate on Eve Martin. What would Eve like to see in her kitchen? And would she agree to take in a boy? But first, and more importantly, once she got here and heard all about this, would she still want to marry him? At least he didn't have a black eye from his encounter with Buck. If he did, she might take one look and get right back on the train.

Eve Martin stared out the window of the railway carriage. The plains were so different from her home back in Pennsylvania. Grasslands spread out on both sides of the tracks, with hardly a tree in sight. Until this journey, she'd been used to forests and gently rolling hills covered with pastures and farmers' tilled fields. This untamed land frightened her a little.

She'd seen such wonders since leaving home, and she'd had several moments when her heart raced and she fleetingly considered turning back. Like the ride across the bridge over the broad Mississippi River. It was over a mile long, and all she could see was murky, swirling water and a few barges and a steamboat puttering along. She'd feared they would never reach the other side—that the bridge would collapse and they would plunge into the roiling, muddy current.

But they'd all survived, and once she was on the Missouri side of the river, she hadn't much heart for crossing it again. So she'd gone on, and the sights that had rewarded her—why, she could scarcely believe half of it. The vast emptiness that was the West awed her. Some of the places they'd stopped had no town at all, just a water tower and sometimes a shoddy little station cobbled together out of poor lumber, with seemingly endless land spreading out in all directions around it.

Was Cheyenne a proper town or just a handful of buildings? She'd seen a few big towns on the way, but settlers hadn't been living out here for more than thirty years or so. There couldn't possibly be a city out here, could there? Forts, perhaps, and little communities where wagon train people had stopped and settled, but she had it in her mind that there were no cities between here and San Francisco. As they drew closer to her destination, she grew more anxious.

What if Caleb wasn't there to meet her? What if Indians crowded about the depot?

She turned to the man sitting beside her. He looked genteel, like a middle-aged banker with graying hair, and he had spoken politely to her after he boarded the train earlier in the day but had not bothered her during their four hours as seatmates.

"Have you ever been to Cheyenne?" she asked.

He smiled. "I've lived there for three years, young lady. Is this your first visit?"

"Yes. We won't see the mountains, will we?"

"Not the Rockies, no, ma'am. The Laramie Mountains aren't far, though, nor the Medicine Bow range, but they're not as big or as splendid as the Rockies."

"I see." Eve thought about that. "I live near the Poconos."

"Ah, Pennsylvania."

She smiled. "That's right. They're impressive, but from what I'm told, the western mountains far outstrip them."

"To be sure. Have you had a pleasant journey so far?"

She wasn't certain how to answer that. "Well, the part where we crossed the Mississippi was frightening."

He chuckled. "Did you cross on the Eads Bridge?"

"Yes, and from all the tales my father told before I left home, I fully expected the bridge to give way and the train to fall into the river."

"Oh no. It's a sturdy bridge. All steel construction."

"So I've heard." Eve sighed. "My father was not convinced."

"Well, it's considered a great engineering feat. Have you heard about how the builders had a circus man take an elephant over it before they allowed people on the bridge?"

"Yes, and I know a lot of trains have passed safely over by now. I think my father was trying to discourage me from making the journey."

"I see."

"Other than that, I admit I've seen some amazing sights. But I haven't seen any Indians, nor any buffalo."

"Not many buffalo left," he said with a sad tinge to his voice.

Eve hesitated then confessed, "This last part has frankly been boring."

She watched the uneven land, like unfenced pasture as far as she could see, whip past for a minute, then turned back to her companion.

"What's Cheyenne like? Is it a good-sized town?"

He laughed. "Oh yes."

"I thought maybe it was a little hamlet, or a fort."

"Why, miss, it's the temporary capital. Cheyenne is a regular city."

"Really?" Eve wasn't sure if that was good or bad.

"There's a fort," he went on, "but the railroad is the heart of things. It draws in all sorts."

"So there are stores and. . . ?"

"Land, yes. Hotels, banks, churches, freight companies, all sorts of businesses. Not as big as St. Louis, mind you, but a healthy, growing city."

"Oh." She eyed him carefully. "And what do you do, sir?"

He grinned at her. "I own two saloons."

Eve swallowed hard. He looked so respectable.

"And what brings you to Cheyenne?" he asked.

Eve felt her cheeks heat. "I'm getting married. My fiancé owns a ranch outside Cheyenne."

"Good for you!" He nodded, his eyes twinkling at her. "Best wishes."

"Thank you."

"My name's Downing," he said. "If you ever need assistance, call on me. You can always find me at either the White Pony or the Willow Tree."

Eve nodded soberly.

Mr. Downing chuckled. "Perhaps you'd best not come to the Pony. It's not the place for ladies. The Willow Tree is quieter, and we serve meals there during the day. Local folks come in for breakfast or dinner. By suppertime it's a rowdier crowd, though, so come early if you want to inquire for me. If you can't find me there, leave a message. It will reach me without delay."

"Thank you. That's kind of you." She doubted she would ever call upon a saloon owner for assistance, but even so, he seemed a thoughtful man, and so far he had treated her with respect.

The train's whistle keened, and Eve jumped. "Where are we now?"

"Just a small place, an outpost really, with water and fuel for the train. We may sit here awhile." He reached inside his jacket. "Allow me to buy you a drink, Miss. . ."

"Martin. But no, thank you." Eve clasped the handle of her pocketbook tightly. Let it never be said that she had allowed a saloon keeper to buy her liquid refreshment.

She turned back to the window. Outside, a few yards away, three mounted men whooped as they drove a herd of about two dozen cattle past the train. Dust wafted in through the open windows, and passengers hurried to close them. Eve pulled hers shut, but not before she sneezed. She rummaged in her pocket for a handkerchief.

"They're bringing those cattle from the holding pens yonder. Probably going to load them on the train right now." Downing rose. "Well, excuse me. I think I'll find something to drink. All this dust, along with the smoke from the engine, makes my throat dry."

She could almost sympathize. If only she'd thought he would bring her water, she would have accepted his offer.

Instead, she sank back in the corner of the seat and watched out the window as the horsemen urged the cattle onward. The herd must be boarding several cars back. She could hear plenty of yelling and lowing as the stockmen did their work. Even with the window shut, she made out a string of curses.

She took a deep breath in an effort to calm herself. Would life be this rough on Caleb's ranch? She had imagined it as a peaceful haven for the two of them, but now she realized he might have some hired men to help him. He raised horses, and one man couldn't do it all alone, could he? He hadn't mentioned any employees in his letters. He had written that he had a quarter section, which she'd learned was a hundred and sixty acres. That seemed like a lot, but maybe he needed that much grassland.

A cowpuncher trotted past on a spotted horse and met Eve's gaze as she stared at him through the glass. He grinned at her, and his expression turned to a leer. He shifted in his saddle so he could watch her a moment longer.

Eve shuddered and forced herself to look away.

Beyond her ability to stand up to the harsher life out here, one thing bothered her. In her letters she had dared to hint at a family skeleton. She was reluctant to put the matter on paper but told Caleb she would if he wanted a full explanation before they were married. In Caleb's reply, he had assured her that he wouldn't judge her on something her kinfolk had done. That relieved Eve's mind greatly, and she had said no more, but now her thoughts began to nag her once again. When he knew what had happened years ago, would he change his mind?

"Next stop Cheyenne!"

She must tell him everything before she married him. If she didn't, she knew it would always haunt her. As desperate as she was to begin a new life, and as fiercely as she wished to become the wife of this upstanding, seemingly kind and forgiving man, she would rather know his reaction now than have him learn about the past later and regret tying himself to her.

Eve pulled in a deep breath. What would she do if he turned out to be mean or dishonest?

No. The man who wrote those letters was a good man. He *had* to be. She couldn't misread things that badly. She had held off for months before she accepted his proposal, asking questions and wanting to be sure she was doing the right thing. She swallowed hard, her throat scratchy from the dust. Caleb would take care of her, and she would help him build his ranch. They would have a good life together.

She closed her eyes for a moment and put her future in God's hands.

The train whistle pierced the air as Caleb halted his team near the depot. He was getting married, or at least meeting the woman he planned to marry. The preacher had assured him that if Miss Martin wanted to wait a day or two to give herself a chance to rest, there was no problem. They could hold the wedding whenever they were ready.

He wished he'd gotten to town earlier so he could check on Willy.

When he'd gone back to the stable yesterday after his trip to the general store, no one was about. The horses were out in Buck's corrals, munching on hay, and there was no sign of the owner or the boy.

Caleb had gone home frustrated. Maybe he should have insisted on taking the boy to the ranch despite what the sheriff said. At this point, he wasn't sure what would have been the wisest choice, and he mulled it over as he kept walking. He'd written out his complaint about Buck's behavior last night, but he didn't have time to deliver it to Sheriff Nichols now. He could hear the train chugging. In just a couple of minutes, it would ease up to the platform, and the brakes would shriek as it slowed.

He'd stocked up on food at the general store and tried to anticipate Eve's cooking needs. He had an old, battered coffeepot at his cabin on the ranch. He'd used it every day for years. But maybe the new Mrs. Blair would prefer a cup of tea. He'd splurged on a china teapot and a pound of the best India tea. What else would Eve like? He had an idea that women set a lot of store by curtains, but he didn't feel qualified to pick out something along those lines. He'd mention it to her and tell her to get something she liked.

He tied up the team, climbed the steps to the platform, and leaned against the wall of the station, letting out a deep sigh. Even though he felt good about the coming meeting, his chest muscles tightened, and he forced himself to breathe slowly and deeply.

He was none too early, but he'd made it on time. A dozen people milled about, some waiting to greet relatives or acquaintances, others prepared to unload freight. He anticipated the moment Eve stepped down from the train. Would she recognize him from the picture he'd sent? Would her eyes light when she spotted him? His pulse picked up, and he breathed again, in and out, as the whistle wailed. Only a minute now.

"I need you to come with me, Blair."

Caleb whipped his head around and stared at Sheriff Nichols. "Now?"

"Yes, now."

"What for?" Maybe Nichols had reconsidered about the boy.

"We need to talk."

"But—" Caleb looked down the tracks. He could see the engine. It was close, and the brakes began to squeal.

"Come on." Nichols seized his arm and tugged.

"But Sheriff, you don't understand."

"I do. Your lady's on the train. I'll see that she's told."

"No! I'll come see you after I collect her. Ten minutes, that's all I need, and we'll both come over to your office."

"Sorry, Blair, but I need you now."

"What's so urgent?"

Nichols's grip on his wrist tightened. "It's Buck Tinan. He's dead."

❧ Chapter 2 ❧

*E*ve clutched the conductor's hand and stepped down onto the platform, her heart pounding. Beyond the station, she could see crowded streets and substantial buildings. To one side was a vast array of corrals, some of which were filled with restless, lowing cattle, beyond them large bins and a grain elevator. Mr. Downing was right—Cheyenne was bigger than she'd imagined. People hurried past her, greeting travelers and claiming baggage. She looked around for the lanky brown-haired rancher who had mailed her his picture.

"Miss Martin?"

She looked up. A red-haired man walked toward her, holding his wide-brimmed hat in his hand. He was considerably older than her, perhaps forty, and his face was broad and somber. Definitely not Caleb Blair. Then she noticed the metal star on the front of his plaid cotton shirt.

"Yes?"

He smiled apologetically. "Howdy, ma'am. I'm Deputy Randall. The sheriff asked me to meet you and let you know that Mr. Blair's over at the jailhouse."

Eve's heart lurched. "I'm sorry?" Surely she'd heard him wrong.

"Caleb Blair? Isn't he the one you're meeting up with?" The deputy gazed at her anxiously.

"Well yes, I expected him."

"He's delayed, ma'am."

"Oh." She felt a little light-headed and glanced about the bustling platform. All around them ranchmen, freighters, railroad men, miners, and travelers dressed in their best surged toward their destinations. Her nightmare had materialized; Caleb was not here to meet her. *Lord, have mercy!*

She gazed at Mr. Randall and inhaled deeply. "What should I do?"

"The sheriff suggested you check in at a hotel or a boardinghouse. He says you can see Mr. Blair in the morning if you want."

"In the—" Eve sucked in a painful breath. "Are you saying Mr. Blair is incarcerated?"

He seemed to consider that, his eyes roaming skyward and then returning to her face. "Yes, ma'am. At least for now he is. The sheriff took him in for questioning."

"I—" Eve reached tentatively toward him as the platform began to sway. "Is there someplace I could sit down?"

"Of course, ma'am." Randall grasped her arm and eased her toward a bench against the wall of the building. "Right over here."

"Thank you." Eve plopped onto it and pulled in a deep breath.

She was short on sleep and food, and now, it seemed, oxygen. But she would *not* faint on the depot platform during her first five minutes in Cheyenne. Her throat constricted, defying her resolve.

"Miss Martin? Are you all right?"

She looked up into her erstwhile seatmate's concerned face.

"Oh Mr. Downing. It's kind of you to ask. It seems my—my fiancé is delayed."

Downing looked at the deputy. "Hello, Randall. What's going on?"

Randall cleared his throat. "Mr. Blair has been detained," he said stiffly.

"He's in jail," Eve blurted. She shot a glance around, fearing she'd just alerted the entire population, but no one else seemed to be paying attention to them.

Downing frowned. "Is that right, Randall? What happened?"

"It's nothing," the deputy said quickly. "It's just that Sheriff Nichols needed to talk to him, that's all."

"No, that is not all." Eve felt stronger now that Mr. Downing was at her side and appeared ready to take her part. "You said I can't see him until tomorrow."

Downing's eyebrows drew together. "Why not, Randall? Too much prenuptial celebrating?"

"No, nothing like that. It's just that someone was killed last night, and the sheriff needed to talk to Blair about it."

"Killed?" Eve squeaked. It got worse and worse.

Downing's shoulders straightened. "Who was killed?"

"That fellow at the stable, Tinan," the deputy said.

"Buck Tinan?"

"You know him?" Eve asked.

"Sure. He's a regular customer at the White Pony." Downing

glanced at her apologetically, and Eve remembered that he'd said the Pony was the less genteel of his two saloons.

"Well, someone put an end to him last night." Randall avoided eye contact with either of them.

"At my saloon?" Mr. Downing demanded.

"No, no. Over to the stable."

Downing's features relaxed a little. "And the sheriff thinks Mr. Blair did it?"

"I didn't say that." Randall squared his shoulders. "Look, I'm just following orders. The sheriff told me a minute ago to come fetch Miss Martin off the train and see her to a hotel, and to tell her she can see Blair in the morning. That's all I know."

Eve stood on shivering legs. "I want to see him now."

"Not until morning, miss."

She turned to Mr. Downing, hoping he could do something for her. He was a businessman, and he was obviously used to taking charge.

"What should I do, Mr. Downing?"

He pulled out his pocket watch and looked at it. "Well, it's getting late. I suggest you let Deputy Randall do as he suggested. Find a respectable place to stay tonight and get some dinner. Then, first thing in the morning—"

"I insist on going to the sheriff's office tonight," Eve said.

Randall sighed. "Can't let you do that, miss."

She raised her chin. "I don't see how you can stop me."

"The lady has a point," Downing said. "It's a free country, and if she wants to walk over to the jailhouse, she has a right." He gave her a kindly smile. "Though I'd be careful, miss. When the sun goes down, things get a little rowdy in town."

"I'll go to the jail first," Eve declared, not sure that was possible

24

but determined to make it happen. "Can I leave my bags here until after?"

"Well, sure, ma'am, you can speak to the stationmaster about it," Randall said, "but it'd be out of your way to come all the way back here for 'em later."

"May I make a suggestion?" Downing asked.

"Of course," Eve said.

"There is a quiet hotel a street or two over from the sheriff's office." He looked pointedly at Randall. "On Brook Street."

"I know the place," Randall said.

"You could have Miss Martin's bags delivered to the hotel while she speaks to Sheriff Nichols."

"That sounds ideal," Eve said. "Thank you, sir."

Randall did not look as happy with the advice, but he merely scowled. "Shall we find your bags then, miss?"

Downing took his leave amid profuse expressions of gratitude from Eve. Within ten minutes, she and Randall had located her trunk, and Randall had arranged with the stationmaster to have it and her valise delivered to an establishment called Wayside Inn. Eve gave the stationmaster fifty cents to ensure this was done. At last they set off on foot.

Eve wondered how far they would have to walk. Her long fasting was beginning to catch up with her, and she felt weak, though she didn't want to say anything. If she started plying Deputy Randall with questions, it might further delay her from seeing Caleb. And she needed to see him, to find out if the accusations against him were true. *What will I do, Lord, if he's killed a man?* She swallowed hard against the painful lump in her throat.

They walked several blocks, mostly on boardwalks, but sometimes on the dusty streets, where she had to lift her skirts and watch out for horse droppings.

"Does it rain much here?" she asked as a wagon lumbered past, raising clouds of fine dust.

"Sometimes," Randall said. "And then again, sometimes it don't."

Why had she asked?

When she thought she couldn't go another step, Randall slowed. "Yonder's the jailhouse."

Eve looked ahead and saw a brick building with barred windows. The wall beside the front door held a placard reading: SHERIFF.

She paused and brushed a weary wrist across her brow. She must look a sight, and she'd had no opportunity to freshen up.

Randall seemed to read her thoughts. "Are you sure you want to go in, miss? 'Cause I can take you round to the hotel, and you can settle in and eat something and come by in the morning when you're rested."

Eve almost believed he sympathized with her, but deep down she was sure he had other motives—like not upsetting his boss, who had told him to keep her away from the jail.

"I'll go in now." She hiked up her skirt and climbed the three steps.

With a sigh, Randall joined her and opened the door for her.

Inside the dim office, a large, middle-aged man rose from behind a desk and squinted at her, then shot Randall a piercing glance.

"This is Miss Martin," Randall said. "That's Sheriff Nichols, miss."

The sheriff scowled. "I told you to help her find lodging."

"I am," Randall replied. "The Wayside. We sent her luggage, but she insisted on coming here first."

"I would like to see Caleb Blair." Eve managed to keep her voice steady.

Nichols came from behind the desk. "You'll have to come

back in the morning."

She cleared her throat. "Sir, I have come thousands of miles to see this man, and I will not be denied."

"I'm not finished questioning him," Nichols replied.

"That is neither here nor there," Eve said. "I must see Mr. Blair."

"You'll have to wait." Nichols held her gaze with a challenging air.

"Fine. Do you have a chair where I can sit?"

"You're not going to sit here all night, miss."

"Well, I'm not leaving until I see my fiancé."

They stood for a long moment, deadlocked in determination. Eve clenched her jaw, afraid she would swoon, and refused to look away.

At last he broke the impasse, turning sharply away, toward his desk.

"Five minutes." He picked up a key ring.

She exhaled. "Thank you, Sheriff."

Caleb could hear voices in the office, but he couldn't make out any distinct words. What was going on? He'd asked for legal counsel, but the sheriff had said there wasn't anyone at hand. Had he found a lawyer? He sat on the edge of the cot, trying not to think what kind of vermin made the smelly straw tick their abode. At least a half hour had passed since the train rolled in, maybe more. What was Eve doing now? She must be frantic.

At last, Sheriff Nichols came in and stopped in the small space in front of the two cells.

"You've got a visitor, Blair. Five minutes, no more."

Slowly, Caleb rose and peered past the man's husky frame. He caught a glimpse of a soft blue hat—a *woman's* hat—with a pheasant feather curling over a wisp of veil that swathed the front of its crown. He caught his breath and stumbled toward the bars as she stepped into the narrow space and the sheriff retreated past her. Nichols left a lantern hanging on a peg in the wall, and its light revealed a woman in a neat, modest dress the same color as the hat. She stood about six inches shorter than him, and her light brown hair gleamed below her hat brim in the lantern light. A smudge streaked her cheek, and her dress was covered with powdery grit.

"Hello, Caleb."

He stepped closer and sucked in a painful breath. The mail-order bride from the picture he'd received, only better. Softer, gentler, and breathing real air. In a jail. On the other side of the bars.

"Miss Martin." He could barely get it out.

"Yes, it's Eve. Are you. . .well?"

He had to think about that, but at last got out, "As well as I can be. I'm so sorry!"

"Can you tell me what happened? We haven't much time."

Caleb tried to order his thoughts, but uppermost in his mind was the fix he'd put her in. "You must despise me—bringing you here, and now here I am in this mess. Eve, you must find a place to stay tonight, and I'll pay for it."

"Don't worry about that, Caleb. The deputy is going to take me to a decent place not far from here. I shall be safe, and you mustn't worry about me. But tell me why you're here."

"It was the boy."

Eve blinked. "What boy?"

Caleb sighed. "He's an orphan boy named Willy. The man at the stable took him in, off one of those orphan trains, last spring."

Eve frowned, and Caleb wondered if she had even heard of orphan trains. Maybe not. They collected orphans from back east and shipped them out here, and folks adopted them. But some only took the children so they'd have free labor, and he feared that was what Tinan had done. A boy to clean out the stable and feed the livestock, without requiring wages. Just a couple of meals a day and a spot to sleep in the hay.

"I was in town yesterday, and I came by the stable," Caleb went on. "The door was open, and I saw Tinan whipping the boy. I made him stop."

"Heavens!" Eve put a gloved hand to her lips.

"That's how I felt. Well, Tinan and I had words. I told the sheriff, but he didn't seem inclined to do much. I stopped back in at the stable later, to check on the kid, but neither one of 'em was in the barn. I went on home and thought maybe we'd look into it today. I had a notion that we might take Willy out to the ranch, and he could stay with us and not get beaten all the time."

Eve's jaw tensed, but she said nothing. What was going on in her mind? Did she think he was a lunatic?

"That doesn't explain why you're in here," she said softly.

"Right. It seems someone else took a dislike to Tinan as well. They found him dead today."

Her eyes grew huge. After a moment, she said flatly, "And the sheriff thinks you did it."

"Afraid so."

"Because you argued with him yesterday?"

"Partly."

She stepped closer and peered at him intently. "What's the other part?"

Caleb hesitated, hating to tell her the worst part. "He was stabbed."

"Oh?"

"With my knife."

Her gaze held his for a long moment. What was going on in her mind? She only stared with those big eyes of hers.

"I missed it last night, after I got home from town," he said. "Figured I'd mislaid it somewhere, but. . .but I didn't do what they're saying."

She nodded slowly. "So, what happens now?"

"I told the sheriff I want a lawyer. He says there's none handy at the moment, but I know there are a couple in town. They follow the railroad, you know?"

She shook her head. "Will they get you someone?"

"I don't know."

She pulled in a deep breath. "I'll come back tomorrow. Maybe I can help if they haven't located anyone."

"No, Eve. I don't want you mixed up in this."

Her eyes shone with unshed tears. "Well, I'm in it."

"You should get on the first train east and not look back."

"I'm afraid they wouldn't sell me a ticket for the little I have in my purse."

Caleb tried to swallow but couldn't. "I'm so sorry. I might have enough for a return fare—I'm not certain. But if you insist on staying after tonight, you can go to my ranch and stay there. That will save you the cost of a hotel."

"We'll see."

The sheriff plodded toward them. "Time's up, miss."

Eve sniffed. "I'll come in the morning."

Caleb nodded. What else could he say?

She turned away and then looked back. "Where's the boy?"

"What?" Sheriff Nichols asked.

Eve turned to face him. "The boy, Willy, that Mr. Blair was

30

trying to help. Where is he now, if his guardian is dead?"

"That's what I'd like to know," Caleb said.

The sheriff cleared his throat. "We haven't located him yet."

"Is there a Mrs. Tinan?" Eve asked.

"No, ma'am. Buck was a bachelor."

"Have you looked for Willy?"

"Yeah," Caleb said. "Did you at least search the stable?"

"I looked around." Nichols wouldn't meet his gaze.

Eve's chin gave a stubborn hike. "If that boy is in danger, you're responsible, Sheriff."

Nichols clenched his jaw.

"Who's taking care of the horses?" Caleb demanded.

The sheriff's eyes hardened. "That's not your concern."

"Well, it better be yours. Those animals need care. And what about my team? You said you'd have someone fetch them from the depot and take them to the livery."

"Shut yer yap, Blair."

Caleb clenched his teeth. Nichols had better see his horses stabled overnight. They couldn't be left standing for hours at the depot.

Nichols turned toward Eve. "Go along now, miss. Randall will take you to your hotel."

"I'll be back in the morning," she said.

Nichols scowled as he reached for the lantern. "Don't come too early. Give us time to give the prisoner his breakfast."

Her gaze met Caleb's through the shadows. "Good night."

His chest tightened. "Good night. Thank you for coming."

They went out, and he slumped down on the cot, his head against the wall. He didn't deserve her. He was pretty sure he still had enough in the bank to send her back to Pennsylvania, and that was what he should do. He had a feeling that she would refuse to go. But he would suggest it again, as soon as she returned.

He pulled his legs up onto the cot and turned on his side.

Don't let her go, Lord.

But that was selfish. Staying here was the worst thing she could do. If they hanged him, she'd be stuck in the middle of nowhere with no family and no income. Young women in that situation never fared well in Cheyenne.

✿ Chapter 3 ✿

$\mathcal{E}$ve's room at the Wayside Inn held only an iron bed, a wash-stand, and a small wooden bench. Her trunk took up most of the limited floor space, and her valise lay open on the quilt. She tugged the bench over near the second-floor window and pushed the cur-tain back halfway. A few lights shone in the street below, and she could hear faint music, but the night was quieter than she had expected. Occasionally muted voices reached her, or the clopping of horses' hooves, but for the most part, this street was undisturbed. She would have to thank Mr. Downing for recommending it.

She'd been able to get a light supper downstairs, and she felt much better now that her faintness had passed. Her thoughts flowed back over the past two hours, past her initial shock when Randall intercepted her, to her meeting with Caleb. He had looked almost the way he had in his photograph, but not so rigid. He was a bit taller than she was, and he had a full head of medium brown hair. He was not, perhaps, the handsomest man she had ever met, but he was far from the homeliest. And he was polite and considerate of her, although he did seem a bit battle fatigued, like her uncle Leo when he returned from the war. Who could blame Caleb, after what he had been through?

A bittersweet smile quirked her lips. She had imagined him meeting her at the depot and sweeping her off her feet. A kiss? On her hand at least—perhaps her cheek. But they hadn't touched each other at all. Instead, they had gazed at one another through the bars of a cell door.

In her reverie, she'd pictured their wedding—small, unpretentious, in a little church with Caleb's minister presiding. She'd brought a new dress for the occasion. White gloves and a wisp of white netting to affix to her hat that day.

She had intended to write her parents a letter tonight, telling them of her arrival. Perhaps of her marriage, or at least of their plans.

Eve sighed. No, she couldn't tell them what had really happened today. It would only worry them. Her father would no doubt send a telegram demanding that she return home at once.

And maybe she should.

If she had enough money, she could get on the next eastbound train and put as much distance between herself and Caleb as possible. But she came here with very little money, expecting to stay. And she didn't really want to go back. Wyoming was frightening, but she was tired of the way her family was treated in their hometown. No matter what the officials said, people continued to look down on the Martins. No, if at all possible, she would not go back.

If she did stay, what would that mean?

She went to the bed and rummaged through the valise, pulling out a stack of six letters tied together with a pale blue ribbon. Caleb's letters. She carried them over to the little bench and sat down.

These few missives contained every word Caleb had written to her—everything she'd known about him before today. Before she'd learned he was accused of murder.

She took out the one that came first, remembering how excited she'd been when the postman left it, and how her fingers had trembled so badly she could barely tear it open. The edge of the envelope was ragged because of her clumsiness. Her heart had pounded, and she'd paused for a moment and thanked God for a response—any response—before she unfolded the letter.

Maybe this was a good time to do that again.

She closed her eyes. "Lord, help me to see what You want me to see, not what I want. I left home believing with all my heart that Caleb was the man for me, the man You had chosen to be my husband. I don't think that's changed, heavenly Father. But I need some reassurance tonight. I don't know what to think about this turn of events, and I don't know how to feel. Show me."

Slowly she unfolded the paper and gazed at his scrawl. *"Dear Miss Martin, Thank you for your gracious response to my advertisement."* She blinked, and a tear escaped the corner of her eye and rolled down her cheek.

He had penned these words before the accusations. Before he'd argued with the stable owner. Before he'd seen the boy being whipped. None of that had happened when he'd opened his heart to her and asked her to leave behind all she knew and share his life with him.

An hour later, she stacked all the letters carefully and laid them and her Bible back in her valise. She had gone over every one of Caleb's messages. His simple, heartfelt words had touched her, as they had the first time she read them.

"My ranch. . . . A fair amount of business. . . . It's a good country out here. . .but I'm missing something. . . . I get lonely. . . . I am praying God will send me someone."

She opened her Bible and read two chapters from Isaiah. The words of the scripture calmed her.

"When thou passest through the waters, I will be with thee;
and through the rivers, they shall not overflow thee: when thou
walkest through the fire, thou shalt not be burned; neither shall
the flame kindle upon thee. For I am the Lord thy God, the
Holy One of Israel, thy Savior."

God had made this promise to the Israelites, but surely He cared as much about her.

If she stayed in Cheyenne, what would she do? Several things came to mind. Uppermost was the thought that she would do as she had intended all along. She would try to help Caleb and support him. She could inquire after Willy and check on Caleb's horses. Without doubt she would ask if the sheriff had contacted a lawyer for Caleb. And she would send her parents a telegram tomorrow, stating simply that she had arrived safely. They would expect a letter to follow, but she would wait on that until she had some pleasant news. The telegram would allay their immediate fears.

She drew in a shuddering breath. The temperature had fallen, and she shivered. The bed with its well-worn quilt looked inviting now, and she thought she could sleep. And she needed to sleep. She had a lot to do in the morning.

After breakfast at the hotel, Eve sent her three-word telegram: SAFE IN CHEYENNE. At fifty cents a word, her parents would expect her to be frugal. Then she set out to find the livery stable. It wasn't hard to find with directions from the desk clerk. As she approached, a young man came out leading a saddled horse. He tipped his hat to Eve, swung into the saddle, and rode off down the street. She turned hesitantly toward the big open door of the barn.

Inside, a wiry, gray-haired man was plying a shovel, loading manure into a wooden wheelbarrow. Eve stepped into the dim, odorous interior.

"Excuse me."

The man looked up and rested his shovel's blade on the floor. "Yes, ma'am? Can I help you?"

"I'm not sure. I was wondering about. . ." She wished she had planned this better.

"Do you need a buggy?" he asked.

"No. No, I heard about the owner being. . ."

The old man walked toward her, dangling the shovel from his hand. "About Tinan being killed?"

"Y—yes. Are you his employee?"

"Not really. I'm just his neighbor. Riley's the name. I used to do a few chores for Buck when he needed help. Before he got the boy, that is. So the sheriff asked me to tend to business here today, since some folks need to come get their horses and so on."

"Oh. Yes. I'm here to inquire about Mr. Blair's team. I believe they were left here yesterday."

Riley nodded. "The deppity brought 'em in last night about nine."

Eve frowned. So Nichols hadn't actually had the team moved from the depot when he'd claimed he sent someone to collect them. What else had he misled her and Caleb about?

"They're out back having their breakfast." Riley spat into the wheelbarrow, and Eve took a step backward. "I heard he's been arrested. You taking care of his place?"

"I also wanted to ask about Willy," she said quickly. "To see if he's all right."

Riley frowned and chewed his plug of tobacco. "Can't say as I've seen him."

"Not at all?"

"Not since Buck was stabbed."

"Oh." She swallowed hard. "Do you know where he lives? Willy, I mean?"

"I figured he was sleepin' here. I never saw him over to Buck's place."

"Where's that?"

"Buck had a cabin near my place, about a mile out of town on the Henshaw Road."

Eve eyed him closely and decided Riley was being straight with her. "Has anyone been over there since it happened? Checked on Mr. Tinan's house, I mean?"

Riley spit into the wheelbarrow again.

"I went over last night. Buck has a yearling colt he keeps out back of his cabin. I made sure he had water last night and this morning. I'll see to him until the sheriff figures out what to do with him."

"But you didn't see Willy."

"No, ma'am."

"All right. I may stop by again later. If you see him, will you let me know? I'm staying at the Wayside Inn."

"Does he know you, ma'am?" Riley cocked his head to one side. "'Cause I don't."

"Oh. I'm sorry. My name is Eve Martin. And no, Willy doesn't know me. But Mr. Blair—Caleb—is concerned about him. We both are."

His expression darkened. "And what are you to Caleb Blair?"

She swallowed hard. "We're going to be married."

"Before or after the hangin'?"

Eve froze for a moment. Icicles pricked her lungs, but her face felt like a furnace. She held Riley's gaze for a moment, then turned and walked as quickly as she could away from the stable.

Once around the corner, she paused and leaned against the wall of a seamstress's shop. She pulled in several deep, slow breaths. So, everyone in town knew the story and was convinced Caleb was guilty.

Several people brushed past her, and a wagon loaded with barrels creaked past. Eve steadied herself and looked around. Which way was the hotel? And which way was the sheriff's office?

She picked what seemed the best option and walked slowly along the edge of the street, beneath overhanging roofs. At the next corner she paused again to orient herself. Between the eaves and tops of other buildings, she caught a glimpse of a steeple. She had no idea what church it was or if she was going up the right street, but she walked in that direction.

It was hard to keep track of the spire, and once she was sure she'd lost it, but at the next break in the tall facades of stores, she saw it again, and it was closer. At the next corner she turned left. The buildings weren't so close together now, and a hundred yards away sat the church. It was made of rough-sawn lumber, and the steeple didn't seem to have a bell, but it was definitely a church, and she hurried toward it as if it had cast her a line and was reeling her in.

She climbed the three wooden steps and tried the door. It wasn't locked, and it swung inward at her touch. Hesitantly, she walked inside. A tall window at the other end of the building let in sunlight. Would the people replace the clear panes with stained glass someday? The pews were wooden benches, and only the first three rows had backs.

Eve was alone in the sanctuary. She sat down on one of the benches and stilled her heart.

Lord, I don't know what I'm doing. Please guide me. I want to help Caleb, but I don't know if I can, or even if I should. Everyone seems to think he killed that man. If he didn't do it, please don't let him be punished for it.

She sat awhile longer, not certain whether she felt better. But God heard her, didn't He? Whether she felt it or not?

At last she rose and went outside, closing the door carefully behind her. On the other side of the building lay a small cemetery. She walked toward it, wondering how long the oldest graves had been here. Of course, there were other churches in town; Mr. Downing had said so. There were probably other cemeteries too.

She rounded the corner of the building and stopped. A woman sat on the ground near a freshly turned grave. Her shoulders shook. Eve felt the urge to go and speak to her, and yet she held back. If she were weeping at a loved one's grave, would she want a stranger to approach her? Probably not.

The woman's hair was a bright, golden color that couldn't be natural, though the idea shocked Eve a little. She looked closer and noticed that the shawl covering the woman's back and shoulders was very fine, perhaps silk, and what Eve could see of her skirt was a garish pink. She shuddered. Probably not someone she should approach.

A wooden cross stuck out of the ground at one end of the grave. It struck Eve suddenly—this could be Buck Tinan's grave. If so, that woman certainly wouldn't want to talk to the fiancée of the man accused of murdering him. Time to leave, before the mourner spotted her.

She whirled toward the street and plowed smack into a man. He was a bit spongy about the middle, so it didn't hurt, but he let out an "oof" that told her she'd at least knocked the breath out of him.

"Oh, I'm so sorry!" She jumped back a pace and met his gaze.

"No harm." He looked to be about her father's age, and he wore a black sack coat and a ribbon tie with his white shirt. "I'm Pastor Viner. Is there anything I can do to help you?"

"Oh no, I—I was just. . ." She looked back toward the cemetery and lowered her voice. "That woman. Is she—?"

"She's Sally Buford."

"And is that Mr. Tinan's grave?"

"Yes it is. We buried him early this morning." He held her gaze, calm and unemotional.

"Is she his wife? I heard he wasn't married."

"No, he wasn't. I believe Miss Buford was a friend of his. She's employed at one of the saloons."

"Oh."

"Did you know Mr. Tinan?"

Eve shook her head. "But I know Caleb Blair."

The pastor's mouth curved upward, transforming his face. Outside of Caleb, he was the first person in Cheyenne who

41

looked happy to see her.

"You must be Miss Martin."

"I am. How did you know?"

"Caleb is one of my parishioners. He told me recently that he was expecting a young lady from. . .Pennsylvania, is it?"

She nodded.

"Yes. He asked me to perform your wedding ceremony, and I was happy to agree."

"You—you know he's in jail?"

"Yes. I heard the news this morning. I was planning to go over there and see him, to find out if there's anything I can do to make him more comfortable."

Eve felt as though her heart would burst, and she thrust out her hand. "Thank you! No one else has spoken a kind word to me since I left the train station. I had no idea you were Caleb's pastor. I just followed the steeple, looking for a place to pray."

He clasped her hand. "I'm so glad the Lord guided you here. Come sit down for a moment and tell me about it."

Eve walked with him to the church steps, and they sat down. The sun had risen higher than the nearby roofs, and it warmed her shoulders.

"I went inside the church," she said.

Pastor Viner smiled. "I saw you come out."

She looked up into the minister's calm hazel eyes. "Caleb didn't kill that man."

"I figured as much. That, or it was self-defense. Were you planning to see him this morning?"

"Yes. That was my next destination."

"Would you like me to walk with you?"

"I would like that very much. I've not got my bearings yet, and to be truthful, the streets here frighten me."

"There's a motley lot in Cheyenne," he said. "Some parts of town are worse than others. Unfortunately, the sheriff's office is in proximity to several saloons and dance halls. Where are you staying, if I might ask?"

"At a place called the Wayside. It's not far from the jail, but it seems to be on a quiet street."

He nodded. "Yes, you could have done much worse. Tell me what you know of Caleb's situation, and we'll pray for him before we set out."

"Thank you." Eve unburdened her heart and told the pastor of her uncertainty the night before. "And so," she concluded, "I've decided to stay and offer him my support. Do you think it's possible God brought me here for that purpose?"

The minister smiled gently. "I think it's very possible."

Caleb sat on his cot, twisting his hands. It must be ten o'clock by now. Was Eve coming? What if she'd left town and he never saw her again? But she'd said she would return, and that she didn't have enough money to go home. Where was she? This was a rough part of town, and he tried not to imagine all the evils that could find her.

He heard the door open in the office and held his breath. Voices—male voices. Sheriff Nichols and who?

Another tone reached him, and his heart surged. That had to be Eve. She'd come back. He stood and walked to the bars, his pulse hammering. Sure enough, the door separating the cells from the office opened.

"Blair, the preacher's here to see you."

His hopes plunged. Maybe the woman's voice he'd heard was

Mrs. Viner's. At least the pastor could tell him how things were going in town and what he'd heard about this mess.

Caleb looked past the big man. Pastor Viner came in with a patient smile.

"Caleb. How are you doing?" He stuck his hand through the bars, and Caleb shook it, infused with a bit of warmth and hope.

"I'm all right, I guess."

"Ruth and I are praying for you."

"Thank you," Caleb said. "Is she here? I thought I heard. . ."

"Oh no, that's Miss Martin." Pastor Viner shook his head. "Lovely girl. I offered to let her come in first, but she thought you might want to see me more than you do her. I assured her that wasn't the case."

"I'm glad to see you both," Caleb said.

Viner smiled. "She seems a very wise young woman, not to mention very pretty."

"Y–yes." Caleb swallowed hard. "I feel as though I brought her out here under false pretenses."

"You couldn't know this would happen."

"I should say not." An accusation of murder had been the furthest thing from his mind as he drove toward the depot yesterday. He flicked a glance at the pastor's eyes. Viner wouldn't hide things from him. "How is she?"

"A bit shaken, but I think she's made of good stuff. We prayed together on the church steps before we came here."

"She found you?"

"By accident—or rather, by providence."

Caleb nodded. "I reckon that's an answer to a prayer I didn't think to make."

"She wants to help you if she can."

"I don't see how." Caleb looked down at the rough board floor. "Did she tell you? They found Tinan in the stable with my knife stuck between his ribs."

"I didn't hear the details. How do you suppose that happened?"

Caleb scrunched up his face and scratched his head. His hair must look awful, and Eve would see him this way. No shave this morning either.

"Near as I can tell, I must have dropped my knife when I tussled with Buck the day before."

"It came to fisticuffs?"

"No. Well, sort of. He was using a whip on that orphan boy he took in. I grabbed it away from him, and then I head-butted him. We both went down. That's probably when I lost the knife. I reckon it fell out of my pocket." He shrugged. "We had a few words. I told him to teach the boy how to do his job, not to beat him. And then I left."

"It's not much," Viner said. "Surely evidence in your favor will turn up."

"I sure hope so."

The minster nodded. "Well, I'll go out and let Miss Martin come in for a few minutes."

"Is she really doing all right?" Caleb asked.

"I think she's doing fine, considering."

"Yeah." Considering the bind he'd put her in.

"Do you need anything?"

"Not really," Caleb said. "They brought me breakfast. A comb, maybe."

Viner smiled and reached into a pocket. "Would you like to use mine? I promise you, I don't have lice."

"Thanks." Caleb took it through the bars and ran the small

tortoiseshell comb through his hair. "I don't guess you've got a razor."

Viner laughed. "The sheriff probably wouldn't let you use it if I did." He ran his gaze over Caleb's head. "I guess you'll pass inspection. While Miss Martin's in here, I'll ask the sheriff about you getting a shave."

"Thank you, but I suppose that's the least of my worries right now." Still, he hated feeling sloppy, especially now that Eve was here. He passed the comb back.

Viner took it and pocketed it, then nodded. "Keep your chin up, Caleb. The Lord knows what happened—and what will happen in the future."

"Thank you. I know you're right."

"I'll try to come back tomorrow if you're still here, but I'll pray for your speedy release."

Caleb watched him go, and almost immediately Eve came in. She looked rested, and her fresh outfit didn't bear the dust and stains of travel he'd noted last night. In fact, her beauty struck him like a mule kick. How could he have landed such a lovely woman—and got himself locked up right when she arrived? He wasn't sure if he was the luckiest or the unluckiest man alive.

"Caleb." She came straight to the door and reached through the bars, laying a hand on his shirtsleeve.

Caleb dared to cover her hand with his. "It's good of you to come."

"Nonsense. How could I stay away?"

He had no answer for that.

"I went by the stable this morning," she said.

"Oh? Was it open?"

"Yes. There was an old man called Riley in there. He said he was

Mr. Tinan's neighbor, and the sheriff asked him to tend the horses."

Caleb nodded slowly. "I know who he is. Old codger with a gray beard. Is there any word on Willy?"

Eve shook her head. "Riley said he hadn't seen him."

Caleb let out a sigh. "I'm worried about Willy. Nobody admits seeing him since that happened."

"I know. I'll keep asking around."

"Do you mind?"

"Not at all."

"I didn't mean to saddle you with all this."

"I know," Eve said. "I can understand why you're worried about him."

Caleb tried to keep back the dark thoughts that had plagued him since late last night, but he couldn't. "I. . .I can't think Willy would have. . ."

She squeezed his fingers, and he felt as though he'd touched a doorknob during a thunderstorm and gotten a hoist off it.

"If he did, I'm sure he had cause. From what you told me, I mean."

Caleb grimaced. "The other thing I'm afraid of is that Tinan might have done something to Willy, and then someone else killed him."

"I'll ask around a bit more."

"Don't if you're not comfortable." Caleb didn't like to think of her poking around alone. It would be dangerous enough under normal circumstances, but if there was a killer out there— "Can you get someone to go with you?"

"I don't like to ask the minister. I'm sure he has a lot to do. And I don't know anyone else. The sheriff says he looked already. I don't think he'll assign a man to escort me around town."

"Do we know where Willy slept?" Caleb asked.

"Riley said he thought the boy stayed at the stable. Maybe I should go back there."

The sheriff opened the door and called, "Time's up, Miss Martin."

"So quick," she said softly, still holding on to Caleb's fingers. "Riley said I can get your horses and wagon later."

"Good. You'll need money. Ask the sheriff to give you what I had in my pocket when he brought me in." Reluctantly, he peeled her hand away. "Pastor Viner or the sheriff can tell you where my ranch is. If you're staying, you might as well go out there and not have to pay for a hotel room. I mean. . .if you want. I was planning on you being there by now."

Her face went a becoming pink. "Thank you."

The sheriff plodded into the space before the cell door. "Your time's up, ma'am. I'm going to have to ask you to leave."

"May I come back later?" Eve looked up at Nichols. "I'd like to bring Mr. Blair a few things. Perhaps a few clean clothes."

She hadn't even asked him what to bring. Caleb hadn't thought about the possibility that he'd be here several more days. Maybe longer than that.

"I'd allow it this afternoon." The sheriff's jaw jutted toward her. "Fifteen minutes, but you've got to respect my rules."

"Yes, sir, I will." Eve threw a glance at Caleb. "A clean shirt for tomorrow, perhaps?"

"That'd be great." Caleb frowned at Nichols. "And maybe a little cash to pay my lawyer. Is anyone coming in today, sheriff?"

Nichols cleared his throat. "I haven't had a chance to line anyone up."

"There's a fellow on Roper Street, isn't there?" Caleb said.

Eve said timidly, "Perhaps I could go around there."

"All right." Caleb glanced at the sheriff then leaned close to the bars. "There's a little cash in an Arbuckle's tin in my kitchen. You can use it for incidentals. And when the sheriff took my wallet off me yesterday, it had twelve dollars in it."

Nichols grunted. "You releasing your belongings to this woman?"

"Yes, sir, I am."

The sheriff hesitated, then nodded. "I'll have you sign a paper saying that."

"No problem there," Caleb said. "Just make sure she gets everything."

"All right, enough of this. Come along, miss."

Nichols herded Eve out so fast they didn't have a chance to say goodbye, but Caleb wasn't overly worried about that. She'd be back later today. What worried him was Sheriff Nichols trying to make a case against him, and the chance he might never walk free again.

❧ Chapter 4 ❧

"Where do you think Willy could be, Reverend Viner?" Eve asked as soon as they were outside the sheriff's office.

"I can't imagine. You say he wasn't living at Tinan's house?"

Eve frowned, thinking about it. "We only have Mr. Riley's word for it. He thought the boy must be sleeping at the livery."

"Perhaps we should go back there and look around carefully," the pastor said.

"I don't want to take up your time. You must have other things to do."

"I don't mind. Willy might not have been one of my flock, but Caleb certainly is."

"Let's go, then." Grateful for his willingness and his protective presence, Eve turned toward the stable.

When they arrived, Riley was out near the pens behind the barn, talking to two men.

"Should we wait?" Eve asked.

Reverend Viner pursed his lips. "I don't see why we can't make some observations while we do that."

She liked this man, and she was sure his sermons must be interesting.

"Caleb saw Tinan with his whip from outside the door as he walked past the livery," she noted.

Reverend Viner considered the wide floor in the middle of the barn between the stalls. "Perhaps over here. . ." He walked toward the stalls on the left side, where the rumps of several horses showed and the animals munched on hay as they stood waiting for riders. "Do you know where Tinan was killed?"

"No. Someplace here at his business, I think. I'm not sure it was inside the barn, but it seems likely."

"Mmm." Reverend Viner's eyebrows drew together, and he glanced toward the open rear door, where the men were still talking. "How about you look around over there, where the harness is hung up, and I'll take a peek in the hayloft?"

Eve nodded and walked as quietly as she could to the back right corner of the barn, where the space that would make two straight stalls was open. Two large barrels stood in the middle, and one had clamps securing the top. The other had a large rock on its lid. A weight to keep rodents from getting at the feed, Eve surmised.

The walls were covered with hooks for harnesses and bridles, and several wooden racks supported saddles of many descriptions—stock saddles, light cavalry rigs, and even a sidesaddle for ladies. Other racks held piles of saddle pads and blankets. But Eve didn't see anything that looked like a boy's spot to sleep in among the equipment, and she didn't see any clothing or other personal possessions that might belong to Willy.

A slash of sunlight came in through the back door, however, and Eve examined the boards at her feet. A dark stain discolored the wooden floor of the harness room. She gasped and stepped back. Could it be Tinan's blood?

"Hey! What are you doing in here?"

She whirled and faced Riley, surprised that the old man could spout such a loud and harsh greeting.

"I—I was hoping to find Willy."

"I told you, that kid hasn't been around here."

"I'm sorry." Eve gulped. The other two men had entered behind him but stood back a couple of paces. They were dressed casually, in twill pants and cotton work shirts. She was relieved when Pastor Viner joined her, brushing bits of hay from his pants. At least Riley hadn't caught him in the loft.

"All right, thank you." She tried to keep her voice as calm as possible. "I also wanted to tell you that Mr. Blair has told the sheriff I can take possession of the team and wagon he left here. I will pay you the fee for keeping them overnight."

Riley gazed at her for a moment. "I'm afraid I'll need more than your say-so on that, ma'am."

Pastor Viner stepped forward. "Hello, I'm the Reverend Charles Viner. I was with Miss Martin at the sheriff's office just now when Mr. Blair signed a release giving her leave to take charge of all his possessions. You can ask the sheriff if you'd like, or go in and ask Caleb Blair himself."

Riley grunted and swung his gaze back to Eve. "You want 'em now?"

"Uh, no, I have to make arrangements with the hotel," she said. "Perhaps this afternoon around three?"

"I'll be here," Riley said.

"Thank you." She nodded as if she was used to concluding business transactions every day and turned toward the front of the livery. Pastor Viner fell in beside her. They stepped out into the sunbaked street.

"Well done," Reverend Viner said softly.

"Thank you for your support," Eve replied. "If you had not been present, I'm not sure he'd have let me take the horses without hauling the sheriff over here."

"I'm glad I was able to help." Reverend Viner glanced back over his shoulder and steered her across the opening to a side street and onto the boardwalk that began on the other side in front of a row of shops. "Did you find anything in the harness room?"

She threw him a troubled look. "There was something dark on the floor. I thought perhaps it was blood, but I didn't like to ask."

He nodded soberly. "And I found a nest in the hay mow. A blanket, a smallish shirt, and a tobacco tin holding a boy's treasures."

"What sort of treasures?" She looked up at him eagerly as they walked.

"A fish hook, a spent shell casing, a few horseshoe nails, and a penny. Not much, but it convinced me I'd found Willy's habitual abode."

"That cruel man," Eve said, thinking of Buck Tinan. "Wouldn't you think people who take in orphans would be required to provide them with a home? An actual place in a house?"

"One would think." Pastor Viner sighed and shook his head. "I suspect the boy is still around, unless. . ."

Eve didn't like the thoughts that his "unless" shoved into her mind. Was Willy hiding somewhere, hurt—or worse?

Reverend Viner stopped at the street corner and pointed. "I

believe that is your hotel."

Eve looked and nodded. "It is. Thank you very much."

"Would you like me to accompany you there?"

"No, but thank you. I'll speak to the innkeeper and see what to do about my trunk. Caleb seems sincere in wanting me to go to his ranch and stay there."

"You would be comfortable if you did," Reverend Viner assured her. "I've visited him several times. The ranch house is more of a small cabin, but it's cozy."

She said goodbye and walked to the Wayside Inn, weighing the options. Staying at the ranch would certainly help her financially, but she would have to drive into town each day if she wanted to see Caleb. Her lack of funds won out, and she spoke to the man at the desk. When she paid her bill, he agreed to have a man ready to help load her trunk shortly after three, when she would bring Caleb's wagon around. She thanked the Lord that her father had taught her to drive back home so that she could drive her family's buggy to the shops.

The hotel didn't serve lunch, so she supposed she would have to find someplace to eat. She had only a few dollars left, and she didn't know how much Riley would ask for at the livery. Of course, she could pay for that out of Caleb's twelve dollars, but she didn't like to spend the money she'd received from the sheriff on herself. Spending it to meet Caleb's needs was a different matter. Down the street she'd seen a bakery. Perhaps she could fill her stomach with rolls cheaply, rather than going to a restaurant.

She soon completed her visit to the bakery, and as she came out carrying a bag of half a dozen warm rolls and an apple fritter, she nearly ran into another woman who was passing.

"Oh, forgive me," Eve cried, jumping back into the doorway.

"It's nothing," the other woman said. She gave a perfunctory smile, and Eve noted that her eyes were bloodshot, though her face was decorated with powder, rouge, and eyeliner. Her lips were a startling red, and as she turned away, Eve noticed her intricate silk shawl.

"Oh," Eve said.

The woman stopped and looked back at her. "Yes?"

Eve's face warmed. Why couldn't she have kept silent?

"I'm sorry. It's just that. . .I believe I saw you this morning. At the cemetery."

The woman eyed her closely. "I was at the cemetery earlier. I didn't see you."

"No, I didn't want to disturb you."

"Did you know Buck?"

"No," Eve said.

The woman frowned. "I'm on my way to work."

"Where do you work?" Eve asked.

"The Willow Tree today."

"Oh." Eve smiled in recognition, then bit it back. "Mr. Downing's establishment."

The other woman's eyes narrowed. "You know Mr. Downing, then?"

"I met him on the train."

"I see. Well, please excuse me."

Eve laid a hand lightly on her arm. "Please, if you'd just tell me—do you know anything about the boy?"

"Boy? You mean Willy?"

"Yes. I'm trying to find him, to make sure he's all right."

Her eyes narrowed. "What's your interest?"

"I'd like to offer him a new home," Eve replied. "And if he's hurt or hungry, I'd like to help him."

The woman with the painted face studied her for a long moment. "Come to the Willow Tree in an hour. And ask for Sally."

"You know where Willy is?"

"I didn't say that." Sally whirled in a flurry of pink skirts and hurried away.

Eve didn't have a watch, but she would make sure no more than an hour passed before she went to the Willow Tree. At least Sally hadn't said the White Pony. The Willow Tree was the more respectable of Mr. Downing's businesses. In fact, he'd said they served meals there, and he'd implied that a lady might get a repast there without mishap. Perhaps she should have gone there for luncheon. But that would cost more than what she'd bought at the bakery. She hurried back to the Wayside. The room was hers for a few more hours, and she would take advantage of that.

She ate one roll and the apple fritter and freshened up. At least half an hour must have passed. She left the hotel and strode down the boardwalk and around the corner. Hesitantly, she approached the Willow Tree. The people going in were mostly men. From out here, it was impossible to tell if it was a saloon or a restaurant. It didn't seem overly noisy. Still, it was midday. It might take on a different ambiance when the sun went down.

Standing outside, she waited until someone came out and she could get a peek through the open door. People sat at tables, talking and eating. And drinking. She could only see two women, one serving diners. She wasn't as flamboyantly dressed as Sally, but she did wear rouge and lip color, and her dress had a neckline that swept low, exposing her collarbone.

The other woman was seated at a table with two men. She was more conventionally garbed, in a daytime dress that would be deemed respectable, though perhaps a bit dowdy, in Pennsylvania.

"Going in, ma'am?" The man who had come out was holding the door and waiting.

"Oh, I—" She gulped. "Yes, thank you."

She stepped inside, and the man closed the door behind her. Eve held her breath, looking around for Sally. Nearly all the patrons here were men, and most of them had some sort of alcoholic beverage before them—mugs of beer, glasses of amber-colored liquid. Some even had whiskey bottles sitting on their tables, though a few were drinking coffee from thick ironstone mugs. The one female customer she'd noticed was drinking beer too. So much for respectability. The woman was laughing at something one of her companions said, and her gaze landed on Eve, who sucked in a breath and turned away.

On the opposite side of the room, a long wooden bar stretched nearly the length of the wall. Behind it stood a bartender clad in a white shirt with sleeve garters—and Sally. She was pouring drinks for a cluster of men leaning on the far end of the bar.

Sally looked up and saw her. She lifted her chin and jerked her head to the right, toward the end of the bar.

"Hey, lady. You want a drink?" a man seated at a nearby table called.

Eve shuddered and moved farther into the room, in the direction Sally had indicated, though that meant skirting the four men at the end of the bar.

To her relief, Sally led her into an alcove where the people in the large room couldn't see them. A small table with two chairs sat in the private corner, and Sally sat down in one, nodding for Eve to take the seat across from her.

"What is it?" Eve asked.

"I talked to Mr. Downing. He said he knew you and that I could tell you what little I know."

Eve blinked, wondering how her travel acquaintance figured into this.

"I was seeing Buck," Sally said. "He came in here once a week or so, or into the Pony. I work there most evenings. And I'd see him outside of work."

"So you know Willy."

Sally nodded. "Two days ago, I went over to the stable. We have a lull around one o'clock or so, when people are done eating, and it's slow until four or five. Mr. Downing lets us take turns having a couple of hours off, so long as there's a bartender and one waitress on duty. I was supposed to show up at the Pony at four to work the evening. I thought I'd see if Buck was busy, and if not, maybe we could walk down to the stockyards."

"Why the stockyards?" Eve asked.

Sally shrugged. "There's always something going on there. Buck goes to the auctions and buys and sells horses there sometimes. He did, I mean." Her eyes darkened. "He knew a lot of people, and it was fun to see what was going on."

Eve nodded to encourage her to keep talking.

"Well, when I got to the stable, I didn't see anyone at first. I thought maybe Buck had stepped out, or maybe he was out back. So I walked into the barn, and then I saw Willy standing in the back, near where Buck keeps all the saddles and harnesses."

"I've seen it," Eve said.

"Willy was standing right there, in the shadows. Made me jump. I asked him if Buck was around, and he just pointed to the floor."

Eve's pulse quickened. "He was there when Buck was killed."

"I don't think Willy killed him, if that's what you mean."

"Nor do I," Eve assured her.

"I ran to Buck and felt for a breath. Willy asked if he was dead. I said I thought so, and Willy ran out the back. That's the last time I saw the kid. I went out to get the sheriff. In fact, I ran into Deputy Randall not far down the street, and he came right away."

Eve studied her for a minute. Sally's use of makeup enhanced her somewhat plain features. Maybe saloon work was the only job she could get in Cheyenne. Waiting on tables didn't seem so bad, compared to other employment for unattached females—but still, Sally had been serving liquor. It was hard to reserve judgment.

"I will continue to look for him," she said at last. "But Sally, why are you telling me this? Do you know I'm engaged to marry Caleb Blair?"

"Mr. Downing told me. He said you seem a decent sort, and that if you want to get Caleb off the hook to marry you, he didn't see any harm in it."

"He believes Caleb is innocent, then."

Sally shrugged. "He didn't go that far. But we all know Buck wasn't the most upright soul. Any number of people might have knifed him. Blair doesn't seem very likely."

Eve eyed her closely, wondering why Sally kept company with Buck if that was her assessment of his character. But that was none of her business.

"Can you think of anyone who seems more likely?"

Sally hesitated. "There's a fellow who comes into the Pony to play cards. Nelson, I think he's called. He lost some money to Buck a week or two ago, and they had words. Nelson seemed to think Buck was cheating. I don't know—I never thought Buck would do that. But the other fella was pretty mad when he left."

"All right. Thank you. Can I give you something for your time?"

Sally waved a hand in dismissal. "I hope you find the kid."

Eve hurried outside, ignoring a couple of comments from men. It chilled her to think that if Caleb hanged for this murder, she could be left without resources, like Sally. How long would it take for her to get used to the stares and rude remarks from the men in places like the Willow Tree? How long before she hired out to employers who demanded that she paint her face and wear revealing clothes?

She had asked directions at the bakery, and now she headed for Roper Street. The lawyer's office wasn't hard to find. A signboard hung near the street, announcing SANDERS & TUTTLE, ATTYS AT LAW. She entered and found herself in a sparsely furnished sitting room. She could hear footsteps and rustling coming from somewhere down a hallway that led farther into the house.

"Hello?" she called.

A well-dressed man of about forty appeared in the doorway. "May I help you, ma'am?"

"Yes. I'm here on behalf of Caleb Blair. He's being detained by the sheriff in connection to Buck Tinan's death. Perhaps you've heard about it?"

"I did hear something. I'm John Tuttle. Won't you come in?"

"Thank you. Eve Martin." She extended her hand and shook his briefly, then followed him into a small office with a window looking out on the side street.

"Mr. Blair is innocent," she said before he could ask questions. "He would like an attorney to visit him at the jail."

"All right. Suppose you give me a few particulars in the case?" Mr. Tuttle took a pen from its rest beside his glass inkwell.

Eve felt more confident than she had to that point. This man seemed efficient and capable. She sat back in the chair.

"What would you like to know?"

❧ Chapter 5 ☙

Caleb jumped up when Eve entered. This time he was able to smile at her.

"Has Mr. Tuttle been here?" she asked without preamble.

"He has. Sheriff Nichols told him my trial will be held in a few weeks. He wanted me held here until then, but Mr. Tuttle is asking for bail."

"What would that mean?" Eve frowned, her smooth brow wrinkling.

"It would mean I could go home until the trial. But the sheriff is against it. He said I'll get a hearing as soon as the judge gets back from his circuit, but by then it will be nearly time for the trial anyway."

Eve sighed. "We mustn't get discouraged."

"That's what Tuttle said. And he's putting together a list of references—friends, that is, neighbors and businessmen who know me—who will vouch for me and swear I'm a decent person and will stick around if they let me out on bail."

"But where would you get the bail money?"

He looked down at the floor. "That could be a problem, depending on how much it is. That's up to the judge, I guess. It's possible he could let me go for nothing, but Tuttle says they usually have you put up something for security. But he'll argue that I'm not about to leave town, since I've established my ranch here, and my fiancée is here, and. . .well, we'll just have to hope the judge sees it our way."

"We'll have to pray," she said softly.

"Yes. Now, did Riley give you any trouble?"

"No," Eve said. "I have the team and wagon outside. He charged me a dollar, and I gave Mr. Tuttle five when I hired him."

Caleb nodded. The lawyer had already told him that much.

"So after I leave here, I plan to stop by the Viners' house," Eve said. "Then I'll go out to the ranch, if you're sure you want me there."

"It would be a relief to know you're out there," Caleb said.

"Do you have any employees?"

"No. I have a small operation, and I trade work with a couple of neighbors when I need it. I'm getting to where I'll need to hire a couple of hands soon though. Of course, if we could find Willy and take him on, he'd be some help."

Eve nodded slowly. "Who's feeding the horses right now?"

"Oh, they're all out to pasture except the ones I drove into town. They should be all right, but I'd appreciate it if you'd check on them if you have time. There should be four horses in the small pasture beside the house, and eight in the big field across the road. A creek runs through there, and they can get water. But the ones in the small pasture might need to have the water trough filled."

"How do you do that?"

"There's a pump right there that will dump into the trough. But I don't want you to have to do it."

"Caleb, if I'm going to be a rancher's wife, I need to learn to do these things. And I worked a pitcher pump back in Pennsylvania."

He spread his hands in surrender. "All right then. Same process. Prime it first."

She nodded.

"You'll pass Josiah Dryden's place right before you get to mine. He's the nearest neighbor, and I suppose if there was a problem with the horses, you could go to him."

"I'll keep him in mind."

"He's a good man," Caleb said. "And Miz Dryden's a fair hand with biscuits."

Eve laughed. "That's important too." She sobered and reached through the bars. She could barely reach his wrist, and Caleb stepped closer and took her hand.

"Caleb, I believe you're innocent."

He looked long and deep into her brown eyes. "Thank you."

"I felt I needed to tell you that."

He nodded, gratitude welling up inside him, and something more. Eve would make a fine wife, and he'd be proud to have her beside him. That is, if he ever got out of here to marry her.

Eve left the jail reluctantly when the sheriff announced that her time was up. Each time she visited Caleb, it was harder to leave him. But she still had a lot to do.

She untied the team and climbed to the wagon seat, glad that her last stop in town would be the minister's house beside the little church. She had made a few more inquiries between her conversation with John Tuttle and retrieving the team from the livery. Most people who admitted to knowing Buck Tinan were tight-lipped and eyed her suspiciously. She hadn't found out any more helpful information. Even though she was glad to have seen Caleb again, she felt a bit discouraged as she walked the horses to the hitching post in front of the parsonage.

As she tied up the team, the front door of the little house opened, and Reverend Viner stepped out onto the stoop.

"Welcome, Miss Martin."

"Hello, Reverend Viner." She smiled wearily and walked toward him.

"My wife is eager to meet you." He took Eve's hand.

"I want to meet her too," Eve said.

"Well, she's got a pot of tea steeping, and some of her shortbread cookies ready."

"That sounds wonderful." Eve realized how tired and hungry she was.

"There's something else too," Reverend Viner said, guiding her to the door. "A little surprise."

Eve stopped and looked up at him. "Oh?"

"I think you'll like it."

Her curiosity was piqued, but she could see from his mysterious smile that he wasn't going to tell her yet, so she went inside, into the dim kitchen. A plump woman with her chestnut hair pulled back in a bun was working at the wood range. She turned and grinned at Eve.

"There now, you're Miss Martin."

Eve walked forward and held out her hand. "Please call me

Eve. I can't thank you and your husband enough for your support. I came here yesterday not knowing a soul, and you've been such an encouragement."

"Well, we've been praying," Mrs. Viner said. "You must call me Ruth."

"Thank you," Eve said.

"Now, before you sit down, come over here and meet our other guest." Ruth turned and led her toward the pine table. Sitting behind it in a corner was a lanky boy of about twelve.

Eve caught her breath. Perhaps this was the Viners' son. But no, she thought not. Ruth had said he was a guest. His hair was shaggy, and a lock tumbled over his forehead, almost obscuring one eye. He wore a rough cotton plaid shirt that looked none too clean. He got to his feet, eyeing her uncertainly, and she noticed his coarse twill pants.

"This," Pastor Viner said with a triumphant air, "is Willy Gilman."

At once, Eve felt a heavy load was lifted. Her lips curved upward, and she held out her hand. "Willy, I'm so pleased to meet you."

Ruth nodded at the lad. "This is Miss Martin, Willy. She's Mr. Blair's intended."

Willy touched her fingers for just a second and ducked his head.

"Willy, Caleb and I want to help you," Eve said. She darted a glance at the pastor. "How did you find him?"

"He was over at the church when I came back this morning. My wife gave him a good lunch, and we made sure he had a place to nap undisturbed for a few hours. I don't think he's slept much the past two nights."

"Willy," Eve said cautiously, "Mr. Blair and I discussed giving you a home now that Mr. Tinan's gone."

Willy pressed his lips together but said nothing.

"I am going out to the ranch now, and I've never been out there before. I thought perhaps you would go with me and help me unload my trunk and check on the horses."

Willy said slowly, "Mr. Blair being the one that took the whip away from Mr. Buck?"

"That's right," Eve said. "He wants to give you a better place to live, if you're willing. He thought you might like living at his horse ranch. We would give you your room and board and perhaps a bit of wages. And you could help him out some. He told me he needs a ranch hand, and I would feel a lot better having a man about the place, since Mr. Blair can't be there for a while."

"Has he got a lawyer yet?" Ruth asked, bringing the teapot to the table.

"Yes," Eve said. "Mr. John Tuttle."

"I've met him," the minister said. "I believe he's honest."

They all sat down, and Eve recounted her day's adventures. "I do hope I can turn up more information that will help Caleb." She smiled across the table at Willy. "And knowing you're safe is a big relief."

Reverend Viner sipped his tea and set down the cup. "I've explained to Willy about Mr. Blair's situation. He knows we believe that Caleb is innocent and that we want to help him in any way we can."

"That's right," Eve said, watching the boy. "He doesn't deserve to be in jail."

Mrs. Viner held out the plate of cookies to him. "Have another, Willy?"

The boy snatched a cookie and drew it to him as though it was a treasure he expected someone to pry from his hand.

Reverend Viner smiled sadly. "There now. Mr. Blair is a good man, Willy. When he came to your defense, he was only trying to do what he thought was best. He protected you. But he wouldn't kill Mr. Tinan, or anyone else, for that matter. If you go with Miss Martin, you will be helping the man who wanted to help you. But if you don't wish to go, I expect we can find a place for you to stay here until the judge decides what's to become of you."

Willy chewed his cookie and slowly raised his gaze to study Eve. She met his eyes with as much openness and trust as she could muster.

"I didn't knife him," Willy said.

"We know you didn't, boy," said the minister. "If you know who did, though, it would help Mr. Blair out of a bad fix."

Willy took another bite of his cookie and chewed in silence.

Mrs. Viner sighed. "Do you have what you need to set up housekeeping at the ranch?"

Eve turned toward her. "Caleb assured me that he'd laid in supplies. I picked up some fresh milk and a dozen eggs in town."

"He's a thoughtful man." Mrs. Viner eyed Willy for a moment. "If you go out there alone, will you be afraid?"

Before Eve could speak, Willy said, "I'll go."

"There now." Mrs. Viner beamed at him. "When you get there, it will be nigh on suppertime. I think I'll send a jar of baked beans with you, and two slices of apple pie."

The minister pushed up out of his chair. "We'd best inform the sheriff that you're found."

Eve drove the wagon over to the jail with Reverend Viner beside her and Willy sitting in the back with the trunk and her other bundles.

When they entered Nichols's small office, the outer room was empty.

"Guess he's out," Reverend Viner said.

"Do you think it's all right for us to go in and see Caleb?" Eve asked.

Reverend Viner looked around and shrugged. "Who's to tell us otherwise?"

The pastor led the way into the back hallway. Caleb was sitting on the cot in his cell, but he jumped up when he saw the three approach. His skin looked gray, but maybe it was just the poor lighting. Eve wished she could speak to him alone, but this time they had other things to talk about.

"Willy! I'm glad to see you." Caleb looked at Eve, his eyebrows arched.

"He came to the church this morning," she said.

"That's a good place to go when things are rough." Caleb eyed the boy. "I'm glad you're all right."

Willy raised his gaze to meet Caleb's. "Thank you for what you done, Mr. Blair."

Caleb was still for a moment, then swallowed. "Couldn't let him tear into you like that, Willy. It wasn't right."

Willy nodded and looked down at his boot toes. "I hate to see you in here."

"You know I didn't kill Buck Tinan, don't you?"

Willy nodded. "Reckon you wouldn't do that, or you'd have done it that day when he was whipping me."

The minister laid a hand on Willy's shoulder. "Can you tell us what you do know, Willy? If you know who did kill Tinan, it might save Mr. Blair's neck."

Willy pulled in a shaky breath, staring down at the floor. "The next day after you fought with him—yesterday, I reckon, or maybe the day before—Mr. Buck sent me to the harness maker to pick up a bridle he'd left to be mended. I went through the corral out back and over the fence. It's shorter." He glanced up, and Caleb nodded.

"When I come back, I went in through the back door of the barn. Mr. Buck was lyin' on the floor in the harness room."

"You see anyone else?" Caleb asked.

"A man was leading out a horse."

"Did he see you?" Reverend Viner prodded.

Willy shook his head.

"Who was it?" the pastor asked.

"I only saw his back. But it wasn't one of the rental horses. It must have been the man's own horse."

"So, who left their horses at the livery that day?" Caleb watched Willy's face.

Willy pulled in a breath and then shrugged. "A lot of folks. I don't know most of the names. There was a gray and a small bay mare—she was still there after it happened—and a grulla dun, and a big ol' spotted gelding. And a couple of horses Mr. Buck rented out with the buggy were in their stalls too."

Caleb said, "Do you remember what the horse the man was taking out looked like?"

Willy pressed his lips together for a moment. "It had a black tail, so maybe a bay? I don't really remember. I ran over to Mr. Buck as soon as I saw him lyin' there."

"Sure," Caleb said. "Anyone would."

Eve cleared her throat. "A woman named Sally said she saw you there."

Willy shot her a glance then looked down. "Reckon so. She come in while I was looking at Mr. Buck. He was lying there kind of funny, not moving. She—she came over and asked what happened. I didn't know, 'cause I just walked in. She felt of his neck, and she was cryin'."

They stood in silence for a moment, and Caleb said gently, "What happened next?"

"I asked her was he dead. She said he was, and—and I ran out the back. I was afraid someone would blame me. So I hid."

"Well, you don't have to hide anymore," Reverend Viner said.

Eve nodded. "Willy has agreed to go with me to the ranch."

Caleb smiled more broadly than before. "That's good. You'll be a help to Miss Martin. Thank you for doing that."

"Do you know Miss Buford?" Reverend Viner asked Willy. "Miss Sally Buford."

Willy nodded, frowning. "She was Mr. Buck's friend. She'd come over now and again, and he'd—"

"What is going on here?" roared Sheriff Nichols from the doorway.

Eve jumped, and they all turned toward the big man.

"Hello, Sheriff," Reverend Viner said. "We came to tell you that Willy is found."

"He is?" Nichols squinted at the boy. "Well now. Where you been, boy?"

Willy swallowed hard. "I slept last night in a haystack."

"He was frightened," Reverend Viner said. "But he came to the church today, and Mrs. Viner and I gave him some dinner."

The sheriff nodded. "You all come out into the office now. You don't got permission to be in here."

"I'm sorry," Eve said, moving toward the door. "You weren't in, and we knew Mr. Blair would want to know." She looked back. Caleb lifted a hand and gave her a sad smile.

In the office, the sheriff rounded on Willy.

"Did you see what happened to Buck Tinan?"

Willy opened his mouth and closed it, looking down at the floor.

"Speak up, boy!"

Willy flinched but said nothing.

Eve stepped forward. "I plan to take him out to Mr. Blair's ranch with me, Sheriff. He'll be a help to me with the livestock."

"Absolutely not."

She jumped at his fierce tone. "But why not? This young man needs a home, and he needs a safe place."

"There is no way that boy can go to the home of an accused murderer."

Pastor Viner stepped forward. "Now, Sheriff, it seems to me that it's an ideal solution. Remember, if Caleb Blair is found guilty, he won't be returning to the ranch, and if he is found innocent, he won't be a murderer. So what's the problem with the boy staying at his ranch? He could be a big help to Miss Martin, and you wouldn't have to ride out there to check on Caleb's livestock."

The sheriff pushed his hat back and frowned at Pastor Viner. "Huh. Well, I suppose. . ." He looked at Eve. "I guess you can take him *temporarily* to the Blair ranch."

"Thank you, Sheriff." Another knot in her stomach loosened, and she sent up a silent prayer of thanks.

Nichols still frowned at her. "I'll have to sort it out with the territorial marshal, and if he says no, then I'll have to remove the boy."

"Where would he go?" Eve asked.

"Well, I'm not sure."

Reverend Viner stepped up. "My wife and I will take Willy in if Miss Martin can't."

"Humph."

Eve dared to make another request. "Is it possible Caleb can be released on bail?"

"Definitely not. I'm waiting for instructions from the judge on that."

Eve nodded meekly.

Nichols glared at Willy for a long moment then opened a drawer in his desk. "I found these things over to the livery. Are they yours?"

He laid a tobacco tin and a ragged shirt on the desk.

Willy looked at them and nodded.

"Can you write your name?" Nichols asked.

The boy's eyes widened, and the sheriff continued.

" 'Cause if you sign a paper saying I gave them to you, you can take your stuff."

Willy stepped to the desk. Nichols laid a list before him and stabbed at the bottom with his thick finger. "Sign right here."

Eve watched as the boy bent and painstakingly wrote *William S. Gilman.*

"Awright," the sheriff said. "Now, tell me what you know about Tinan's death."

Willy hesitated, his mouth working.

Pastor Viner laid a hand on Willy's shoulder. "It's all right to tell the sheriff what you know, Willy. He wants the truth, same as we all do. Even if he's got the wrong man in jail, he wants to know who did it."

"Let's hear it." Nichols sounded impatient, but Reverend Viner patted the boy's shoulder again.

Slowly at first, Willy retold his story, gaining speed as he went and rushing to the end.

"And then I ran out the back and hid. I was scared."

72

"Where did you hide?" The sheriff's eyebrows met above the bridge of his nose as he glowered at Willy.

"Different places. But I was hungry. I didn't want to steal nothing, and I thought maybe the preacher could help me. So I went over to the church."

Nichols frowned. "I'm not sure I should let you go."

"He's a good boy, Sheriff," Reverend Viner said.

"He'll stay with me," Eve said firmly, "and if you need to speak to him again, he'll be right there. Won't you, Willy?"

Willy nodded.

"You won't run away and hide again?" the sheriff demanded.

Willy shook his head.

Nichols sighed. "All right, get out of here."

"Thank you." Eve touched Willy's shoulder. "Let's go." The boy scooped up his belongings, and they hurried out to the wagon. Willy climbed into the wagon bed.

"I'll drive you home," Eve said to the minister.

Viner smiled but shook his head. "I'll walk. You'd best get going so you can get settled before dark."

"Thank you," she said. "For everything."

He nodded and waved at Willy. "I expect I'll see you soon."

He was right. Eve would be back tomorrow to see Caleb. Sheriff Nichols couldn't keep her away. Quickly, she got the team moving in the direction of the ranch. Reverend Viner had given her explicit instructions and told her of several landmarks she would pass. She knew they would find everything at the ranch to meet her and Willy's physical needs, but she couldn't help wondering how this would all turn out.

❧ Chapter 6 ❦

*E*ve stepped into the modest ranch house and looked around. One large room served as kitchen and sitting room. Two doors opened off it. She crossed to the first one and opened it, with Willy right on her heels. It proved to be a storeroom with three barrels inside, several piled crates, and shelves holding an assortment of supplies, boxes, tins, and tools. Another door, secured with a metal hasp, led outside.

"Well, he seems to be a neat man," she murmured as she closed the storeroom.

"He must be rich," Willy said.

Eve looked at him. "Why do you say that?"

"He's got a lot of stuff in there. And this is a nice place for one man living alone."

"Do you think so?" Eve opened the second door. This room was obviously Caleb's bedchamber. The bed had a spoked iron headboard and footboard. She walked over and prodded the mattress. A straw tick, topped by a featherbed. Could be a lot worse. Neatly made up, the bed was covered by a woolen blanket. She smiled thinking of how the Carolina Lily quilt in her trunk would look when she spread it out on top. The room also held an upturned crate beside the bed, holding a Bible and a lantern. A highboy dresser of cherry wood stood against the far wall, seeming out of place in the rough house.

"Can we look at the barn?" Willy asked. "I reckon I can sleep out there."

"Yes, we should look things over before it's dark." The sun was already low in the west, and Eve wanted a good idea of the out-buildings while she still had daylight.

The barn was small, with only two horse stalls that opened into the yard. Both were empty. To one side was an enclosed room that held a stock saddle, a couple of bridles, odds and ends of harness, and a large wooden barrel. Overhead was a loft, and wisps of loose hay peeked out over the front edge. Not too substantial, but adequate. She remembered that Caleb had written in one of his letters that he hoped to enlarge his barn.

"Remember, Mr. Blair said we need to water the horses in the small pasture," she told Willy.

The boy ran without hesitation to the gate on the side nearest the house. A few feet inside the fenced enclosure was a tall pitcher pump with a wooden trough beneath it. Four horses lifted their heads from where they were grazing and ambled toward it.

Willy took a can of water from the pump's base and poured it down into the top. He lifted the handle and began working it up and down quickly. The horses nickered and gathered about the trough. They looked lean but well muscled. Eve wondered if these were Caleb's working horses. She and Willy could unharness the team and turn them in here with the others.

A sharp neigh and pounding hoofbeats demanded her attention, and she turned to gaze out over the larger pasture. Several horses galloped up to the fence and stood watching her. One large bay whickered and pawed at the ground.

"Well, hello." Eve strolled across the dirt road and patted the bay's muzzle. "Been wondering where your master is?"

By now, half a dozen animals had gathered, eyeing her curiously. She looked out over the pasture. A line of trees in the distance must mark the course of the creek. She and Willy could check it tomorrow to make sure the water was adequate for the herd.

"Where should I put the team?"

She turned to find Willy behind her.

"Oh, are you done with the water?"

"Yes'm. Weren't hard at all to get the pump going."

"There's supposed to be a creek on this side that these animals can drink from," Eve said. "Mr. Blair didn't say which pasture to put the team in."

Willy frowned in thought. "I reckon if we put them in the small pasture, it'll be easier to get them tomorrow when we want to go into town."

"I agree. But I also think we should check the creek tomorrow morning to see if it's flowing well."

He shrugged. "Ain't been too hot, ma'am. Don't s'pose it would dry up in two or three days' time."

"You're probably right." Eve was relieved by his commonsense approach. "All right, let's unharness the team and put them inside the fence."

"I can do it," Willy said.

She started to object but stopped. This was what Willy had done for Buck at the livery stable. She smiled. "All right then. Call to me if you need any help, and I'll go start our supper."

He grinned. "Sure sounds good, ma'am. And we can get that trunk in after I'm done with the horses."

Bolstered again by his confidence and his assumption that things would go well, Eve took a box Reverend Viner had given them from the wagon bed and headed into the house. She set it on the small maple drop-leaf table a few feet from the cookstove. She pulled out the jar of baked beans, one of pickles, another of jam, and a pie plate covered with a linen towel. She smiled and set Mrs. Viner's pie aside. Caleb's rough kitchen had a wide workspace over shelves of pans and dishes. An enameled dishpan sat in a recess of the drain board, and a clean cloth was draped over the edge. A soap holder with a bar of soap in it sat nearby. On the stove was a large teakettle, and a bucket half-full of water sat next to the range.

Eve was about to go out for her satchel and retrieve an apron from it when she spied a half apron hanging by its ties from a peg on the wall. She smiled and took it down. The patchwork skirt was sturdy. In fact, it looked new. Caleb must have bought it for her. She closed her eyes for a moment. *Thank You, Lord, for giving me such a thoughtful man. Show me what I can do to help him in return.*

She lit the stove. While the beans were heating in a skillet, she took stock and rummaged in her new kitchen, finding nearly everything she could have asked for in utensils and staples. To her surprise, a blue-and-white porcelain teapot sat on the shelf with Caleb's thick ironstone plates and mugs. Carefully, she lifted it down. A tin of tea sat behind it, and she wondered if Caleb drank tea or if this was just for her.

She slipped outside for the milk and eggs she'd bought in town and stirred up a batch of biscuits. She was just putting them in the oven when Willy came in, flushed and a bit grubby.

Eve smiled at him. "Everything all right?"

"Yes'm. Everything's fine." He brushed back his unruly hair.

"Good. Willy, I believe I'll take you to the barber tomorrow when we go in to see Mr. Blair."

He eyed her doubtfully.

"Now, wash up for supper. It's nearly ready."

He didn't move, so she poured some hot water from the teakettle into the washbasin and added a dipperful of cold from the bucket.

"Soap's right here, and a towel." She stepped back.

Willy squared his shoulders and walked over to the drain board.

"How long since you've had a bath?" Eve asked as casually as she could.

His eyes grew huge. After a moment, he turned toward the basin and grabbed the soap. "It's been awhile, ma'am."

"Ah. Well, after we wash the dishes, I think we should heat more water so you can have a good scrub. What do you say?"

Willy didn't speak while he lathered his hands, rinsed them, and dried them on the towel. After hanging it up, he turned to face her. "Whatever you say, ma'am."

Willy had protested much over joining the school on opening day, stating that Mr. Buck never mentioned school, except as a threat. For more than a week, Eve tried to convince him that school was a wonderful place and that he would learn amazing things that would help him all through life. Willy thought otherwise.

Finally, she poured out her heart to Caleb during one of their fifteen-minute visits.

"Let me talk to him," Caleb had said.

Eve didn't think it would make a difference, but she sent the boy in alone and waited outside the jail. Willy had complied with every request she'd made except this one. He willingly went about the chores she set him and submitted to the haircut and regular washing. He even agreed to sleep in the main room of the house after Eve told him she felt uneasy alone in the ranch house at night. But he had put his foot down when the topic of school was raised, and no reasoning or cajoling had changed his mind.

To her surprise, when he emerged from his talk with Caleb and walked out to the wagon, his first words were, "I'm sorry I was rude, Miss Martin. I'll go to school Monday if you want me to."

"Thank you, Willy," she replied. "I do think it will benefit you. And now, would you like to drive us over to the mercantile?"

Willy's eyes lit. "I would."

Eve saw that she had given him a reward he loved.

"Then take the reins. I'd like to talk to some of the people at the businesses near the livery—people who knew Buck Tinan—to see if they know of anyone who might have wished him harm." She also wanted to buy Willy a new shirt, since she planned to take him with her to church the next day, but she would bring that up when they reached the store.

Willy worked at the knot in the reins and freed them from the hitching post. "You might want to talk to Joe Hinckle."

"And who is that?" Eve asked.

"He's the bartender at the White Pony."

"Oh." Eve mulled that over. "I don't think the Pony is a good place for a woman to make inquiries."

"Perhaps not," Willy said.

"What made you think of Joe Hinckle?" she asked.

"Mr. Buck always stopped at the Pony in the evening, after he closed up the stable, and he and Joe got into it sometimes."

"What do you mean, they got into it?"

Willy climbed up to the driver's seat and positioned the reins in his hands. He threw her a sidelong glance. "They fought sometimes."

"Over business?"

"Over Mr. Buck's drinking, and whether he'd paid his bill or not."

"I see."

"He went there a lot." Willy pulled back gently but steadily on the reins, and the horses backed up. He turned their heads toward the livery and chirped to them, and the team set out in a synchronized trot.

"Mr. Blair has well-trained horses," Eve noted.

"Yes'm, they're better behaved than most."

Eve let him concentrate on his driving for several minutes. They were getting close to the livery when she asked, "Willy, how do you know that Joe and Buck argued?"

He glanced her way, then straight ahead.

"Don't tell me you were present in the saloon?"

"Sometimes," he admitted.

"Surely Mr. Buck didn't allow you to drink, did he?"

"No'm. I was mostly there to make sure he got home after."

"So. . .he drank to excess."

"Sometimes."

Eve shook her head. "Mr. Downing shouldn't have allowed you in there."

"Well. . ." Willy scowled. "Once or twice he did tell Mr. Buck not to bring me. After that, Mr. Buck would look inside the saloon first, and if the owner was there, he'd tell me to wait for him outside."

"I see." Eve wished her Caleb had taken an interest in Willy earlier. "How long were you with Mr. Tinan?"

"A year last spring."

"And where did you come from?"

"Brooklyn, New York. All the kids on the train I came on were from New York. Some from the city, some from Albany, some from White Plains."

"Did Mr. Tinan adopt you?"

"No, ma'am. He told the train people he would, but every time the subject came up, he had some reason to put it off." Willy's shoulders sagged.

Eve wondered if he'd really hoped to become the drunkard's legal son, but she didn't ask. It grieved her that Buck Tinan was the only person he'd had to offer his loyalty and affection to. It seemed he'd gotten little in return.

Willy halted the team a little past the mercantile.

"The Pony's yonder." He nodded down the street, and Eve could make out the signboard for the notorious saloon.

"I think I'll wait on that." Eve wasn't about to storm the saloon. Perhaps she could talk to Sally again and get her help in arranging to meet Joe Hinckle.

On Monday Eve sat in the wagon and watched as Willy approached the schoolhouse with dragging steps. He paused irresolutely. Children ran about the school yard. A cluster of young boys were kicking a ball about, and girls gathered in small groups to gossip and laugh. A couple of boys Willy's age huddled near the building. One of them nudged the other, and they stared at the newcomer.

Willy looked over his shoulder at Eve. He was still close enough that she thought she could call out to him without being overheard by the other children.

"Would you like me to go in with you?" She had spoken to the schoolmaster on Saturday, and he was expecting Willy.

The boy shook his head, squared his shoulders, and walked toward the steps. He looked fine in his new shirt. From his polite behavior at church the previous day, Eve was sure his mother had taught him manners when he was a child. She didn't think he would misbehave, but she knew he was frightened and still begrudged her a little bit for instigating this. A lot would depend on how the other students reacted to him. But surely he wasn't the only new pupil.

The front door opened, and a man dressed in a dark suit came out. He rang a handbell, its musical peal beckoning the children. They stopped what they were doing and hurried toward the steps.

Willy let most of them pass him and mounted the treads slowly. When he reached the porch, the schoolmaster spoke to him with a smile. Willy responded and shook his hand. They both turned to the door.

Eve was satisfied. She could only pray that Willy would some-how be drawn in by the lessons and lose his resentment. She clucked to the horse and headed for her prearranged meeting with Sally. She hadn't told Willy about it, fearing he would use it as an excuse to delay his entrance into school.

Sally was inside the emporium looking over bolts of cloth when Eve arrived. Eve joined her, though most of the styles Sally seemed to favor were far gaudier than Eve would want to wear.

"Thank you for coming," she said with a smile.

Sally nodded and turned her attention back to the fabrics. "I don't know if I can help you."

Eve sighed. "I've tried to talk to other people who knew Buck, but I haven't had much success. All of them claim they were nowhere near the livery on the day he died, and most of them seem to want to be left alone."

"Can't blame them," Sally said. "Nobody wants to call attention to themselves in a murder case. I only agreed to talk to you because I want Buck's killer put away. That Mr. Blair isn't a killer."

"Thank you," Eve said. "Do you have any suggestions? I tried talking to that gambler you mentioned—caught him when he finished his lunch at the Willow Tree a few days ago. But he wouldn't even admit having played cards with Buck."

"Figures." Sally fingered a shimmering satin so red Eve thought it would blind her in direct sunlight.

"Willy said he sometimes fought with the Pony's bartender, Joe Hinckle," Eve said. "I hoped you could help me get to meet him outside the saloon."

Sally shook her head.

"Why not?"

"I don't want to get on the wrong side of Joe. He could get me fired."

"Mr. Downing seems a reasonable man."

"Yeah, mostly, but Joe's a good bartender, and he's been with Downing a long time."

"At least tell me when he's at the Pony," Eve said.

Two other women approached the fabric display, and Sally grasped Eve's arm and drew her into the next aisle.

Sally faced her and lowered her voice. "He'll be in by two, and he stays late. The Pony's open all night, but another bartender comes in after midnight. I'd go early if I were you. The place gets rowdy by suppertime."

Eve exhaled slowly. "Will you be working tonight?"

"I have to be there by four, when it starts to pick up. I'd as soon you made your visit before then if you insist on going."

"I'd rather you asked him to step outside for a minute and talk to me."

"That's not going to happen."

Eve eyed her stony features. "All right. I'll try to go around two, before Willy gets out of school."

Sally's painted eyebrows shot up. "You put him in school."

"Yes, why?"

Sally nodded soberly. "Probably the best thing for him. Well no, I take that back. If you and Mr. Blair can get him to stay on that ranch with you and lead a normal boy's life, that'd be the best thing for him. He's a good kid. I'm sorry about what happened to Buck, but he wasn't a good father—for Willy or any kid."

Eve glanced around. The other women had made their selection and carried two bolts of cloth to the counter.

"Sally, what attracted you to Buck? I mean, if he wasn't trustworthy. . ."

Sally's blackened eyelashes lowered. "Every woman working in a saloon hopes to get out, to have some different kind of life. I'm not sure I'd want to answer to a man like Buck for the rest of my life, but it would be better than answering to a hundred different men every day."

Eve nodded gravely. She didn't know the indignities and wounds Sally suffered, and she was glad, but her empathy for the young woman had grown since their first meeting.

"Thank you again."

Sally shrugged. "I hope you get something out of Joe, but I doubt you will."

"You *what?*" Caleb immediately regretted his condemning tone when Eve flinched and stepped back from the bars. "I'm sorry," he said quickly. "I just can't believe you went in that place unattended."

The White Pony, while not the lowest, vilest tavern in Cheyenne, was certainly not respectable. He'd never been inside and had no desire to do so. But Eve, it seemed, in her attempts to help him bolster his defense, had walked right into it, in the middle of the day, when any number of people might have seen her.

"I'm sorry," Eve choked out. "I was only trying to help."

"I know, but—" Caleb looked away. "Perhaps it's better to let Mr. Tuttle sniff these things out. It's his job, after all."

Eve drew her shoulders upward and raised her chin. "Much as I respect Mr. Tuttle, I don't think he has an investigator out talking to Tinan's cronies."

Caleb tried not to scowl. In his opinion, Mr. Tuttle probably had good reason for that. He didn't like to think ill of Eve, but her recent endeavors seemed a bit misguided. And what did Eve know of investigators? Had she been reading dime novels? He pulled in a deep breath.

"Forgive me. I simply think you might bring harm to yourself, either to your person or your reputation, if you keep on like this."

"If I—" Her face crumpled, and he was afraid she would cry. "Oh Caleb, I want you out of here. Do you truly want me to stop trying to find out the truth? I only want my husband to be free!"

His stomach lurched. She thought of him as her husband, and he hadn't so much as kissed her yet.

"I do appreciate your efforts. Truly. But I'm so afraid of what might happen to you. I can take whatever they hand me, but Eve, if something happened to you, I don't think I could stand it."

A red tinge colored her cheeks. She took two deep breaths. "All right. I think I understand. Thank you for your concern."

Caleb's gut wrenched, and he clutched the bars between them. "It's more than concern. Don't you see? I care about you. I care—deeply—what happens to you. And there's Willy. Did you stop to think what will become of the boy if either one of us is incapacitated now?"

"Inca—" She fell mute and stared at him for a moment. "Do you really think someone would do me bodily harm?"

"Why not? Someone killed Tinan, and now you're sniffing around, asking about the circumstances of his death."

"Oh."

She stared at him with those huge brown eyes. Caleb longed to pull her to him and crush her to his chest. To protect her. To assure her that all would be well. But the sheriff had not yet allowed them to meet without the bars separating them, and Caleb had seen no evidence that he would be freed. His lawyer had visited him three times, and each time Tuttle had insisted he was doing all within his power to prepare for the trial. He'd filed some motions, for example, but Caleb wasn't really sure what that meant or if it would help. He just wanted this over with.

Eve pressed her lips together and stepped closer. "Caleb," she whispered. "Willy and I need you."

"Is everything all right at the ranch?" he asked.

"Yes. A man came by yesterday, wanting to look at a horse. Willy showed him the ones in the small pasture, but I had no idea what you would ask for them, or even if those were ones you wanted to sell."

"I'd better make you a list," Caleb said. "There are three or four

I wouldn't part with, but the rest could go if the price was right."

"Could you do that today?" Eve asked.

"I'll ask the sheriff for a pencil and paper and give it to you tomorrow." He eyed her sharply. "You are coming tomorrow, aren't you?"

"Of course."

He smiled. She had come every day, sometimes twice a day. Willy usually came too, although he probably wouldn't see as much of the boy now since school had started.

"I hope it's not wearing you down, all this running back and forth."

She shook her head. "Willy's very good with the horses. It's really not that bad. But it will be so much better when you're free."

"Eve." He gazed down at her, longing to hold her and to comfort her. "If I'm convicted—"

"Don't say it."

"I must. Look, I don't have a will, but when Tuttle comes again, I'll have him draw one up. I want to leave the ranch to you."

Tears glistened in her eyes. "You don't have to."

"It's what I want if the worst happens."

One tear trickled slowly down her cheek. "No, I mean, you don't have to, because you won't be dying soon."

"Still, it's good to have it in place." He forced a chuckle. "Even if I get out, I could break my neck any day, tussling with an ornery horse."

She blinked rapidly. Time to change the subject.

"So, what did Joe Hinckle say?"

Eve met his gaze. "That he didn't know what I was talking about. Said he never fought with Buck, though he did have to see him out of the Pony once or twice when Buck had too many."

"Did you believe him?"

"No." Eve laughed ruefully. "I don't think that man could tell the truth if he wanted to. And he looked at me like—" She shuddered and looked away.

"Don't go there again," Caleb said.

"All right, I won't."

"I'll ask Tuttle to have a conversation with him."

"If you think it will do any good."

"Time's up," Deputy Randall called from the doorway. Caleb was sure he'd given them a few extra minutes in the sheriff's absence.

"I need to go get Willy," Eve said. "School will be out soon."

Caleb reached through the bars, and she put her hand, soft and warm and pliant, in his. The breath he pulled in was painful.

"Thank you," he said.

"I didn't accomplish much."

"But you're trying. And I will discuss all this with Tuttle."

She nodded and slipped away, dodging the deputy on her way out. When he heard the outer door close behind her, Caleb called, "Randall?"

The deputy appeared in the doorway.

"I'd like a pencil and paper, please."

Randall muttered something under his breath, but half a minute later, he brought the items Caleb had requested. Sitting down on the cot, Caleb forced himself to think about his livestock and write a detailed description of each horse and the price he thought it should bring. But his mind kept going back to Eve and the way she'd looked standing on the other side of the bars, gazing at him with the sheen of tears in her eyes.

Chapter 7

Eve sat up late reading by lamplight. Willy was settled on his pallet in the next room, and she could hear his rhythmic breathing. She took the Bible that sat on the crate by the bed and opened it to the front. Caleb had mentioned that she could use it if she liked, but so far she had read from the one she had brought with her.

"James A. Blair" was written in bold script. Caleb's father? She turned to the pages between the Old and New Testaments and found, not surprisingly, a place for family milestones. James A. Blair married to Alla Bornstern, June 8, 1847.

On the next page, she found the record of Caleb's birth two years later. Another birth was listed, in 1852. Deborah. Caleb had a sister? No other babies were listed. It struck Eve again how little she actually knew about Caleb.

She flipped through the pages and noticed several passages were underlined in pencil. Was that Caleb's doing, or had someone else in the family marked them?

A folded sheet of paper lay between the leaves in the Gospel of Matthew. With just a flicker of guilt, she took it out and opened it. The single sheet was written in a delicate hand.

> *Dear Caleb, I trust all is well with the ranch. I'm pleased that you're making a go of it. You asked me to visit, but honestly, I think my bones are too weary to make that journey. I need to be here, near your papa's grave. I see your sister at least once a week, and her children are a joy. The Lord has been good to me in that way. I will have to leave it to you to come back sometime. Until then, I think we do pretty well with writing, but we do miss you. I pray for you every day.*
>
> *Love,*
> *Ma*

Eve's eyes stung with unshed tears. How lonely Caleb must be!

But not anymore, Lord. You've brought me here to help him feel less alone, as he will help me.

His mother sounded like a wise, godly woman, and her love for Caleb was obvious.

Once more Eve felt the need to press on with her endeavor to clear his name. Going into town every day was tiring, and the lack of progress depressed her. And yet Caleb's mother was out there praying for him. That thought bolstered her. Had he told his family about her yet? She had written to her parents at last, describing the ranch and what a fine man Caleb was. But she hadn't summoned up the courage to tell them why the wedding had not yet taken place.

She had to find something that would exonerate him. If only she could see some results on her inquiries. The people she'd asked about the murder—merchants, shoppers, the gambler, and a couple of other men heading into the Willow Tree—hadn't been able to tell her a thing.

She could see Willy's discouragement too, although he seemed to love the ranch. She could tell that he was happy when he was out in the pasture with the horses. He had gotten Caleb's permission to ride most of them. Only the colts, the stallion, and two mustangs that needed more training were off-limits. When he was not at school, Willy rode about the ranch, exploring every corner of the pasture.

She didn't want to think what they would do if Caleb was convicted—refused to even consider her and Willy's future.

You can make us a true family, Lord. Please don't take that promise away.

Caleb's pulse stampeded the next morning when Eve entered the jail. She looked prettier than ever. She must be getting into a routine at the ranch, and the life seemed to agree with her.

"How's Willy?" he asked. "Is he at school?"

"Yes," Eve replied. "How are *you*?"

"Same as ever."

She eyed him closely. "Has Mr. Tuttle been round?"

"He came after you left yesterday. I told him about your talk with Hinckle. He told me to advise you to keep away from the Pony."

Eve frowned. "Someone has to talk to these people."

"Easy now," Caleb said. "Tuttle says he'll handle it. Just take care of yourself and Willy. Are you eating well? Finding everything you need?"

"We are. And I haven't used any of the money from your stash, except to pay Mr. Tuttle."

"He'll probably need another payment soon," Caleb said.

"I guess lawyers are expensive." Eve's disheartenment showed in her eyes.

"Not as expensive here as they would be back east, I'm sure."

She seemed to take that at face value. Holding out his large Bible, she tipped it on edge so it would fit between the bars.

"Sheriff Nichols said I might bring you this. He's examined it to make sure I hadn't hidden any contraband in it." She smiled faintly, but she didn't seem to think it was really funny. "I read from it last night, instead of my own."

"Good. What did you read?"

"Besides a few chapters in Matthew, I read the letter from your mother that's in there. Caleb, she sounds like a wonderful woman. Does she know about me?"

His heart sank. "My mother passed on last year. I never did get back to see her."

"I'm sorry."

Her eyes told how sympathetic she felt, and Caleb hastened to reassure her.

"It's all right. I know she's in a better place, and that when I die, I'll see her again." That was the only thing keeping him from going mad in this place, knowing that if God let him hang for this crime, he'd soon be in paradise. That hope and Eve's loyalty kept him from despair.

"Your sister," Eve ventured. "Deborah?"

"Yes. She's fine. I hear from her now and again." He managed a smile. "So. Are you staying in town today while Willy is in school?"

"I thought I'd go home and do some laundry. Willy assured me he can walk home or catch a ride with a neighbor." Eve squinted up at him. "Do you think it's too far?"

"I've walked it before," Caleb said. "Three miles is a good hike, but it shouldn't do him in. And if he does meet up with someone driving that way, so much the better."

"All right then. I suppose I should let him ride one of the horses to school." She threw him a quick glance. "I thought I'd try to see Sally Buford again."

Caleb didn't like her getting tangled up with the saloon girl, not one bit. "Why?"

"She's not telling me everything."

"How do you know that?"

Eve shrugged. "It's just something about her manner that makes me feel she's holding back. And she sent me to Joe Hinckle as though she was sure he had information, but Joe was no help at all."

Caleb struggled to keep his voice low and gentle. "I told you, my dear, Mr. Tuttle will deal with that."

She sighed. "All right. I'll head home then. If I get the laundry done, maybe I'll come back in for Willy."

"You should rest."

"That's hard to do with you in here. Is there anything you'd like me to bring you next time?"

When she left, Caleb lay down and tried not to dwell on the things she'd said concerning his situation. Better to delve into the scripture and claim God's promises. He must remember that the Lord was with him, even if he had to give up his life.

Although Caleb had urged her to stop interviewing Buck's acquaintances, Eve felt compelled to keep on with her work. She dared to go back to the White Pony and linger by the entrance to the alley that led to the back door, though she'd promised not to go inside. Sure enough, a young woman overdressed for the streets approached and started to duck past her into the alley. Maybe she could shed some light on Buck's situation. There might have been someone who had his eye on Sally and resented Buck's attentions to her.

"Excuse me." Eve jumped in front of the young woman, who had to pull up short to avoid slamming into her. "I'm sorry," Eve said. "I wondered if you could help me."

"How's that?" The woman gazed testily at her through eyes rimmed in dark makeup. "You want a job here?"

"No, no thank you." Eve's cheeks heated, and she glanced around quickly to be sure no one was listening to the conversation. "Are you acquainted with Sally Buford?"

"Yeah, I know Sal. You want to speak to her?"

"No, I—" Eve swallowed hard. "I wondered if you could tell me more about her. Does she have a special man she's seeing?"

The woman frowned and pulled back a bit. "Jealous of Sally, are you?"

"What? No!"

"Humph. Best leave that one alone." She turned and stomped down the alley, knocked on a door, and disappeared inside.

Eve let out her pent-up breath. This angle didn't seem to be working. Not only was she getting no information, but people were starting to think she was jealous of a saloon girl. Caleb wouldn't want her here making these sordid contacts, she knew that.

She'd better get back to where she'd left the horse and buggy. She wanted to get some work done before Willy got home.

He had fussed and complained a little after his first day in class, but after a couple of days, on their rides home and in the evenings, he'd begun telling her some anecdotes about the teacher and the other children. Eve had decided that he didn't totally hate school, but he wanted to register his objections to the institution on principle.

When he'd mentioned a story the teacher had read to them in the afternoon, his voice went soft and wistful. Eve was certain the tale had caught his interest. It was a chapter from a book called *The Silver Skates*, and Eve remembered she had read the same book a few years earlier.

"Oh, I like that story," she'd exclaimed, and she and Willy spent the final mile of their drive that day in a lively discussion of Hans Brinker and the other characters.

She hoped the teacher continued the story today, and that Willy found other things to interest him. He hadn't said much about the other boys, and she decided he was still sizing them up and not sure how to react to them yet.

At half past four, Willy arrived at the ranch. Eve was taking down dry linens from the clothesline. She was relieved to see him come into the barnyard.

"Did you have to walk the whole way?" she called.

"No, Mr. Jarrett was passing by when I was only halfway home. He lives about a mile north of here. He gave me a ride."

"I'm glad," Eve said.

Willy lowered his schoolbooks to the stoop. "Need help?"

"No, I'm fine. Why don't you see to the livestock? There's an apple for you on the table, and I'll have supper ready in an hour."

"Thanks." Willy picked up the books and bounded up the steps.

Eve looked forward to a quiet meal with him and a report on his day, after which she would oversee his schoolwork. Willy seemed more content today. If only Caleb could come home soon and complete their family.

The next morning after her visit to Caleb, Eve walked down the street and let her thoughts roam. She came to the hitching rail near a small shop called Price's, where she had left the wagon. As she untied the reins, she heard a thunk and whipped toward the store wall behind her. A knife with a wicked five-inch blade was stuck into a solid plank of the wall.

✤ Chapter 8 ✤

Trembling, Eve grabbed the end post of the hitching rail for support. She stared at the knife for only a second, then she ducked inside the store and out of line of fire or sight from the doorway. She stood shivering and looked around. She was in a stationer's shop. Only a couple of customers occupied it. One was speaking cheerfully to the bald man behind the counter, and the other, a heavyset woman, was browsing letter paper.

Eve took a deep breath, uncertain whether she should speak of the incident to these strangers or not. She spotted a shelf of books and stepped toward it. Perusing them would give her a chance to settle her nerves and decide what to do.

If she told the shop owner about the knife, chaos might ensue. If she told Caleb, he would only worry more and would probably forbid her to come into town again before his trial. If she told Sheriff Nichols, he might look into it, or he might not. But how could she get safely to the sheriff's office to tell him? The person who had thrown the blade at her might be lurking out there, ready to try again. There were others whose help she could enlist—Reverend Viner, for instance, or attorney John Tuttle. But again, how could she reach them without the possibility of being attacked on the way?

She closed her eyes for a moment and formed a prayer for wisdom in her mind.

"Help you, ma'am?"

She opened her eyes. The man from behind the counter was standing two feet away from her, eyeing her with concern.

"Oh, I—I was going to look over the books you're offering."

He nodded. "Got a few new ones in this week. Got poetry and sermons." He reached past her and took a volume down from the shelf. "*The Housewife's Companion.* That's a popular one. Tells you all sorts of receipts and hints for keeping house."

"Oh, thank you." She took it from his hand.

"If you need anything, I'll be here."

He started to turn away, and Eve reached a sudden decision.

"Oh, please, Mr.—"

"I'm Ethan Price, the owner."

"Of course. Mr. Price, I confess I ran in here for safety."

"Oh?" His face took on the tautness of an alert man ready to act. "From what, may I ask?"

Eve gulped in a quick breath. "I had left my wagon out front while running another errand, and when I returned, someone"— she looked up at him, wondering if he would believe her wild story—"someone threw a knife at me."

His eyes widened. "A knife?"

"Yes, sir. It lodged in the side of your building."

He stared at her for a moment then strode to the door. He poked his head out and looked around, after which he stepped out onto the boardwalk. Eve followed him timidly, fearful to expose herself again.

"I don't see any knife." Price was examining the wall before the hitching post.

"It was over there." She pointed to the other side of the door, near the corner of the building, but no knife decorated the board siding anymore. "Oh dear, it's gone." She glanced around and stepped out, following Mr. Price to the spot.

In the wood, a slit marred the siding.

"It was right there." She pointed. "Do you see it?"

"Yes." Price fingered the gash in the wood, raising a sliver on the edge of the cut. "Hmm. Well, whoever threw it seems to have retrieved it." Again he looked about. "Did you see this person?"

"No, sir. I heard the impact, and I saw the knife. My only thought was to get inside, out of danger."

"Of course. But are you sure he was throwing at you?"

"Well. . ." Eve couldn't be sure, but she figured whoever did this was trying to stop her from making further inquiries. However, she didn't wish to lay out the entire story to the stationer.

"Could it have been an accident?" he asked.

"I hardly think so. Who would practice their weaponry in an area where people walk every minute, and with horses so close by?"

"Hmm. Yes." He straightened. "I can ask Sheriff Nichols to look into it, I suppose, but there's no proof, really."

"You see that it was there."

"Well yes." He seemed none too certain.

"Never mind," she said. "If you will stand here for a few moments, I will get in my wagon and drive over to the sheriff's office myself. But I'd appreciate it if you'd watch to be sure I get down the street safely."

"Certainly." He seemed to like this solution that required no real effort on his part. Eve thrust the book she was still holding into his hand and hurried to untie the horses.

At the jail, the sheriff was in. Eve insisted that he accompany her into the cell area so that she could tell both him and Caleb what had happened.

Caleb was shocked, as she'd feared he would be. "Eve, you must give up this pursuit. Let Mr. Tuttle handle things, I'm begging you."

"And why do you suppose anyone would try to hurt you, ma'am?" Nichols asked.

"Because of the inquiries I've made about Buck Tinan's death," she said.

"Hmm, would the people you talked to include Joe Hinckle over to the Pony?"

"Well yes," Eve said.

Nichols gave a curt nod. "He told me to keep that nosy eastern woman away from his place. I figured it was you."

"But don't you see?" Eve turned to him without much hope of aid. "This means someone out there doesn't want the truth to come out. Someone who knows what really happened doesn't want to see Caleb exonerated."

Caleb reached toward her between the bars. "Go home, Eve. Please."

"I can't leave Willy alone to walk all that way to the ranch after school. What if someone attacks him?"

"Willy can take care of himself," the sheriff said.

"I'll ask someone to bring him home," Caleb added. "Maybe Reverend Viner would do it if I pay him for his time."

Eve couldn't help fretting as she went to retrieve the wagon. It seemed all the people who should be helping her—the sheriff, the attorney, even Caleb—wanted her to stop making inquiries. But how would Caleb's name be cleared if she gave up now? The knife incident only reinforced her belief that the guilty person wanted to stop her.

She thought of one other person who might possibly help her. She went back to Mr. Price's stationery shop and hurried inside to purchase a pencil and a sheet of writing paper.

When she had thought carefully about her message, she walked three blocks to the Willow Tree and went inside. A few customers were having late coffee or an early luncheon. No one stood behind the bar. Maybe it didn't open until later—although a quick assessment told her that a couple of the male customers were drinking beer. Maybe the bartender was out back eating lunch, or perhaps the waitresses got the drinks for the few patrons this time of day.

She didn't see Sally, but she recognized the other waitress who had been working on her previous visit. The woman had wispy brown hair caught up in a bun, and her face showed lines of care and fatigue. Eve waited for her to finish waiting on people and headed her off as she walked toward the kitchen door.

"Please, could I have just a minute of your time?"

The waitress's lips puckered. "You here to eat dinner?"

"No," Eve said. "I need to get a message to Mr. Downing. He's not here, is he?"

"Not likely."

Eve held out her folded message. She'd kept it vague so that if anyone else read it, they wouldn't understand her inquiry, yet she hoped it was specific enough to grab Mr. Downing's attention.

You said on the train that if I needed assistance, I could call upon you. That time has come. I am staying at my fiancé's ranch, but I am in town most mornings to visit him at the jail.

Yours truly,

E. Martin

She hesitated and then rummaged in her handbag. She opened her coin purse and took out a quarter.

The waitress frowned and took the note and the coin. "I can't promise you nothin'."

"I understand, but Mr. Downing assured me that a message left for him here would reach him speedily."

The woman's face softened, and Eve realized she was younger than she'd first thought. "I'll do my best." She tucked the envelope into her apron pocket and hurried away.

Eve was suddenly very tired. She wasn't sure her legs would hold her up for the walk back to the wagon. She sank down in the nearest chair and pulled in a deep breath.

A couple of minutes later, the waitress appeared at her side. "You want something else?"

Disregarding the waitress's rudeness, Eve managed a weary smile. "A cup of tea, if I might."

"Sure." The woman dashed away, whisking some dirty dishes off the next table and onto her tray before going to the kitchen. Soon she was back with Eve's teacup, full of steaming brew. "I sent the boy who washes the dishes to take your message to Mr. Downing."

"Thank you so much." Eve's smile felt more genuine now. She hoped the boy got at least a nickel out of the two bits she'd handed over.

"My name's Rhoda."

Eve met her gaze. "I'm Eve Martin."

Rhoda nodded. "I'm here most days until about four o'clock."

"I'll remember. Thank you again."

The waitress nodded, her face still grim. Eve wondered what her story was and why she had changed her mind about helping her. She seemed almost friendly now, as though she was reaching out for something, but what?

"Rhoda," a man called from across the room, "how about another piece of that cake?"

Without a word, the waitress whirled away to serve him.

Eve sipped her tea, trying to decide what to do next. Perhaps it would be best to do as Caleb wished and go home.

Home, she thought. Over the past couple of weeks, she had started to think of the little cabin and the ranch as her home. Would she ever get to share it with Caleb? Right now, what little evidence the lawyer had to work with seemed to point toward his client. She drank the rest of her tea and stood. Doing anything was better than doing nothing.

She looked around. Several new customers had come in, and Rhoda was setting plates out before them.

Eve walked slowly back toward the wagon. Would it do any good to visit Riley at the stable again? She doubted it; he hadn't been exactly forthcoming on their first meeting. There must be something else she could do before leaving town. She knew what Caleb would say to that. She'd probably better head home and do some baking. Later she could take some treats to Caleb at the jail and show him that she hadn't been stirring up more trouble.

As she crossed the end of an alley between the stationer's and a milliner's shop, a flicker of movement caught her eye. Before she could turn, a man leaped toward her and yanked her off the street and into the alley. Eve thrashed against his hold and tried to scream, but his hand was clamped firmly over her mouth. She could barely breathe, and the smell of him soured her stomach. Was this the end? Was she going to be murdered with Caleb still in prison? She flung herself wildly about, hoping to kick her assailant, but he was too strong. His iron grip around her midsection felt as though it would crush her lungs.

Chapter 9

I told you to keep away."

Eve froze. She recognized that gruff voice. She tried again to cry out, but he held her firmly and hauled her back from the street. Finally, he shoved her away from him and against a wall. She hit hard on her shoulder and hip, then slid down to the ground.

"What do you want?" she gasped.

"Stay out of what ain't your business."

"Meaning Buck Tinan's death?" She clutched her side and turned her head to look up at him, but every tiny movement hurt.

His eyes hardened. "If you know what's good for you, you'll keep your trap shut. This is your last warning."

Eve caught sight of a man striding into the alley behind him.

"What's the meaning of this?" Mr. Downing barked.

Deputy Randall turned with his right hand hovering near his gun, but Downing already had a revolver in his hand.

"Pete Randall?" Downing's eyes flickered past the red-haired deputy to Eve, who still sat sprawled on the ground against the wall, her skirts billowing around her.

"It's nothing," Randall said. "Go on about your business."

"I'd hardly call it nothing." Downing lifted his chin and met Eve's gaze. "Are you all right, Miss Martin?"

"I'm a bit bruised." With a hand against the wall to steady herself, she staggered to her feet.

"All right, Randall, let's go." Downing's voice held an edge of steel.

"Where to?"

"The sheriff's office."

"Let me explain, Mr. Downing," Randall said quickly. "This is official business."

"Then you won't mind explaining to the sheriff. You can tell us all about it once we get over to the jail." Downing looked to Eve. "Are you able to follow us, ma'am? I think you'll wish to file a complaint."

Eve's heart still lodged in her throat. She brushed the worst dirt and debris from her skirt. "Yes, I'll be right behind you, sir."

What would Caleb say when he learned that she had defied his wishes and continued her inquiries, with this result? He wouldn't be happy, that was for certain. She tried not to think of the disappointment in his eyes.

But she was sure now that Randall was involved in Tinan's murder. If this episode led to evidence in Caleb's favor. . . More than anything, she wanted to free Caleb. Second on her list of goals was to give him reason to be proud of her. She didn't want to give him any reason to think she would not make him a good wife. She may have gone too far this time.

A sudden thought chilled her. If Deputy Randall was mixed up in this, could they trust Sheriff Nichols?

Nichols was just coming out of his office as the trio approached. He smiled and started to call out a greeting when he saw the gun in Downing's hand as the saloon keeper herded his deputy toward him.

"What's going on here, Randall? Downing?" Nichols frowned at the two men, and when he glanced at Eve his scowl deepened.

"I think we'd better take this inside," Mr. Downing said. "We can discuss it more privately there."

Nichols looked around and saw the onlookers who had paused to watch the procession. "All right." He led the way inside and turned to face Downing. "Now, what's this all about?"

"Perhaps you should relieve Mr. Randall of his sidearm before we talk."

"Mr. Randall is my sworn deputy." Nichols nodded curtly at Downing. "Just out with it."

"Your deputy attacked Miss Martin in the alley by Price's shop."

"What do you mean, attacked?" Nichols rounded on Randall.

"It wasn't like that." The deputy's eyes roamed the room, unable to meet Nichols's gaze. "She stole something from Price's. When she came out, I stopped her, and she—"

Mr. Downing cut him off in loud, angry tones. "I witnessed an assault, Sheriff. Miss Martin had not been in Price's shop. She'd just left the Willow Tree. This man snatched her as she walked down the street minding her own business. He dragged her into the alley and threw her down, and then he threatened her."

Nichols stared at his deputy for a long moment. Randall stood there, gazing at the floor.

"This is about Nancy, isn't it?" Nichols said at last.

Randall's cheek twitched. "It was his fault."

Eve tried to puzzle that out. To whom was Randall referring? And who was Nancy? She shot an anxious glance toward Mr. Downing, but like her, he was keeping quiet and waiting for an explanation.

Nichols let out a deep sigh. "The judge will have to sort it out. Come on." He took his key ring from the desk and walked into the back room.

Randall walked stiffly after him, and the sounds of metal on metal and a cell door swinging open reached them.

Downing holstered his revolver and gave Eve a thin smile. "So sorry it came to this, Miss Martin, but I guess we know who's behind Buck Tinan's death now."

"Who's Nancy?" she asked.

"I don't know Randall very well," Downing said, "but I believe she was—"

A cell door clanged shut in the other room, and Caleb said, "Sheriff, what's going on?"

"I'll get to you," Nichols snarled. He came back into the office carrying Randall's gun and badge. He stood beside his desk, his shoulders slumped.

"Sheriff, I expect you'll want us to write down what happened," Downing said.

"Yeah." Without another word, Nichols put the gun and badge in a drawer and took out two sheets of paper. He handed one to Eve and one to Downing, along with short pencils that looked as though a beaver had sharpened them with its teeth. He walked outside, leaving the door open.

Downing waved toward the desk. "After you, Miss Martin."

Eve sat down in the sheriff's chair, her mind whirling. She wanted to run into the back room and tell Caleb about the attack, but Randall was in there. She didn't want him to hear her discussing it with her fiancé. But Caleb probably heard most of it. He must be frantic. Her heart went out to him. With all her poking and digging, her only regret was the worry she had caused him. When Caleb placed his advertisement, he had only wanted a woman to love him and share his quiet life. She could do that when this was over. She wanted to do that. Her face felt hot as she thought of how their life together would be once he was released from jail. More than anything, Eve wanted that sweet, quiet life with him.

Maybe when Sheriff Nichols returned—if he did—she could ask to speak privately with Caleb. Not that he would give her that concession.

Downing had already begun to write his account, hunching his tall form over the side of the desk. Eve bent over her paper and wrote, *"I left the Willow Tree restaurant. . ."*

After they finished writing out their statements for the sheriff, Eve went to Roper Street and asked Mr. Tuttle to come to the jail. On their return, she was surprised to find Mr. Downing was still there, leaning against the wall opposite the sheriff's desk. He gave her a solemn nod.

"Sheriff, I'm here to see my client," Tuttle said, "but first, Miss Martin would like to see Mr. Blair in private."

Sheriff Nichols scowled at him but picked up the keys and stomped into the back. A moment later, he brought Caleb out.

"Sit there." He gave Caleb a little push toward his chair and stood back. "Five minutes," he said to Eve.

Mr. Tuttle bristled at that. "Surely Miss Martin, who has been very patient throughout this whole thing, should be allowed more than that."

"Five minutes."

"It's all right," Eve said, stepping toward Caleb. His whiskers had softened into a short beard, and his clothing and hair were rumpled, but she didn't care. In spite of their audience, she lifted her arms to him. After a moment's hesitation, Caleb stood and enfolded her in a warm embrace. She didn't look to see how the sheriff reacted. She was past caring.

"Don't you think the couple should have some privacy?" Mr. Downing asked, edging toward the door as Eve pulled slowly away from Caleb.

Nichols grunted and brandished the key ring at Caleb. "I'll be right outside. Don't try anything, Blair."

Tuttle touched the sheriff's arm and urged him toward the door. "My client has no reason to run, Sheriff. We all know he's innocent."

The door closed, and Eve turned her attention back to Caleb.

"What happened?" he asked, holding her hands firmly in his. "Why is Randall in jail?"

"Mr. Tuttle can fill you in. I'm sure he'll have more than five minutes."

"Eve, I—"

He hesitated, but she didn't. When he bent toward her, she rose on tiptoe and accepted his kiss. Heat shot through her, and she very daringly raised her hands to encircle his neck. Caleb's arms slid around her, warm and solid.

"Mr. Tuttle says that the judge can't help but set you free now," she whispered.

"But why?"

"It seems Mr. Randall's wife, Nancy, was killed in a carriage accident a couple of years ago. Mr. Tuttle told me about it on the way here from his office. She was driving an unruly horse rented to her by Buck Tinan."

"And that's what started all of this?"

"Apparently. And when Randall heard you'd wrangled with Buck and found your knife lying on the stable floor, he saw the perfect chance to get even—and blame it on you."

"But—"

Eve raised a finger to his lips. *"Shhh."*

Caleb apparently realized the shortness of time left to them and swept her back in for another, more passionate kiss.

Eve was still in town when it was time for school to let out. Mr. Downing had insisted on treating her to lunch at the Willow Tree, leaving Mr. Tuttle to explain the legalities of the situation to Caleb and work things out with the sheriff. The food was good, and Eve ate with a good appetite.

Mr. Downing revealed that he had come into the place through the back door just as Eve was leaving that morning. Rhoda had told him earlier how hard Eve was seeking the truth, and he had followed her out, hoping to talk to her about it. Eve was glad to see Rhoda again and have a chance to thank her for her help, though her thoughts of Caleb distracted her through the entire meal. When they'd finished, Downing walked Eve back to the jail.

"Can't let him go until the judge signs off," Sheriff Nichols said with a stubborn air. "And he won't do that until morning."

Eve was mightily disappointed, but Mr. Tuttle came from the back room and assured her that Caleb would be free as soon as the judge signed the paperwork.

"But will Mr. Randall come right out and confess?" she asked. "We know he assaulted me, but will he admit to the murder?"

Sheriff Nichols's face was gray, and he hadn't risen from his chair since Eve had returned. He and Randall were probably friends, and today's events seemed to have aged the sheriff a great deal.

He said in a flat tone, "He did it. I should have seen it sooner. He's been cut up about it ever since Nancy died. Tried to file charges against Buck for renting her a wild horse, but the judge dismissed it. Said the horse might have been stung by a bee or anything." He shook his head. "I've told him many times to let it go, but he's held a grudge all this time. I should have known he was behind this."

"Then Caleb should be freed," Eve said.

Nichols shook his head. "It's a capital case. Have to do the paperwork and get it right. Come back in the morning."

He let her see Caleb for a few minutes, but she had to go to him this time. Randall sat on the cot in the second cell and stared at her dolefully. She and Caleb spoke for a minute or two in low tones, but Eve was uncomfortable.

Caleb patted her hand through the bars. "Go get Willy. Tell him the good news. I'll see you both in the morning."

She went out to the front room. A man she'd never met sat at the sheriff's desk. Dark haired, about thirty years old, he wore a tin star like the one Randall had worn.

"Has the sheriff gone?"

The new deputy nodded. "Over to see the judge."

Eve hesitated. She had intended to ask Nichols to also question

Randall as to whether or not he had thrown the knife at her outside the stationer's shop that morning. Mr. Tuttle would probably remember.

"Thank you." She went to the wagon and drove to the schoolhouse. The children were just streaming out. Willy caught sight of her and jogged toward the wagon, his books dangling by a strap from one hand.

"Climb up," she said. "I have a lot to tell you."

"Want me to drive?"

"Thanks. You can head home." She waited until Willy turned the horses toward the ranch and got them trotting along steadily.

"Well?" He looked over at her.

"Caleb will be released tomorrow."

"On bail?"

"No." She couldn't help grinning. "He's going to walk free. Deputy Randall has confessed to killing Buck."

All the way home, they discussed that day's happenings. Willy was appalled when she told him about Randall's attack in the alley.

"I should have been there to help you," he said.

Eve touched his sleeve. "God sent Mr. Downing, so it's all right. But thank you."

Willy frowned. "We should have stopped at Reverend Viner's."

"I suppose he'd like to hear the good news."

"Don't you want to have the wedding tomorrow? You said you two was getting married as soon as Caleb got out of jail."

Eve's breath whooshed out of her, and her pulse ran riot. "Well, I—" Neither she nor Caleb had mentioned that today, but she knew what she wanted, and she was fairly sure she knew what Caleb wanted too.

The sheriff's heavy tread brought Caleb awake.

"Come on, Blair."

He sat up on the edge of the cot and fumbled for his boots. "Where we going?"

"The judge says you can go. Miss Martin's out front."

"Really?" Caleb felt a bit sluggish, but he jumped up. At last he could go home. He glanced at the man who was sleeping on a straw tick on the floor. He was still snoring loudly. The sheriff had brought two drunks in last night. Rather than put Caleb in Randall's cell, he'd stuck one inebriated prisoner in each. Caleb was grateful. If he had to spend a night with a lawbreaker, he'd rather it was a stranger than the man who tried to blame him for a murder.

After three weeks in the jail, he was feeling a bit rank, though he'd washed up every day. And his beard—well, Eve hadn't seemed to mind it when he kissed her yesterday. He couldn't help but smile at the memory.

"What you grinning at?"

He shot a glance through the bars at the cowboy who'd shared Randall's cell last night.

"I'm going home." Caleb ran his hands through his dirty hair. He couldn't wait for a plunge in the creek. Or to hold Eve in his arms again.

He heard her voice in the office. He could always tell now when it was Eve. Nobody else's voice sounded like her sweet, melodious tones. He tried to breathe slowly and calm himself. Who was she talking to? The sheriff was in here. The new deputy, maybe.

Nichols closed the cell door behind him, and Caleb followed him out, he hoped for the last time. Eve and Willy stood together, smiling as he approached. Both looked clean and combed. Eve wore a dress he'd never seen before, a shimmery green fabric that looked expensive, and Willy, he would swear, had on a brand-new shirt and a ribbon tie.

"No school today?" he asked, feeling a bit stupid and very unkempt.

"It's Saturday," Willy said.

"Oh right. Guess I lost track." He managed a smile, but he still felt disoriented. "You both look very nice."

"Thank you," Eve said, and Willy nodded.

Eve looked at Nichols. "Are we all set, Sheriff?"

"Yep, you can go anytime."

Eve slipped her hand through Caleb's arm. "Let's go then."

Willy ran ahead of them out to the wagon. The team looked shiny and well fed.

"You're taking good care of the stock," Caleb said.

"We'll take good care of you too." Eve paused on the boardwalk and turned to face him. "Caleb, I know we didn't discuss this, but I brought along a change of clothes for you. Reverend and Mrs. Viner would be happy to let you have a bath at their house, and then the pastor says we can use the church."

"The church?" Caleb gazed at her for a moment, and then her meaning dawned. "Oh." He grinned. "Today? Now?"

"If you want to. Willy suggested it. But if you'd rather wait awhile—"

"I wouldn't."

Her eyes opened wide, and a slow smile curved her lips. Then her lashes lowered, and she sobered. "There's one thing though. You know I told you in my letters about some unpleasantness in my family. . ."

"I don't care about that," Caleb said.

"Perhaps you should."

He gazed at her for several seconds, then said, "All right, tell me if it will make you feel better."

"My grandfather Martin. He. . .he was accused of stealing from his employer. He lost his position because of it, and he spent several years in prison."

Her cheeks were scarlet, and she couldn't seem to look him in the eye.

"That was him, not you," Caleb said gently.

"Don't you care? Even if he was guilty? Because everyone in town gossiped about it. They shunned my family for the longest time."

"Eve." He tipped her chin up until she met his gaze. "Everyone here has been talking about me being in jail too. What's the difference?"

Her brow furrowed. "My parents were so hurt. People were cruel."

"But that doesn't affect us now. Nobody out here has ever heard of your grandpa Martin. And they won't hear about him from me."

"Thank you."

"Are you ashamed of me because I was in jail?"

"No, but you were innocent."

"Even so, people will talk about this for a long time."

She nodded slowly. "I guess you're right."

He smiled. "Come on. This is a happy day, not a sad one."

Eve sniffed and blinked hard. "I agree. I'm very happy."

He squeezed her hand and helped her into the wagon. Willy had climbed in back, so Caleb took the reins. It felt good to hold the lines in his hands again.

They paused for a moment in front of the Willow Tree, and Willy ran inside. When he climbed back onto the wagon, he said, "Miss Rhoda will get Miss Sally and meet us at the church in an hour. And Mr. Downing, if they can find him."

Caleb eyed Eve in surprise.

"I hope you don't mind," she said softly. "They were all so helpful."

"I don't mind. Any other friends you'd like to invite?"

"I can't think of any. But what about you? You've lived here several years. Is there anyone you'd like to ask?"

"Just the Viners, and—" He caught sight of a familiar figure striding down the sidewalk and pulled back on the reins. "Whoa!"

The wagon stopped in the street. John Tuttle waved and took a few more steps, bringing him even with the wagon.

"Well, hello, Blair. I was coming to see you at the jail."

"The sheriff just let me loose," Caleb said. "We're planning a wedding in an hour. Are you interested in attending?"

"I'd love to," Tuttle said.

"Fine then." Caleb named the church, and Tuttle nodded.

"I know where it is. I'll see you there."

Caleb drove on. He was starting to relax. A deep joy was settling over his heart, and he reached for Eve's hand. She squeezed his fingers and gave him a smile that seemed almost shy, which was hard to believe after the way she'd accosted a multitude of strangers, ferreting out information to help him.

To his surprise, the Viners had a washtub all set up in the privacy of their bedroom, with several kettles of water steaming on the cookstove. Eve handed him the valise she had brought along.

"Where did this come from?" he asked.

"I had it for my train journey. Your clean clothes are in there."

Not just clean, he soon learned. She had included a new shirt and socks, along with his Sunday pants and jacket. No razor was included, so he guessed that would have to wait. At least he could wash his hair and beard.

When he emerged feeling a little more like a groom, Willy was waiting for him in the kitchen.

"Miss Eve went across to the church with Reverend and Mrs. Viner," the boy said. "Folks are starting to come."

"Well then, we'd better get over there." Caleb put a hand on Willy's shoulder. "Will you stand up with me, Willy?"

"You mean—?"

"My best man. I can't think of anyone I'd rather have."

Willy grinned. "Sure. Oh, and Miss Eve forgot to tell you—when we got home yesterday, that man came again about the horse. The pinto mare."

"Right, he was interested in her before."

Willy nodded. "Well, he bought her. Gave the price you said. So Miss Eve didn't think you'd mind if she bought me new boots. Mine were getting too small. And shirts for you and me."

Caleb smiled. "That's fine. You look mighty fine, Willy."

The boy looked away, smiling. "So do you, Mr. Caleb."

Caleb clapped Willy on the shoulder. "You did well. Let's get over there."

The next day, while Caleb and Willy worked with the young horses, Eve sat down to pen an overdue letter to her family.

Dear Father and Mother,
    Yesterday was an auspicious day for us. Mr. Caleb Blair

and Miss Eve Martin were married in Cheyenne, Wyoming, attended by Mr. William Gilman and Miss Sally Buford. William is Willy, the boy I told you about. He is happily living at the ranch. Caleb plans to build an extra room onto our small house this fall so Willy won't have to sleep on the sitting room floor. Miss Buford is a new friend I made since coming here.

The judge made us Willy's legal guardians yesterday as well, shortly after the wedding ceremony. By God's blessing, we are now a family. I do hope that you can visit us someday on the ranch, or that we can all travel back for a visit, so that you can meet Caleb and Willy. I expect to have a very happy life here on the ranch.

Your loving daughter,
Eve Blair

Susan Page Davis is the author of more than eighty Christian novels and novellas. Her historical novels have won numerous awards, including the Carol Award, two Will Rogers Medallions for Western Fiction, and two FHL Reader's Choice Awards. She lives in western Kentucky with her husband. She's the mother of six and the grandmother of ten. Visit her website at susanpagedavis.com.

Romancing the Rancher

by Linda Ford

Chapter 1

Broken Arrow, Montana Territory, 1886

Amelia Pressly looked at the brave false front of the store in Broken Arrow, Montana Territory, and hoped she could put on an equally brave false front. She left her trunk and crate by the door, hitched two-year-old Daisy higher on her hip, took a deep breath, and stepped inside the JD Mercantile Store. She blinked as her eyes adjusted to the dimmer, cooler interior. Scents—familiar and strange—surrounded her. Jute, dill pickles, and coal oil were the first she recognized. She also caught the fainter odor of animals, which might have accompanied her indoors from her long journey on the stagecoach.

This was the smell of the West.

Her gaze lit on the tall man leaning against the counter

speaking to the storekeeper who stood with his back to the shelves full of canned goods and red syrup tins. The storekeeper looked to be about the age her father would have been by now. He had a kindly face that strengthened her faltering courage.

She knew the man talking to him was the man she sought. Zach Taggerty. His letters had given her enough information to recognize the man she had come to marry.

If I had to describe myself, I'd say my jaw is often set too tight. I am taller than most. Could add a few pounds to my body, but I have always been too thin, even though Ma tried hard to fatten me up.

He turned and saw her. Tipped his hat in silent greeting. Hadn't he recognized her? She'd done her best to describe herself in her letters, but it had proven difficult. She gathered up her false courage and crossed the floor.

"Mr. Taggerty, it is I, Amelia Pressly, and this is Daisy."

"Nice to know." He smiled at the baby in her arms, "Hello, Daisy."

Nice to know? They had never met, but surely their months of sending letters back and forth meant they weren't totally unfamiliar with each other.

"Hi." Daisy didn't usually answer strangers.

What Zach Taggerty hadn't told Amelia was how dark and bottomless his eyes were. Of course, he might not see that when he looked in a mirror.

He turned back to the man with the white apron and wide-eyed interest. "Someone sent for me. Said it was urgent. I was to meet them here. I guess I missed them."

The storekeeper's gaze went to Amelia and back to Zach. He opened his mouth, looking about ready to venture an opinion about why she stood there boldly confronting this tall, handsome young man—something else he hadn't been accurate about.

I look like most cowboys. A little dusty, not always clean-shaven, and smelling like I've spent the day on the back of a horse. Which I have.

"I'm the one you are supposed to meet," she said with far more boldness than she felt. "Have you forgotten our arrangement?"

Zach straightened. Didn't she have every right to call him by his Christian name in her mind? His eyes narrowed. He looked her up and down.

"Ma'am, not only have I not forgotten any arrangement between us, but I don't recall ever making one. I have no notion of who you are."

If the floor had opened up right then and swallowed her, she wouldn't have been any more surprised.

"Hi," Daisy said again.

Zach spared a quick glance and a fleeting smile at the child. "Hi, yourself." No smile remained when his gaze returned to Amelia. "I think you've mistaken me for someone else." He tipped his hat and looked at the door behind Amelia.

She shifted to block his view and any escape he considered. If he'd changed his mind, he could at least be honest about it. "Are you Zach Taggerty? Do you have a sister named Kathy? A father who doesn't remember things very well? Did you lose your mother six months ago?"

"Who told you that?"

"You did. Let me show you." She stood Daisy beside her, hoping the unfamiliar surroundings would keep her from wandering away. Amelia put her hand luggage on the counter and opened it. All the letters were tied together with a red ribbon, which now seemed rather foolish, but she ignored the heat in her cheeks and pulled the latest note from the stack.

She held it toward him. "Here, read this."

He skimmed it and handed it back. "I didn't write it. Nor any of those." He nodded toward the bundle in her hands.

"But your name—Zach Taggerty." She pointed to the name on the page. "You answered my ad as a mail-order bride. We wrote. You sent for me. Said we would marry."

"Marry? Ma'am, you most certainly have the wrong fella. I don't have time for one more problem." His gaze went to Daisy. "Make that two. Now I best be on my way."

Amelia stuffed the letters into her traveling case, took it in one hand and Daisy in the other, and followed Zach. "I have no place to go."

Zach turned, sighed, and walked back to the counter. "You got any ideas, John?"

The man turned to Amelia. "I'm John Daniels. Welcome to Broken Arrow." The storekeeper reached for Amelia's hand. She hoped the kindness in his blue eyes and the welcoming smile on his face meant he would help her.

She shook his hand. She'd heard that name before. *"Wilma Daniels was my ma's closest friend."* It was all she could do not to hang on to the storekeeper's hand and beg for his assistance.

John Daniels turned to Zach. "You could take her home."

Zach jerked back. "You don't think my life is complicated enough already?"

Amelia drew herself up, bristly enough to scrub the inside of a potato pot. "I am not now, nor have I ever been, a problem or a complication." She had half a mind to leave the store and set out on her own. She might have too, except she couldn't drag Daisy up and down the streets begging for a place to sleep.

Zach looked around the store as if hoping a miracle would emerge from the dark corners. His gaze stopped at the post office wicket. "Where did you say you found this ad about me?"

"You found me in the *Matrimonial News*. It's a paper. . ."

"Like this?" He held up a copy of the *Matrimonial News*.

"Yes, but a different edition."

He flipped open the pages. "I don't see my name. There's nothing but numbers. I don't understand."

She remained silent. Surely he could see that the ads were posted anonymously and replies sent to the paper were forwarded to the specific person.

He paused to search the page before him. "Ah ha. Here is the answer to your problem." He folded the page back and read, " 'Farmer in the Dakotas, near the badlands, seeks a marriageable young woman. Nice farm. I'm a churchgoer. Promise to be a good provider.' There. Write him, and he'll marry you."

Someplace between "farmer in the Dakotas" and "provider," Amelia had lost her voice. And her brave front. And the strength in her legs. She clutched the counter. Now would be a good time to remember to pray, though not a thought formed in her head apart from *God, help me*. Never before had three words been so heartfelt.

"John, can you give the lady some paper and ink? Oh yeah, and an envelope, please. Put it on my bill."

Mr. Daniels didn't move. "Zach, I don't like the way you're handling this."

Zach crossed his arms and leaned back. "What would you suggest?" Before the man could answer, he added, "Besides taking her home."

"I'd say she deserves a chance."

"You got paper or not?"

Mr. Daniels handed Amelia the writing material. "Miss Pressly, I am so sorry about this."

"It's not your fault." She bent her head over the paper and concentrated. She needed a place to live, so it behooved her to make sure this letter provided all the right information. Enough about her family to reassure the man. Of course, she had to mention Daisy. *She's my sister's child and very sweet natured.* She went on to list her qualifications as a potential wife. *Although I am only eighteen years old, I have had much experience. I took care of my grandmother in her final days and tended her house since I was twelve. I am a churchgoer too and believe strongly in God's love and care.* She was about to sign her name when Zach spoke.

"Best add that you're able-bodied and pleasant to the eyes."

She hadn't realized he read over her shoulder. She jerked so hard a blob of ink landed on the envelope Mr. Daniels had provided. Her hand shaking, she added that she was able-bodied.

"Where shall I tell him to contact me?" She had no home, no address, no bed upon which to find rest. And how was she to find food for the two of them while she waited for a reply?

"He can send it to my address." Zach seemed to think this was satisfactory.

She did not, but she affixed her signature, blotted the ink, and waved the page to dry before she folded it, inserted it into the envelope, and glued it shut. She added the address for the *Matrimonial News*. The paper would forward it to the Dakota farmer. She handed the envelope to Mr. Daniels.

He stared at it. "Zach, this doesn't seem right."

"Don't seem right for someone to pretend to be me then not show up."

Mr. Daniels lifted the letter in a sign of agreement, or perhaps confusion at this drama taking place in his store. He glued on a stamp and set the letter in the pile of outgoing mail.

Zach nodded, satisfied. "Well. That's that." He again headed for the door.

Amelia considered her options, but she had none. "Guess Daisy and I will stand here and wait for a reply from that man. Mr. Daniels, how long do you suppose it takes to get a letter to this place in the Dakota Territory and a reply? I expect we will have to correspond back and forth for a few months."

Zach stopped, his back to her.

"Oh, don't worry about us, Mr. Taggerty." She knew her voice was sharp, perhaps a bit accusing, but she couldn't help it. She had been misled far worse than he. "We'll be just fine. Yes, just fine. Daisy is such a good girl, I'm sure she won't fuss at all when we sleep outside and beg for food scraps."

"Zach." Mr. Daniels's voice carried a warning note. "What would your ma want you to do?"

Zach ground about. "She'd want me to look after my sister, my father, and the ranch. But no doubt she'd think I should show a little Christian charity." He managed to make it sound like he'd swallowed some bitter seeds and couldn't wait to spit them out. "Very well. You and the young one can stay at the ranch until you hear from this man. That your trunk on the step?"

"Yes."

"It all you got?"

"That and the box beside it." She clung to her traveling case.

"I'll give you a hand." Mr. Daniels hurried around the counter to help Zach. "Good thing you brought the wagon."

"I had to pick up a few things while I was in town."

Holding Daisy by the hand, Amelia went to the wagon. Her day had started out so full of promise as she anticipated marrying a man she thought she had grown to love in the weeks they had corresponded. But there was no such man. Only disappointment and, if she were honest, a large dose of fear. Had God abandoned her? No, her circumstances might have taken an unexpected and unpleasant turn, but God's faithfulness had not changed. *Never will I leave thee nor forsake thee.*

Never before had she felt her faith more severely challenged.

Mr. Daniels helped her up to the wagon and lifted Daisy to her. "Things will work out. You'll see."

"Thank you." But it would take more than the pleasant words of the storekeeper for that to happen.

Zach studied the woman out of the corner of his eyes as they left the dusty town of Broken Arrow behind and continued down the dusty trail toward the ranch. If they didn't get rain soon, everything would turn to dust. He'd about worn out his hope that God would listen to any of his prayers. How many had he uttered about Pa's mental state, about the ranch, the need for rain, and his sister, Kathy? At twelve years of age, she had turned into a rebel. Ma would be so disappointed. Not only in Kathy, but also in Zach, though he was doing his very best to handle everything.

None of his prayer requests had been answered. None since his ma's death. Maybe God only listened to Ma's prayers, and with her gone. . .

He knew his thoughts were foolish, which signified the depth of his discouragement.

Daisy shifted in Miss Pressly's lap and studied Zach. The child was sweet-looking with fair hair sticking out from under her bonnet and unusual green eyes like some kind of a gem.

"Bird," Daisy said, pointing to a crow flapping in the air.

"Yup, a crow."

"Bird."

Miss Pressly laughed. "Daisy, a crow is a bird."

Zach's gaze connected with Miss Pressly's over Daisy's head. She had the same green eyes as the little one. Her hair was considerably darker though still not quite brown. No doubt there was a proper name for the color, but he'd settle for something between brown and blond. He almost snorted as he thought how the young lady would react if he described her hair as dirty blond.

"Is Daisy your daughter?"

"If you'd read my letters, you'd know she is my niece. My sister died, and I'm her guardian."

He'd missed that bit of information as he'd glanced at the letter she'd moments ago penned. "I would have read your letters if I had gotten them." Someone was playing a cruel trick on both of them. It hit him that it was an inconvenience for him, but for her, it was more like a disaster. He felt sorry for her predicament, but he didn't intend to marry her to correct it.

"Well, someone got them and wrote back to me." She faced forward, her lips pressed into a disapproving frown.

"Are you suggesting I got them but am pretending otherwise?" He didn't give her a chance to answer. "How am I to know you aren't making this all up?" Except she knew about Kathy and his parents. But how hard would it be for her to get that information by simply asking around?

"Mr. Taggerty, even if I didn't have Daisy to consider, I would not be so foolish as to arrive in western Montana without believing I had a home waiting for me."

"I suppose not." They rode on in silence except for Daisy pointing to things and calling the name of them, though he was mostly guessing that what she said carried a meaning. He slanted a look at her. He could remember when Kathy was learning to talk. So sweet and innocent. Now look at her. He sank down into his troubled thoughts.

Miss Pressly leaned forward. "There's the turnoff to the ranch. Just like you described it. The big trees on either side of the gate. The sign over the top. Bar T. You said you wanted to put some flowers here in memory of your ma. Guess you never got around to it."

"Guess I never knew I planned it in the first place." But it was a good idea. If this drought ever ended, he would do that.

They turned off the road and on to the trail leading to the ranch.

Miss Pressly sat back, her arms around Daisy, her fingers intertwined. Her knuckles were white. For a moment, he allowed himself a little pity toward her and her situation.

She sucked in air. "Is your pa any better?"

"What do you know about Pa?"

"What you told me."

"I wish you'd stop that."

"How else do I explain it? In the letters you wrote, you told me how he'd been slowly losing his ability to remember or to think clearly. Last letter I got said he had wandered off and it took you half a day to find him."

"My cook is supposed to watch him. Make sure he doesn't wander away."

"Gil, right?"

"I have to admit it kind of bothers me to hear you talk about my family like you know them. Kind of scrapes along my nerves, if you know what I mean."

She looked at him, her green eyes as hard as whatever that gem was called. He bet it took a lot of heat and many hard blows to soften that gem. Sure hope it didn't mean the same for dealing with this woman.

"I know what you—your letters—or whoever wrote them—told me. You are nineteen years old. Your mother is dead. You hired Gil to help, but he has a fondness for liquor so can't always be counted on. You have a new neighbor who is doing his best to drive you out. I know the layout of your house. I know where it is in relation to the barn. I know you have a thousand head of cows on free range." Her eyes glittered. "Anything I've forgotten?"

He shuddered visibly, letting her know how much this disquieted him. "And I know almost nothing about you."

"In my letters I told you I am eighteen."

Young, just like him.

"My sister and I were orphaned when I was ten and she was twelve. Our grandmother took care of us in Righteous, Ohio. My sister died shortly before we started to correspond."

"How long ago was that?"

"Three months." Her voice caught as if her throat had closed off. Her loss was so recent. He understood how it pained her to speak of it.

"I'm sorry for your loss."

"Thank you." Her voice was low. The words broken.

He understood how sorrow could do that to one's speech and again felt a reluctant pity for her.

They would soon arrive at the ranch. His nerves twanged like frosty wire at the dread of what he might find. "Seems I never come home without some disaster awaiting me."

"I know."

"How much did this person posing as me say?"

"He was pretty frank."

Zach squirmed. "Please tell me he didn't present me as a whiner."

She laughed.

He kind of liked the sound.

"Not at all."

"I have one question for you. Why would you want a mail-order marriage? Surely there are lots of young men in Righteous, Ohio."

She kept her eyes focused on the approaching buildings. Then slowly answered. "None who would welcome Daisy." She tightened her arms about the child and kissed the top of her head.

He dipped his gaze to the little gal who smiled up at her aunt. "That seems odd. Why do I get the feeling there is something you aren't telling me?"

She puffed out her cheeks and looked at him. "I guess it won't provide a reason for you not to marry me, seeing as you've already refused to do so. My sister—" She swallowed hard and blinked twice. "Daisy was born of my sister's immoral life."

Zach examined each word for its meaning. "Immoral life? You mean she was a. . ." He sought for a polite way of saying it.

"A soiled dove." Her rock-hard gaze held his like a vise— waiting for his response. She pulled Daisy harder to her chest. "My niece carries the shame of it. That's why I did not stay in Righteous. The people there would not accept her. The men either rejected me or thought I was like Callie. That's my sister. It was Grandmother who said I should seek marriage elsewhere. She thought I should keep the truth of Daisy's mother a secret, but I can't do that. All I ask is that whether you find that taints her in your sight or not, you keep the facts to yourself. I know I can trust you to do that." She gasped. "I'm basing that on what I know of you from your letters, but I'm trusting a man I don't know."

He wanted to argue, but what could he say? She thought she knew him from correspondence that someone posing as him had sent.

Who had sent those letters?

❧ Chapter 2 ❧

The knowledge that she had left every bit of security to journey to Montana on a false belief and was now riding into a situation fraught with all sorts of dangers left Amelia stunned and immobile.

I will trust and not fear.

She repeated the words over and over. It was easy to trust God. Mostly easy to trust the Zach she had grown to know through his letters. But this Zach. Who was he?

They arrived at the ranch, and she looked about with a sense of familiarity. The house, just as it had been described to her. A two-story log structure. The logs weathered to gray. Not large, but warm and homey. To her left, the barn, the corrals, and beyond that, the bunkhouse, *"where we have up to a dozen men in the spring and fall, especially for the roundup."* Next to that, the cookhouse, which she understood would not now be in use. The men would be out and their meals prepared at the chuck wagon.

So many details she knew.

Zach pulled up to the house. He glanced toward the corrals and groaned.

"Kathy," he yelled, causing Daisy to jump and whimper. "Get away from that horse."

Amelia saw the girl. Dressed in dungarees and a faded red shirt, with a cowboy hat mostly taming a mane of black hair that tangled about her shoulders. As she turned, the hat fell to her back. She saw Amelia, her eyes widened, and she grabbed the bridle hanging from the fence and climbed to the top rail.

In the corral, a horse snorted and pawed the ground.

"Wait here," Zach said. "While I drag my little sister away from certain death." He ran across the yard and grabbed Kathy before she could swing both legs over the fence.

He held her under his arm and carried her back, kicking and swinging her fists.

"Put me down, you big, overgrown hunk of stupidity."

"Don't talk to me about stupid. I told you to leave that horse alone. He's wild. It will take an experienced man to break him."

"I'll be experienced once I've ridden him."

"No. You'll be dead or crippled. And I sure don't need either one."

Amelia climbed down and set Daisy on the ground beside her. The child clung to Amelia's side as they watched the pair wrangle their way across the yard.

"I told you. I intend to be a cowboy. The sooner you accept that, the sooner I can get on with my plans."

"Don't know if you realize it." Zach's voice was as dry as the dusty road they had traversed a few moments ago. He brought

Kathy as far as the wagon and set her on the ground, keeping a firm hold on one arm. "But you ain't never going to be a cow*boy*."

Kathy had eyes as dark as her brother's. The two scowled at each other.

Amelia pressed her fingers to her mouth to stifle her amusement.

Kathy jerked toward her. "Who are you?"

Zach's voice rumbled in his throat, a clear warning for his sister to mind her manners.

Amelia wasn't offended. "I'm Amelia, and you're Kathy. Pleased to meet you."

"I'm not Kathy. I'm Kat."

"Hi, Kat." Amelia thought the name most appropriate. The girl seemed all fangs and claws. "This is Daisy. Daisy, say hello."

Daisy managed a quick greeting and then buried her face in Amelia's skirts.

"She scared of me?" Kat demanded.

"She might be." Amelia wasn't going to point out that Kat's yelling and fighting was reason enough for a child to experience some fear.

" 'Course she's scared of you. She thinks you're some kind of wild animal." Zach looked around. "Is Pa in the house?"

"Pa's gone."

"Gone?" He jerked her arm. "Where? When? Where's Gil?"

"Gil's behind the house. In the shade. With a bottle." She broke from Zach's grasp. "She planning to stay?"

"For a bit," Zach said. "I have to find Pa. I'll deal with Gil later."

"Have fun." Kathy started to flounce away then stopped. "What-cha gonna do with them?"

Amelia knew Kathy meant her and Daisy. Zach's sister's words were far from welcoming.

"Would you show her to a room? Help her take her things inside."

"Why me?"

"Could you please just do it?"

Amelia thought the strain of holding his temper must do strange and frightening things to this man's brain.

Zach didn't wait for Kat to agree to his request. He got halfway to the barn when a horse rode toward them.

"Here comes trouble." Kat's disgust filled her words.

Amelia picked up Daisy and held her tight, half expecting the man to pull a gun. But the man looked like he had purchased his clothes a mile from town. Not a speck of dust clung to him. His hat looked equally new. He rode a fine-looking bay horse. She checked his boots. Yes, exactly as the letter writer had described. *"Boots that haven't seen anything but a clean floor."*

"It's Mr. Sobel, your new neighbor, isn't it?"

Kat fairly spit out her words. "Neighbor by closeness but not by any sort of kindness. The man is nothing more than a well-dressed crook."

They both listened openly as the man rode up to Zach, who waited with his arms akimbo and his brow furrowed in grooves deep enough to plant potatoes.

"Good to find you home." Mr. Sobel sounded pleasant enough. If one didn't hear the mocking undertones. "Too bad you aren't out looking after your cows." He leaned over his saddle horn. His voice grew hard. "Boy, I've said it before, and I'll say it again. This isn't a job for a youngster. Sell out while you have cows to sell. Move to town, where you can tend to your sister and addled father."

Zach had dropped his hands to his sides, and his fists curled and uncurled. "I ain't sellin', and especially not to the likes of you."

"There'll come a time you'll be glad to let me take what's left of your cows off your hands."

"What do you mean, what's left of them?"

"With this drought there isn't enough grass for the both of us." The man reined about, saw Amelia, and stopped. "Well, well, well. You're a pretty addition to the place. Allow me to introduce myself. I'm—"

Amelia handed Daisy to Kathy. The little one squirmed. "Hold her. I don't want her running after me." Amelia lifted her skirts and strode toward Mr. Sobel. "I know who you are. You're the man who is making life miserable for this family. I detest such unkind behavior."

Mr. Sobel leaned back and laughed.

Still grinning, though Amelia detected a hint of malice in the man's pale blue eyes, he looked at Zach. "I see you've found yourself a little spitfire. That ought to prove interesting." He doffed his hat.

Three cowboys thundered in on lathered horses. "Boss, Boss," they called. "The cows are way to the east, miles from water. They're standing around with their tongues out."

"You have to choose whether to be nanny to your kid sister and father or take care of your cows." With that Mr. Sobel rode from the yard, seemingly pleased with this turn of events.

Zach stared after him, his jaw muscles bunching. "Get my horse. And do something with the horses you're on before you ruin them."

The cowboys wheeled toward the barn.

Zach looked heavenward and let out a long, weary breath. "I still have to find Pa and sober up Gil."

"I'll look after your pa and the cook. You take care of the cows," Amelia said.

"You? You just got here."

"You forget I have learned a great deal about your family. Leave them to me."

The cowboys led a horse toward Zach and waited.

She watched him trying to decide if he could count on her or not. If he'd read her letters, he would know the things she'd had to deal with. "Your experience is with cows. Mine is with hurting, sick people. Let's each do what we're best at."

"I seem to have little choice. None, in fact." He swung into his saddle and rode off without a backward look, the three cowboys in his wake.

It was a far cry from the welcome Amelia had expected, but she wasn't about to sit around and mope. The man needed help even if he didn't welcome it from her.

"You're going to take care of Pa and Gil?" Kat sounded more doubtful than impressed.

"I'm going to do my best. Now where would your pa go?"

"I don't know. Sometimes he wanders down the road. Sometimes he goes to the trees over there or there." She pointed west and then north. "Sometimes he just sits and stares into space. But if you call him, he doesn't answer."

"I'll find him. Can you watch Daisy for me?"

Kat studied the wide-eyed child in her arms. "Do you think she likes me?"

"Of course she does. What's not to like? Just don't let her run away. You might give her some water and maybe a biscuit or a piece of bread and jam."

"Okay."

Amelia took Daisy's face between her hands. "You stay with Kat until I get back. Be a good girl."

Daisy looked around. "Kitty?"

Amelia chuckled. She turned Daisy's face toward Kat and rested her hand on Kat's head. "This is Kat."

"Hi, Daisy," Kat said.

"Hi, Kitty." Daisy stroked Kat's hair where it draped over her shoulder.

Kat and Amelia chuckled.

"You two take care of each other. I'll be back when I find your pa." She looked about. North, west, trees, rocks. Where would he go? How far would he roam? *I found him five miles from home sitting on a fallen tree looking lost and forlorn.* She decided to try the trees first.

As she walked, she took in the scenery. Zach's letters had been full of praise for the rolling hills, the richness of the grass in the draws, the abundance of trees and water, and the mountains, so blue and majestic, *"like guardians of the land."* She smiled at the memory of those words.

Who had written them?

She traipsed down a hill. The grass was brown. Little puffs of seeds and yellow fluff blew up at each step. So dry. In his last letter, the writer had mentioned his concern for the drought.

The ground rose, and she climbed to the top of the rise. The trees were to her right.

"Mr. Taggerty," she called, then listened. No answer. She didn't know his given name. She called again. "Mr. Taggerty." Kat had said he sometimes stared straight ahead and didn't seem to hear, so Amelia circled the trees of mixed deciduous and evergreen and then went deeper. "Pa, Pa," she called, hoping the title would more likely elicit a response.

She had searched the entire grove. He must have gone elsewhere. Then she saw him, almost invisible in the dabbled sunlight, sitting in the shadow of a large tree.

He seemed unaware of her presence. Not wanting to frighten

him, she approached slowly. "Mr. Taggerty." No response. "Pa." His head came up. Good. She knelt in front of him. "Hi, how are you?"

He smiled and touched her shoulder. "Do I know you?"

"Maybe not. My name is Amelia, and I've come to take you home."

He looked about. "I can't remember how to get back."

"That's okay. I know the way. Will you come with me?" She held out her hand.

He took it, and she led him from the trees. "We go down this little hill and up the other side, and then you'll see home."

"Good. How long have I known you?"

She didn't think loading him with details would do any good. "Not nearly long enough."

"Okay."

They climbed to the top of the hill and paused to catch their breath. She pointed. "Do you see home?"

"Oh yes, yes I do." He set off at a trot.

"Slow down. Wait for me."

He stopped. "I'm sorry. I got excited."

She chuckled and tucked her hand around his arm. "Let's walk together." As they approached the house, she glanced about. Where were Kat and Daisy? She gave the corrals a quick study and let out her breath when she didn't see them there.

Mr. Taggerty rushed for the door and into the house. He stopped and backed up a step.

"What's wrong?" Amelia asked.

"Maybe this isn't my home." He pointed toward the table. "I don't recall a baby."

Amelia patted his shoulder. "That's my little girl. Her name is Daisy. Daisy, say hello."

" 'Lo." She waved. Red jam circled her mouth and dotted her fingers.

"Hi, Pa." Kat watched her father with a good deal of wariness. The poor girl had been dealing with the uncertainty of his behavior a long time.

"Thank you for taking care of Daisy." Amelia led the man to the table as she spoke. "Kat, would you give your pa some bread and jam?"

Kat sprang up to do so and poured him coffee from the pot on the back of the stove. The liquid was black and thick. How long ago had it been made?

She'd make some fresh just as soon as she got things under control. "Now where can I find Gil?"

Kat nodded to the side of the house.

"Will you keep an eye on these two while I deal with him?"

Kat's eyes lit. "I'd sooner see how you handle him."

Amelia didn't say anything, just waited for Kat to answer her question.

"Oh, very well." The words were anything but gracious.

"Thank you." Amelia went outdoors and around the house. She could have followed her nose to the man. He sat with his knees drawn up and his head lulled to one side. A bottle hung from his hands. He didn't hear her approach.

She stood in front of him. "Gil." She spoke sharply, not knowing if the man was passed out or sleeping. Either way, he was as drunk as a miner in town with a poke of gold and nothing to spend it on but liquor.

Gil jerked. His legs jolted outward, and he stared at her, struggling to focus. He opened his mouth then closed it, but before he could find his voice, she spoke.

"Zach was good enough to bring you here, give you a home and some dignity in exchange for cooking and watching his pa. You agreed not to drink while you're here. Now look at you. You're a mess."

He looked at his clothes and patted his pant legs, sending up puffs of dirt.

"You're sitting here drinking while Mr. Taggerty roams away on his own."

Gil found the bottle where he'd dropped it when she frightened him awake. Before he could lift it to his lips, she took it and poured the contents on the ground.

"Tha's mine."

"Not while you're here."

Gil struggled to his feet, swayed, and groaned. "Maybe I won't stay."

"You have no other place." Zach had found him behind the saloon. Said he'd begged or scavenged food from what the hotel dining room threw out.

"I ain't nothing but a drunk." The exact words Zach—only, she reminded herself, it wasn't Zach—had written in his letter.

He used to cook for the men, but Pa let him go when he went missing a few too many times after a weekend in town. I found him sleeping off another weekend behind the saloon. He looked terrible and smelled worse. I poured black coffee into him. He said, "Heard your ma died. Sorry. She was a good woman." I explained about Pa and the new neighbor. He got riled at that. I asked if he wanted to come back to work. His eyes lit up, and then he shook his head. "I ain't nothin' but a drunk."

She repeated Zach's answer. "You can change that."

"Trying."

"Sitting at the side of the house downing the contents of a bottle isn't trying. Now this is what you are going to do." As she spoke, she steered him toward the house. "You're going to get sober and stay sober and do the job Zach hired you to do."

They entered the kitchen. "Kat, would you take Daisy out to play, please?"

"Aw. I'd like to see what you do."

"And I don't want Daisy to witness this. Please."

Kat sighed, a sound that carried a whole world of grievances. "Come on, Daisy, let's go."

Pa remained at the table. He looked at Gil as he sat across from him. "You smell awful."

"But I feel good." Gil's laugh was wobbly. "Mostly."

"You'll feel better when you drink this." Amelia emptied the coffeepot and set the cup before him. "While you do, I'll make some fresh."

A little later, he was sober enough to make sense. And Pa was right. Gil smelled bad. "Go wash up somewhere and put on clean clothes. You aren't fit to be around decent company."

Scowling and muttering, Gil stalked from the house. She didn't know where he'd wash, nor did she care. So long as he didn't have another bottle stashed somewhere. With that in mind, she watched him cross to the barn, remove his boots, and step into the water trough, fully dressed.

"Now to get my things inside." She went upstairs and poked her head into the five bedrooms. He called this a small house! She found one empty except for a bed, a table at the bedside, and a large wardrobe. It would do just fine. Though she might make Daisy a bed on the floor so she wouldn't worry about her falling out of bed.

Back downstairs, she went outside. "Kat, can you help me with my trunk?"

The two girls played on a swing.

Reluctantly, slowly, letting Amelia know just how put out she was about this, Kat stood Daisy on the ground and sauntered over. Daisy followed on her heels.

"How long you staying?"

They struggled up the stairs with the trunk and into the bedroom. "I don't rightly know."

Back downstairs and out to the wagon. The crate was easier to take up to the room.

As they descended, Mr. Taggerty waited at the bottom of the stairs. "Have you come to help?"

His face puckered up with trying to sort out this change in his household.

She smiled. "Yes, I'm here to help. Is that okay?"

He thought on it a minute then smiled. "I like that."

Amelia turned to Kat. "How about you? Are you okay with that?"

Kat shrugged. "Don't matter to me. I aim to be doing some cowboyin'."

"Good. Then I have just the job for you."

Kat brightened. "Yeah? Sounds good."

"You can help me take care of the horses." Zach had left them hitched to the wagon, no doubt expecting Gil to take care of them.

"That ain't cowboyin'. That's chorin'."

Amelia managed to get the girl to the door as they talked. "I spent a week traveling here, and in that time, I saw lots of cowboys. Never saw one who would neglect a horse."

"How many did you see?"

Amelia took Daisy in her arms as they led the animals to the barn. She told Kat of some of the cowboys she'd seen. They took care of the animals then returned to the house. Pa stood at the window watching for them. At least he hadn't wandered away.

Gil emerged from the bunkhouse, his hair slicked back, his whiskers brushed into place, and wearing clean, albeit wrinkled, clothes. He didn't return to the house but sat on the steps of the bunkhouse, his head in his hands.

That left Amelia to prepare supper, and she set to it. Pa sat at the kitchen table. Kat and Daisy played a finger game.

She explored the kitchen, opening cupboards and looking into bins. Zach had said little about this room in the house. She paused and smiled as she recalled what he had said.

Ma always made the kitchen a place where we gathered as a family. Some of my fondest memories are sitting around the table, laughing and talking. Things changed after she passed. And especially with Pa not being himself. I miss those times.

It sounded idyllic. Everything she had dreamed of, planned for, and expected.

Except for one small detail. Zach was not the one who wrote her, nor was he the slightest bit welcoming.

Who had written those letters? Was that man waiting for her? But unless Zach had a twin brother with a life the same as Zach's. . .

Was there some way she could sort this out and keep a roof over her head, for Daisy's sake?

ᘉᕗ Chapter 3 ᘂᕐ

It was almost dark as Zach made his weary way home. His stomach kissed his backbone. He was hungry enough to eat the bark off the trees he passed. He'd missed dinner in order to take care of the cows, and now he was set on missing supper. Those at home would have eaten supper a long time ago. Though he didn't know if they would have had a proper meal, what with Gil drinking again. They might have had to scrounge for whatever they could find in the kitchen.

What he wouldn't give for Gil to stay sober and cook a decent meal.

While he was wishing for the impossible, he might as well wish Kathy would turn into a sweet young gal and Pa would be well enough to take over some of the responsibility of running the ranch.

His stomach growled. If only Ma were alive. But he might as well wish for rain from the cloudless sky.

God in heaven, our land is suffering for want of rain. Could You please send some our way?

He knew God did not always provide the answers a man sought. His ma would have said God had bigger, better plans, but Zach couldn't see how that was possible. Without rain, the grass would wither, the cows would lose weight, and the weaker ones would die. How was he to take care of his family if he lost his livelihood?

The house came into view. A light flickered in the kitchen window. He rose in his stirrups and studied the place. One of his worries was that Pa might accidently start a fire. He nudged his horse to a faster pace. The light focused on the table. Soon he could make out a lamp. Had someone forgotten to put it out?

He went directly to the barn and took care of his mount, then ran for the house and threw open the door.

"Welcome back."

He skidded to a halt at the cheery greeting. "Miss Pressly, what are you doing up?" A calming beat of his heart. "I half forgot you were here." Truth was he had pushed away every thought of the young lady because he didn't want to deal with another problem in his already troubled life. What was he supposed to do with her?

"First, let's dispense with the formality. You've addressed me as Amelia in your letters."

Before he could protest, she held up a hand. "Or at least I believed you did. So please, call me Amelia. And the reason I'm up is to wait for you."

Just like Ma used to do. Except Ma wouldn't have ignored his comment about forgetting about Amelia. She would have pointed out that either he was pretending or he was being rude. In this case, it was a little of each.

"I didn't know if you would eat at the chuck wagon, but I saved you a meal just in case you were hungry."

His stomach rumbled. "I'm starved." And he wasn't about to turn away good food just because the woman offering it posed a problem to his tidy little life. He barely kept a snort from erupting. Tidy life? He hadn't seen such since Ma died.

Amelia got a plateful of food from the warming oven and set it before him.

"Thank you." Mashed potatoes and pork chops drowned in rich gravy, turnips, and peas. "Did Gil sober up enough to cook?" He dug in without waiting for her answer.

"I made it."

He nodded. "It's good. Thank you." He glanced toward the stairs. "Pa?"

"I found him in the trees to the west. He's home and sleeping soundly."

"Good. I gotta say I was worried about him. I didn't know if—"

"If I could manage him?"

He nodded then thought better of it and shook his head.

"He was agreeable. Seemed to like having company. Daisy is calling him *Gampa*."

"That's nice." *I guess.* But wouldn't it confuse Pa even more to have them move in and then move out? "I take it Gil was too hung over to cook."

"He sobered up enough to join us for supper, then went to the bunkhouse. I hope he doesn't have a bottle stashed there." She sat across the table from him.

Gil had bottles hidden in half a dozen places, but there was no point in saying so. Zach cleaned his plate and looked about. Ma always made dessert, but no reason to expect it now.

Amelia brought a large serving of apple crisp to the table. "Were you able to deal with your cows?"

"We found a hundred head hours away from water and had to drive them back slowly. Lost six."

"How did they get so far? Doesn't seem natural."

He cleaned his bowl and resisted an urge to lick it clean. "It's not. Someone has been systematically separating them out a few head at a time and driving them away."

"Where was your foreman? Morgan Grant. Right?"

He stared at her. "How do you know that?"

"From the letters?"

"The letters I didn't write?"

She chuckled, and her green eyes caught the lamplight in glittering sharpness. "You don't by any chance have a twin no one knows about?"

"If I do, I think it's about time he started pulling his share of the workload around here."

She laughed, and he stared. As if he'd never heard a woman laugh before.

"About the foreman?" she asked again, her eyes becoming more serious.

"He's been busy at the river, fighting Sobel's men to allow the cattle to drink."

"Aw. That's not nice. I've not liked this Sobel man since you—" She stopped before she could again say he'd written her. "Since I first heard of him. But you got everything sorted out, didn't you?"

"For now. But Sobel is determined to make me quit. He thinks he'll succeed because, in his eyes, I'm nothing but a boy."

"Just as I'm nothing but a girl, and yet I've taken care of my grandmother as she declined in health. I took care of her estate after she passed. I nursed Callie when she came home dying. I will raise Daisy as my own daughter." Her voice grew firmer with each word. "And I traveled west to get married." The fire in her voice died and she stared at her hands.

"I feel at a disadvantage. Someone has told you all about me and my situation, but today is the first I've heard of yours. You've had a lot to deal with." Not unlike himself. He felt a tremor of connection that he dismissed before it could take up residence.

She lifted her head and gave him a look full of determination. "No more than have you."

Their gazes fused as he recognized in her someone who had been forced to grow up early and fast. Again the thought—not unlike himself.

This time he couldn't as easily dismiss the notion, and in that moment, he felt they shared something he'd been unable to share with anyone else. He couldn't understand why it should be, but the idea calmed his soul and strengthened his spirit.

"Did you get settled into a room upstairs?" His gaze sought the steps that rose to the second story.

"Kat helped me move into the next to the last."

Zach had the first, Pa next to him, and then Kat.

"Kat helped you?" He couldn't keep the disbelief from his voice. "Lately, she's balked at helping do anything but eat."

Amelia laughed. "I'm not about to claim she was overjoyed, but she helped. She and Daisy played together, and that helped as well." She looked about. "Your home is every bit as lovely as I expected. What I've seen of the countryside is peaceful. I can see why you called the mountains 'guardians of the land.'"

"I said that?"

"Well, whoever wrote the letters and signed them 'Zach Tag-gerty' did. I'm still having trouble thinking of that person not being you." She pressed her fingertips to her forehead. "Who would do such a thing, and for what reason? It puts me in rather an awkward position, wouldn't you say?"

Him too. He tried to think how to answer, but everything that came to mind sounded unkind. "Someone will want to marry you."

"Of course they will. After all, I'm a good worker. I made a good meal, didn't I? I tended the horses with Kat's help, and I settled your pa. By the way, your pa thinks I'm here to help."

"What does Kat think?" She could make life difficult for them all if she chose to.

"I think she was glad to have someone take charge of Gil and your pa and supper." She gave him a look that made him blink with surprise. What had he done to earn a silent challenge?

"I hope you don't mind that I took over things."

"You said you would, and I left you to do so." He pushed back from the table. "I appreciate coming home to a hot meal. Thanks." He stood behind his chair and looked down at her. "But it doesn't change anything. I don't have time for courting, or for tending to a wife's needs. Truth is, I don't even know if I'm going to be able to save this ranch from ruin, and not just because I'm a kid, as Sobel constantly reminds me. Between the drought, the men—" He didn't know what the author of those letters had told her about the men, but he certainly didn't intend to whine about it.

She rose and faced him, her hands clasped to the top rung of the chair. "What about the men? The letters mentioned they didn't feel they should obey your orders, but I thought getting Morgan as the foreman had fixed that problem." She waited a heartbeat. Two. When he didn't answer, she pressed. "Did it not?"

"Not entirely."

"How much did it not help? Are the men refusing to obey your orders?" Her eyes narrowed. "Are they in cahoots with Sobel? How much do you trust Morgan?"

They studied each other over the table that had been the site of many family meetings. Pa had included Ma in all the decisions. *"It's as much her life as mine,"* he'd said. *"Besides, she has some good ideas. You should listen to her as well."*

He didn't expect any wise words from Amelia. After all, she was a newcomer to the situation. Nor did he expect an easy answer, but he sure didn't mind sharing some of his worries, even if this woman waited for another man to write from the Dakotas and offer her marriage. "I have wondered if one or two aren't working for Sobel, but I haven't found any evidence to prove it. As to Morgan, I trust him completely, but he has his hands full dealing with Sobel's men at the river. It's the only place for the cows to water."

"Zach— Sorry, in my mind I have known you as Zach for several weeks."

"Zach is fine."

She continued. "I had no idea things were so hard still. But at least I am here to help with Kat and your pa." She grinned. "And maybe Gil from time to time."

"I don't like to take advantage of your misfortune. Soon enough this Dakota farmer will be courting you by mail."

Amelia nodded, though her expression was tight, as if the skin on her face had shrunk. "In the meantime, I might as well keep busy." She stepped back. "Now, if you'll excuse me, I will retire to my bedroom." She crossed the floor in even steps and climbed the stairs.

He watched until the door closed behind her.

Why did he get the feeling he had said something wrong?

Amelia checked on Daisy and smiled at the way the baby sprawled out, a corner of a blanket clutched in her fingers. Thankfully, she was a happy, contented child.

Amelia's smile fled as she prepared for bed. What did Zach mean he didn't have time for courting? Did he not understand that she had put aside any expectation of that when she came here to marry him?

Only it wasn't him. She had to continually remind herself of that. Who would perpetrate such a cruel joke? Sobel? For what purpose other than to torment them both?

Or perhaps Sobel hoped to divert Zach from his ranching for courting and tending a wife.

Neither was going to happen. If Sobel had been the author of those letters, he'd be sorely disappointed at how things had turned out.

She sat on the edge of the bed. Somehow what she knew of Sobel and even with the few minutes of contact she'd had, she couldn't see him writing the letters she'd received. In her opinion, the man didn't have a kind, gentle bone in his body. He would be incapable of penning such wooing words.

But someone had. Someone had made her fall in love with a man who was unaware of her existence. Her heart twisted. It was a cruel turn of events.

Tomorrow she must ask Zach if he had any idea who would do such a thing.

The smell of coffee jerked Amelia from her sleep the next morning. She checked to make sure Daisy was safe. The baby sat in the middle of her tangled blankets and smiled at her.

"Mama. Mama."

"Hi, sweetie." She'd taught Daisy to call her "Mama" since Callie died.

She'd overslept, thus putting to naught her noble plans of being the first up and having coffee and breakfast ready when Zach appeared. Now she'd have to hurry to make up for it.

She dressed herself and Daisy, then rushed down to the kitchen. She stared at the man before the stove. He certainly looked better than when she'd last seen him.

"Morning, ma'am."

"Gil, you look mighty fine this morning. And the food smells delicious." She looked around. No one else was in the room. "Are we the only ones up?"

"The men are out doing chores."

So much for being an early riser.

"Ain't seen hide nor hair of Kathy yet." Gil's chuckle rasped. "She don't 'xactly like mornings." He smiled at Daisy. "Don't believe I've met this young lady."

Amelia introduced them.

Gil patted Daisy on the head. "She's gonna be a looker when she grows up. Like her mama." The weather-worn cowboy shot a shy smile at Amelia.

Zach stepped into the room in time to hear Gil's comment, and chuckled. "Gil, don't be embarrassing Amelia. How's breakfast coming?"

"It's ready, Boss." He scurried back to the stove.

Amelia looked at Zach, wondering if he objected to Gil's comment. But his smile said otherwise, and self-conscious heat stung her cheeks. Callie had always been the more beautiful sister. Amelia had grown used to being a pale afterthought. She'd explained that in the letters she'd written to Zach. Letters that had gone elsewhere.

Pa followed Zach into the house. His eyes filled with joy when he saw Daisy. "How's the little gal this morning?"

"Down," Daisy said.

Amelia put her on the floor, wondering what she meant to do. The little girl went to Pa. "Gampa."

"Hi." Hand in hand the pair walked to the table and sat down, their hands folded on the tabletop as they waited for their breakfast.

Zach laughed. "Guess who's hungry?"

Grinning, Amelia met his gaze. Something flickered in his eyes. A slow, sweet smile drew up the corners of his mouth.

Was he seeing her, really seeing her? Perhaps finding something he liked? Without Callie for comparison, did he see a desirable young woman?

She mocked her thoughts.

She'd settle for being seen as useful.

"Better call your sister," Gil said.

Zach went to the stairs and hollered, "Kat, get down here."

When he returned to stand next to her, Amelia told herself not to let it mean anything. She simply happened to be in a spot that was convenient for him. Pushing her errant thoughts into submission, she nudged him and pointed toward the pair at the table. Both had big eyes, startled expressions, and their hands were clutched together. "I think you scared them."

"Never meant to. I'll have to be more careful in the future."

There was something he needed to realize and understand the impact of. "Your pa and Daisy have already formed a special relationship." She couldn't keep the displeasure out of her voice. "It's going to hurt her when we leave. She's already lost so much."

"It's going to hurt Pa too, and he's lost so much. I think losing his mind is probably the hardest."

At least he was sympathetic to her concern. Though if whoever wrote those letters portrayed him accurately, she could expect that. "I don't see any way to protect them."

He crossed his arms and studied the pair. "I don't either."

She shrugged. "Then I guess we'll make the best of it."

"Right. And deal with the end when it comes."

Feeling frustrated and yet somehow comforted by his casual acceptance of the matter, Amelia helped Gil serve the meal despite his protests.

Kat clattered down the stairs, her hair unbrushed and her clothes wrinkled, as if she'd slept in them. Like a cowboy would, no doubt. She plunked down across from her pa and Daisy.

They all sat down, Gil too, at Zach's insistence. Gil sat by Kat, and Amelia ended up sitting across from Zach. Thankfully, the table was square, so she didn't feel she had taken over the position of a wife.

Amelia folded her hands on her lap. Grandmother had always asked a blessing before meals and before that, her papa. She'd prayed with Daisy when it was the two of them. She waited. From the letters she'd received, she understood that Zach had reluctantly taken his pa's place as head of the house. *"It pains me to do so. I want the pa who was strong and sure of himself to come back. I understand it isn't going to happen, but I still long for it."*

Zach turned to his pa. "Would you like to say the grace?"

Pa's face brightened. "Can I?"

"Of course."

If Amelia wasn't mistaken, Zach's words were laden with emotion. Her thoughts did a hard turn. Watching his pa deteriorate must pain him deeply. She would do her best to share some of that load, at least until she heard from the Dakota farmer.

If he would let her.

They all bowed their heads, and Pa prayed.

"God is great. God is good. Let us thank Him for our food. Amen." He beamed as he looked around at the others.

Tears tugged at Amelia's eyes. Sometimes it took so little to give others a bit of pleasure.

Daisy was next to her, and Amelia cut her food into pieces. The child ate neatly for someone so young, so at least she didn't have to worry about Daisy offending anyone. She had told the pretend Zach all these things. She looked across the table at him. He was a stranger and yet not one.

They finished, and he pushed away from the table. "I need to check on the cows."

Pa pushed back too. "I'll go with you." He sounded as if he had a moment of clarity.

Zach remained in his chair, his lips pursed.

Amelia could tell he didn't want to take his pa with him but didn't have the heart to refuse him. She'd have to rescue Zach. "Pa, would you mind staying home and helping look after Daisy?"

Pa looked from Zach to Amelia. "Daisy?" Total confusion in his mind.

Amelia's throat tightened. The poor man. Poor Zach looking like he'd been gut shot. Poor Kat. Her head down, hiding behind her mop of hair. Poor Gil, no doubt wishing to bury in a bottle the pain of seeing the man like this.

She pushed back her shoulders. "Daisy, say hi to Gampa."

Obediently, ever the cheerful child, she touched the elder man's arm, and he turned to her. "Hi, Gampa."

"Hi, yourself." Pa's face crinkled in a smile. "Your mama says she needs help with you."

Amelia felt Zach's surprise. She looked at him and shrugged. There was something special about the connection between the young child and the older man.

He tilted his head to one side and gave a crooked grin.

It was a moment of sweet understanding.

She could do with more of those as she navigated her way through this unexpectedly strange situation.

"What do you need me to do?" Pa asked.

Amelia shifted her attention back to the older man. "Would you play with her while I help Gil clean the kitchen?"

"Okay." Hand in hand the pair went into the living room. Pa found a basket of toys in the cupboard.

"You have toys?" Amelia couldn't help being surprised.

"They used to be mine," Kat said.

"Do you mind her playing with them?"

"Nope. A cowboy ain't got no use for playthings."

Zach rolled his eyes and strode from the house.

"I best be going too." Kat followed, her exaggerated swagger tickling Amelia's funny bone.

Gil groaned. "That gal needs a mother." He turned to study Amelia. "Or someone like you to make her see sense."

Amelia ignored him and watched the pair from the window. They seemed to argue. Zach pointed to the house. Kat shook her head. Zach went into the barn, Kat on his heels. He emerged in a few minutes, leading a horse. Kat followed, waving her arms and yelling, though Amelia couldn't make out her words.

She wanted to intervene, try and draw Kat back to the house, but she couldn't be certain it wouldn't make things worse, so she watched and prayed for wisdom. What did the Bible say in Ecclesiastes? *"There is. . .a time to keep silence, and a time to speak."*

Was this a time to be silent?

"To every thing there is a season. . ."

Was this a season of waiting for whatever God had planned for her?

The assurance that God had a plan eased a knot in Amelia's stomach that she hadn't been aware of.

Zach rode away, leaving Kat waving her arms and yelling. The girl stomped her feet and headed for the corrals.

Her heart in her throat, Amelia watched. *Please don't go near that mustang.*

Kat climbed the fence and sat on the top rail. The horse raced to the far corner and wheeled to face her, tossing his head.

Amelia must have gasped, for Gil joined her at the window. "Crazy fool girl is trying to get herself killed."

"She won't really go near the horse, will she? Should I try and stop her?"

"I dunno. Seems to me the more attention she gets for acting badly, the more she does it."

"Wise words. But what if something happens? Zach will surely blame me."

"Guess if he wants to make sure she's safe every minute of the day, he should take her with him."

"Why doesn't he?"

"That boy don't need any more reason for the men to judge him unfairly. Taking a girl with him would give them plenty of reason to do so."

This was a new bit of information for Amelia. Zach's letters had said he struggled to take over his pa's role. Her heart went out to the tall cowboy who was trying so hard to cope with the challenges of his life. She ached to help him, but would he let her? Really, there was no way he could stop her while she was here. With renewed determination, she turned to assist with the kitchen chores.

As she helped Gil clean the kitchen, she glanced out the window as often as she could. She didn't breathe easy until Kat got down from the fence and wandered away.

The kitchen done, she took water and rags and began to scrub the living room. Judging from the layers of dust, she knew it had been a long time since it had last been cleaned.

Pa and Daisy gave her a pained look at the interference with their play and took the toys outside. She left the door open so she could hear them and keep an eye on them.

The dust on the bookshelf was thick enough to make her sneeze. She took off every object and cleaned everything thoroughly. The plank floor wore a coat of ground-in dirt. She went to the kitchen for a bucket of hot water.

Gil watched her. "The place hasn't had proper cleaning since the missus passed away."

Amelia didn't say she would have guessed it.

On her hands and knees, she tackled the floor with a scrub brush.

"Mama." Daisy leaned over Amelia's back.

Amelia sat up and hugged the child. "Where's Gampa?"

"Gone."

"Gone? Gone where?" She was on her feet and out the door,

Daisy in her arms. She looked to the right. No Pa. No Pa to the left either.

"Kat," she called. Waited. Called again. "Kat, I need you."

Gil came to her side. "What's wrong?"

"Pa is missing. I have to find him. I need Kat to watch Daisy for me." She yelled again.

Kat sauntered around the side of the barn. "Ya hollered?"

"That girl needs something, and I ain't saying what, but my ma would've used the strap on her," Gil muttered, returning to the kitchen.

"Kat, have you seen your pa?"

"Last I saw, he was right there." She pointed to the spot where Amelia had last seen him.

"Did you see him wander away?"

"Nope. I was busy."

Amelia did her best to push back her impatience at the girl even though she herself was as much at fault as Kat. She should have been more attentive.

"I'm going to look for him. I need you to watch Daisy for me. Don't let her wander away." Amelia shuddered at the idea of Daisy lost. "Can you do that for me?" She wanted to add, and no playing cowboy, but knew it was one of the things best left unsaid.

"Sure."

She slipped in to let Gil know what was going on.

"I'll watch them," he said.

She knew he would so long as a bottle didn't call him. Remembering the dryness of her throat yesterday, she filled a canteen and hung it over her shoulder. "Do you have any idea where I should look?"

"Wish I did."

She stepped outside and looked about, hoping to see Pa sitting nearby, lost in his thoughts. Nothing. She looked for clues in the grass as to which way he had gone, but the grass was dry and worn and provided no information. If she were Pa, where would she go? It was impossible to guess, because Pa didn't think along normal lines.

Following her heart, she went past the bunkhouse. That brought a snort. Following her heart had landed her right here in Montana, unexpected, unwelcome, and with no future. She looked up at the mountains. The scenery almost made it worthwhile.

She reached the trees where she had found Pa the day before, but a thorough search convinced her he wasn't there. That meant retracing her steps as far as the hill and veering to the right to another grove of trees. Again, she did not find him.

Standing in the open, she looked all around, seeing nothing but dusty grass, blue sky, and majestic mountains. She lifted her face to the sky. "God, You are all-seeing. Guide me to Pa."

She followed the valley for a time. Surely he hadn't come this far. She climbed the hill and looked about. The sun was high overhead. She was hot and hungry, but she would not stop until she found him.

Maybe he'd gone the other direction entirely. She retraced her steps, past the outbuildings and to the house, stopping long enough to grab some food. Gil packed more to take with her.

"He'll be hungry when you find him."

"Kat, are you okay looking after Daisy? I'm sorry to leave her with you."

"I'd sooner look after her than look for Pa."

"Thank you. She should have a nap after she's eaten." Amelia was on her way out the door, eating a sandwich as she walked.

Two hours later, she still had not located the man. She fell to her knees, tears wetting her face. *Please God, help me find him.*

She rested a few minutes then resumed the search. After a bit, she spied some rough terrain. A person could break a leg trying to get through the maze of rocks and bulges of ground.

She stepped around a boulder. "Pa," she whispered. He sat on a clump of grass, his back to a rock, his gaze fixed on the distance. She approached slowly, conscious of the fact she might frighten him. Skirting another boulder, she circled around and sat down facing him.

He looked her direction, but it was obvious he didn't register her presence.

How long had he been this way? Should she call him back to the present?

As she considered what to do, she uncorked the canteen and quenched her thirst. Poor Pa must be terribly thirsty.

"Hi, Pa." Her words were soft, barely more than a whisper.

He gave no indication that he heard her.

Praying she would say and do the right thing, she began to talk, keeping her tone gentle. "It's a nice day. I like the sunshine, though I know we desperately need rain. I like the intense blue of the sky and the mountains. Guardians of the land."

He jerked at those words. "That's what my wife said." He stared at Amelia. "You aren't Evelyn."

She guessed that to be his wife's name. "I'm Amelia. Evelyn sounds like a very nice woman."

Tears filled Pa's eyes. "I can't find her."

Her heart went out to him. She wanted to hug him but feared how he would react. "I brought some food and water. Would you like some?"

"A picnic." He rubbed his hands. "Isn't that fun?"

"Yes, it is." She handed him the canteen. He drank deeply, and then she offered him the sandwich Gil had prepared, breaking off a quarter for herself only because she worried Pa wouldn't eat if she didn't.

They ate in silence as she waited for him to indicate where his thoughts had gone.

"Who did you say you are?"

"Amelia."

"Do I know you?"

"I'm here to help you."

He finished the food and wiped his hands on a red handkerchief he pulled from his pocket. But he showed no sign of moving.

"Would you like to go home now?" She rose and held out her hand to him.

He drew back. "I'm waiting."

She sat again. "What are you waiting for?"

"Evelyn. She went picking berries and said she would come right back."

Amelia tried again. "Please let me take you home." But when she held her hand out to him, he turned his back to her.

"I won't leave until Evelyn returns."

Amelia tried everything she could think of. She suggested Evelyn waited for him at home. She reminded him of Daisy, of Kat, said supper would be ready shortly. Said Zach would be coming home. She even took his hand and attempted to pull him to his feet. He jerked away, anger filling his eyes. She didn't want to aggravate him, so she waited.

Two hours later, nothing had worked, and she sat with her elbows on her knees and her chin in her palms. *Please, God, help him come round so we can go home. Please keep Daisy safe.*

Her heart thudded with fear as she worried about Daisy. It was all she could do not to picture Kat deciding to ride the mustang and Daisy wandering off.

Zach would surely come looking for them once he got home. Yesterday it had been almost dark.

At least they were safe here. A rustle behind her made her neck twitch. Were they alone? Were there wild animals prowling nearby? Or worse, wild men?

❧ Chapter 4 ❧

Zach had spent the day checking on the men and cows. After telling Amelia his suspicions about a couple of the men, he had found them at the fringes of where they should be and asked them to join Morgan near the river. He had sent two others to take their place on the western side of the range. What he needed around him were people he could trust.

That brought Amelia to mind. Someone had acted dishonestly, representing himself as Zach. Who and why?

It was coming toward suppertime when he rode toward home with more anticipation than he'd known for some time. Knowing Amelia would have things under control was a nice feeling.

He tended his horse then strode toward the house and stepped inside. Kat and Daisy played at the table.

Gil looked up at Zach's entrance. "We been hopin' you'd get back soon."

Amelia and Pa weren't in sight, and Zach's nerves twitched. "What's wrong?"

Gil and Kat both tried to tell him at the same time.

"They've been missing most of the day?" What disaster had befallen them?

Daisy patted his leg. "Mama?" Her bottom lip quivered and tears clung to her lashes.

He picked her up. She buried her face in his neck and sobbed. He patted her back. "Hush, baby. Your mama is okay. I'll go get her now." He tried to put her down, but she clung to him. What could he do but sit and hold her until she stopped crying?

Her sobs ended, and she tipped her face up to him. "Find Mama?"

"I will."

"Gampa?"

"Him too. But I need you to stay with Kat. Can you do that?"

"Want you." She pressed her head to his chest.

His heart refused to beat. His lungs stopped working. How could she trust him so readily? It made him feel both powerful and weak at the same time.

"Kat?"

His sister lifted Daisy from his lap. "Would you like a biscuit and jam?"

"Okay."

Kat sat her at the table as Zach rose to leave.

"Bye." Daisy waved.

Zach chuckled at how quickly she switched from teary to cheery. "Bye. I'll be back."

Gil had said the last time he saw Amelia she headed south, so he went that direction. He scanned his surroundings, hoping to see them, hoping for some idea of where they had gone. Nothing provided any clue. He rode one direction, saw nothing, turned, and rode back a mile. He continued to sweep the countryside for almost an hour before he reached an area they had nicknamed the Giant's Ball Game because of the huge lumps and boulders that had made his ma say it looked like giants had had a fight that involved tossing stone balls at one another.

He circled the section of land, knowing how perilous it was to ride a horse through the area, all the while keeping a sharp lookout for any indication of Pa and Amelia. A flash of gray color caught his attention, and he reined in.

"Pa, Amelia."

Amelia popped up. "Over here."

Where was Pa? Zach didn't see him. He dismounted and zigzagged his way on foot through the lumps and rocks. All sorts of possibilities raced through his mind. Pa was hurt. Or worse.

He stepped past a mound of dirt, and his breath whooshed out. Pa sat in front of Amelia.

Zach's relief lasted but a second. Then he saw the faraway, blank expression on his pa's face. He sidled up to Amelia. "How long has he been like this?"

"Since I found him. I've tried to talk to him and get him to go home, but I've failed." She caught his arm as he moved toward his pa. "He's waiting for your ma. Thinks she's picking berries."

Zach stopped to consider what to do. He had to get his father home as soon as possible. Being in his own house would surely bring his mind back. At least to a degree. He squatted in front of him. "Pa, how are you?"

His father didn't seem to notice him.

"Pa? Do you hear me?" He took his pa's hands and rubbed them. "Pa, it's time to go home."

His father slowly brought his gaze to Zach. "I can't go. I'm waiting for Evelyn."

"Why don't we see if she's gone home?"

Pa rocked his head from side to side.

Zach gave Amelia a helpless look. What was he to do?

Amelia stood at Zach's side and placed a hand on his shoulder. Her touch comforted him in a way he couldn't explain. It was nice not to have to deal with this alone.

"What's his favorite song?"

He stared at her. "Why?"

"I just had an idea. I wonder if we sing it, if it would make him willing to move."

"It's worth a try. Both he and Ma liked 'Amazing Grace.' "

She began to sing, nodding at him to join her. Their voices blended perfectly. As if they were made to sing together. How foolish of him to think so. It was simply the emotion of the moment that made him consider such a thing.

She took one of Pa's hands. He took the other, and they drew the older man to his feet.

Pa looked from one to the other, a distant expression still in his eyes, and yet he followed along without hesitation.

They reached the horse. Zach caught up the reins and led it.

The three of them—four, counting the horse—marched across the dry, grassy field toward the house, two of them singing along the way.

Gil stood on the doorstep watching. Soon Kat joined him, Daisy in her arms.

Daisy waved and called, "Mama. Gampa. Mis'er. Hi."

Mister, huh? Seems he should have had a better title than that, but what? Would Amelia object to the child calling him Zach? Probably. How about Uncle Zach? He didn't think he much cared for that title either, but it was preferable to *mister*.

Gil and Kat stood back as they reached the door

Zach handed Kat the reins. "Look after my horse, would you?"

Amelia took Daisy.

Kat, to her credit, took the horse without arguing.

They led Pa into the kitchen and to a chair. He sat, blinked, and looked about him.

"Hi, Gampa," Daisy said again.

Amelia sat the child on the chair next to Pa. Zach could tell she was prepared to snatch the little one away if either one seemed unsettled. But Pa looked at Daisy. "You hungry too?"

Daisy nodded.

Pa took her hand and looked to Zach. "Is supper ready?"

Zach dropped to the nearest chair as relief sucked away his strength.

Amelia sat down as well and dropped her head to her chest.

He touched her shoulder. "You must be tired." She'd been out almost the entire day.

She nodded. "Tired, but so grateful he's home safe and sound."

"Thank you for keeping him safe." He squeezed her shoulder.

She shook her head. "I should have been watching him more carefully."

"I'm not blaming you. It only takes a minute for him to disappear."

Kat skidded into the house. "Is everyone all right?"

Pa looked up at her and smiled. "Why wouldn't we be?"

"Yes, Kat. Why wouldn't we be?" Amelia said with a wagonload of irony in her words. She grinned at Kat, and the two of them started to laugh.

Zach saw the humor in the situation and laughed with them.

Pa and Daisy joined in, though probably as much for the simple enjoyment of the moment as anything.

Gil stared at them. "You all been out in the sun too long."

A few minutes later, Gil set a meal before them. Pa ate like a starving man.

Zach looked at Amelia, and they grinned as they shared a thought. It was nice to have Pa back to this state instead of staring into space waiting for Ma. Zach studied Amelia, saw the weary lines around her mouth. It had been a difficult day for her. He must do something to make up for it.

He did chores while Amelia helped Gil clean up from the meal. When he returned to the house, she was headed upstairs with a sleepy Daisy in her arms. Afraid she might decide to go to bed at the same time, he said, "Would you join me for a walk after she's settled?"

Amelia studied him a moment, as if trying to understand what his request meant. Then she nodded and continued into the bedroom she shared with Daisy.

Kat sat on the bottom step watching him. "You courtin' her?"

He blinked. "Why would you think that?"

"Well, I just don't understand why she's here, is all."

"She mistakenly came to Broken Arrow and has no place to go until other arrangements can be made."

Kat shrugged. "It's nice to have someone around to help with Pa and all." She sauntered away before Zach could think of how to answer. But she was right. And he meant to thank Amelia.

Amelia slipped from the room. "Is Kat around? I need her to listen for Daisy."

Kat reappeared. "I'll stay here."

Amelia squeezed her hands. "Thank you. I don't know if you realize how much help you've been. While I was out with your pa, I knew Daisy was safe with you."

"I didn't do nothin'." But she grinned as she returned to the bottom step.

Zach had no intention of correcting her grammar and ruining the moment. He led the way to the door and held it for Amelia. That's when he realized he had no notion of what he wanted to do. He gave a chuckle that sounded self-mocking, even to himself. "I wanted to go for a walk with you, but after the hours of walking you put in today, it seems foolish. What would you like to do?"

"I'd like to enjoy the view of the mountains. Don't suppose I'll see much of them in the Dakotas."

"Guess you won't." He'd almost forgotten about the farmer with a desire for a wife. He decided he would forget about it a little longer, but in a few days, he would send one of the men to town to see if a letter had arrived for Amelia. "Let's go past the barn. There's a nice view of the mountains there." Side by side, they walked past the barn. From there, the ground dipped away to reveal rolling hills and the mountains. He indicated a grassy spot, and they sat down.

"Blue and majestic, guardians of the land. You said that in the letters you didn't write. I've been wanting to ask who you think wrote them."

He leaned back on one elbow. "I've given it some thought. From what you tell me, it has to be someone who knows me well. But Pa couldn't do it."

"Kat?"

He chuckled. "Kat has never written one word except under threats from Ma. Besides, she's more into cow*boying* than letter writing."

Amelia laughed. Their gazes held after their amusement ended. His heart swelled with the pleasure of sharing the moment.

Slightly dizzy, he turned away and looked at the mountains. It was gratitude he felt. Nothing more. "I want to thank you for taking care of my Pa." He saw she was ready to protest. "I know I said it already, but it doesn't hurt to repeat it. I guess I feel sort of the way you do with Kat and Daisy. I can go about my business knowing you'll be watching him."

"I don't know how you can say that. He wasn't safe. He was lost."

"Lost more in his mind than unable to find his way back to the ranch. That's not your fault, and I don't hold you responsible. I just wish—"

"Oh Zach, I know how you feel. You wish you had your pa back, sound in mind, sharing in the work of running the ranch."

He shifted so he could study her more closely, saw how her green eyes held the warmth of a summer day. "How do you know that?"

"You said so in the letters you didn't write." Her smile spread to her eyes, and she laughed.

He sputtered a half-hearted protest before he laughed too, then flung himself on his back and stared at the sky. "He started to forget things before Ma died, but after that it was like part of his mind had died with her."

"He misses her." She lay on her back beside him, a circumspect twelve inches between them. Her arms were at her sides. "I miss my grandmother and Callie."

The tightness of her words made him ache for her. He shifted his arm and covered her hand with his. She didn't move. "Tell me about Callie."

"Callie was two years older than me. She was twelve when our parents died."

"How did they die?"

"I told you. Oh right, you didn't get my letters. They died when their horse was frightened by a train and they were thrown from the buggy."

"I'm sorry. That's when you went to live with your grandmother?"

"Yes. I'll never forget the funeral. We both had new dresses—black with a high collar that scratched my neck. Tight cuffs on the wrists. The material rustled when I moved, and each time it earned me a warning frown from Grandmother. I thought the funeral was bad enough, but the next day was worse. Not because I didn't like Grandmother. I did. She was gentle and sweet. But she marched into our house and straight to our bedroom. She was still wearing her black dress, and it said *shush, shush* every time she moved. A man I had seen in town followed with a trunk on a squeaky-wheeled trolley. She opened the trunk and began to dismantle our room and pack our things into it.

"I watched, feeling as if my insides were bleeding.

"She told us to help as she gathered up our books and toys. I tried hard to keep from crying. Callie crossed her arms and refused to move until Grandmother reached for an object, then she snatched up her things and put them in the trunk.

"We followed her to the sitting room where the man from town stood with a little black book in which he wrote notes with a stub of a pencil. He had a black line on his lip from licking the pencil from time to time. Grandmother pointed to a little bookshelf and said she would take that with her. Two men carried it to the wagon. She circled the room telling the man to take one thing after another. She pointed to Papa's chair and Mama's little table. I thought she was taking all our things with us, but then she pointed to the kitchen table and chairs and said they could be sold. The men carried more and more things outside. Slowly our lives were dismantled. Bits and pieces went to Grandmother's wagon. The other things were taken by the man with the black notebook. I wondered how many destroyed homes were listed in that book.

"My insides were like fragile glass, cutting me to pieces because of the way our life was being torn apart." She paused as if lost in her painful memories.

"I could see Callie was upset too. When Grandmother pointed to a painting on the wall and said it was atrocious and would have to be sold, Callie jerked the picture from the wall and wouldn't let her have it. It was painted by our mama's mother and was special to all of us."

Amelia shook her head. "I had never seen Callie so angry, so ready to do battle."

Zach felt an incredible urge to hold her. Speak words to ease the strain in her face. But they were practically strangers, although she had the advantage of knowing him through those letters.

She sucked in air as if she'd forgotten to breathe. "Grandmother let us keep the picture. I think she realized if she insisted on selling it that Callie would have fought her. My insides trembled as I watched all this, and then I had a fearsome thought. What was happening to our animals? Grandmother said Mr. Earnest would take care of them. I thought she meant until we came back, but Grandmother said we wouldn't be coming back. The news practically slammed me to the ground. I raced out to big, gentle Pierre and leaned my face against his shoulder. I loved the farm. I think in the back of my mind I've always hoped to get back to one like we had." Amelia was silent, and Zach waited, wondering if she was done.

She drew in a long breath and continued. "Callie followed me, and she said if she had a gun she would shoot him. I knew she meant Pierre, and I clung to the horse's leg and asked why she would do that. She said because our parents were dead and our home was being torn apart and we had to go live with Grandmother all because the stupid horse was scared of a train whistle.

"I tried to make it seem better and pointed out that train whistles are loud, and besides, what was wrong with living with Grandma?

"I'll never forget her answer. She said, 'Oh grow up, Amelia.'"

Amelia sighed. "I don't know how many times I heard her say that over the years." Another beat of silence before she continued. "Callie saw the tears on my cheeks and said she guessed I would have to now. No more being coddled by Mama and Papa. Her words hurt, but I've often wondered if she meant them for me or herself."

Zach listened to the sad story and wished he could comfort her. He ached for comfort too. Since his ma's death, he had been forced to be strong when sometimes he longed to be a boy again. All he could do was squeeze her hand and listen to her words. "What happened to the picture? Did she get to keep it?"

Amelia chuckled. "I still have it. I'll keep it and give it to Daisy."

"You can hang it here if you like."

She shifted to look at him. Her eyes were damp.

He wiped his finger along her lashes to dry away the tears clinging to them. He withdrew his hand, alarmed at how easily he'd reached for her. Touched her so freely. Would she be offended?

She held his gaze, her eyes full of depth and searching. He didn't shift away even though he knew he should. How could he deny her a bit of understanding? How could he deny himself the feeling that she understood him?

Her thoughts shuttered. She looked toward the sky. "I will wait and hang it in my permanent home." Longing filled her voice.

He could offer her permanency, but along with it, worry about Pa and Kat, concerns about the future of the ranch, and a whole lot of aggravation from the neighbor. He simply wasn't much of a bargain.

"What was it like living with your grandmother?"

Amelia chuckled. "She was set in her ways and a collector of things. One of our chores was to dust her knickknacks every Saturday. Callie hated it and broke more than one 'accidentally.' I hated when she did that. Grandma would look sad, and Callie would act like she didn't care. They would end up scowling at each other. I finally said I would do the dusting. Callie could mop the kitchen floor. Even that she purposely did wrong. It seemed she did her best to make Grandma angry. When they fought, Grandma would say, 'I should have let you go to an orphanage.' I did my best to keep peace between them. Callie said she didn't care. What difference did it make if she lived there or somewhere else? she'd say.

"She spent a lot of her time visiting her girlfriends. By the time she was fourteen, her circle of friends had widened to include boys. By the time she was sixteen, she bragged she got paid to offer them more than a kiss."

Zach watched her cheeks turn red. Callie's actions had doubtlessly affected Amelia in many ways.

"When Grandma learned what she was doing, she was horrified and told her it must stop. Instead, Callie moved away to a bigger town where she could earn more money. That was three years ago. A few months ago she returned with a year-and-a-half-old child. Callie was sick and died within a few weeks. It wasn't long until everyone in town knew about Daisy. People I thought were my friends turned away from me. I had a beau. He stopped calling on me and avoided me, so obviously I knew there was no hope for us."

His belly ground painfully at the pain in her voice.

"It was Grandma who suggested I seek a mail-order marriage. Everyone in Righteous knew the circumstances of Daisy's birth."

"Amelia, I am so sorry for your troubles."

She sat up. "Seems we have that in common—troubles."

He shifted closer and reached out, intending to put an arm about her shoulders.

She jumped to her feet. "Enough sad stories. Show me the patch of flowers that was your mother's favorite place."

"Sorry. I didn't mean to frighten you. I only wanted to let you know I feel bad about what you've had to endure." How could he begin to think she would welcome him being so free with his touches? A terrible thought surfaced. Would she think he saw her as offering the same thing her sister had? Hadn't she said there had been those who treated her that way? He should apologize. Explain it wasn't like that. But what could he say that wouldn't make the situation worse?

She faced him, her eyes hard. "I will provide Daisy with a secure home where she is accepted. It is all that matters to me."

"And keeping my family safe and saving the ranch are what matters to me." He believed the words, and at one time it had been all he cared about. But lately he'd become aware of a hollowness inside that he couldn't ignore.

He broke free from her look, even though part of him wanted to delve deeper into her thoughts and feelings. "You want to see Ma's flower patch, as she called it. I doubt there are many flowers right now. Not with the drought." He led the way across the edge of the hill they were on until the dip of ground lay before them. He stared in disbelief.

His voice rang with his surprise. "It's filled with flowers."

Amelia rushed forward and fell on her knees in the bright patch of bluebells, little white trumpet-shaped flowers, yellow daisy-like flowers, and pink ones with five flat petals. "Oh, I wish I knew the names of them all." She kept her head down, not wanting him to see the ache in her eyes. When he had held her hand, her heart had filled with longing. To belong, yes. To be safe and secure, yes. But more. To be loved as she had been as a child. But Daisy's needs came first. She had to give the child a permanent home.

Zach was not prepared to offer that.

She'd seen his intent to put his arm around her shoulders and couldn't help but wonder if telling him about Callie made him think he had the right. She'd come west fully expecting to enter into marriage with him, knowing full well that involved physical intimacy. But she wasn't prepared to offer any favors outside of marriage. She would not follow Callie's example.

She knelt among the flowers until the sunset streaked the sky with a riot of colors, and then she pushed to her feet.

Zach sat on the slope of ground, watching her.

"We need to get back," she said. She had lingered far too long.

They fell into step as they returned to the house. She thanked Kat for watching Daisy.

"Gil and Pa have both gone to bed," Kat said, yawning.

"Thanks, Kat." She patted the girl on the shoulder and knew from the way Kat leaned toward her that she longed for loving touches. Amelia would gladly give them for the time she was there. Then what? Kat would have to grow up the same way Amelia had. Without a mother's hugs and without a father's touches. Regret and wishes twisted together into a knot in the pit of Amelia's stomach.

"Good night," she murmured, and hurried up the stairs before the tears pushing at her eyelids could escape.

In her bedroom, she sank to the edge of the bed and took slow, deep breaths.

Life wasn't easy. No one had promised it would be. She found the Bible Grandma had given her the Christmas she turned sixteen and opened it to the story of Joseph. All the bad things that happened to him. Yet the scriptures said the Lord was with Joseph.

"The Lord is with me too. I will trust Him to bring me to a place of permanency for Daisy and me."

The next day was Saturday. Zach left right after breakfast. She fully expected he would be gone all day. She set to work determined that when she left, he, Pa, Gil, and Kat would notice her absence.

She finished cleaning the sitting room, thankful that Gil had at least emptied the bucket of dirty water yesterday. Speaking of Gil, he had gone to the bunkhouse shortly after breakfast. Hopefully, not in search of a bottle, but she had no intention of trespassing into his quarters, so she would have to wait and see.

In one of the letters she'd received, the author had mentioned that Zach had a fondness for a certain boiled raisin cake that Gil didn't make. He'd sent the recipe, saying he'd copied it from his ma's notes. She had made it several times in anticipation of making it for him. Her plans had been to do it as his wife and to earn gratitude that he would express with a kiss and maybe by sweeping her into a big hug. Her cheeks burned at how wild her dreams had been.

How far removed was the reality.

However, she still intended to surprise Zach, and it was perfect timing with Gil gone.

She mixed up the ingredients and put the cake into the oven to bake.

Kat wandered into the kitchen, as if drawn by the aroma. "Smells good. Whatcha making?"

"Boiled raisin cake." She waited for Kat's reaction and wasn't disappointed.

The girl blinked, stared hard at Amelia, then jerked away, but not before Amelia caught the glisten of tears.

She longed to hug Kat but knew she had to bide her time or Kat would withdraw into herself.

"Ma used to make a boiled raisin cake."

"Did you like it?"

"It was my favorite. Zach's too. And Pa's." Kat brought her gaze back to Amelia. "Funny that you decided to make it." She narrowed her eyes. "Bet it's not as good as Ma used to make."

"I wouldn't expect it would be."

Kat's expression hardened. "Why not?"

"Because your mother made the cake with love. Love for you and Zach and your father. That makes all the difference." Amelia touched Kat's elbow and felt her shudder. "But perhaps I can offer it as a memory of her love."

Kat shuddered again then bolted for the door.

The sun was high overhead when Zach rode toward home. No doubt some of the cowboys would be putting his early departure down to laziness or an inability to cope. It was neither. He told himself he was simply checking on his pa. But that's why he'd hired Gil. However, it wasn't Gil he trusted to be watching out for his father. It was Amelia, and that knowledge had him all tangled up inside. He'd told himself he didn't have time for courting and didn't need any more complications in his life, yet here he was thinking life had improved with her arrival.

He was surely mistaken in that thought and meant to prove it. That, he firmly informed himself, provided the reason for him riding home at noon.

Dismounting as he reached the yard, he led his horse into the barn to unsaddle him. He stiffened at a strange sound and tilted his head to locate the direction. A figure huddled in the far corner. Gil. Drunk again. He strode across the floor. Only it wasn't Gil. Kat sat with her head pressed to drawn-up knees. The sounds were sobs, though he knew she would deny it. He hadn't seen her cry since Ma died.

He stopped. "Kat."

"Go away."

He sat beside her.

"Go away," she mumbled.

"Can't."

"You got a broken leg or something?" She did her best to sound confrontational and hard but fell short.

"Nothing broke. But I can't leave my little sister alone when I see she is upset about something. Care to tell me what it is?"

She sniffed, lifted her head, and swiped her nose on her sleeve. "Maybe I don't."

"I can wait."

"Sometimes you're a pain in the neck."

He chuckled. "I've been called worse. So what happened? Did Amelia do something to upset you?" Why did he hope Kat would say yes?

"She made boiled raisin cake." The words were so full of disgust that Zach wanted to laugh. "How'd she know that was my favorite?

Yours too? She said maybe it would give me memories of Ma's love."
Kat snorted. "Like I need more." She lowered her face to her knees.

Zach rubbed her back. "Kat, we will never forget Ma. How could we?"

"Pa does."

"Sometimes, yes. But I don't think we want to be like that."

She shrugged. Her shoulders quivered.

Zach had tried to comfort her before, and each time she had shaken him off or just run. But he decided to risk it again and pulled her into his arms. She slowly relaxed as he rubbed her back.

"Why'd Ma have to die and Pa forget who he is?"

"I could as easy answer that as I could answer why it doesn't rain. We simply have to trust God."

"Don't see why we should."

Zach had fought a similar battle. "I thought the same, but the alternative is to think we are lost in a great big sea without a rudder, without a pilot, and without hope."

Kat shuddered. "Maybe we are."

"I don't believe that, and neither do you."

She didn't argue, which meant she reluctantly agreed.

Zach held her a minute longer. His stomach growled. "Boiled raisin cake, you say? Did it smell good?"

"Good enough to pull me into the house."

"Let's go see if it tastes as good." He rose and pulled her to her feet.

"Won't taste as good as Ma's."

"Guess it won't."

"You know what Amelia said? She said she didn't expect it would, because Ma's was full of love for us." Her voice squeaked at the end.

Zach's throat tightened, and he was grateful he didn't have to say anything.

They stepped into the house. The cake did indeed smell wonderful. He knew how she'd known to make that flavor. No doubt whoever wrote those letters had informed her. He tried to think who would know so much about him. Pa, for sure, but Pa couldn't have written them.

Gil maybe, but Gil could barely write his name.

Amelia turned at their entrance, and Zach forgot musing about the letter writer.

She had a bit of flour on her cheek. Looked like a spot of molasses on her apron. She wouldn't know it, of course, but he'd often come into the house and seen Ma the same way.

Amelia smiled. "I didn't expect you back so early."

It wasn't quite the greeting Ma would have given, but it sure felt good.

"I hope you don't mind."

She laughed. "Why should I? It's your house."

He glanced around. Pa and Daisy sat at the table. Crumbs before them indicated Amelia had given them something to tide them over until dinner. "Where's Gil?"

She glanced toward the bunkhouse. "I haven't seen him since breakfast."

He groaned. "I'd better go check on him." He trotted across the yard and up the wooden steps into the bunkhouse. The place reeked of liquor, and Gil lay on his bed, his arm across his eyes.

Zach shook the man. "You've been drinking again."

"Only had a mouthful." The slurred words said otherwise.

Zach spotted the bottle beside Gil and shook it. It was empty. "Gil, you need to stop drinking." He left the man, knowing he would take a few hours to sober up.

What was he going to do about him? Once Amelia left, Gil was all he had to cook and look after Pa. Trouble was, Gil was not to be counted on.

He left the bunkhouse and was drawn back to the kitchen by the smell of a cake full of raisins and molasses. He couldn't wait to sink his teeth into it.

The table was set, and a plate piled high with biscuits sat in the middle. Around it were various other offerings—fried potatoes, bacon, a salad of grated carrots and raisins—another of Zach's favorites. His mouth watered. Gil was an okay cook, but his usual fare was baked beans for dinner.

Zach sat down. He glanced at Pa, but Pa was smiling at Daisy. Zach didn't think he looked ready to ask the blessing, so he bowed his head and offered up a quick prayer. The meal was good and he said so, but he longed to try the cake.

After the meal, Amelia cut generous slices and gave one to each of them.

Zach savored his first bite. "Just like Ma used to make."

Kat pushed aside her piece. "Don't think I want any."

But when Zach reached to take her plate, she slid it out of his way. "Might have it later."

Zach chuckled. "You'll enjoy it."

Kat scowled at him, but he knew she was being stubborn out of principle and a mistaken belief that she would do their ma a disservice if she admitted the cake was as good as Ma's. Which it was.

"Thanks," he said to Amelia, then headed outside to tend to the chores.

Zach had hoped to spend more time at home while Amelia was there, but the next few days he ended up spending most of his time with the herd. He even spent a couple nights out there, trusting that she took care of Pa and anything else needing attention. Sobel went out of his way to create problems. His cowhands continued to push Zach's cows from the river. There were frequent confrontations at the water. Zach was downright tired of it and anxious for a break. The thought of boiled raisin cake drew his thoughts homeward. The last of the cake would be gone by now. But Amelia and Daisy would still be there.

Finally, Morgan said he could handle things if the boss wanted to go home.

Zach wondered if his edginess had been that apparent. He looked around, deciding things had settled down, though he wondered what Sobel had up his sleeve next. He rode home, ready for a cup of coffee served in a china cup.

"Welcome home." Amelia's greeting brought a smile to Zach's mouth and heart.

Daisy trotted up to him, and he swung her into the air, earning him a throaty giggle.

"More," she said, and he did it again.

Kat came around the house. At least she wasn't hanging around the mustang.

Gil stood at the stove and nodded a greeting. Sober. For how long?

Pa sat at the kitchen table paging through the Bible.

A sense of peace filled Zach. This was the sort of home he wished he could hope to return to every day.

"Coffee?" Amelia asked. When he nodded, she filled a white

china mug and set it on the table along with a plateful of cookies. Soon everyone sat around the table eating cookies and drinking coffee or milk.

"Anything new around here?" he asked.

Kat and Pa vied to tell him about the coyote that had sat nearby and watched them one evening.

"Daisy thought it was a dog," Kat said.

"Doggie. Want doggie."

Zach met Amelia's amused gaze across the table and again thought this was the way he had dreamed his home would be.

The sound of an approaching horse drew his attention. He went to the door and watched a rider approach.

His neck tensed. Could it be Sobel again, bringing along more troublesome news? Then he remembered he'd sent someone for the mail, and his muscles twanged even more.

What news would be in the stack the cowboy carried? Would there be a message from the Dakota farmer?

❧ Chapter 5 ❧

Amelia followed Zach out of the house, tension creaking along her neck as a cowboy rode in from the direction of town and handed Zach a stack of mail. It looked to be mostly newspapers.

With a touch of irony, Amelia wondered if one of them was the *Matrimonial News*.

Zach sorted through the stack. Paused to study one item. "It's for you."

She took the envelope, knowing it was from the farmer she'd written to. Her fingers clenched the missive. How could she have already received a reply? She thought it would take weeks. The man must have been standing in the office of *Matrimonial News* when her letter arrived. His eagerness should be a good sign. After all, didn't she want to be that important to someone?

"Aren't you going to open it?" Zach asked.

There was no reason not to share the news with him. They were alone in front of the house. She opened the letter and read:

"Dear Miss Pressly,
You sound exactly like the sort of woman who would make
a perfect helpmeet for me."

He went on to describe his home and his farm.

"It sounds like what you want. A place like where you lived as a child." Zach seemed to be pleased with the letter.

She finished reading it.

"Please send me information about where you live, and tell me
more about yourself and the little girl. She is more than wel-
come. A good beginning to our family.

Awaiting your reply,
Jacob Wells"

Amelia couldn't speak. A farm. A man with a strong-sounding name. Wasn't it what she had always wanted? And yet if Zach would offer one hint—no matter how small—that he wanted her to stay, she would write and tell Mr. Wells she had changed her mind. But even his favorite cake, made from his ma's recipe, didn't seem to have caused him to reconsider asking her to stay.

"You'll want to write him immediately." Zach's words certainly didn't contain any hope that he had changed his mind.

"I'll write back this afternoon. Which reminds me. Tomorrow is Sunday. Can we go to church?" They hadn't gone last week because Zach was away.

"Sure, then I could give your letter to John, and he would post it for you."

Getting him to agree to go to church had been easy. Writing the letter, she discovered an hour later, was difficult. In the end, she answered the questions Jacob Wells had asked and did her best to anticipate hearing from him again.

The one thing she could write with complete honesty was, "*Your farm reminds me of the one where I lived as a child. I loved it.*"

She sealed the envelope and set it on the table at her bedside. Tomorrow would see it on its way.

Sunday morning, she prepared herself for church, set out Daisy's best little dress, then descended to the kitchen.

Gil was there. Whatever he'd done the day before, he seemed ready to work today. He looked at her dark blue cotton dress with the Victorian collar and lace-trimmed cuffs. "Bit fancy for frying pork, ain't it?"

She chuckled. "We're going to church."

"Who's 'we'? I ain't going. Seen enough people scowling at me and shaking their heads without going there."

"Not everyone is the same." It was easy to say. Harder to believe, having experienced judgment herself after Daisy arrived in Grandma's house.

"I'll have to take yer word for it, as I ain't about to see for myself. Who did ya say is going?"

"I didn't. I guess I don't know."

Zach stepped into the house from doing the morning chores and overheard enough of the conversation to know what it was about. "I think we'll all go. It might be good for Pa and will certainly be good for Kat."

"I'm not going," Kat insisted when she heard the news.

"Yes, you are." Zach spoke firmly, as if he hoped to end the argument before it started.

"You can't make me. You aren't my pa."

At that, her pa looked up. "We'll all go to church. Your mother would expect it."

That ended Kat's protests as they stared at Pa. He was clear in his mind at the moment.

Amelia shared a look with Zach and knew he was as surprised as she was and as hopeful that Pa's clarity would last.

"I'll stay home and make a Sunday dinner like your ma used to make," Gil said. No one protested, though Amelia wondered if having them all away would give Gil opportunity to do something besides cook. Not that having them at home proved a deterrent.

After breakfast and after everyone had changed into their Sunday best, Zach drove the wagon to the house and helped them into it. Pa chose to sit in the back with Kat, who had managed to find a dress that wasn't torn and soiled.

Zach helped Amelia to the bench, and she held Daisy. Almost like her journey here just a few days ago.

"Do you have your letter?" Zach murmured as he sat beside her. As if he couldn't wait for her to be gone.

"Right here." She patted her little drawstring bag. At least she could hope for a welcome with Jacob Wells. The thought did nothing to ease the way her insides tightened.

As they approached Broken Arrow, she found breathing increasingly difficult. What would people think of her with the Taggerty family? What would they think of Daisy? Would they ask questions about the child? And most of all, did she want to mail the letter in her bag?

As soon as they reached the small, white church, the Taggertys were surrounded by friends. Kat ran off with some girls her age. Zach and Amelia stayed on either side of Pa.

As more and more people greeted him, Amelia could feel the tension and confusion growing in the man.

"Let's get inside," Zach said, and they hurried into the church.

A couple spoke to Pa inside the sanctuary.

Amelia recognized John Daniels. He introduced his wife, Wilma, a plump, smiling woman. Mrs. Daniels turned to speak to Pa.

"Norm, it is so good to see you. How are you doing?"

Pa looked at her. "Have you seen Evelyn? I can't find her."

Mrs. Daniels patted his hand. "You'll see her soon."

"Your letter," Zach reminded Amelia.

She dug it from her bag and handed it to Mr. Daniels and asked him to post it. Any hope that Zach might see some value in asking her to stay disappeared with the letter that Mr. Daniels slipped into his pocket.

They led Pa to a pew and sat on either side of him. Daisy sat quietly but reached out and took Pa's hand. He smiled and visibly relaxed.

Couldn't Zach see the calming effect Daisy had on his Pa? Didn't that mean anything?

The church filled up, and the preacher took his place. His gaze lit on Amelia. "I see the Taggertys have company. Welcome. I'm Pastor Morrow." His gaze shifted to Pa. "And welcome to Mr. Taggerty and the rest of the family. Now if you would turn to number—" He announced the first hymn.

Amelia and Zach held a hymnal in front of Pa. Amelia knew

from singing "Amazing Grace" with Zach that he had a fine voice, and she prepared to enjoy the service.

Pa sang too, a deep rumbling bass that surprised Amelia. Her eyes stung. This was a hint of the man he had once been and the one Zach missed.

The song service ended, and Pastor Morrow announced his text. "Hebrews thirteen, verses five and six. 'I will never leave thee, nor forsake thee. So that we may boldly say, The Lord is my helper, and I will not fear what man shall do unto me.' " His message of encouragement was exactly what Amelia needed.

But Pa grew restless. He and Daisy twiddled fingers.

Amelia glanced at Zach, seeing her concern reflected in his eyes. He draped his arm around his Pa's shoulders and squeezed.

As soon as the pastor gave the benediction, Zach helped Pa to his feet, and they hurried for the door.

Several called out to them, no doubt wanting to meet Amelia, but they needed to get Pa home before confusion overtook him.

"Kat," Zach called.

She looked up from where she visited with her friends. She might have argued, but she glanced at her pa and rushed toward them.

They got everyone into the wagon and drove from town.

Kat poked her head between Zach and Amelia. "He's getting real restless."

They looked back. Pa sat up, clutching at the sides of the wagon as if he meant to jump out.

Zach reached back. "Pa, sit down. We'll soon be home."

Pa shook his hand off. "I have to go."

"Go where, Pa?" Kat asked. Her fear and worry were palpable. The poor child.

"Stop the wagon," Amelia said.

"If I do, he'll get out."

"Hold him while I get in the back." She handed Daisy to Kat. "Pa, look, Daisy wants to sit with you."

He glanced at the baby, smiled, and then seemed to forget her as he rose, trying to climb out. Zach held him while Amelia got into the back. She sat beside Pa and pulled at his arm to get his attention. "Sit with me and help me sing. What's your favorite song?"

He looked at her. He began to sit but then grabbed the side of the wagon again. Zach held his shoulder so he couldn't climb out. Amelia took his hand and began singing "Amazing Grace." Pa slowly relaxed, and she pulled him down to sit beside her.

Zach joined in the singing. Then Pa. Kat rolled her eyes as if this was too silly for words, but then she sang too. Her voice was clear and sweet.

Tears stung Amelia's eyes both at the power of the words and the knowledge that if she left, Zach and Kat, and maybe Gil, would deal with this on their own.

Was there any hope he would ask her to stay?

If Zach needed any more reason not to ask Amelia to stay, this trip to church provided it. Pa was requiring more and more care. It was not the sort of life a decent man would ask a woman to share. No, he would have to find a man capable of caring for Pa.

They reached home, and he guided his father inside.

There was no just-like-Ma-used-to-make dinner ready. The stove was cold and Gil was missing.

"I'll stay with your pa while you find Gil," Amelia said. She led Pa to the table and had him and Daisy sit side by side. The two immediately reached for each other's hands.

Zach stared at the pair of clasped hands on the tabletop. If only he could grab a hand and find such comfort. But he had to accept the reality of his life.

Amelia started a fire in the stove and set the coffee to boil, then looked in the cupboards for something for dinner.

Things were under control for the moment, so Zach went in search of Gil. He found him in the bunkhouse, sleeping or passed out. From the smell of alcohol, Zach guessed it was the latter. He drained the little bit left in the bottle and searched the place for hidden bottles. He found two that he disposed of but knew Gil likely had others hidden in places much harder to find.

He stepped outside and breathed in the clean air.

What woman in her right mind would want any part of this life?

Pa was tired from the morning out and went to bed after the meal Amelia had put together. She put Daisy down for a nap, then descended the stairs.

"Kat," Amelia said, "I hate to ask it again, but could you listen for Daisy and your pa? I want to talk to your brother."

"Gonna tell him he's gotten too big for his britches?"

Amelia laughed. "I don't think so."

"Shucks." Kat brightened. "Guess I'll have to be the one to do it."

"Not right now. Would you?" She glanced to the rooms upstairs.

"Sure. Can we have cookies when they wake up?"

"Yes. Even if I'm back, you can have them."

Zach studied Amelia. What was it she wanted to tell him? Likely that she'd had enough of his crazy life and was going to stay in town. He knew Wilma would welcome her.

"Shall we?" she said, waiting at the door.

He pushed aside his long-empty cup and got to his feet and followed her outside. "What did you have in mind?"

"A walk. I know the morning was difficult for you and thought a change of scenery would help."

He glanced around. "Looks the same to me." He meant to be funny, but really he sought to hide how much he wished he could change things for the better.

"And you couldn't ask for anything more beautiful."

"I suppose not. I don't wish to change the landscape."

"But you wish you could change the circumstances of your life?"

They passed the barn, and he realized they were retracing their steps to his ma's favorite place. He didn't respond to her question. What could he say that didn't sound like whining? A man didn't whine.

They reached the flowers and sat side by side on the slope of the hill.

"It's beautiful and peaceful here. I expect that's why your ma said it was her favorite place."

He leaned over his knees. "She would often come out here. Said it was her special place to think and pray."

"What did she do in the wintertime for a special place?"

Zach had to think for a moment. "I saw her sitting in the rocking chair and knitting or mending. Often she looked lost in thought, and we had to call her a couple of times to get her attention."

"She sounds serene."

"That describes her all right."

Amelia grew quiet. She seemed like his ma often did, far away and lost in thought.

"What are you thinking?" he asked.

She blinked and met his gaze. "I was trying to think of why this reminds me of home."

"You mean with your parents?"

"Yes. One day Papa took us all for a walk to show us the new crop coming through the soil. Row after row. So green and bright. 'This is our land,' he said. I held his hand and filled my lungs with the smell of hope and promise. He went on to say they would live there until they were old, and maybe us girls would get married and farm with them. I remember how he chuckled as if pleased with the possibility. He said he would build a bigger house and grow more crops. Raise more cows. I asked if we would have more chickens."

Amelia smiled at him. "I loved the chickens. I could picture us all there. So happy. Pa asked Callie what she would like, and she said she would grow row upon row of flowers. Red and pink, purple and blue, every color under the sun."

Amelia stopped when her voice thickened. She cleared her throat and continued. "Mama and Papa laughed, and Mama said it would be beautiful. Papa took off his hat, held it to his chest, and prayed, thanking God for His many blessings." She released a soft sigh. "I felt like God had showered His love down upon us like a warm summer day."

Amelia plucked a pink flower and studied its petals. "Sadly, it came to an end a year later. I think Callie was remembering her dreams when she named her baby Daisy." She stroked the petals of the flower. One fell to the ground, and she tossed the flower aside. "I want to give Daisy that feeling of security I had at that moment."

Zach thought of the Dakota farmer. It sounded much like the life she sought. He would not in any way interfere with the fulfillment of her dreams, though he couldn't imagine how he would cope—how any of them would cope—when she left.

It was time he started to advertise for a man to take care of Pa.

Amelia leaned back on her elbow. "I came out here planning to help you forget about the morning. I know it was trying. Instead, I'm talking about myself."

"I can't think of a better way for me to put aside the problems of the day."

She chuckled. "Don't try and make me feel like I was thinking of you." She sat up, tucked her legs to one side, and faced him. "I told you one of my favorite memories. Now you tell me one of yours." Her eyes matched the color of the nearby leaves of a pink flower.

Her intensity and interest reached into his heart and squeezed it until he wondered it didn't burst.

He tried to shift his gaze away, but it was locked to hers. And it stayed there as he recalled a special time with Pa. "When I was ten, Pa took me on a roundup with him. I rode the range with him, camped with the men, and studied the steers ready to sell. He taught me how to rope, how to cut out a cow, how to do all the things he said I would need to know when I grew up. I admired Pa so much. I saw how the men respected him and how he respected them." Zach shrugged and looked away. "I liked feeling a part of something big and wonderful."

"You still are." Her softly spoken words drew his gaze back to her. "You're doing exactly what your pa prepared you for."

"I don't feel ready." His words were barely a whisper. "I feel like a kid."

She reached for his hand where it lay in his lap and took it between her fingers.

A flood of emotions raced through him. All of them demanding things that were out of reach. But he could no more pull his hand from her grasp than he could order rain from heaven.

"You've been thrust into a situation you didn't ask for. Nothing could have prepared you for all the things occurring in your life right now. Last night I read the story of Joseph again. Such awful things happened to him. But the scriptures say, 'The Lord was with Joseph.' The circumstances of our lives change. Sometimes they are almost more than we can bear. But God doesn't change. Like Pastor Morrow reminded us, God will never leave us or forsake us."

Her look went on and on, searching into the deepest corners of his heart and brushing away the cobwebs to reveal new life, new hope.

He squeezed her hands between his. "Thank you for reminding me that I am not alone in this struggle."

A smile brightened her eyes. "Often God sends people alongside us to help us."

"Like the Dakota farmer for you."

She withdrew her hands and turned away to study the flowers. She didn't put any more distance between them than had been there before, but nevertheless, he felt her withdrawal.

Was she that impatient for the man to offer to marry her?

He closed his eyes and forced himself to pull in air past the lump in his chest. The man had a farm, a nice house, and no complications.

Zach had nothing but troubles and trials to offer. He could hardly blame her for being anxious to leave.

The pain in his chest increased. He pressed his hand to it, but it didn't help.

Being able to talk to her about his life, to tell her about his day, to walk with her and enjoy the scenery with her had done a lot to make his life more bearable.

How was he to go back to dealing with all this on his own?

Amelia stared at the flowers without really seeing them. Seemed Zach thought the Dakota farmer was ideal for her. In a sense, he was. His farm sounded like the one she had grown up on. His life certainly sounded simpler than life here on the ranch. Wasn't it everything she wanted for Daisy?

And yet if Zach asked her, she would stay. But he only reminded her to think of the Dakota farmer.

She picked a bluebell and studied it. These sturdy little flowers bloomed despite the drought and winds. She must do the same—whether in the Montana or Dakota Territory. No matter where she went or what challenges she encountered, the Lord was with her. Life was made for living, loving, and laughing, if one chose that way.

Laughing, she bounced to her feet and grabbed Zach's hands, and they ran down the slope into the middle of the flowers, where she stopped and took both his hands to swing them in a circle.

He laughed. "What's come over you?"

"Life." She told him how she realized it didn't matter where she was or what life sent her way, the Lord was with her. "It's a shame to let disappointments and challenges rob us of happiness. Life and love and laughter are meant to be enjoyed."

They stood a foot apart, in a green bowl of land, surrounded by flowers of many colors, a canopy of blue sky above them. She smiled at him, wanting him to realize that he too could enjoy life despite the heavy burdens he bore.

"Life, love, and laughter, you say?"

She nodded, letting his hungry gaze search her. Would he see, understand, accept all that her words meant?

He grinned at her, grabbed her hand, and pulled her after him as he ran up the hill, across the field, not slowing until they reached a grove of trees. He lifted his hands over his head, tipped his head back, and laughed.

She bent over, trying to catch her breath. When her lungs no longer struggled for air, she joined his laughter. He caught her hand again.

"Tell me we aren't having another race," she said.

"Nope, we're going to enjoy a bit of life and laughter."

She couldn't help notice he'd left out love. "How are we going to do that?"

"By playing." He dropped her hand and, still facing her, danced away. "See if you can catch me."

She stared at him.

"Have you forgotten how to play?" he teased.

"It's been a long time." She pretended to give the idea serious consideration then leaped toward him.

He sidestepped behind a tree. She reached for him, but he darted from tree to tree as she chased him.

She laughed so hard that she finally collapsed to the ground.

"Give up?" He eased closer. Waited. Came closer still.

She waited until just the right moment and lunged for him, catching him around the ankle.

He crashed to the ground, landing on his back. The air whooshed from his lungs. He lay so still she jumped up and rushed to his side. "Zach, are you okay? I didn't mean to hurt you."

His eyes were wide, beseeching.

"Can't you breathe? What do you want me to do?"

He crooked his finger, and she leaned over him. He caught her wrists and pulled her to his chest.

She could sprawl on him or lean on her upper arms. She wanted to do the former but wisely chose the latter, her elbows cradling his ribs on either side like a hug. He held their clasped hands over his heart. Did he do it on purpose, silently telling her that's where she belonged? But of course he didn't. And of course she didn't belong there.

His pupils were so wide there was only a brim of brown iris in his eyes. His hat had landed behind him, and a lock of his hair dipped over his forehead.

She didn't move. Couldn't. This was where she wanted to be. To belong. And she didn't mean the ranch, though it was part and parcel of who Zach was. She meant his family. But most of all, she meant Zach.

"I caught you." His words rumbled from his chest, vibrating through her fingers, up her arms and into her heart. Oh, if only it meant what she wanted it to mean.

"I didn't know I was being chased," she murmured.

"Weren't we playing a game?"

He might have been, but she wasn't now.

"I thought you might have hurt yourself." She freed herself from his grasp, left behind the heart-to-heart connection that was in her mind only, and sat up.

He grunted as he sat beside her. "I might have been hurt just a little."

She turned her head to study him. "Really?" She sounded uncertain, not knowing if he had been bruised or if he teased.

"Yeah. I never expected you to play such a dirty trick on me." Oh, what hurt he managed to put into his words, though she wasn't convinced.

"All's fair in love and war."

"War, is it?" He puffed out his lips. "I know who I'm at war with, but who are you warring with?"

Several answers sprang to her mind. None of which she could give voice to. She was at war with his reluctance, with disappointment, and even with her own goal, which was first and foremost to give Daisy the kind of security that she herself had known as a child. Besides, it wasn't war she was thinking about. It was love. But Zach watched her, waiting for her to answer.

"I'm at war with how people will judge Daisy."

"I can't believe anyone would look at that sweet child and judge her for something she had nothing to do with. But I know they will. Giving her a father will help a lot. Especially if the man is supportive and protective of her."

"I know." She thought of how Zach often held the child. How Daisy pressed to his chest with such free affection. And Kat, Pa, and even Gil all adored the little girl.

She got to her feet. "I'd better get back and make sure she's okay."

Zach fell in beside her, and they returned to the farm. As they passed the barn, Amelia pulled Zach to a halt. "Look." The sound of laughter carried to them as Kat chased Daisy, catching her and swinging her into the air then putting her down to do it again. Both of them laughed with abandon. And Pa sat by the house watching and chuckling.

Zach squeezed Amelia's hands. "So nice to come home to them enjoying themselves." He glanced toward the bunkhouse. "I doubt if Gil has sobered up yet."

"Let him sleep it off. I'll make supper. What would you like?"

He seemed surprised by her question. A slow smile, right from the depths of his heart, made her blink. "Ma made a real nice supper of creamed peas and hard boiled eggs and served it on biscuits." His words deepened. "I haven't had it since she died."

"You'll have it tonight," she promised.

Together they crossed the yard to the house. Daisy saw them and ran straight for Zach. Seeing her intent, he held out his arms and caught her.

Amelia's throat tightened until she couldn't get in a satisfying breath. If only Zach would change his mind and see her and Daisy not as a complication but as a blessing.

She made biscuits and creamed peas and eggs.

Zach sighed his pleasure and thanked her. Pa ate about half his serving then put his knife and fork down. "Evelyn must be home."

Tension grabbed Kat and the two adults at his words. They all knew to tell him she wasn't back could well send him into a dark place. But if he went looking for her. . .

"I made the creamed peas," Amelia said, praying her words wouldn't upset him. "Did I do as good as Evelyn would?"

"I don't know." He took a mouthful and considered the taste. "It's pretty good. But you know, I don't think anyone could be as good as my Evelyn." He looked about. His gaze rested on Amelia, and she wondered if she sat where Evelyn once had. She resisted an urge to shift over beside Kat.

Pa looked at Daisy, who was blessedly unaware of the drama around her, and sighed. "I sure do miss her." He returned to eating.

A collective sigh followed his words and actions.

When the main course was over, Amelia glanced around at the others. "What do you want for dessert?"

Kat and Zach grinned at each other and answered in unison. "Jam and biscuits?"

Thrilled at the connection she'd seen between brother and sister, Amelia grinned at them as she brought a pint of raspberry jam to the table.

Kat stared at the jar. "I helped Ma make this last summer."

Zach gave Amelia a look full of pleading. She understood he wasn't sure how to comfort his little sister.

Amelia hugged Kat. "What a privilege to have been able to work with your Ma. She'd be so proud of how you are doing."

Kat tipped her head back to look at Amelia. "How can you say that? You didn't even know her."

"That's true. I never met her in person, but I see her in the missing and loving in your pa's eyes. I see her in the way you smile and how kind you are to Daisy." Amelia shifted her gaze to Zach. "I see her in the way your brother takes care of you."

Zach's eyes darkened, and she remembered the moment out in the field of flowers and all the longing that had tugged at her heart. Useless feelings unless Zach opened his mind to accepting her. She looked past him to the rest of the house.

"I see her in the afghan hung over the rocking chair, in the dishes that were hers, and in the pictures on the wall and the books in the bookcase."

Kat sniffled. "That's pretty."

"It sure is." Zach's voice had deepened.

Amelia returned to her place, split a biscuit, and put jam on it for Daisy.

After supper Kat helped Amelia clean the kitchen. It was the first time the girl had offered to help, and Amelia thanked her and hugged her around the shoulders.

"Is it Daisy's bedtime?" Kat asked.

"She can stay up a bit longer."

"Good. Come on, Daisy. Let's play."

The pair headed outside. Pa followed.

Zach moved to Amelia's side. "Your words really helped Kat. Thank you."

She smiled, knowing her heart and all her feelings filled her eyes. But she didn't care. She wanted him to see.

He beckoned to her. "Come on outside too. It's a nice evening."

Disappointed but not surprised, she followed him. Would he ever see how helpful she was? Or perhaps he did but it wasn't enough.

She almost stumbled. Because of the letters she'd received, she knew he'd had a girl he courted a bit.

I blush to tell you this, but I serenaded Miss Nellie Newell under her window. She was duly impressed. Her father threatened to sic the dogs on me though. You might well wonder where she is now and why I'm not still courting her. But I got so busy on the ranch that I didn't have time for courting, so she took up with someone who did. That's why I'm doing the mail-order thing. I don't have time for serious courting.

He'd told her again in person too when she showed up expecting a marriage, that he didn't have time for courting. What he hadn't bothered to ask was, did she expect courting? She didn't. And besides, they had grown to know each other in the time she'd been at the ranch.

But neither had she asked if he had taken to pursuing another young lady.

It was a question she must ask even if she dreaded the answer. Though why should it matter to her? She knew she wasn't welcome here, and to think of another woman taking her place pained her mightily.

❧ Chapter 6 ❧

Zach wondered what had caused Amelia to stumble and then gasp. But she seemed fine as they went outdoors.

Kat and Daisy chased back and forth in a noisy game.

Pa sat by the corner of the house, watching them.

Zach thought of sitting by Pa, but Amelia seemed restless and several times glanced toward Ma's wildflower patch. He grinned. Maybe she wanted to repeat the fun they'd had this afternoon. It was more than the fall to the ground that had made it impossible for him to catch his breath. Her arms across his chest were like a sweet hug. Her hair had come loose from the coil she wore to church and fell across his shoulders, brushing his face. Her eyes gleamed like hot emeralds. It took every ounce of his self-control not to pull her closer and kiss her.

He had no right. A Dakota farmer courted her. Albeit by mail. But no matter how Zach looked at his life, it was not the sort that a man with any pride or any scruples could seriously ask a woman to share, even though having her here had eased his burden considerably. That was simply looking at it selfishly.

"I'm going for a walk," she said.

"Do you want company?" He fell in at her side without waiting for her to answer. They reached the flower patch before either of them spoke.

"Is something troubling you?" he asked.

She picked a bluebell and studied it, her head down so he couldn't see her face. "In the letters you didn't write"—she gave a mirthless chuckle—"you told me about Nellie and how she chose someone else to be her beau."

Zach sputtered. "Is there anything this person who isn't me didn't tell you?"

Her head came up. Her gaze was direct and challenging. "You— he—didn't say whether you have a new girl you're interested in."

He certainly did, and she stood before him. "Amelia, you can't be serious. First, when would I ever have time to court a woman? These last couple of days are the first since Ma died that I haven't been needed in at least two places at the same time." Mostly thanks to Amelia, but he wasn't going to make her feel she was obligated to help him. "Above that, I have a pa who needs constant watching and careful handling. I have a sister who is continually threatening to ride the wildest mustang in three counties." Except she hadn't bothered him near as much since Amelia came. Seemed she enjoyed playing with Daisy. "I have a cook who does his job about half the time. A drought and a selfish neighbor are threatening my cows. If it doesn't rain soon, it might be like Sobel said. I might wish I'd sold out to him while I could."

Her eyes remained on him, never jerking away, never dipping in the least.

"This is not a situation that I could with honor ask a woman to share with me."

She crossed her arms and fired him a hot look. "It sounds to me like what you need is someone to help you." She climbed the hill, long strides eating up the distance.

Before he caught up to her, she turned. "Zach, is it honor or pride that you are talking about?"

"Pride?" He swallowed to stop himself from sputtering. But she steamed on, not allowing him a chance to answer. Not that he had an answer.

But by the time they reached the barn, he could no longer keep quiet. "I thought you, of all people, might understand."

She jerked about to face him. "Why? Because my situation back in Ohio made me realize how unacceptable I was? Am." The pain in her eyes sliced through him. "But at least I'm not too proud to seek an arrangement that will benefit Daisy and me."

He caught her arm, stung by the acknowledgment of how being judged by her sister's actions had hurt her. "You are not unacceptable." He drew her closer, wanting to quench the hungry sadness in her eyes. His gaze went to her mouth and back to her eyes. A kiss might convince her that she was desirable.

Or it might make her think he saw her just as those who judged her as being like her sister.

He leaned back on his heels, putting a discreet distance between them. "Your Dakota farmer will see you as the best thing since man discovered honey."

Amelia flicked him a look that made him cringe, then hurried away. She scooped up Daisy and headed into the house.

Kat stared after them then confronted Zach. "Okay, big brother, what did you do?"

"Do? Me? All I did was walk her back to the house."

"Don't think I didn't see you two arguing by the barn." She studied him, her face screwed up in disgust. There was no doubt how she felt, even though she didn't know any of the details.

"Come on, Pa." She stomped into the house with Pa at her heels.

Zach had half a mind to spend the night in the bunkhouse. He would have, except Gil smelled a little ripe, and Zach liked to be where he could hear if Pa decided to wander during the night.

But he sure wasn't going into the house right away.

He tended to the animals that were kept at home. He wandered about the corrals, pausing to watch the mustang. He'd hoped by keeping the animal at home it would grow accustomed to people. Seemed to be working. The horse glanced up at Zach's approach and then resumed grazing.

No time like the present to start working the horse. There was still lots of light left, so he went to the barn and got a rope. He stepped into the pen and tossed a loop over the animal's head and wrapped three loops around the post in the middle of the pen. As expected, the horse snorted and bucked. As soon as the rope snugged up enough to stop him, Zach eased in and slipped on a halter. The mustang rolled his eyes. Zach removed the rope from around the horse's neck. Now he had some control over the horse without worrying about hurting it.

The mustang reared and struck out with his front hooves.

Zach was ready and jumped out of the way. He stood in the middle of the pen and let the animal circle the perimeter.

They worked for the better part of an hour, by which time the shadows were long and gray. He freed the horse and backed up to the fence.

"I was afraid you were going to get hurt."

He startled at the sound of Amelia's voice close to his ear. "How long have you been here?"

"I watched from the window a bit, but I was too far away should anything go wrong."

He didn't know whether he should laugh or hug her. In the end, he did neither. But he studied her a moment. "What did you figure to do if something, as you say, went wrong?"

"I'd do whatever needed to be done."

It was almost laughable to think she might jump into the pen and fight off the horse or drag Zach's battered body out, and yet he didn't, for one minute, doubt she wouldn't do it. Or at least try.

He swung over the fence and landed by her side. "I thought you might be mad enough at me to hope the horse would teach me a lesson."

She ducked her head. "I apologize for my behavior. I had no right."

She didn't say exactly what she had no right to, and he wasn't going to ask. Nope. He wasn't about to start up any more disagreements between them.

"Want to watch the sunset?"

"I'd love to."

He led her past the barn to the slope where he'd previously shown her the view of the mountains, and they sat side by side in companionable silence as the sun disappeared behind the mountains and the sky colored. "Ma always said it was like the sun threw out colored banners as it departed. She said she once saw a May Day dance where the dancers carried colored streamers that dipped and rolled behind them. She said that's what the sunset was like."

Amelia leaned back on her hands. "You have such lovely memories of your mother."

"I do. I miss her."

"It hasn't been very long for you. My parents have been gone eight years. I've never stopped missing them, but I've grown used to it."

He rested his hand over hers and squeezed. "I'm glad to hear it gets more bearable."

She rose and held out a hand to help him up. "I think your mother would want you to be happy."

It was something to think about as they made their way back to the house. He bade her good night and waited until she closed the door to her room before he went upstairs. As always, he peeked into Pa's room. He slept on his back. The big bed seemed so wide with just one person in it, but Pa seemed to find comfort in familiar things. Even the bed he had once shared with his wife.

Zach watched him for a moment. Asleep, he looked like the strong, sure Pa that Zach remembered.

He closed the door gently and tiptoed away. There was no point in wishing things were like they had been. This was his lot in life.

Recalling what Amelia had said about Joseph, he opened his Bible to Genesis and read the story. In all the dreadful things Joseph had endured, the Lord was with him. It was enough for Joseph, and it was enough for Zach.

Over the following days, they settled into a routine. Pa occasionally wandered, but Amelia got him to return before he got too far away. Daisy and Kat played. Pa also played with Daisy. Gil must have run out of hidden bottles, because he remained sober.

Zach spent his days with the men, seeking better pasture, fighting Sobel to allow the cattle to water, and was constantly on the lookout for anyone trying to cut out some of the Taggerty stock. At the end of each day, he rode homeward, his thoughts already at the house, seeing Amelia waiting for his return.

One night he reined in and realized how eager he was to see her smile. He couldn't continue this way. The longer Amelia stayed, the harder it was to think of letting her go.

He considered packing his things and staying at camp with the hired hands. But that would leave Amelia to cope with everything on her own, and wasn't his desire to protect her from having to do that his reason for not asking her to stay?

Pain shafted through him, and he bent over, waiting for it to pass. How could he let her go?

How could he be so selfish as to ask her to stay?

Amelia was grateful for the calm days. The best part of the day was when Zach returned. Often, after supper, they walked together, usually to his ma's flower patch. As days passed with no rain, many of the flowers withered and died. She and Zach kept their conversation to mundane things. What Daisy had said or done that made them smile. How Kat had been eyeing the mustang again and how that worried them both. How Pa's day had gone.

Inside, she felt like those flowers. Drying up and dying for want of things she must deny herself.

Tomorrow was Sunday. "Are you going to go to church?" she asked Zach on their customary evening walk.

"If Pa seems good in the morning."

So the next morning, she helped Gil prepare breakfast. The man kept looking out the window. Twice he opened a cupboard need-lessly. She knew he searched for a bottle.

When Zach came in, Gil said, "Boss, I thought I'd ride over and visit my old friend Buster, if you don't mind."

Zach studied Gil. "I wish your old friend didn't have alcohol to offer you."

Gil shrugged his shoulder. "Ain't seen him in a long time. A man can't work all the time."

Zach nodded. "You deserve your days off."

"Thanks, Boss." Gil was suddenly laughing and moving at a pace Amelia had never before seen.

He hurried them through breakfast and left Amelia with her hands in soapy water, washing dishes.

She watched from the window. Zach spoke to him before he rode away.

"Do you think he'll be back?" she asked Zach when he returned to the house.

"He'll be back, but I don't know what condition he'll be in." He glanced at the clock behind the table. "I'll get the wagon. Is every-one about ready?"

Pa descended the stairs, his suit coat buttoned crookedly, his hair slicked back with an abundance of oil.

"We'll be ready." She went to Pa. "Don't you look nice." She adjusted his buttons and wiped his hair with a towel.

They were soon on their way, Daisy between Pa and Kat in the back, Amelia beside Zach on the seat. How many more trips like this would she enjoy? She did not like the answer.

Not nearly enough.

This time they were ready and hurried into the church with Pa between them.

John and Wilma Daniels sat in front of them. They turned around to greet all of them but especially Pa. Then Mrs. Daniels turned to Amelia. "And how are you liking the ranch?"

"Very much, thank you."

"You don't find it too much work?"

"Goodness, no. I enjoy every minute of it." She hoped Zach was listening and taking the words to heart.

"That's good to hear. Isn't it, Zach?"

"Indeed."

Amelia thought he might have sounded happier about it.

"I haven't seen any letters for you from the *Matrimonial News*," she said to Amelia.

"Wilma." Her husband sounded shocked. "The mail is private."

"Oh pshaw. I'm just expressing an interest." But at her husband's frown, she sighed and turned around.

Then she looked over her shoulder to Amelia. "Seems to me if a man was interested, he would write back posthaste."

He husband jabbed his elbow into her side, and she jerked back to the front.

Amelia could not think past the woman's words. What if Jacob Wells had found something in her letters that he didn't like?

A bubble of anticipation pressed against her ribs. Wouldn't Zach then have to keep her?

The bubble burst. She didn't want someone to *have to keep her*.

What did she want?

Security for Daisy, she insisted, though the argument felt watery and weak.

Pastor Morrow rose to welcome everyone present and announce the first hymn. Amelia shoved aside all her troubling thoughts as she and Zach shared a hymnal with Pa between them and Daisy and Kat on Amelia's other side. She loved singing with Zach. Their voices blended perfectly.

He smiled at her as if he enjoyed singing together as much as she. Hardly reason enough for him to ask her to stay.

She kept her eyes on the hymnal for the next three hymns and straight ahead to the preacher as he opened his Bible.

"Over and over, the great men of God we read about here"—he tapped his Bible—"faced great trials. Often they failed and did foolish things. But through it all, they learned that God is faithful." As he delivered the rest of his message, Amelia breathed in encouragement to face her own challenges. Wherever He led, she would trust Him.

It was easy to be committed to those words the rest of Sunday as Zach stayed near the house. He played with Daisy and Kat. Amelia saw how Kat enjoyed time with her big brother. Zach sat beside his pa and talked about the cows. Sometimes Pa followed and made wise comments. But mostly he didn't seem to comprehend the conversation.

Amelia sat on the other side of Pa, as much for Zach's comfort as Pa's.

They were seated around the table for supper when Gil rode in, singing loudly, his condition apparent in the way his words slurred.

Kat and Daisy looked worried.

"It's okay," Zach said. "He'll go to the bunkhouse."

Amelia wondered if he'd be up to make breakfast the next morning. She planned to be down early to start the meal.

When she rose Monday morning, she smelled coffee and hurried down the stairs, leaving Daisy asleep. The child knew enough to come down on her own when she awakened.

It wasn't Gil in the kitchen but Zach.

He handed her a cup of fresh brew, and without any need for talk, they leaned against the cupboard and enjoyed a few minutes of peace and quiet before the day began. It was a wonderful way to start the morning, and the sense of shared satisfaction carried Amelia through preparing breakfast.

They ate the meal, and Zach left. Gil came in and drank three cups of coffee.

"I'm fine now."

Amelia didn't point out the bloodshot eyes as she washed dishes.

Kat burst into the house. "Zach's working with the mustang!"

He'd spent a bit of time each day with the horse, but something in Kat's voice made Amelia think it was more. She hurried from the house in time to see Zach easing a saddle onto the animal's back.

She caught up Daisy and raced to the corrals, Kat hard on her heels.

Panting, she leaned against the fence. *Please don't get on that horse's back.* But she kept the words silent for fear of breaking Zach's concentration.

Her lungs filled when he simply let the horse get used to the feel of the saddle.

Out of the corner of her eye, Amelia saw that Pa had joined them. Zach saw them lined up at the fence.

"There's no danger," he said, keeping his voice soft so as not to alarm the horse. He turned his attention back to the animal.

Daisy wanted down, so Kat took her back to the house. Pa followed, and the three were soon playing.

Amelia stayed at the fence. *Just in case,* she told herself. Not because she enjoyed watching Zach and didn't want to miss this opportunity.

Zach looked past her. "Wagon coming." He came to the fence and leaned his arms on the top rail as they watched the approaching wagon. A man drove it.

"No one I recognize," Zach said. "I wonder what he wants. One way to find out." He swung over the fence, and they strode toward the wagon.

The men spoke to each other. Zach gestured toward her, and the stranger nodded.

Amelia forgot to breathe. Who was he, and what did he want with her? She didn't have long to wait. He left the wagon, and he and Zach crossed to her.

Zach cleared his throat. "Miss Pressly, this is Jacob Wells."

The man from the Dakotas. Her face felt cold. Her hands clammy. She forced herself to concentrate. Mr. Wells was tall and slim, well built. He was clean-shaven. His skin darkened by work in the sun. His hair was the color of rich soil and his eyes a pale gray.

"Miss Amelia—may I call you Amelia?"

She couldn't move, but he took her silence for permission.

"I knew as soon as I read your letter that you were the right woman for me. I couldn't wait for more letters to make their way back and forth, seeing as we both want to get married and get on with our lives. So here I am. They assured me in Broken Arrow that there's a preacher who would marry us. And then I'll have the pleasure of taking you to your new home." He rattled off the words. Words she had longed to hear. Home. Belonging. Someone who wanted her.

She shifted his gaze to Zach. Why couldn't he want her?

"I'll leave you two alone to make your plans." He disappeared into the barn.

Amelia's gaze followed him out of sight, then she forced in a strengthening breath and brought her gaze back to Mr. Wells.

Though she supposed she must call him Jacob.

"Can we walk a ways and talk?" he asked.

She certainly couldn't fault his manners, nor his way of talking. Though why was she trying to fault him? She found her voice. "Certainly." But she would not take him to the slope where she and Zach had watched the sunset. Nor to the hollow of flowers.

Instead, she indicated the trail past the bunkhouse.

"This looks like a nice place. Is this where you grew up?"

"I was raised in Ohio, but I came here expecting—" How did she explain this without making the man think he was second choice? Which was not a good way to start plans for a marriage. "I came here by mistake."

"I see. But no matter. How soon can you be ready to leave? I don't wish to rush you, but I need to get back as soon as possible."

It didn't seem she could ask for a week or two, or even a day or two to get used to the idea of marrying this man. There was no reason for delay.

Except one. Seeing a man ready to marry her and take her away might jar Zach into action.

"Would tomorrow morning be soon enough?"

Would it be long enough for Zach to realize that she cared for him, that she wanted to stay and help him with his family and so much more?

❧ Chapter 7 ❧

Zach stood inside the barn, hidden in the shadows, and watched Amelia and the Dakota farmer wander past the bunkhouse. The farmer spoke and Amelia nodded. No doubt they were making travel arrangements and—

His ribs closed in, threatening to crush his heart.

They would be making wedding arrangements.

He closed his eyes and tried not to think of them standing before Pastor Morrow vowing faithfulness to each other the rest of their lives. Slow, deep breaths did little to calm his erratic heartbeat.

The pair retraced their steps and headed toward the house. Amelia glanced toward the barn. Zach drew back into the shadows. He would not interfere with her chance at the life she'd dreamed of. A farm like the one she'd grown up on. A life she was familiar with. Her own sweet little family.

Amelia lifted Daisy and introduced the child to her prospective new father.

Zach groaned and leaned against the nearest post at the thought of another man getting the baby's affections, watching her grow into the beautiful young lady he knew she would become. He didn't want to watch any more of Amelia with her future husband, but he couldn't stop himself. The man touched Daisy's cheek, and she pressed her face into Amelia's chest. It would take time for her to warm up to the stranger.

But hadn't she come almost immediately to Zach?

Not that doing so meant anything.

Amelia introduced the man to Pa and Kat.

Kat's expression grew hard. Pa looked confused. His gaze went to the horizon.

Zach understood that Pa wanted to escape this upset in his routine. When Amelia left, he would have to keep a close eye on his father to make sure he didn't wander off.

Amelia handed Daisy to Kat then headed Zach's way. He glanced around, but there was no place to hide.

"Zach?" Then her eyes adjusted to the dimness. "There you are. He wants to stay overnight so we can start out first thing in the morning. Is that okay?"

No. Send him away. Tell him you don't want to marry him. But what could Zach offer to compare to what the Dakota farmer had? Nothing but worry and uncertainty. It just wasn't fair. She deserved the life she'd always wanted.

"Sure, it's fine. You're happy with this arrangement?"

She didn't answer. Her face revealed nothing, and it was too dim inside the barn for him to be able to read anything in her eyes.

Finally, she spoke. "I expect everything will work out. After all, isn't that what Pastor Morrow meant when he said God is faithful no matter where we go or what befalls us?"

If she meant the words to reassure him, they fell far short of the mark. But then, what need did she have to reassure him?

"Let's go see to arrangements for the night." Back at the house, Mr. Wells—asking them to call him Jacob—said he would sleep in the bunkhouse.

Gil had prepared a hearty dinner, and they gathered around the table, but Zach didn't feel very hospitable. The others seemed quieter than usual.

Gil poked a finger in Zach's shoulder as he filled his cup with coffee. "Seems a man should know a good thing when he has it."

Zach ignored him. Just as he ignored Kat's scowling glances. Pa seemed happy enough to have Daisy's company.

The rest of the day stretched before him. He had no desire to watch Jacob courting Amelia. "I'll check the cows this afternoon."

Kat followed him to the barn. "You gonna let her go with that fella?"

"That's the plan."

"Why?"

"It's what she wants."

Kat blocked his escape from the barn. "How do you know? Did you ask her? Are you going to go back to Pa wandering away? What about me? I need her." She sucked in air. "You talked about being lost in a great big sea without a rudder, without a pilot, and without hope. Seems to me God sent Amelia to help us get safely to shore."

Kat's words stung. He wished he could believe that was the way it should be. "Kat, we can't selfishly stand in the way of her finding happiness."

His sister snorted. " 'Pears to me she's happy. You're just too selfish to ask her to stay."

Selfish? If she only knew. "You're too young to understand." He swung into his saddle.

She grabbed his leg. "You don't see what's right in front of your nose. Sometimes you act like a silly kid." She stomped away, and he rode to the cows.

The condition of the grassland had steadily deteriorated due to lack of rain. He'd had the cowboys move the cattle farther up the mountains. Sobel had done the same thing, so the fight over grass continued. So far the Taggerty cowboys had been able to get the herd to water despite Sobel's attempts to keep them away.

Zach joined his foreman, and they rode the area, looking for better grass.

"How's that pretty little gal settling in?" Morgan asked. He'd seen Amelia twice when he came to the ranch to speak to Zach.

"She's leaving tomorrow."

"Leaving? Don't tell me you're letting a good woman like that get away?"

Zach tried for a laugh but wondered if it sounded more like a wail. "She's set on marrying a Dakota farmer. He came for her today. They leave in the morning."

Morgan shifted in his saddle to give Zach a hard look up and down his whole length. "Did you give her any reason to stay?"

"And what reason would that be?"

"Maybe because you need her and want her?"

Zach rode away without replying. He had thought of joining the men at the chuck wagon for supper, but he couldn't endure the way Morgan kept shaking his head and muttering about being too stubborn to ask.

But he made certain it was late before he got home. When he saw a lamp glowing in the kitchen window, he pretended his heart didn't jolt against his ribs to know Amelia had left it burning for him. He took care of his horse then hurried to the house. What was the harm in enjoying it one last time?

"Have you eaten?" she asked as he stepped into the kitchen.

"No."

"I saved you a plate." She pulled it from the warming oven.

"Thanks." He glanced around. "Where's your young man?" Ironic to call him that when he was likely ten years older than Zach. Another thing in the man's favor.

"Gone to the bunkhouse. He wants to get an early start tomorrow."

He let the words hang in the air, wished they would stay there, but they settled in the pit of his stomach like hot rocks. His appetite had departed, but he cleaned up his plate.

"Will you come to town to see us married?"

It was only his imagination that made her sound weary, resigned. Or perhaps an echo of his heart.

"I'll see." He pushed from the table and hurried upstairs.

He was tired enough to sleep like a bear in hibernation, but sleep refused to come.

Words circled in his head. Was he being stubborn, prideful, and childish in not asking her to consider staying?

"Ye have not because ye ask not."

It was a scripture verse that had nothing to do with him and Amelia.

Yet the words hammered inside his head with a persistence that was almost painful.

There was only one thing to do.

Ask. He'd do it tomorrow morning before she left.

Amelia lay awake long into the night praying. *Please, God, let me be certain of this.* How could she think of marrying Jacob when she loved Zach? There. She'd admitted it. If only Zach would ask her to stay.

She was packed. On the top of her things in the trunk, she'd put the picture her maternal grandmother had painted and Callie had rescued from being sold. She'd hang it on the wall of her new home. To her it signified permanency and security.

The next morning, when she went downstairs to join the others for breakfast, Jacob sat at the table and smiled at her.

Zach kept his head down as if he cared about nothing but the food about to be served.

If he would utter even one word to indicate he wanted her to stay. . .

They were almost finished eating breakfast when a rider thundered into the yard.

Zach rushed out to greet one of his cowboys.

They all overheard the message. "Boss, the cows have been stampeded. They're all over creation."

"Saddle my horse." Zach returned as far as the door. "I'm afraid I have to leave. All the best to all of you." His gaze slid over Amelia and rested a moment on Daisy, and then he was gone. Along with any hope that he might have even a sliver of the affection for her that she had for him.

That left her nothing but the farm in the Dakotas.

Once it would have been enough.

Jacob pushed from the table. "Thank you for the hospitality." He addressed Pa, who looked confused.

Who would watch to see that Pa wouldn't wander off? Gil didn't keep a close enough eye on the elderly man, and Kat often spent time at the corrals, oblivious to her father.

Jacob smiled at Amelia. "Are you ready to go?"

"I have a trunk and crate upstairs. I'll need help bringing them down."

He followed her up the steps and grabbed a handle of the trunk. She took the other, and they lifted it. He backed from the room and made his way to the top of the stairs.

"Stop." She let her end drop to the floor.

"Is it too heavy? Maybe I can get Gil to help."

"It's not too heavy. It's too far."

"I don't understand."

"I know, and I don't expect you to. But I can't go. I am needed here."

Jacob stared at her. "Are you saying you won't marry me? That you are going to stay here?"

She nodded.

"Is Zach going to marry you?"

She shrugged. "I love him. But even if he won't marry me, I will stay. This is where I belong."

"That's for sure," Kat said.

Amelia looked over the bannister to see Kat, Pa, Gil, and Daisy grinning up at her. "I'm sorry," she said to Jacob.

"Me too, but I'm glad you're honest with me. I want a wife who loves me and is true to me even in her heart. I'll be on my way."

They waved goodbye to him at the door, and Amelia returned upstairs. There was something she must do. She lifted the painting from her trunk and took it downstairs. She found a hammer and nail and hung it where it would greet everyone who stepped inside the house.

Zach reached the cowboys at the camp, where Morgan was giving orders. Morgan turned toward Zach. "Did you ask her to stay?"

"I was going to but got your message that the cows had been stampeded."

"So you're choosing your cows over that young lady?" Morgan said.

Zach felt the stare of every man in the camp. Was it so obvious to everyone else? Suddenly he saw that it was. He was letting his circumstances dictate his choices. He knew he would regret doing so every day for the rest of his life. She'd proven she fit into his life, supported him, and didn't mind the challenges she must deal with. Why was he being so stubborn? Prideful? Stupid? "No, I'm not. You lot can handle the cows. I've got a girl to marry."

As he rode away, a cheer rose from the camp.

He galloped all the way home. The yard was empty and silent. He jumped from his horse in front of the door and ran inside. "Is she gone?" he hollered.

No one answered. The house was strangely quiet.

Zach took a step, saw a painting of flowers on the wall facing him. "Where did that come from?"

Amelia stepped into view. "I hung it there. It's my mother's picture."

"You're still here? I thought you would be gone."

"I belong here. That's why I hung the picture. I know you're afraid your life is too complicated to share with a woman, but I'm here to stay."

"Why?"

She smiled, her eyes full of green gentleness. "I could say because you need my help. Or because I care about Pa and Kat. All of which would be true. But the biggest reason is because I love you."

"You'd willingly stay and deal with my crazy life?"

"I'd willingly stay no matter what."

"Because you love me?"

"With my whole heart."

He whooped and pulled her to his chest. "Amelia, I have been fighting my love for you from the day you showed up claiming I was to be your husband."

"That seems like a waste."

"It was. Amelia Pressly, I love you as much as one heart can. I love Daisy, and I propose we get married and become one happy family."

"I accept."

He lowered his head, and they sealed their love with a kiss that contained the promise of both their dreams fulfilled.

That very afternoon they put on their Sunday best, put their family members into the wagon, and rode to town.

To everyone's surprise, Gil asked to accompany them. "Amelia has made me see how good churchgoing people can be."

Zach grinned. "She's made a difference in all our lives." He had two people in mind to act as their witnesses and stopped at the store to invite John and Wilma Daniels.

"Since you're Ma's oldest friends, I'd like you to come to our wedding."

John hung a CLOSED sign on the door, and they went to the

church, where Pastor Morrow awaited them.

He smiled at Zach and Amelia. "It is good to see two people uniting their lives to take on the responsibilities you both bring with you."

It was the first time Zach had thought that the responsibilities went both ways.

They exchanged the customary vows, then Zach said, "I want to add something." He turned to Amelia. "I not only take you as my wife. I take Daisy as my daughter."

Tears glistened in her eyes.

He wiped her lashes.

"I have something to add too," she said. "Zach, I take you as my husband. But I also take Pa as my pa and Kat as my sister." She waved them both forward and kissed their cheeks.

Kat sniffled and hugged Amelia.

Pa beamed to be part of the happy occasion.

"Normally, I say you may now kiss the bride," Pastor Morrow said.

"No need." Zach wrapped his arms about Amelia and kissed her. It was a kiss full of promise.

Wilma Daniels sighed. "I knew it would all work out. That's why I wrote—" She broke off as she realized she was about to say more than she intended.

Zach laughed. "So it was you. I wondered who would know so much about me."

Wilma nodded. "When I saw how little time you had for courting, I knew this was the answer for you. You needed someone who didn't mind helping with your family and someone who needed a home and family."

Amelia hugged Wilma. "And most of all, we both wanted love,

and we have found it. Thank you for being our matchmaker."

Zach held Amelia back as the others left the church. "I think we should name our first child after her." He chuckled when Amelia's cheeks grew as pink as the blossoms she'd admired in the field.

She laughed too. "A good idea."

With a sigh of contentment, she looked about. She had found the home her heart longed for.

"Look," Zach drew her attention to the horizon. "I believe there's rain coming." He hugged her. "We better make a run for it." They hurried into the wagon and drove home, making it to the house as the heavens opened with the blessing of rain.

But in Amelia's mind, nothing was more of a blessing than belonging to her new family. And the man who loved her.

Linda Ford draws on her own experiences living in the Canadian prairie and Rockies to paint wonderful adventures in romance and faith. She lives in Alberta, Canada, with her family, and she writes as much as her full-time job of taking care of a paraplegic and four kids, who are still at home, will allow. Linda says, "I thank God that He has given me a full, productive life and that I'm not bored. I thank Him for placing a little bit of the creative energy revealed in His creation into me, and I pray I might use my writing for His honor and glory."

The Marriage Sham

by Vickie McDonough

Chapter 1

Persimmon Hill, Texas, May 20, 1888

> *Husband of good character wanted for Christian
> woman aged 24. I can cook, sew, and maintain a home
> well. I'm not overly pretty but not ugly either.*

Zola Bryant wadded up the copy of the *Matrimonial News* that
contained the ad she'd placed six months ago and tossed it into the
fire. The dreams of love and happiness she'd had before she and
Henry married were dried up and dead now. Loneliness was her
constant companion. Only her family Bible brought her peace and
comfort—that and an occasional visit from her friend Alice.

She stirred the pot of boiling water that held the rabbit she'd
been fortunate to snare, mixed with the last potato and carrot from
her garden. The little hare hadn't been full grown, and she hated to

eat the poor thing, but she desperately needed food. If Henry didn't return soon, she might starve to death.

And yet she dreaded his coming home. The "man of good character" she'd sought was rough, crude, and demanding. If she didn't need the food and the piddling money he brought home each time he was away, she would— No, she could never divorce Henry, no matter how bad things were. It just wasn't done.

Zola lifted the frayed curtain and stared out. Henry had been gone two weeks this time. In the four and a half months they'd been married, she never knew where he went or when he'd be back. He never told her a thing about the type of work he did, and she learned not to question him. She touched the cheek he had bruised the last time she asked about his employment.

Blowing out a sigh, she looked about her pitiful one-room home, checking to see if anything was out of place. The wedding ring quilt she and her mother had made before her mama's passing was the sole spot of color in the shabby cabin. Two chairs, a table, a washstand, and a small bed filled the tiny room.

A glance in the water bucket revealed it was low, so she grabbed it and headed down to the creek. Already the hundreds of night creatures nearby were singing. It would soon be dark, so she quickened her steps. She hated being out at dusk. Everything was so different in the West than it had been back in Chicago. Things sounded different. There were no lights save the one lantern in the cabin. And so many unfamiliar creatures.

Zola brushed the top of the water to clear it of insects, then she dipped in the bucket. She ought to water the garden, but nothing was growing anyway. The spring had been long, dry, and hot. Her first attempt at growing her own food had not gone well. Hopefully, next year would be better.

As she stood, the crickets stopped. Zola's heartbeat leaped. She had learned that when the birds and insects got quiet, something was about. Was it man or some kind of beast?

She held her breath, not sure which she wished it was. If only she had a gun, but Henry wouldn't allow it.

A horse snorted in the direction of the cabin. So it was a person. She tiptoed across a patch of dirt, avoiding the dry grass and twigs that could alert the stranger to her presence. If Henry were home, he'd yell for her as soon as he saw she wasn't in the cabin.

When no holler came, the hairs on her arms stood on end. Had one of Henry's cronies come by thinking he could get special favors? It had happened more than once. The last time Henry had beaten her for tempting the man, even though she'd done nothing but lock herself in the cabin.

"Mrs. Bryant? You here? It's Marshal Taylor."

The marshal? What could he want at this hour? Her first thought was that he was probably on his way back to town and was hoping for a meal. Her heart sank. If that's what he wanted, she'd have to pretend she'd already eaten, because there wasn't enough stew for two.

Ah, well. It wasn't the first time she'd gone hungry.

"I'm over here, Marshal. I was getting water." She stepped into the clearing, lugging the heavy bucket.

He hurried forward. "Here, let me get that for you."

"No, it's—"

He tugged the bucket from her hand.

"Um, thank you."

"Happy to help."

He carried the bucket to the door and set it down.

Zola hated that she was happy he didn't ask to go inside.

There was barely enough light left in the darkening sky to see his craggy features. She guessed the tall man must be near fifty. She'd seen him in Persimmon Hill the few times she'd been to town.

He tugged off his hat and frowned. "I hate to be the bearer of bad news, ma'am."

Zola couldn't imagine what he must be referring to. Henry was away. She had no other family. "What's happened?"

"There was a stage holdup this afternoon. I'm sorry to tell you that your husband was shot and killed."

Henry was dead? She felt instant remorse that she had no grief over his passing. What kind of woman was she? "But. . .why was he riding the stage when he has a horse?"

The marshal shuffled his feet and blew out a deep breath. "There's no easy way to say this, ma'am. Henry wasn't riding *in* the stage. He was one of the robbers."

Zola lifted her fingers to her mouth as she reached for the door-jamb with her other hand. "Surely there must be some mistake."

"Sorry, ma'am, but he was caught red-handed. The shotgun rider said he recognized Henry. Your husband had on a ring that was taken from a man in the last robbery."

She remembered that ring. She'd wondered how Henry had been able to buy it when they had so little. "Was anyone else hurt?"

"The driver was winged in the arm, but he'll live. Two of the three thieves were killed, but one got away."

"I can't believe it. Henry robbed the stage?" But now things made sense. Henry gone for weeks at a time, only to return with a fresh supply of cigars and whiskey, as well as a few cans of food. No wonder he never wanted to talk about his work. He was an outlaw. She leaned against the house for fear her shaking legs would fail her.

Thank the good Lord her parents weren't alive to learn about this dreadful turn of events.

"I brought you Henry's horse. Would you like to gather your things and go stay in town?"

She shook her head. "I'll be fine here. Thank you for returning the horse."

His eyes were kind. "If you're sure."

"I am."

He looked as if he had something else to say but decided not to. "I'll tend the gelding then be on my way. You got a barn out back?"

She shook her head. "Only a lean-to. Around that way." She gestured to the right.

The marshal turned away, paused, then started walking again.

"Would you care for a bite of supper before you go?"

"Thank you kindly. But my wife will most likely have a meal waiting for me."

"All right." She stepped inside, closed the door, then crossed the room and dropped onto the bed.

What was going to become of her?

How could she not have known Henry was an outlaw? His elusiveness should have given her a clue. She was so stupid. So naive.

Zola hated that she wasn't the least bit sorry she was a widow. She felt bad that Henry had died and had never known God, but he refused to allow her to talk about her faith.

She blew out a sigh. How would she survive? She could sell Henry's horse, but if she found employment in town, she would need the animal. The cabin was too far from town for her to walk there, especially when she didn't have a weapon.

Zola reached for the family Bible she kept on the table next to the bed, lifted it, and hugged it to her chest. *Father God, I don't know what to do. Please heal the stage driver who was injured, and please help me.*

A knock at the door made her jump. "Y–yes?"

"It's just me, Marshal Taylor. There's something else I need to tell you."

Zola set the Bible on the bed, swiped at her moist eyes, and crossed to the door. She pulled it back, illuminating the lawman. "Is the horse all right?"

"He's fine." The marshal rubbed his jaw. "That's not it. I don't rightly know how to tell you. I thought about not mentioning it, but it's something you should know."

Zola tightened her grip on the door. What more could he possibly tell her?

He rubbed his ear, then shuffled his feet and stared at the darkness. "Turns out that the man who married you and Henry was a buddy of his."

"Yes, I knew that."

The marshal finally looked her in the eye. "But what you don't know is that he isn't a real preacher. Henry paid him to pretend."

The skin on Zola's face tightened as the blood drained from it. She grabbed the doorframe, suddenly understanding the meaning of what the marshal had said. "You m–mean Henry and I were never. . .m–married?"

He nodded. "I'm truly sorry."

Dreadful thoughts buzzed her like angry wasps. "But how do you know that?"

He leaned one hand against the house, his gaze filled with compassion. "Henry confessed as he was dying. Said he wished he'd treated you better."

A deathbed confession. It must be true.

The horrible ramifications of Henry's lies swarmed Zola. She was a fallen woman, and her marriage was nothing but a sham. She closed her eyes as darkness surrounded her.

Sunlight filtered through the ruffled curtains in the bedroom. Zola stretched as she looked around the pretty room. She was in the marshal's house. Suddenly last night's events came rushing back.

Rolling over, she buried her face in the pillow. How could she face the townsfolk? Did they know her marriage was a sham? That she was a fallen woman, although not of her own accord? Few people in Persimmon Hill knew her, since she'd been to town only two times—on the day she arrived and married Henry, and once when he had a bit of money and brought her to town to purchase supplies.

Tears burned her eyes. How could Henry have done such a thing? Why had he ordered a wife when he was hardly ever home? Had he hoped to change his ways? Was it just a game to him?

She'd probably never know. But she'd bear the scars of their union forever.

Needing air, she turned over. What was she going to do now? The only things of value she had was a cameo that had belonged to her grandmother, which she could never part with, and Henry's horse. The cabin wasn't even hers, since they rented it. Zola bolted up. When was the next rent payment due?

She squeezed the bridge of her nose. So many things to think about. Decisions to be made. And she needed to ask the marshal how Henry's burial would be handled. Would she be responsible for that?

Her mother always said, "Nothing gets done by sitting around thinking."

Zola blew out a loud sigh. If only she could stay in this room until news of Henry's ill deeds had died down, but she couldn't. She rose and quickly dressed, then made the bed and folded the nightgown Mrs. Taylor had loaned her. She looked in the mirror at her splotchy face—the face of a woman in mourning. But it wasn't her deceased husband she grieved. It was her virtue.

A knock sounded. Zola quickly splashed water onto her face and grabbed the towel. "Come in."

She dried her face and forced a smile as Mrs. Taylor peeked in. "Good morning. Do you feel up to eating breakfast? Mr. Taylor is gone to work, so it's just us."

Zola folded and rehung the towel, pinched her cheeks, and walked to the door. As much as she longed for a good meal, she wasn't sure she could eat. Still, she didn't want to offend the woman who'd been so kind to her. "That sounds nice. Thank you."

Zola managed to eat more than she expected of the eggs, bacon, biscuits, and gravy. She placed her silverware on her plate. "That was delicious. Please allow me to wash the dishes for you."

Mrs. Taylor swatted her hand in the air. "Nonsense. You're my guest. Would you care for more coffee?"

"No, thank you. I'm stuffed." She looked around the cozy two-bedroom home. The furnishings had seen better days, but the house was tidy. The kitchen smelled of bacon and the yeasty scent of rising bread dough. Sky-blue gingham curtains blended with the braided rug, which had darker shades of blue. A couch, two chairs, and a pair of side tables filled the small parlor. She could have been quite happy in a little house like this one. She could have been content with her shack had Henry been nicer. Her eyes burned, and she turned her gaze to the open window.

Mrs. Taylor took their plates to the kitchen counter, then refilled her coffee cup and returned to her seat. "I'm so sorry for what's happened to you, dear. It simply isn't right that a man could do such a thing to an unsuspecting bride."

Zola's chin wobbled. She couldn't cry. Wouldn't. She'd shed too many tears already, and all they'd done was make her head hurt, her nose run, and her face look like she'd been stung by a dozen bees.

"I know it's probably too soon to ask, but what do you plan to do? Can you return to your parents' home?"

Zola shook her head. "My mother and father are both deceased. I have no siblings or other living relatives."

Mrs. Taylor laid her hand on Zola's back. "You poor dear. You're welcome to stay here a few days while you make plans."

Zola placed her hands in her lap. "I very much appreciate your kindness, especially how you cared for me last night when I was so upset, but I should return home."

"What will you do there? I'm guessing that if you had any means of support, you'd never have become a mail-order bride." The woman's kind blue eyes looked into Zola's with sympathy. Her brownish-gray hair was pulled back in a loose bun.

"I suppose I'll need to find some kind of employment."

Mrs. Taylor pursed her lips, and Zola couldn't help but wonder if she was thinking how nobody would want to hire a fallen woman, except the kinds of places Zola refused to work. She'd starve to death before that.

"Persimmon Hill is not a large town, but perhaps you could find work at one of the cafés or take in laundry, although that would be difficult with you living so far from town."

"God will provide. But I need to do my part, which includes looking. So I best get at it. May I leave my horse in your barn a bit longer?"

"Of course, dear. As I said before, you are welcome to stay here for several days while you look for work."

"That's very kind of you, but I don't want to impose. I'll go out and see what I can find."

"I truly think you should wait a day. You've had some very disturbing news, and that can take a toll on your body."

Zola's neck ached with tension, and she did feel overly tired. When she'd checked in the mirror this morning, the area around her eyes was still puffy and reddish. Who'd want to hire her looking like that? "I suppose you're right. Perhaps I'll rest today then venture out tomorrow."

Mrs. Taylor smiled. "I think that's the wise thing to do. Feel free to lie down or read if you want. Mr. Taylor has several well-read novels on the shelf in the parlor."

Zola smiled. "Thank you so much."

The kind lady pushed to her feet. "Think nothing of it. I'm delighted to get to visit with another woman. I have been lonely since our daughter married last year."

"I've been lonely too."

Mrs. Taylor patted her hand. "You rest now, and then we'll have a nice chat over lunch, if you're feeling up to it."

"Would you mind if I sat on the porch for a while?"

"Of course not."

"Let me help with the dishes first."

Mrs. Taylor shook her head. "Thank you, dear, but you're my guest. You go on outside. Perhaps I'll join you when I'm done and work on my mending, if you don't mind the company."

Zola rose and gave her a quick hug. "I would love for you to come out too."

A few minutes later, Zola stepped outside, her heart pounding.

The Taylors' house was only one block off Main Street. She lowered herself into a faded rocker and glanced down the road. The chair creaked as she set it into motion. Had word about Henry's indiscretions made it around town? News traveled so quickly in this small town that didn't even have a newspaper. And exactly what had people heard? That Henry was an outlaw?

Or that he had faked their marriage?

❦ *Chapter 2* ❦

*E*van Clayborne used the bootjack to slip out of his muddy boots, then set them near the back door of his house. He removed his dirty, torn shirt and dropped it in the clothes basket in the mudroom. Mrs. Crocker wouldn't be happy that a cranky calf had caught a hoof in his pocket and ripped the same shirt she'd mended last week.

He opened the door softly and tiptoed in, hoping to make it to his room before she saw him. The delicious aroma of a pie baking made his mouth water. Clanking in the kitchen alerted him that Mrs. Crocker was there, probably preparing supper.

Once again, he was glad he'd had a second door installed in the mudroom so that he could get to his bedroom without going through the main part of the house. It also came in handy when one of his ranch hands needed him in the wee hours of the night. With the coast clear, Evan hurried down the hall, relishing the silence. Too many times he'd come home and walked in on an argument between his twelve-year-old sister, Amy, and her caregiver.

After washing up, he snagged a shirt from his wardrobe and put it on. His stomach growled, reminding him he'd skipped lunch. That calf, stuck in a bog, had kept him busy for too long.

His gut warned him things hadn't gone well today between Amy and Mrs. Crocker, but perhaps he was wrong. The last thing he needed was for the latest caregiver to quit. She was the sixth one this year, and he was running out of people to ask. Add that to the reputation Amy had for causing trouble, and he'd likely have to hunt out of state for a new worker next time he needed one. And he didn't doubt there would be a next time.

Blowing out a loud sigh, he tucked in his shirt and walked down the hall to Amy's room. He loved his sister, but having her live here was a challenge and added to his already busy workload as a rancher. But she was family—the only one he had left since the carriage accident that took his parents. Only Amy had survived.

He paused in the doorway and found her in her wheelchair by the window, reading. His heart clenched as it did most times he saw his vivacious baby sister stuck in that chair. He longed to see her running around and his mother calling after her to behave like a lady. His lips tilted in a sad smile. Five months had passed since the accident, but Amy still couldn't walk. Would she ever?

Amy snapped the book shut, making him jerk. She grinned. "I thought you'd fallen asleep on your feet."

He straightened. "Oh, I see. Rather than let this hardworking rancher rest a moment, you thought you needed to be my rooster call."

She lifted a thin hand. "I merely closed my book. I could have screamed bloody murder, but then Mrs. Crocker would come running and chew me out."

"I'm sure she would." He moved into her room and sat in the chair next to the bed. "How'd things go today?"

Amy tossed her book onto the bed. "Boring, as usual."

"Did you do your schoolwork?"

She lifted one shoulder.

"Amy?" he said, trying to sound stern.

"What's the point?" She slapped the arms of the wheelchair. "I don't need an education. I can read just fine. I don't need to know higher math or other harder subjects when all I'll be doing is sitting in this stupid chair for the rest of my life."

Evan struggled for a response. He wasn't a father—what did he know about raising a troubled girl? "If your math skills improve, I could use your help with the ranch's accounting."

His sister rolled her dark blue eyes. "I don't want to do book work. I'd rather herd cattle or groom horses. Book work is boring."

Everything was tiresome to Amy. But he could sympathize to some extent. If he were cooped up in the house like she was, he'd go stir-crazy too. "How about I wheel you out to the barn after supper?"

"Truly? I would love that. You promise?"

Quick footsteps sounded down the hall. Mrs. Crocker paused in the doorway, her pursed lips making him wonder what had gone on today. He stood and glanced at Amy, who was struggling to hide a smile.

"Dinner is served—no thanks to your sister."

"What does that mean?" Evan rose.

"Just that she managed to spill sugar all over the floor and then knock her glass of water onto it. Can you imagine how difficult it was to clean up that wet, sugary mess?"

He couldn't. "Sounds to me like it was an accident."

"Humph!" She turned and started back down the hall. "You'd think this place was haunted with all of the *accidents* in this house."

Evan eyed Amy again. She had her sweet, innocent face on, which meant she was most likely guilty.

He sat down again to be eye level with his sister. "You do know it took me a whole month of advertising to find Mrs. Crocker? I need you to be pleasant so she'll stay."

Amy's lips quirked.

"I mean it, squirt. I can't stay home and care for you when I have so much to do already."

"You're gone all the time." She crossed her arms.

"I have a ranch to run. It takes lots of work."

"Fine. Just go do what you must."

Evan stood and wheeled Amy to the kitchen. Trying to get her to see reason was as impossible as getting a bull to bear a calf. He lifted his gaze to heaven. *I could use Your help here. You blessed me with my sister living through that accident, but I need You to show me how to live with her.*

A few minutes later they sat at the large kitchen table. Mrs. Crocker had already set the meal on the table. Evan said the prayer, then they ate mostly in silence. Mrs. Crocker's lips puckered each time she glanced at Amy.

If he were a betting man, which he wasn't, he'd guess Mrs. Crocker's days were numbered. He'd best pull out the short list of names he'd kept just in case.

Though his stomach had been satisfied with fried ham, potatoes, gravy, green beans, and biscuits, it gurgled again when Mrs. Crocker set a golden brown pie on the table.

Amy placed her silverware on her plate and rubbed her stomach. "I don't think I can eat another thing. I'm stuffed."

Evan stared at his sister. Was she getting sick? Probably not, since she'd eaten plenty for supper. But she almost never turned down dessert.

Mrs. Crocker slid an oozing piece of apple pie in front of him. His mouth watered. One thing he could say about his current cook—she could bake.

After cutting herself a smaller slice, Mrs. Crocker took her seat. Almost at the same time, they forked a bite into their mouths. Evan's gaze suddenly collided with the cook's as salt battered his taste buds instead of the sweetness he'd expected. He grabbed his napkin and spat out the pie. He shifted his gaze to his sister. Her napkin hid most of her face except for her twinkling eyes.

Amy burst out laughing. "Oh. . .you should have seen your face." She puckered up, imitating him, then giggled again.

Mrs. Crocker gulped down the last of her coffee, slapped her hands on the table, and stood. "I've had enough of your shenanigans, young lady. I don't deserve to endure your pranks, not after all my hard work to cook, clean, and care for you." She turned her angry brown eyes on Evan. "I quit. First thing in the morning, I'll expect a ride to town." She threw her napkin on the table and stomped off.

Evan closed his eyes. Not again. He should have trusted his gut. It rarely ever failed him.

He took a steadying breath so he wouldn't lambast his sister. Finally, he regained his composure. "You may spend the evening in your bedroom, after you help with the dishes."

"But—"

Evan stood and placed his hands on the table so he could stare his sister in the eye. "No 'buts.' What a shame to waste what could have been a delicious pie. Food is too hard to come by to ruin with your pranks. Once we finally get another cook, you will not get dessert for a month."

Amy crossed her arms and scowled. "That's not fair."

"Too bad." Evan rose, grabbed the pie, and dumped it in the slop bucket, although he wasn't sure the hog would eat the salt-laden pastry. He crossed his arms and stared out the back window. Looked like he'd be searching for a caregiver and cook again. How long would it take to find one this time?

After eating breakfast with the Taylors, Zola had insisted on helping clean up. Then she spent some time reading her Bible and praying, giving business owners time to open for the day. Zola took a deep breath and knocked on the door of the doctor's office. She stared down the street at the businesses she'd already stopped at. The few people who hadn't turned up their noses at her didn't need help.

Word had definitely gotten around town about her sham marriage. Several ladies had seen her coming, murmured to themselves, then crossed to the opposite side of the street, while throwing her looks that could have curdled milk on a chilly day.

A man cleared his throat. "I'm Dr. Parkhurst. Can I be of assistance, ma'am?"

Zola squeezed her hands together. "I'm Mrs. Bryant." The name left a bitter taste in her mouth, especially since it wasn't her true name. "I'm seeking employment and wondered if perhaps you needed someone to assist you or tend your books. I can even cook and clean." She closed her mouth, realizing how needy she sounded.

The doctor removed his spectacles, wiped them with a cloth he had in his pocket, then put them back on. "Do you have any medical training?"

She ducked her head. "No, sir."

"Well, even if you did, I probably couldn't hire you."

So he too looked down on her because of what happened. She had thought a doctor would be more understanding.

"You see, I mostly get paid in food stock, like a ham, baked goods, or a chicken now and then. I wish I could help, but I truly don't need an assistant except on rare occasions."

"Thank you. I'm sorry to have bothered you."

He offered a kind smile. "It's never a bother to chat with a pretty lady."

The man must need new spectacles if he thought she was pretty. Still, she returned his smile, grateful for his kindness, and continued down the street.

Zola skipped the marshal's office, knowing he wouldn't have any work for her. Next was a lawyer's office. She paused at the window then hurried on past it. What did she know about law? She couldn't even get married properly. The last two businesses were the Dos Vaqueros Cantina and the livery.

Heart heavy, she turned back the way she'd come and headed to the marshal's home for lunch and to get her horse.

Persimmon Hill was similar to the other small Texas towns the train had stopped at on her trip here. The buildings were one or two stories, with fancy, sometimes colorful, facades, while the sides were wood or brick. As she walked, she studied the businesses across Main Street. She passed a general store, millinery, and a dressmaker's shop. Farther down were a café and bakery. Perhaps she would have had better luck if she had started on that side. Ah well, she'd save that for tomorrow.

As Zola passed the bank, the door opened, and a trio of women stepped out. The shortest of the three was talking. One lady looked at Zola and stopped suddenly, causing the other two to do the same.

The chatty lady slammed her mouth closed, puckered her lips, and glared at Zola. "Well, I never. Come, ladies."

They skirted around Zola and sashayed off. She wasn't sure, but she thought she heard the word *hussy*. Threatening tears burned her eyes. She needed to get out of town.

She made her apologies to the marshal's wife for not staying for lunch, retrieved the horse, and headed home. Half an hour later, she reached the cabin, and the tears hadn't stopped. Fortunately, she lived in a remote area, so she didn't pass a soul on the ride back.

She dismounted then struggled to remove the heavy saddle and get it on the tree stump that Henry had always used as a mounting block. She made quick work of brushing the horse, and then she put it in the lean-to. Finally, she returned to the cabin and closed the door. Relief washed over her. At least she was safe from scornful looks and snide remarks here.

She dropped onto the chair, blew her nose on her handkerchief, and rested her cheeks in her hands. Her head throbbed. She knew without looking that her face was red again. What was she going to do?

Would she starve to death in this tiny shack with not a soul caring what happened to her? It was all so unfair. Few jobs were available to women except for those places where she refused to work, like a house of ill repute or a dance hall. She'd rather starve. She had tried to do the right thing by marrying. Why had it gone so badly?

She had prayed before answering Henry's letters. Why had God led her here to marry—no, not even marry—an outlaw? Did God care for her anymore?

Tears fell again. Zola crossed to the bed and collapsed. If only her parents hadn't died. Things would have been so much better.

A short while later, a loud knock at the door caused Zola to bolt up in the bed. Who could that be? It was nearly suppertime—or possibly past, by the way her stomach was grumbling. Had she fallen asleep?

She hurried to the water bucket, washed her face, and walked to the door. Her heart leaped. She hadn't barred the door when she came in earlier. "Who's there?"

"It's Frank Gibbons."

Her mind raced. She'd heard the name before but couldn't remember meeting him. "Yes?"

"I. . .uh. . .need to talk to you. Could you open the door?"

She drew in several deep breaths. Here she was alone, without any sort of weapon. Her gaze landed on the cast-iron skillet, and she rushed to grab it. She held it behind her back, opened the door, and peeked out. "How can I help you?"

The man yanked off his hat, glanced at her, then his eyes widened—probably shocked to see her splotchy face. "I know it's a bad time with your. . .uh. . .man just dying and all." He cleared his throat and glanced at his horse. "I don't rightly know how to tell you this, but I own this piece of land. Henry owed me two months' rent. Unless you can catch it up, I'll need you to clear out."

She sucked in a sharp breath. She had no money. Where would she go? But hadn't she known this would happen sooner or later? She blinked, refusing to cry again. "Could you possibly give me a few days to make arrangements?" Not that she had any idea what those might be.

"All right. Seeings as you're a recent widow—I mean. . ." His ears reddened, and the stain spread across his tanned cheeks. "Well,

I heard what Henry did. Downright disgusting if you ask me."

"Um. . .thank you for your concern. I'll be out by Saturday."

He nodded, slapped on his hat, and made a bowlegged jog toward his horse. The man had looked as uncomfortable as she felt.

She closed the door and sat down on the chair, staring at a crack in the wall where the chinking was gone.

All her life she'd gone to church, listened to the preachers, and tried to walk the straight and narrow path. She thought things couldn't get any worse, but they had. Whatever was she going to do?

She looked at the Bible that she'd salvaged before the auctioneers had sold off her parents' possessions to pay for the back taxes. Not only had she lost her parents, but everything else that was familiar. She'd been allowed to keep several dresses and her unmentionables, but that was all. Thank goodness her mother had given her the cameo already, or it would be lost.

For once, she had no desire to hug the Bible that had given her comfort in the past. She felt numb—listless. She needed to eat, but she had no appetite.

She trudged back to the bed, flopped down, and stared at the ceiling. What would become of her now that God had deserted her?

Chapter 3

The morning sun shone in Zola's window, illuminating the words in the Bible. *"For I know the thoughts that I think toward you, saith the Lord, thoughts of peace, and not of evil, to give you an expected end. Then shall ye call upon me, and ye shall go and pray unto me, and I will hearken unto you. And ye shall seek me, and find me, when ye shall search for me with all your heart."*

The passage in Jeremiah 29 had encouraged her in the past, and she hoped it would once again. When she'd risen this morning, she'd felt a heap of guilt over thinking that God had abandoned her. Circumstances were about as bad as she'd ever encountered, but God still reigned, and she chose to believe that He would make a way for her. That He wouldn't forget about her.

Still, it was hard to keep her spirits up while searching for employment when she kept getting the door slammed in her face. She finished off her dried biscuit and read the rest of the chapter. Feeling a wee bit better, she rose and dressed.

One glance in the mirror made her cringe. Her face was pale and her nose red from so much crying. She hoped by the time she reached town her complexion would return to normal.

She looked around the shack. Should she pack her things and go stay with the Taylors, as they had offered?

Shaking her head, she decided to wait to see if she found work today.

A knock on the door made her spin around, her heart pounding. "Who's there?"

"It's Alice."

Relief washed through Zola as she hurried to the door. She and Alice had ridden to town on the same stage on a chilly January day. She was Zola's only good friend in Persimmon Hill. "Alice! What are you doing way out here?"

"I came to check on you."

Zola stepped back to allow her friend to enter. "That was kind of you."

Alice's gaze made quick work of scanning the small cabin. "I. . .um. . .heard some things in town."

Zola motioned for Alice to sit. "Would you like a glass of water? A biscuit?"

"No, thank you. I ate earlier."

Zola took the other chair, dreading what she had to ask her friend. "What did you hear?"

Alice stared at the floor. "People are saying awful things."

"They're probably true."

Alice lifted her hazel eyes. "Henry was an outlaw?"

Zola nodded, wishing she could be as carefree as the birds happily chirping outside. "That's what the marshal told me."

"And the other?" Alice's cheeks pinked, and she looked out the window.

Zola sighed. At least her friend's expression was sympathetic embarrassment and not disdain. "It turns out that one of Henry's cronies posed as the minister, so our marriage was never real. Just a sham."

Alice laid her hand over Zola's. "I can't imagine how dreadful that is."

No, thankfully she couldn't. No woman should ever have to feel so filthy. "It's terrible. I'm a fallen woman through no fault of my own."

"I'm so sorry. Surely people will be understanding, considering the circumstances."

Alice was a naive, eighteen-year-old schoolteacher, who had come to Persimmon Hill to work. She hadn't seen the rough side of life that Zola had experienced. Hadn't felt the derisive stares she had.

Alice squeezed Zola's hand. "Well, this is a terrible place to live. I want you to come stay with me."

Zola blinked. "In your tiny cottage?"

"Yes. We will make do."

"That's very kind of you." Zola picked flecks of loose paint off the table. "My landlord showed up yesterday and told me I had to be out by Saturday."

Alice smiled. "Well, there you have it. Let's pack up, and you can come now. I rented a buggy, so there's room for your things, but we need to hurry so I can get back in time for school."

Zola looked around the cabin. There was nothing holding her here. But she had to think of Alice. "Associating with me could put a smear on your reputation."

"Oh." Alice's eyebrows puckered. "I see what you're saying. Well, I can always return home if I lose this job."

"That's true, but you might have a difficult time finding another teaching position if the board here doesn't give you a good recommendation."

Alice nibbled her lower lip, obviously wrestling with the situation. "But I want to help you."

"Perhaps you could deliver me to Mrs. Taylor's house."

"The marshal's wife?"

Zola nodded. "She offered to let me stay while I looked for work. If I don't find anything here, I'll sell Henry's horse and go to another town."

"Something will work out. I know it will." Alice cocked her head and smiled. "Perhaps you'll find another man to marry."

Zola rose, not believing her friend could even say that. After marrying a man who was crude and demanding and abusive, only to find out their marriage wasn't real, she had no desire to marry again. Not unless she had no other way to survive. "I'd better start packing. I want to have plenty of time to search for employment."

Alice hopped to her feet. "What can I do?"

"Would you mind folding the bedding while I go saddle the horse? I can tie him to the back of the wagon and ride up front with you."

"Certainly."

Zola smiled her gratitude then headed out to the lean-to. She sure wouldn't miss this dumpy place, although she didn't like the insecurity of not knowing what the future held. Still, God had provided a place to stay for the next few nights. He'd even sent Alice to help her take her belongings to town. She would accept that and be grateful. And she would try not to worry about the future.

Evan tapped his toe, hoping the man talking to the postmaster would hurry up and finish. He'd ridden to town to see if the last woman on his list had written back. The other two on his list were no longer interested in the caretaker position.

He scratched his neck, thinking of all the tasks he'd fallen behind on since he had to stay home to watch over Amy. If she were better able to tend herself, he could leave her alone more often. But with her being only twelve and stuck in a wheelchair, he didn't dare leave her unattended for longer than it took him to run out to the barn for a few minutes.

He glanced at the mailboxes behind the postmaster, and his heart bucked. He had a letter. He hoped it was the one he was waiting on—and that the response was positive.

Less than a week had passed since Mrs. Crocker left, and both he and Amy were already sick of his cooking. Not to mention his sister was getting old enough that she didn't want a man helping her dress, thus she still wore the frock she had on the day Mrs. Crocker left. He'd have to burn the thing if she ever took it off.

"Warm weather we've been having, right, Carl?" The man in front of him leaned one arm on the counter, looking like he was settling in for a long chat.

Pete, the youngest of his ranch hands, loved books, so he'd left him on the front porch with Amy, reading *Treasure Island*. Evan tapped his toe. He had to get back soon. He cleared his throat. "If I could get my letter, the two of you could continue your chat, and I can get on with my business."

The man stepped aside, although his frown showed he wasn't

happy being interrupted. Evan recognized Jess Pershing, now that he'd turned around.

"I don't mean to be rude, but I've got to get back home—you know—because of my sister."

Carl Hopkins nodded. "I heard your latest helper quit. That's a shame."

No kidding. Mrs. Crocker must have started the gossip train when she came back to town to await the stage.

Carl stroked his long, scraggly white beard. "You know, there's been a gal poundin' the streets, lookin' for work."

"She that outlaw's wife?" Jess curled his lip.

"Whoa!" Evan held up his hands. "I don't want any outlaws near my sister or my ranch."

Carl thumped the counter. "It ain't like that. Scuttlebutt says she didn't know he was one."

How could a woman not know her husband was a robber?

Jess straightened. "I heard tell they wasn't even married."

Evan's eyes widened before he schooled his expression. They must think he was really desperate to consider hiring a woman of such low morals. It was time he broadened his search to towns farther away—if the final woman refused his generous offer.

Carl shook his head. "No, that ain't the case exactly. I heard the deputy say that Henry Bryant sent for a mail-order bride, then when she arrived in town, he got one of his outlaw buddies to pretend to be a preacher. He married them. So she thought they was wedded, but they weren't actually."

Could that be true? Evan's sympathy rose for the woman he had just looked down on. How could a man do such a heinous thing to a poor, unsuspecting bride? On the other hand, the truth had a way of getting skewed when lips started flapping. No telling how much of the woman's story was true.

The postmaster turned, grabbed the letter from Evan's box, then handed it to him. "I feel sorry for her. She stopped in here, asking if I needed help, but I don't. After she left, I watched her for a bit. Several ladies turned up their noses and crossed the street just so's they didn't have to walk past her. Mrs. Bryant was polite and seemed nice—and a bit sad—when I talked to her. It ain't right that she suffer for what that snake of a husband did."

"She ain't a missus, and that's simply the way of things," Jess said.

Evan nodded at the men and stepped outside to scan the letter. Another refusal. He wadded up the paper then shoved it in his pocket. What now?

Blowing out a frustrated sigh, he surveyed the town. It looked much the same as it always did. Too bad there wasn't a woman around who needed a job.

His thoughts shifted to the outlaw's wife. Was she as innocent as Carl said? If so, she sounded like she was in a difficult position and might be glad to work for him. He shook his head. What was he thinking? Yes, he was desperate, but not enough to hire a woman who may well be an outlaw.

Evan pushed his boots into action. His next step—to wire several ranchers he had dealings with and see if one of them knew of a woman looking for employment—was a long shot.

As he neared the telegraph office, Marshal Taylor stepped out of his office and stretched.

"Nap time, marshal?" Evan chuckled.

The marshal patted his belly. "Nope. Lunchtime."

At the mention of a meal, Evan's stomach rumbled. He longed to eat in town, but he really ought to get home.

"What brings you to town midweek?"

"Checking my mail to see if the woman I'd written to about helping with Amy had written back. She did. Said no." He pursed his lips. If only his sister wasn't so hard to get along with. She'd been a sweet thing when she was younger, but the accident had changed her.

The marshal rubbed his jaw. "I've got a woman staying with me and Etta that's looking for work." He frowned and shook his head. "It's a shame what men do to women sometimes."

"What do you mean?"

"Just that she came to town as a mail-order bride, thought she'd married Henry Bryant, but he'd arranged for a phony minister. Then it turns out that Bryant was one of the thieves that's been robbing stages and trains in these parts. I feel sorry for her. A man oughtn't toy with a woman's virtue."

"How do you know she wasn't part of the outlaw gang?"

"She's too sweet and innocent, for one." He tugged on his vest and nodded at a rider passing by. "I'm a fairly good reader of people, and I can tell you, she was completely shocked at the news about Henry being a thief. When I told her about the fake marriage, she passed out at my feet. I had to tote her home for Etta to care for her. Couldn't exactly leave her alone way out yonder all by herself after delivering that kind of news."

The marshal came across as tough, but evidently he had a soft side.

"Do you think she'd be able to care for Amy, as well as the house?"

"Mrs. Bryant's been staying with us the past three days, and I ain't never seen Etta happier. Our guest is a good cook and makes my wife sit and relax while she does the work. I'll kinda be sorry to see her leave when the time comes, although I will enjoy it only being me and Etta again. With my hours varying so much, I'm always afraid I'll walk in at the wrong moment."

He could understand that. There had been a few embarrassing times when he'd walked into the kitchen and found the caregiver in her nightgown.

"Hey." The marshal nudged him. "Why don't you come to lunch? That way you can meet Mrs. Bryant without her knowing you're looking to hire someone. You can see for yourself what she's like."

Evan rubbed the back of his neck. "I oughta be getting back. Amy might need me."

"You don't have to stay long. I usually eat fast so I can return to work. You can too. C'mon. Be good to have another man to balance things out."

"All right. You talked me into it."

Evan wrestled with his choice as he walked alongside the marshal. A home-cooked meal would taste wonderful. And just maybe this Mrs. Bryant was the woman he was looking for.

Chapter 4

Zola peeked at the handsome man across the table while he chatted with Etta and the marshal. She couldn't help wondering why Marshal Taylor had brought him home for lunch, but that was none of her business.

"How is your sister doing, Mr. Clayborne?" Etta buttered a biscuit as she cast a glance at the stranger.

" 'Bout the same. Her health seems stable, but she keeps running off her caregivers."

"Why do you think that is?" Etta asked.

Mr. Clayborne shrugged. "I sure wish I knew, then maybe I could stop it."

Etta looked at Zola. "Amy, Mr. Clayborne's sister, was injured and is in one of those wheeled chairs. Mighty handy contraption, that is."

"I'm sorry." Zola glanced at the man across from her, then just as quickly looked away. She wondered how old his sister was but thought it rude to ask. It was none of her business anyway.

Etta shook her head. "Such a sad thing for one so young to have to live in a chair. Is there no chance she'll walk again?"

"Dearest, that's none of our business." The marshal scowled then dug back into his meal.

"I don't mind the question. The doctor Amy sees in Dallas says the injuries she got from the accident have healed, and he can find no reason that she can't walk. He also admits there are many things about the body that still have physicians flummoxed. I keep praying God will heal her and give her the will to walk again."

Zola ached for Amy. How awful not to be able to stroll through a field of wildflowers, cook a meal, or enjoy life as God meant for a woman to.

"So, you're in the market for a caregiver, eh?" The marshal's lips twisted in an odd way.

Mr. Clayborne frowned at him. "You could say that."

Zola's heart leaped. She needed work, and Mr. Clayborne needed help. Dare she hope he'd hire her?

Just as fast, her heart dropped. What man in his right mind would hire the wife of an outlaw to watch over his ill sister? She placed her folded napkin on the table and rose to get the coffeepot so the others wouldn't notice the unshed tears stinging her eyes. It was so unfair that she had been labeled a loose woman because the man she'd trusted had tricked her.

She refilled Etta's and the marshal's cups then stopped beside the stranger. He looked up, smiled, and nodded. His dark blue eyes immediately captured Zola's and held her gaze for a long moment. She felt her cheeks burning, then focused on the cup so she didn't spill any coffee. My, but the man had pretty eyes. They reminded her of the bluebonnets that had bloomed this past spring.

After Zola returned to her place at the table, Mr. Clayborne cleared his throat. "So, Mrs. Bryant, what did you do before coming to Persimmon Hill, if you don't mind me asking?"

Zola managed to swallow her coffee without choking. Stalling while she gathered her composure, she wiped her mouth on her napkin. "I lived with my parents in Chicago. But they both died last November. When the doctor informed me their illness was most likely terminal, and then Papa told me they had no money and that I needed to make arrangements, I starting searching advertisements for men looking for a"—she swallowed the lump in her throat—"mail-order bride." Heat blistered her cheeks. Surely Mr. Clayborne had heard that she was never truly married.

She hopped up again and took her dish to the counter, her appetite gone. She retrieved the dessert plates and the rhubarb pie she'd made and turned back to the table, hoping to keep her gaze off the guest. But his compassionate expression drew her eyes to him again.

"I'm sorry about your parents. Amy and I lost ours not too long ago, so I understand the pain of that."

"Thank you."

She quickly sliced the pie, served everyone, and took her seat. If only she could retire to her room.

The men talked about town issues while the pie was devoured. Etta rose and began clearing the table, so Zola joined her. Once the dishes were on the counter, she grabbed the bucket and headed outside for fresh water. Behind her, chairs squealed as the men stood.

She drew in a breath of fresh air as she walked to the pump. It had become clear that she was going to have to leave town to find work. But how could she manage when she had no money and didn't know a soul in any other town?

The pump handle creaked as she jerked it up. A soothing splash hit the bucket, and after a few more pushes, it was full. She was reaching for the handle when she saw movement out of the corner of her eye. Zola screeched and jumped back.

Mr. Clayborne stared at her with wide blue eyes. "Uh. . .I'm sorry. I only meant to carry that for you."

She smoothed down her skirt, once again striving for a calm demeanor. "I didn't hear you come out."

"I apologize." He ducked his head for a moment then looked at her again. "I need to ask you a question."

Her heart tripled its pace. "What is that?"

He pursed his lips then nailed her with a stern stare. "Did you honestly not know your husband was an outlaw?"

Zola sucked in a sharp breath. Definitely not the question she had hoped for. "I did not. At least not until the day Marshal Taylor arrived and told me about Henry's unscrupulous activities. I asked Henry several times about his work, but he refused to talk about it." She didn't mention that Henry slapped her the last time she'd asked.

Mr. Clayborne rubbed the nape of his neck. "I find it hard to believe you wouldn't figure it out."

Zola sucked in a sharp breath. "I assure you that I did not. Many men travel to find work. It's not uncommon."

"All right. I believe you. But I had to know for sure."

"Why?" It was really none of his business. She glanced at the door, anxious to get away from him.

He removed his slouch hat, forked his fingers through his hair, then blew out a loud breath. "I'm in need of help. Amy can't fend for herself. I can't tend my ranch and give her the time that she needs. Can you cook and teach a twelve-year-old the things she'd be learning if she was in school?"

Oh yes! She tried not to let the eagerness she suddenly felt show. "Why doesn't Amy attend school?"

"She's stuck in a wheelchair." Mr. Clayborne stiffened and scowled. "I don't want her subjected to the cruelty that kids her age dispense."

No wonder Amy was lonely. She probably took her frustrations out on her unsuspecting caregivers. "I'm sure I could teach her most of the things she needs to know. What are her interests?"

He shook his head and shrugged. "Besides pie and fried chicken, I'm not sure."

Fried chicken. Zola loved eating it too, but she'd never had to pluck a hen. Would she be expected to do that task too? Her papa had bought their meat from the butcher. However would she manage that?

"What is it?" He narrowed his gaze at her.

"Nothing. What else would you expect me to do?"

"Cooking, cleaning, the wash, and caring for Amy. That's all."

That's all? Working hard to keep a straight face, Zola decided the man actually wanted a wife—without the fringe benefits. She swallowed hard. Surely he didn't expect *that*. Could that be the real reason why his other caregivers had left? Was she jumping out of the frying pan into the fire?

Still, she trusted Marshal Taylor. She'd learned enough to know he wouldn't bring Mr. Clayborne home if he couldn't vouch for the man.

"Are you interested?"

"Are you offering me the job?"

He put his hands on his hips. "Isn't that what we're talking about?"

The neighbors' fat black-and-white cat lapped up water that

had spilled from the pump. Then it strolled over and wove its way through Mr. Clayborne's legs. The tall man reached down and scratched the critter then straightened. That action spoke volumes to Zola. A man who was kind to animals was surely kind to people.

He rubbed his hand down his face. "I reckon I should explain what you get out of the deal. You'll have your own room, next to Amy's, all the food you can eat, a small salary, and you'll be under my protection."

"That's very generous. I apologize if I'm slow to answer, but the last man I trusted did me very wrong. It's a bit hard to trust another stranger."

His expression softened. "What that scoundrel did was inexcusable. Don't judge all men by his example. Most around here are kind, decent men. Ask the marshal about me. He and I have been friends for years. The pastor at First Christian Church knows me, as well as most anyone in town. You want to go visit the pastor?"

Zola's eyes widened. Surely he wasn't talking marriage. "What for?"

"So the man can vouch my character."

"Oh." She wasn't used to talking with a man she didn't know. His nearness and the fact that they were alone rattled her. The cat lumbered back toward its own house, and she wished she could go with it.

"The thing is, I need to get home to my sister soon. I left her in the care of one of my ranch hands, who was reading a book to her. You need to know that taking care of her won't be an easy task. She's run off half a dozen ladies in the five months she's lived with me. I brought Amy home shortly after the accident that injured her and killed our parents."

"I'm sorry she had to go through all of that." Still, she couldn't help wondering why so many caregivers had left his service.

"Me too. She used to be such a happy child. She loved visiting the ranch and riding horses."

"If she has an interest in horses, perhaps I can use that to get her to learn."

"So, you'll come?"

"Let me talk with the marshal first, if you don't mind."

"Go ahead. I'll fetch my wagon and pull around front." He started to walk away then paused and turned around. "Thank you. I don't know how to express how grateful I am that you're willing to take the job."

Zola watched his long-legged stride eat up the distance. Then he disappeared around the front of the neighbors' house. She hadn't told him she'd take the job, but he seemed to think it was a done deal. Was his standing in town so good that he knew the marshal wouldn't have anything negative to say?

Only one way to find out.

Evan drove the wagon down the road that led to his house. Would Mrs. Bryant be impressed? He'd worked hard to build a nice house and had hoped to have a wife and children to fill it one day, but those plans had been abandoned once Amy came to live with him.

One thing for sure, Amy would drill Mrs. Bryant about her marriage to Henry if she ever found out. If nothing else, his sister was curious, not to mention tenacious. He should probably warn his newest employee. "Whoa there."

Mrs. Bryant's eyes widened as she looked around. "Why are we stopping here?"

"My house is over the next rise, and I need to tell you something before we get there." He brushed his hand over his jaw, making a rasping sound. "Amy is extremely curious."

"That's a good thing in a child."

"Well, I thought you might want to keep your experience with

Henry quiet. Otherwise, she'll pester you with questions."

"Oh." She twisted her hands together. "About that. Um. . . well. . .since I wasn't officially married to Henry, I probably should switch back to using my maiden name. It doesn't seem right to go by Bryant when it was never truly my name."

"That makes sense. So, what is your maiden name?"

"Zola Allasandra Francesca Barbieri."

"Barber what?" He'd never remember half of that. What was wrong with a simple name like Pearl or Maude?

Zola's dark eyes twinkled, and she looked to be holding back a grin. She was lovely when she wasn't so serious. "Barbieri. It's Italian, and as a matter of fact, it means barber."

Evan blew out a sigh. *Italian.* That explained her dark, exotic features. His ranch hands would be making excuses to come to the house just to stare at her. "Talk about a mouthful of a name. How about you call me Evan, and I'll call you Zola? Makes things so much easier."

"Are you certain?"

"Sure as the wind blows across the Texas plains."

Zola smiled. "Using our Christian names would make things easier and less formal. All right. As long as you don't mind."

"I don't. Amy will appreciate not having to say your last name too. Anything else we need to discuss before we get home?"

She tapped her finger to her lip, and Evan couldn't help staring. His stomach did an odd jig. He scowled and looked away. He couldn't afford to become attracted to Amy's caregiver. No telling how long this one would last.

"Do you attend Sunday services?"

"Used to, before Amy came to stay with me. She doesn't want to go because she doesn't like people staring at her."

"I understand that, but don't you think she needs a Christian upbringing? It would help her with the issues she struggles with, especially if she knew where to turn in the Bible for help."

Evan clucked to the horses, and they moved forward. He really should have made Amy go to church, but things had been in an uproar since she arrived. His whole schedule changed, and not attending church had been one of the easiest changes to make, not that he didn't miss it. Maybe it would be good for Amy to attend services. She shouldn't spend the rest of her life hiding in the house.

Zola sucked in a breath, and he glanced at her. He realized she was staring at the house. Next to his growing ranch, the soft yellow clapboard house was what he was proudest of. "The place was originally a two-story, six-room house. My office, a guest room, and a washroom are on the top floor. After the accident, I had two more bedrooms built downstairs—one for Amy and one for me, so I could be close in case she needed me. There's also a bedroom for you on the first floor." The crowning feature of the house was the wide veranda that wrapped around both floors.

"It's incredible. I love the porches."

"It's a nice place to sit and watch the sunset."

"I can imagine."

The wistfulness in her voice tugged at him. What horrible things had she gone through that a house would create such longing in her voice?

He glanced at the front porch, and his heart lurched. "Shoot!"

"Shoot what?" Zola's gaze scoured the area, as if she were searching for a wild creature.

He might have chuckled if the situation hadn't been so serious. "Amy is supposed to be on the porch with Pete, but they're both gone."

Chapter 5

Zola followed Evan onto the wide porch. He stormed into the house, shouting his sister's name. Zola paused at the front door, not sure whether to enter or wait for an invitation. But if Amy was injured, Evan might need her assistance. She opened the door and stepped in. After her eyes adjusted to the dim lighting, she studied the comfortable parlor.

A sofa sat against the wall facing the big picture window. On the far wall was a large, stone fireplace with two comfortable-looking chairs on each side. Three small tables had been placed around the room to hold the hurricane lamps and several small decorations. A Navajo rug warmed the center part of the room, giving the place a western, but inviting feel. *Homey* described it well. The big room was three times the size of her parents' parlor. She hadn't realized

Evan Clayborne was so well off. Not that it mattered.

She wandered into the dining room where a regal, dark walnut table with carved legs and eight chairs filled the center of the room. A matching sideboard and china cabinet completed the set.

Zola looked out the window to a pasture where more than a dozen horses grazed on the side of a hill. She thought it odd that the room didn't have any curtains or drapes covering the windows, but with the ranch house being so far from town, they probably weren't a necessity.

She peeked into the kitchen and frowned. Dirty dishes and empty food cans littered the countertop. Things could stand to be tidied up. A thrill ran through her when she turned and saw the near-new Home Comfort stove. What a treat to cook on it. The old stove her parents owned had been passed down from friends and didn't have half the features this one did. She'd never considered her parents' modest home to be on the poorer side, but looking at Evan's fine abode made her suspect that was the case.

She wondered where her room was but didn't feel comfortable venturing further into the house. She peeked down the hall off the kitchen, but raised voices made her halt. She turned around and made her way back to the parlor to wait.

A red-faced young man marched down the hall, barreled past without seeing her, and stormed out the front door, causing the screen to bang shut. Zola winced as the glass in the lamps rattled, and she reached out to silence the nearest one.

"You know better than to allow a man to come in the house when I'm gone," Evan said, his voice raised.

"But I got hot—and we'd finished the book. I just wanted to show Pete my library so he could pick out another book for us to start."

"Regardless, he shouldn't have been alone in the house with you. Think of your reputation."

"Well, you were gone a lot longer than you said you would be. And besides, the only reputation I have is that of a cripple."

"Don't say that."

Zola could imagine Evan rubbing his neck in frustration, as he had when questioning her. She pondered going in to see if she could defuse the situation but decided against it. Maybe in time she could be a mediator between Evan and his sister, but not yet.

"I was gone so long because I found another caregiver for you."

"Horse feathers! I told you I don't need a babysitter."

"You know I can't watch you all the time. I have a ranch to run."

Zola couldn't hear all of Amy's soft response, but it included the word *stupid*.

"At any rate, you need to come out and meet Miss Barbaria."

Zola smiled at how he butchered her surname.

"What kind of name is that? Is she a foreigner?" By the sound of Amy's elevated voice, Zola figured she wanted her to hear.

"She's Italian and very nice. You are to treat her kindly and with respect."

Amy didn't comment. Zola could imagine the girl scowling with her arms crossed. She understood Amy's desire for independence, especially with her being almost in her teen years. She had to find ways to help the girl be as independent as possible. That meant keeping a keen eye open and watching Amy's daily routine.

The clump of boots came her way, and Evan tramped into the room. He looked at Zola and shook his head. "I don't understand why God took my parents. Amy needs them far more than she does me." He shoved his hands to his waist and sighed. "I don't know what to do with her."

"It will help when you can go back to being her brother and not tending her all day. She craves your love, comfort, and time together. I will see to her daily needs, and that will help the strained situation between you two. At least I believe it will."

"I sure hope you're right." He rubbed his neck and smiled. "I'd rather wrestle a loco bull to the ground than have an argument with my sister. It seems I can't ever win with her. I never say the right thing."

Zola reached out and patted his arm. "Ask God for wisdom."

He sobered and glanced down at her hand. Zola's cheek heated, and she yanked her hand back. Her family had always been quick to hug or offer a reassuring touch, but perhaps that wasn't the case here.

Evan cleared his throat. "Thank you for your encouragement. That alone is more help to me than those other ladies gave. I reckon if you want to meet Amy, you'll have to go to her. She isn't budging at the moment."

Zola smiled, although her insides still quivered at the contact with her boss. He couldn't have meant what he said about the other caregivers, but her heart warmed to think that what she'd said had cheered him. "I don't mind reaching out to her. Lead the way."

Evan clomped down the hall to the first room, then stepped back to allow her to enter before him. Zola quickly took in Amy's cheerful room before her gaze landed on the brooding girl. She looked pale and small for a twelve-year-old, but maybe the chair disguised her actual size. Amy's hair must have been blond when she was younger, judging by the ends of the strands. Although it had started to darken, Zola doubted it would ever be black like her brother's. "It's a pleasure to make your acquaintance, Amy. I'm Zola."

"Humph. I don't care who you are." Amy frowned, staring her

up and down. "Are you an Indian? I don't want to have to worry about my scalp."

"Amy! That was rude. You apologize right now."

A tiny smirk danced on the girl's lips as she slid her gaze from her brother to Zola. "You can leave now or wait until I make you completely miserable."

"A–aa–mee." Evan ground out the short name, making it sound much longer. "You have manners. Use them."

Amy scowled at her brother then instantly plastered on a somewhat pleasant expression. "Nice to meet you, ma'am. I do suggest for your own safety and sanity that you have my brother return you to town immediately."

Zola worked hard to not show a reaction. She liked Amy's spunk. At least the girl had some fight in her, and that would help her in the long run. Still, Zola couldn't help wondering what dreadful plots Amy had planned for her. Probably the same things that had worked on her other caregivers.

She smiled. "Thank you so much for your kind warning, but I do believe I'll stay. I'm sure I can handle whatever you're capable of dishing out, but I should warn you, I used to have a brother, and I learned some things from him. I have a few pranks of my own in my arsenal, should I need them." Zola spun around, leaving both Amy and her brother with gaping mouths. She strode out of the room, her heart beating like the wings of a frantic bird caught in a trap.

When she reached the parlor, she took a deep breath. Had she just gotten herself fired?

Evan stared at the empty doorway. If Amy hadn't been in the room, he might have chuckled at Zola's gumption. Good for her for not letting a peevish malcontent of a child cause her to tuck tail and run.

Making sure there was not a smidgeon of humor in his expression, he turned on his sister. "You had no call to talk to Zola that way. That was rude and embarrassing behavior. You were taught better than that."

"Why do you call that woman by her first name when you always insisted I use surnames for those other riffraff babysitters?"

Leave it to Amy to try to deflect him with a question. "I can't say her last name, so it is simpler to use first names. *You* can call her *Miss* Zola. And you can stay in your room until suppertime since you can't seem to locate your manners and behave properly. I suggest you search your room and see if you can find them somewhere before I decide to ship you off to boarding school."

He spun and marched out of the room, his gut clenched at the sound of Amy gasping. He had never mentioned boarding school before, and he knew he could never send her away, but it was all he could think of to get her to toe the line and treat Zola with a measure of respect. Zola was his last option, and he aimed to keep her for a long while.

He slowed his steps as he walked into the parlor and didn't see her. Had she changed her mind and decided to leave?

A creak through the screen door alerted him that she was on the front porch, rocking. Perhaps she was out there waiting for him to take her back to town. His gut tightened. Caring for such a cranky child was too much to ask of a stranger. Would she stay if he offered her more money?

He dropped into a chair beside her and sighed loudly. "You see what I'm dealing with?" He swatted at a fly buzzing his face. "I sure wish I knew how to help her."

"She's angry, that's for sure. But exactly what it is that upsets her is the real question. If we could figure that out, then maybe we'd know how to help her be more pleasant."

Evan's heart bucked. "You're not leaving? When I saw you on the porch, I thought. . ."

Zola shook her head. "I think Amy needs someone to reach out to her and help her in more than just physical ways. I was sitting here praying that God would give me grace and wisdom. That He would show me how to help Amy."

Evan felt a shaft of pain that he'd been so busy since Amy had arrived that he hadn't prayed for his sister or the situation. Perhaps he was still angry with God that his parents had been taken and Amy injured.

"Do you have any suggestions on how I can help her?" Zola asked.

Her dark, intense gaze made his stomach jittery. He attempted to ignore that unwanted sensation and tried to concentrate on her question. "Um. . .no, I don't. I've tried everything I know. Short of her being healed and getting out of that chair, I don't know what would make her happy. The only suggestions I have are to be patient—and watchful."

"Watchful? You mean, make sure she doesn't get hurt?"

He rubbed his jaw, grinning a tad bit. "No. I mean watch out for snakes, mice, spiders, and the like. I don't know how Amy manages to catch so many critters when she's in that chair, but every lady that's worked here has met them in her bed, bags, and uh. . .unmentionables."

Zola's eyes widened. "You can't be serious."

He nodded. "Serious as a tornado in summertime."

"All right then. Thank you for the warning. I'll be extra cautious."

They sat in comfortable silence for several minutes, then Evan cleared his throat. "Did you mean what you said about having a brother?"

Zola's lips pursed as she stared in the direction of the barn. "I did. Angelo was four years younger than I and used to pester my friends and me to death. Every kind of critter you can think of somehow found its way into my room. I often wished I'd been an only child. And then, sadly, one day I was."

"What happened, if you don't mind me asking?"

"Angelo was a typical boy. He'd romp and play with his friends and often come home bleeding, not that it seemed to bother him like it did Mama. But one time, the scratch didn't heal properly, and then Angelo got real sick. He died when he was only nine years old."

"I'm sorry. My mother lost several babies between me and Amy, but I don't suppose it's the same. I never got to know those siblings."

"A child's loss hurts, no matter what the age."

Evan nodded. He remembered his ma crying for weeks after losing a baby. Neither he nor his father could do much to soothe her. Only two things seemed to help Ma—reading her Bible and the passing of time. And then Amy had come along, and they'd all been so happy. He didn't even mind that he had a sister instead of a brother. With fifteen years between them, it hardly mattered. He just enjoyed seeing his ma happy again.

"So, you had no other siblings?" he asked.

"No."

His heart went out to Zola. So many awful things had happened in her life. She seemed like a kindhearted, caring person, but time would tell if that was true. He thought again about how her husband had been an outlaw. He hoped he hadn't made a mistake in hiring her.

She waved at the corral where Pete and Buck were working with a green-broke filly. "I see that you have several ranch hands. Will I be cooking for them too?" She turned to look at Evan. "I'm only asking so I know how much food I need to prepare."

"Nope. Ramon's a fair cook, and Smitty is too, so they fix their own meals."

She nibbled her lip. "Would it be all right if I made some baked goods for them on occasion?"

Evan smiled. None of Amy's other caregivers had given a thought about the men who worked so hard to make the ranch a success. "I doubt anyone would complain, and I'm sure you'd quickly make some friends."

Her eyebrows puckered as she frowned. "I wouldn't do it to make them like me. I just thought it would be something nice they might enjoy."

"I have no objection, as long as you keep some for us."

She grinned and lifted her brows. "You have a sweet tooth, do you?"

The way her dark eyes danced intrigued him. He placed a hand on his chest and tried to look solemn. "Guilty as charged."

The chair Zola sat in creaked softly as she started rocking again. "What kind of desserts do you like?"

"All of them, but I have a particular fondness for apple, cherry, and custard pie—not all together, mind you." He chuckled. "And then there's rhubarb pie, apple dumplings, molasses cake, mmm. . ."

Zola's eyes twinkled.

Evan's gut tightened. What was he doing sitting here chatting when he had so much work to do? He jumped to his feet, and Zola immediately stopped rocking. "Let me show you around the kitchen and the cellar. Then I need to get to work."

"Of course." She stood and followed him, but her cheerful demeanor was gone.

He almost hated ending their talk, but he had no business sitting around in the middle of the day, especially when he'd been gone for hours this morning. If he didn't watch out, he might be hunting for excuses to stay home so he could make Zola's pretty eyes dance again.

~ Chapter 6 ~

Zola stared at the pile of dirty dishes for a moment, then spun toward the hall door and headed to Amy's room. Evan sure perplexed her. One moment he was joking about all the desserts he liked, then the next, he was on his feet and all business again. She'd racked her brain trying to figure out what she'd done or said, but nothing came to mind.

She paused at Amy's door, wondering if she should walk on in or knock, even though the door was open.

"What do *you* want?" The girl's sourpuss tone made Zola want to sweep her from the room and go on an exciting adventure that would cause Amy to smile and laugh. Her second thought was to remember to try not to sneak up on the sharp child.

Zola drew in a deep, steadying breath then walked in. She

glanced at Amy where she sat staring out the window, then at the room again. The walls were painted a soft blue, with white eyelet curtains that fluttered on the warm breeze. A pretty sunshine and shadow quilt in pastel colors covered the bed. A large bookcase on the northern wall held probably a hundred books. "Your room is quite lovely."

"You wouldn't think so if you had to sit in it day after day."

"I don't suppose I would. Is there anything I can get for you? Water? A snack?"

"I don't want anything from you. Just take your bags and leave."

"I don't plan to go anytime soon."

Amy peered over her shoulder and glared. "It's your life."

Zola struggled not to react. "Well, if you think of something, please call me. I'll be in the kitchen." She didn't wait for the girl to sling another snide comment her way.

As she walked down the hall, she thought of how the wide doorways and hall made sense. They allowed for Amy's chair.

Zola prayed for her ward while she worked on the mess of dishes—that God would heal Amy and help her to have a better attitude. That He would show Zola how to help her.

After the kitchen was clean, she searched through the crocks, bags, and containers to see what supplies there were for preparing meals. To her delight, she discovered much more to work with than there had ever been at her parents' home. She selected two cans of apples, flour, and sugar, and went to work making a pair of pies. Once she had those in the oven, she started on the evening meal.

With the potatoes peeled and sitting in cold water and the bacon ready to fry, she returned to Amy's room carrying a glass of the milk she'd found in a pail in the cellar.

The poor child hadn't moved from her position. Zola set the glass down and studied the sleeping girl. She looked much more innocent while resting. Zola straightened the doily on the drum table nearest Amy's wheelchair, then walked over to the bookcase and scanned the shelves. She selected books that might interest Amy and turned to put them on the table where she could reach them easily.

An ear-piercing scream rang out.

Zola jumped, and the books flew up and then dropped to the floor in a disheveled mess. She stared at Amy, who was laughing.

"That was great! You jumped about a foot." The girl kept snickering.

Zola bent, picked up the books, and smoothed out the creased pages as she struggled to regain her composure. She set them on the table, albeit a bit hard. Then she picked up the glass of milk and faced the girl.

Amy reached out her hand.

For the briefest of moments, Zola was tempted to toss the milk in the frustrating child's face, but that was certainly not behavior she wanted Amy to model. Instead, she took a drink. "Mmm. . .this cold milk is so refreshing on such a warm day. Exactly what I needed after working in the kitchen."

Amy's eyes widened then she scowled. "Hey, that's mine."

"Not anymore. You need to learn that when you behave badly, there will be consequences."

"That's not fair. I'm thirsty, and I can't get my own drink."

Zola nodded at the cup on the table. "You still have water."

"But it's hot."

"Maybe you'll think next time before you consider pulling

another prank." Zola headed for the door.

"You won't get away with this. I'm going to tell Evan, and he'll fire you. He believes whatever I tell him."

Zola wondered if he really would let her go, but perhaps her pie would soothe his ruffled feathers after he heard whatever story Amy concocted.

"Wait, I'm *sooo* thirsty."

If Amy thought a whiny, pleading tone would work on her, she had another think coming.

Evan quietly entered through the back door and hung his hat on a peg. He peered in the pitcher, pleased to find fresh water. He poured some into the bowl then washed his face and hands, all the time listening for any signs of a problem.

All he heard was the clattering of kitchenware and soft humming. Things couldn't have gone too badly if Zola was in a pleasant enough mood to hum.

He stepped into the kitchen and inhaled a deep breath of air, scented with the aroma of bacon laced with something sweet. Had she made pie? His stomach rumbled in hope.

Zola put the lid on a pot on the stove. She turned toward him, paused for a brief moment, and then smiled. "Oh good. You're home. I wasn't sure what time to have supper ready." Her brow wrinkled. "If we discussed that, I don't remember."

"I'm not sure we did." Evan poured himself a glass of water and took a sip. "I try to be home by five thirty. But things do happen at times, so I'll be later if a problem arises. If I'm not home by six, you and Amy go ahead and eat. Just save me a plate." He smiled. Zola looked quite at home in the calico apron his other caregivers had used. She had cleaned up the kitchen nicely. He hated that it was such a mess when she arrived, but there were only so many hours in a day. Amy and the ranch came before dishes.

"Of course I will save your supper. Everything is ready. Should I get Amy, or would you rather do it?"

"I'll get her. How did things go today?" He watched Zola's expression. Ofttimes he could read something in one of his worker's faces that wasn't expressed in words.

"Well. . .I didn't see a lot of her since there was so much to be done in the kitchen, and you had said she was to stay in her room. I took her fresh water several times and offered her a snack, but she wasn't hungry."

Zola nibbled her lip and looked away. Ah. . .there was something. What had Amy done?

"I should probably tell you that I took Amy a glass of milk," she said in a quieter than normal voice. "I thought she was sleeping, so I went to the bookshelf and selected several books I thought she might like for when she woke up. But she wasn't actually asleep and screamed suddenly. It startled me and caused me to drop the books, and Amy laughed. I wasn't really upset—at least not after my heart stopped pounding—but I took Amy's milk. And drank it myself."

Amy's actions were not surprising, but what Zola did was. "Why did you do that?"

A rosy shade tinged Zola's olive cheeks. "I felt she needed a consequence for her bad behavior, and that's all I could come up with at the time."

Evan grinned. Yes sir, Zola had gumption. She just might make it here.

"You're not upset?"

He shook his head. "It sounds like Amy had it coming."

Zola shrugged. "I figured I should tell you before she did, because her story might not be quite the truth."

"I appreciate that. And you're probably right. Amy's been known to exaggerate."

Zola turned back to the stove, so Evan took that as his cue to go get his sister. He strode down the hall and to her door. Amy sat in the same spot by the window, reading a book. His heart ached for her. He enjoyed a good book too, but he sure wouldn't want to have to read day in and day out and do little else. "Howdy."

"It's about time you got home. You left me with that dragon lady. How could you do that?" Her eyes glistened with tears. Were they real or manufactured? Had Zola been the one to stretch the truth? Had she done something awful to his sister?

He hurried to her side and squatted down on his heels. "What happened?"

"I scared her like I did all the others." Amy shrugged. "But then she threw milk in my face and said I needed to learn some manners."

Anger surged through Evan. Had Zola really done that after telling him a much milder version of the tale? He looked at his sister, whose eyes had that innocent please-believe-me expression. Then he noticed Amy's dress. It was the same one she'd been wearing this morning. He rose, leaned over, and sniffed.

"Hey!" Amy pushed back into the chair. "What are you doing?"

"Checking to see if your dress smells like spoiled milk. It doesn't."

Amy's cheeks pinked as she glanced down. Evidently she hadn't thought of that when concocting her story.

"I don't appreciate you lying to me."

Amy shrugged as she stared out the window.

He clenched his fist, trying to be patient. His sister needed to learn manners, but he didn't know how to get her to learn them. "It's time to eat."

"I'm not hungry."

"Well, you're going to eat anyway. You have to keep up your strength." He walked behind the chair and wheeled it around. At the table, he lifted Amy out and placed her in the armed chair with a footrest that he'd had made for her. Though Amy was light, he wondered if Zola would be able to lift her. He probably should have thought of that before hiring a smaller-sized woman, but then he really hadn't had a choice.

He took his place and stared at the steam rising off the bacon, onions, and fried potatoes. His belly complained again, making him anxious to taste the food. If Amy had been in her room all day as he'd ordered, the meal should be safe to consume. Still, he wasn't quite ready to take a heaping spoonful of his first bite.

Zola placed a plate of golden brown corn bread in front of him, then returned to the counter for a bowl of green beans. She took the seat across from him with Amy on her right side. Then she looked at him.

He blinked and stared back.

"Do you pray before meals?"

"Sure, if you'd like. It's just that Mrs. Reynolds didn't care for out-loud prayers, so I kinda quit saying them."

"If you don't mind, I would like us to pray. We have much to be thankful for."

He nodded and bowed his head, intrigued with her use of "we." Amy made a scoffing sound in the back of her throat, which he chose to ignore. "Heavenly Father, we ask that You bless this meal and the hands that prepared it. Thank You for guiding me to Zola and a special thanks that she agreed to help us. Amen."

He glanced up to see Amy frowning and Zola smiling. He blew out a soft sigh, knowing that was probably how things would be for a long while.

He took conservative servings—just in case the food had been tainted. After he served Amy, and Zola had filled her plate, he finally speared several potato cubes on his fork. He glanced at Zola then Amy, whose nonchalant expression made him wary. He took a tiny bite, waiting for the wrong flavors, but instead, the tasty delight of bacon, potato, and onion teased his tongue. After a small sampling of the green beans, he dug in with full gusto. If all of Zola's cooking tasted this good, he'd be thrilled that he'd hired her.

He was going to fire her. At least that was Zola's thought when Evan took such tiny first bites, as if he was afraid her cooking would be disgusting. Had the other women been such awful cooks that he had to be so cautious? He must have liked what he tasted, because now he was eating as she'd expect a hardworking man to eat.

He selected a large square of corn bread, buttered it, and once again took a puny bite. His eyes brightened, then closed as if in delight, and he took a mouthful this time. She'd never seen anyone sample his food that way, except for Angelo, who'd been an extremely picky eater. Perhaps she ought to get a list of the things he liked to eat so that she didn't make too many things he despised.

Amy pushed her food around on her plate as if she had no appetite.

Was that a common occurrence, or was the girl still upset with her? "Don't you like this meal?" Zola asked.

Amy merely shrugged.

"Would you care for a glass of milk instead of water?"

The girl's gaze crashed into Zola's as if looking for deeper meaning in the simple question. Amy frowned and shook her head.

"You oughta drink milk. I read that it's good for your bones and things." Evan pushed back his chair, snagged a glass off the shelf, and went down into the cellar. He returned shortly with a full glass of milk.

"I could have gotten that." Zola reached for her water and took a sip.

"It's no problem." He set the glass in front of his sister and took a seat. As he reached for his fork, he sent an odd look Zola's way. Was he trying to tell her something?

They stared at one another as Zola tried to interpret what he meant.

Amy cleared her throat.

Zola broke Evan's stare, which had set her heart to thumping, and glanced Amy's way. "Do you need something?"

"I need you to keep your eyes off my brother. He's not available."

Zola sucked in a sharp breath at the same time Evan shouted his sister's name.

"Amy! Behave, or you'll be back in your room."

She merely rolled her eyes.

Zola watched Evan's face as different expressions crossed it. Was he embarrassed by his sister's behavior? Did he wonder what Zola thought about it? She hated that Amy made things so difficult when Evan worked hard all day and needed a place he could rest.

"You're grounded from dessert for a month because of what you did to Mrs. Crocker, but I'll lift that punishment just for tonight since this is Zola's first day with us."

Amy's eyes lit up. The girl must love sweets as much as her brother.

Evan lifted a hand. "But I want you to clean your plate and treat Zola with respect. She worked hard to prepare this meal for us."

"All right."

Evan cleared his throat.

Amy looked as if she'd started to roll her eyes but then decided against it. "I mean, yes, sir."

Zola kept her head down for several minutes. After she finished her meal, she looked up. "I thought if you could let me know which foods you prefer, I could make those. That way you won't have to sample everything to see if it's to your liking."

Amy snorted and started giggling.

Evan sent her a stern look. "My sampling has nothing to do with your cooking."

"No?" Zola wrinkled her brow. "Then what?"

"My sister has been known to sabotage a meal a time or two."

"How—? I mean, *why* would you do that?"

"I'm resourceful, that's how." Amy lifted her chin as if proud of her actions.

Zola shook her head. "My family didn't have a lot of money, and we treasured the food we had. I can't imagine anyone purposely tampering with good food. That's a terrible waste."

For a smidgeon of a second, Amy actually looked penitent. But evidently her remorse was fleeting. She took her last bite and set her silverware on her plate. "There. I ate it all. Now I want dessert."

Evan narrowed his eyes at her.

"I mean, I would like some dessert."

"Amy. . . ," he growled.

"Please."

Zola felt bad for Evan. Amy's use of the word *please* sounded so awkward. Unfamiliar. She had to find a way to reach his sister and get her to see how her bad behavior affected everybody. But then maybe that was the point.

Chapter 7

Zola sat on the porch, enjoying the coolness of the evening while recuperating from helping Evan get Amy ready for bed. She'd helped Amy wash. Then the girl had squawked at her brother for looking, although he had kept his eyes focused on the ceiling while she helped Amy change into her nightgown.

Zola watched the horizon, breathing in the fresh air of the evening. The beginning of twilight and the beauty of the setting sun as it cast glowing shades of pink and orange on the clouds was mesmerizing. The sunset was something she'd dearly missed while living in the woods. At least the noise of the tree frogs and insects wasn't deafening here, as it had been at the cabin.

The screen door squeaked as Evan came out onto the porch. He took the rocker next to hers. "That went much better with you there."

"It did?" She didn't know what she'd expected. The thing that had surprised her the most was that Amy could actually put some weight on her legs without them crumpling underneath her, albeit only for a few seconds as she pivoted onto the bed. But it gave Zola hope.

He chuckled. "Can you imagine how difficult it was for me to help her dress by myself when I'm not supposed to look at her?"

Zola smiled, grateful that he could find humor in a difficult situation. "She's at an age where girls like their privacy."

"I don't know a speck about what a half-grown female likes."

"That's where I come in. It helps to have been a girl at one time. What kind of things did Amy enjoy before she was injured?"

Somewhere near the barn, an owl hooted, and a horse whickered, as if answering it.

He shrugged. "I didn't see her all that much, since she lived with Ma and Pa. They'd visit the ranch in the summer, sometimes staying for several weeks, and then they'd either come here for Christmas, or I'd visit them when I could get away."

"What did she want to do when she was here?"

"She would have lived in the barn if Ma had let her. Amy loved riding and caring for the animals. She didn't even mind mucking stalls, but Ma quickly put an end to that when Amy went inside smelling like a barnyard." He chuckled. "Sis finally gave up cleaning stalls because she hated having to take a bath each time she did it—and Ma always insisted on it."

Zola tapped her lip, an idea firing in her mind. "I wonder if you could rig up something like you did with the chair at the table. Something with sides and a belt."

"What for?"

Zola looked at him in the waning light. "To attach to a saddle.

So Amy could ride again."

Evan turned toward her, eyes widened. "Ride? Are you loco?"

"Not at all. I think it would be good for her. It would certainly lift her spirits and give her something to look forward to. I don't mean she would go riding off on her own, but you could lead her around inside the corral."

He shook his head. "I can't risk that. Too dangerous."

Zola hated disagreeing with her new boss, but the repetitive motion of riding just might help Amy in some way. If nothing else, the sunshine would help her pasty complexion. "How is it risky? And what could happen if you were there, leading what I'm sure would be your tamest horse inside the corral. Just think how happy it would make Amy."

"Nope. That isn't going to happen."

Zola resisted sighing. If he was going to be so protective of his sister, it would make helping Amy become more independent very difficult. The little stinker presented enough of a barrier with her bad attitude. "I should probably turn in, but first, could you please explain Amy's daily routine?"

"Sure. After I get up and get dressed, I go in and help Amy with her basic needs and then get her dressed and situated in her chair." He rubbed his jaw, making that intriguing bristling sound again. "I've been fixing breakfast lately, but you'll be doing that. After eating, I usually wheel her into the parlor and get whatever book she is reading for her. I always make sure she has some water within reach."

He stretched out his arms in front of him and yawned. "Excuse me. After lunch I put Amy in her bed on her stomach. That helps to prevent bedsores and gets her out of the chair. I usually come back in an hour or two and get her up again."

Zola pursed her lips. No wonder Amy picked at people. She had nothing to interest her other than books. Not that there was anything wrong with a good novel, but she needed other interests. "Do you know if she's ever helped with the cooking?"

Evan glanced at her as if she truly was loco. "And just how is she supposed to do that?"

"There's nothing wrong with her hands. She could easily shell peas or snap beans into a bowl. Or if she was sitting at the table, she could cut vegetables or fruit. She could even dry the dishes. I know she's capable, especially if she's managed to taint food in the past."

He grunted. "I hired you to do all that."

Yes, she knew that. "I can do it all by myself, but Amy needs things to occupy her time other than simply reading books. Also, the more help I have with my duties, the more time I'll have to work with your sister."

"Maybe so, but I can't see her helping in the kitchen."

"So. . .you're not opposed to it if I can find some things that she is easily able to do? Safely."

"I'm not opposed if she's willing, but therein lies the problem."

As long as *he* was agreeable, that was all the incentive Zola needed. She'd find a way to interest Amy, somehow, with the Lord's help.

She rose. "Thank you, again, for giving me the chance to work for you and your sister. I will strive hard to make things easier for you and to help Amy."

"I appreciate that." He nodded. "Evening."

"Good night." She stepped inside and quietly closed the screen.

She made a detour to the kitchen to double-check that everything was still clean, got a quick drink, and then set the glass in the basin. She blew out the lantern and walked down the hall. Pausing at Amy's door, she peeked in, glad to hear the girl's soft snores. After a day spent in that chair with just a book for company, Amy probably relished going to sleep. At least one wasn't bored when sleeping.

Zola entered her room and glanced at the nice furnishings. The bedframe, wardrobe, and desk and chair were oak. The walls were painted white, and the drapes were made from a rose-patterned fabric, which also covered the comfortable-looking wingback chair. She turned up the lantern and walked over to the bed, where her satchel sat. Cautiously, she opened the bag and peered inside. She tilted it toward the light, more than a little relieved not to see anything crawling in it. After she removed her nightgown, she pulled out her spare dress.

She reached for the knob of the wardrobe then paused. What if there was a snake inside? She put her dress down and retrieved the lantern. Very slowly, she opened the door a crack, held up the light. Relief surged through her to find it empty, except for several shelves. She repeated the action with the other door and discovered a bar with hangers for her dresses. But no unwanted critters. She blew out a loud sigh.

After checking under the bed, she returned the lantern to the desk then hung up her dress and changed into her nightgown. She walked over to the nearest window and opened it to allow in the fresh evening breeze. The room must have been closed up since the last caregiver left, because it was a bit stuffy.

Zola yawned as she walked over to the lantern to turn it down. As she reached for it, she paused as a chilling thought intruded. She returned to the bed, grabbed the edge of her quilt, and jerked it off, along with the sheet. She yelped and jumped back.

More than a dozen crickets hopped across her bed.

With breakfast out of the way and the dishes washed, Zola returned to her room, retrieved her sewing tin and the floral picture she'd been stitching, and joined Amy in the parlor. Evan had positioned his sister so the light from the window shone on her book while also giving her a good view of the ranch yard in front of the house. From there she could see the men working with horses in the corral or their comings and goings from the barn. Amy stared at her book and didn't look up as Zola found a seat.

From the child's smirk at breakfast, Zola guessed Amy was well aware of the crickets in her bed. Had she heard Zola's yelp and actions following her discovery? She had managed to sweep a number of them to the back door and outside, but several escapees had woken her up more than once with their chirping. She was determined not to let Amy know how just how much they had disturbed her.

How had Amy managed to collect so many crickets and get them in her bed without getting caught? Her chair was a new model, which allowed her to maneuver it on her own, but it was a bit difficult for her to get it moving and awkward with the other furniture to skirt around. And how could Amy have gotten into Zola's room without her hearing? In truth, she doubted the girl had enough strength to wheel the chair that far.

Which meant Amy had to have a cohort in crime. But who? Surely Evan wouldn't participate in such childish pranks, especially when they had resulted in him losing the women he'd hired to care for his sister. Perhaps it was Pete, the ranch hand who had watched Amy while Evan had gone to town. That made the most sense.

While she stitched a pretty pink rose, she shifted her thoughts on what she could prepare for supper. She glanced at Amy, who was successfully ignoring her. Zola cleared her throat, but Amy didn't move a muscle.

"I was thinking about supper. Is there anything in particular that sounds good to you?"

Amy shrugged.

"Sliced ham steaks? Stew? Soup? Pot roast?" Zola suggested.

The girl finally looked up. "Fried chicken. Now please be quiet so I can read."

Zola lifted a brow at her impudence, but she kept quiet. Fried chicken. Did Amy suggest that because she knew how much work was involved? She probably thought Zola would be squeamish about plucking a hen, and in truth, she was. But Amy didn't need to know that. An idea blossomed.

"I'll make you a deal. I'll prepare the chicken if you will pluck it."

Amy's blasé expression turned horrified. "Me? Why, I can't do that. It's terribly messy. And besides, you have to do it outside."

"All right then. What else would you like to eat?"

Frowning, Amy picked up her book and started reading.

Zola counted that as a small battle won. At least she didn't have to strip the unsuspecting hen of its feathers either.

Just as Zola finished stitching the rose, Amy laid her book in her lap. "You know, if you ask Evan, he'll have one of the hands kill and pluck a bird. That way neither of us has to do it."

Joy shot through Zola, and she smiled. "That would be quite nice for us both. So, you weren't joking about wanting chicken?"

Amy stared out the window for a long moment, then looked at Zola with an almost civil expression. "I was serious. We haven't had it in a long while."

"All right then, I'll go ask your brother if we can." She folded her picture and laid it with her sewing tin on the end of the couch.

As she walked out the door, she couldn't help smiling. One small victory—as long as somebody had time to put an end to a poor hen's life.

Zola crossed the wide yard and slowed her pace as she neared the corral. One man held the halter of a horse whose hooves never stopped moving. Evan shinnied over the fence and climbed on the horse. After several moments of getting situated on the fidgety beast, Evan nodded. The ranch hand released the horse, stepped back, and then quickly crawled through the fence rails, just as the horse exploded in a fury of movement and scattering dirt. Zola clung to the fence, her mouth dry, as the horse bucked Evan up and down, then twisted in a circle. She feared the horse would fall and land on him. He was tossed around like a rag doll, but as she watched, she realized that he was actually somewhat in control. Not so much where the horse went, but in his leg actions. He actually kicked the horse when it slackened its gyrating. Crazy man!

After what seemed an eternity, the horse's bucking slowed to a trot with an occasional crowhop and then finally to a rough walk. Evan grinned like he'd won a race.

"Whoo-ee! That was one fine ride, Boss." The ranch hand slapped his hat against his pants.

Evan finally noticed Zola, smiled at her, then dismounted. He handed the reins to the ranch hand and walked toward her. As he neared, his smile wavered. He slipped through the railing. "Something wrong? Is Amy all right?"

Zola realized she was shaking. Her hands were white on the fence rail. She forced herself to let go and turned on him. "Are you crazy! How could you do such a dangerous thing? Amy just lost her parents. She can't afford to lose you."

"Whoa now," Evan said in a soothing voice like he might use on a frightened horse. "It's not like I don't know what I'm doing. I've broken over fifty horses."

"Do you stop to think of Amy? I don't know that she'd survive if anything happened to you."

He reached up under one side of his hat and scratched. "I don't have a choice, Zola. Breaking and selling horses is how we make most of our income. Yes, we raise cattle, but with stock prices low, we need the income the horses bring."

Zola's cheeks burned as she realized that she'd just lambasted her new boss. "I'm sorry, Mr. Clayborne. It's really none of my business." She turned back toward the house.

"Wait. It's Evan, and why did you come out here?"

"Oh." She faced him again. "Amy would like fried chicken for supper. Would it be possible for you to have someone kill a hen and pluck it?" She shrugged. "I don't know how, and I'm not sure I have the stomach to do that task."

He tipped his hat to her. "Happy to."

"Thank you." She headed back to the house at a quicker pace than when she came out.

"I appreciate your concern," Evan called after her.

Zola's gut clenched. Henry would have walloped her if she'd talked to him like she had Evan. She tried to analyze her reaction to seeing him ride. Why had it upset her so? It wasn't simply her concern for Amy. Zola didn't want to admit the truth—she was attracted to her boss and didn't want to see him get hurt. And besides, Amy did need him. She could feel his gaze on her back, so she didn't stop to acknowledge his comment and hurried into the security of the house.

Amy must have gone back to her room, because she was no longer in the parlor. Zola sat down and reached for her sewing again. She unfolded the fabric and gasped. The stitches on the rose she had just finished had been ripped out.

❧ Chapter 8 ❧

Zola had wrestled with her feelings over Amy's destructive actions all afternoon. The girl had no idea of the importance of the floral picture. Zola considered not giving her any chicken at supper, but she couldn't bring herself to do that. Instead, she'd busied herself making an extra nice meal. Keeping busy helped her not to march into Amy's room and say something she might regret.

What could have inspired Amy to do such a mean deed? Zola had always tried to get along with people. Sure, she was opinionated about certain things, but more often than not, she'd keep her thoughts to herself. Henry certainly hadn't cared about her opinions. She learned to keep her mouth shut so that it didn't result in getting slapped or her hair yanked. She rubbed her cheek at the painful memory. Henry had only wanted two things from her—food and loving.

She shuddered at the thought of being intimate with Henry. He had never loved her—just used her. She was a jezebel. Ruined. No man would want her now. She reached down and rubbed a hand across her stomach. What if she was carrying Henry's child? Would Evan turn her out if he discovered she was pregnant? Sure, she could keep things quiet for a while, but her conscience wouldn't allow her to keep it a secret. He had a right to know.

Well, there was nothing stopping the inevitable. If she was carrying a baby, she'd deal with that when she knew for sure. As she coated the chicken, she tried to decide how she'd feel about carrying Henry's child. Of course, she would love him or her, but it would certainly make things harder, whether she stayed here or had to go somewhere else. A part of her longed to ask God to keep her from being with child, but her heart wouldn't allow it.

An hour later, Evan stomped inside and removed his hat. "I've been smelling that chicken for the past half hour, and my mouth and belly are about to drive me loco. Is it ready?"

A thrill sped through Zola at seeing Evan so excited about her cooking. What a joy to cook for a man who appreciated a nice meal. "Yes, it is. Do you want to get Amy while I put things on the table?"

"Sure." He crossed to the counter where the platter of chicken sat and pinched off a piece of the crispy coating. His eyes twinkled as he plopped the absconded bite into his mouth. "Be right back."

Zola smiled at his boyish antics. She'd always been attracted to men with blue eyes, probably because her whole family had brown ones, even her grandparents. Evan was a fine-looking man, but it was his kindness to her and his love for his sister that she admired most. Many men would have sent a younger sibling to a home for the sick and injured rather than keep the child with him.

"Yay! Fried chicken. I can hardly wait." Amy clapped her hands as Evan lifted her into her chair.

Zola hadn't seen her so animated since coming to stay with the Claybornes. Once again, she thought about depriving Amy of the chicken because of what she'd done, but it didn't seem right, and she didn't want to ruin the happy atmosphere. She set the bowls of potatoes and corn on the cob on the table, then added the platter of meat to the mix, and returned to the counter for the biscuits and butter.

She took her seat, and Evan prayed. As soon as he was done, Amy snagged a chicken leg off the platter. She bit into it and closed her eyes. After she'd chewed her food, she smiled. "I could eat this every day."

"Me too, but we'd soon run out of hens, and then we wouldn't have any eggs."

Evan placed two thighs on his plate and passed the platter to Zola. He bit into the bigger thigh, and his eyes closed. "I may have to buy more of those pesky birds. This is like stepping into heaven."

"I'm glad you two like it so well."

"It's perfect. So is the rest of the food." Evan smiled, waving his spoon at the potato bowl. "How did you get the spuds so creamy?"

Zola shrugged. She couldn't very well tell him she was beating out her frustrations on the spuds. Her heart warmed at his enthusiasm. That was what a real marriage should be like. A family enjoying a meal together. Gratitude, rather than stern orders about the food and other duties, and then only complaints if something wasn't to Henry's liking.

"So, what did you two do today?" Evan reached for another biscuit.

Zola glanced at Amy.

The girl's cheeks darkened to a rosy shade. "Oh, the usual. Eat, read, sleep, read."

"Sounds engaging." Evan grinned.

Amy rolled her eyes.

Zola's heart tripped when Evan looked at her.

"What about you?"

"I. . .cooked." She glanced at Amy, who had a wary expression. "I also sewed a little on the picture I'm embroidering. It has a rose pattern and will have a scripture when I finish." She caught Amy's eyes, and the girl actually leaned back as if preparing for a scolding. "The piece was one my mother had started but didn't get to complete before she died. I made a promise to myself to finish it in honor of her."

Amy's eyes widened, and she ducked her head.

"That's a nice thing to do. I'd like to see it sometime." Evan snagged another piece of chicken. "Have you started schooling Amy yet?"

Zola shook her head. "I thought it better to get settled in with my other duties and to get to know Amy a bit first. I also needed a chance to look over the books you have and see where Amy is in her schooling. I thought we'd start next week."

"That sounds good."

After dinner, while Evan spent some time in the parlor with Amy, Zola did the dishes. When she was done, she picked up the plate of cookies she'd made for the ranch hands and walked down to the bunkhouse. She knocked on the door. Smitty opened it. His eyes lit up when he saw what she was carrying.

"Miss Zola, you're going to spoil us for certain." The sound of booted feet hitting the floor echoed through the big building. Three other men crowded around the door.

"That's my intention, Smitty." She smiled and stepped back so the others could come out. "You men work so hard to make the Clayborne ranch a success, that I think you need a treat now and then."

"That's mighty kind of ya, ma'am." Pete grinned and licked his lips. The youth's reddish-brown hair spiked up, going in ten different directions.

"It's my pleasure." Zola allowed each man to help himself to a handful of cookies, then she cleared her throat. "I would ask a favor."

Four eager pairs of eyes looked her way.

"What can we do for ya, ma'am? Ask us anythin'." Pete took another bite.

"I would like whichever of you is providing Amy with critters to please stop it." Three blank stares met her gaze, including Pete's. So much for him being the culprit. Smitty ducked his head.

"It weren't me," said the dark-complexioned man whose name she didn't know. He ducked back into the bunkhouse with Pete and Dean.

Smitty shuffled his feet. "I'm sorry, ma'am. I didn't mind scaring those other ladies since they all treated Miss Amy so poorly, but I felt bad about doing it to you. What with how nice you've been to us and all. None of them other women ever gave us as much as a kind glance."

"I'm sorry." She lowered the plate now that it was empty. "It's not for me that I'm asking, but I want to help Amy, and by being her cohort in crime, you're not helping her to improve her actions."

He scratched his chest, head still down. "I just wanted to make that little gal happy. She used to be so bouncy and excited to ride the horses. When the boss was busy, I was tasked with leading her around. Hated it at first, but then I kinda got to lookin' forward to it." A gentle smile tugged at his weathered lips. "That little squirt talked a mile a minute back then."

He lifted his head, his eyes filled with pain. "The only time I ever see her smile now is when I help her scare you ladies. But I won't do it no more."

"Thank you. I aim to find ways to make her happy again, and then you'll get to see her smiling."

"That would make my old heart happy." He patted his chest.

"Me too. And just so you know, I didn't bring the cookies as a bribe. I'll keep bringing other treats from time to time."

"I'll be looking forward to it."

"I'm glad you enjoy them. Good evening, Smitty." She turned back toward the house.

"Uh. . .ma'am."

Zola paused and glanced over her shoulder. "Yes?"

Smitty shuffled his feet again, and his ears turned bright red. "There, uh, might be a snake in your clothes cupboard. Just a little one, mind ya."

Zola's heart thumped. A snake! "Thank you for the warning."

Back at the house, she deposited the plate in the kitchen and went straight to her room. She grabbed the broom, still in the far corner of her room since the cricket incident, then opened the wardrobe door. Her dresses hung on one side with her satchel sitting on the other. She used the broom to move her bag out and froze. There was the offensive critter. What to do? The slippery thing would slide right off the broom handle. She slammed the doors shut and went to find Evan.

He was in the kitchen, pouring a fresh cup of coffee. He took a sip, and his eyes crinkled at the corners as he noticed her.

She wrung her hands together. "Could you help me for a moment?"

"Sure. What do you need?"

"There's a snake in my room."

He thumped his chest. "King of the snake catchers at your service."

The scare of finding the varmint lessened at his jesting. "It's in my wardrobe."

He frowned. "That's an odd place—" His gaze narrowed. "Did my sister plant it?"

Zola lifted one shoulder. "I don't think so, but I also believe there won't be any more invaders, at least not those purposely placed in my room."

His mouth quirked. "If that's true, congratulations. You'll be the first to put an end to the shenanigans. By the way, did you have crickets in your room the other night? I found several in mine."

Zola nodded as she headed down the hall. She couldn't see the end of the critters fast enough. Of course, there would be the ones that happened in through the open windows, but at least maybe they wouldn't find their way into her bed and clothes closet. She opened the wardrobe and stood back, behind the door, peering around to see if the intruder was still there.

"Well, that's just a little fellow. It's only a baby bull snake."

Zola made a scoffing sound in her throat. "It still belongs outside."

Evan picked it up behind its head. "You should like this little guy. He eats mice, rats, gophers, and such."

"Yes, well, I'll like him much better when he's outside."

She followed him down the hall and to the front door. He walked out into the twilight and set the varmint down a good ways from the house, then he strolled back.

"There you go. Would you care to sit a bit?"

"What about getting Amy ready for bed?"

"Done. You were gone, so I took care of it."

She lowered herself into a rocker while his hand steadied the top. "I took that extra batch of cookies to the bunkhouse."

He sat beside her. "I sure hate to see those yummy treats go, but I bet you made the guys happy."

"Yes. They were so grateful. It's a pleasure to bake for them."

"Hey!" He reached out and laid his fingers on her arm. "I'm grateful too."

She smiled in spite of the fact that her stomach was dancing a jig at the intimate touch. Though Evan was all man, he was also gentle. Respectful. Two things Henry never was. "Have no fear, you'll get your desserts."

He pulled his hand back, and she wished she could reach out and tug it over again. "You have no idea how happy that makes me."

Zola ducked her head to hide her smile. He was like a child where sweets were concerned.

Evan blew out a loud sigh. "I really enjoy sitting out here with you. I never did that with the other women, but then they rarely came outside except on laundry day. They generally retreated to their room once Amy was in bed."

She could understand that. It was about the only chance she had time to herself, but she would just as soon spend it with him.

He cleared his throat. "Amy told me what she did today."

Zola's lips drew up. The action still hurt. Not so much having to redo the rose, but that Amy had wanted to lash out at her. She needed to give her more time and be patient.

"That was an awful thing for her to do. I'm really sorry."

"It's not your fault."

"I somehow feel it is. I should know better how to make her behave."

"Why? You've never been a father. Don't be so hard on yourself."

"Thank you. I've never had anyone other than Smitty to talk to about these things, but he was mostly too embarrassed to chat about my sister. It's nice to have someone else who cares about her."

"I believe things will get better. It simply takes time. Amy's had so many changes to deal with. And I can tell you that a girl misses her mother when she's gone."

"Yes. I miss my folks too."

She thought about the difficult choices she had to make after her parents died. Perhaps she should share some of those with Amy. Then maybe she'd see that they had something in common.

Zola turned her thoughts to the book she'd been reading whenever she got the chance—a book about muscles and other parts of the body. She'd scanned a section on electrotherapy, but after reading a bit, she shuddered at the inhumane treatment and thumbed back to the index. Next, a chapter on strengthening muscles had caught her eye. "I read something in one of the books I found in the parlor cabinet. It's a medical book. One of the contributors thinks the muscles of paralyzed people should be manipulated and exercised daily. I admit I've wondered how that could affect anything in a person who can't feel or use their limbs, but possibly it might in Amy's case. She can move her legs a tiny bit and stand long enough to pivot onto the bed. Do you think it would help if I exercised her legs somehow?"

"I read that book. I honestly don't know, but I'm not opposed to you giving it a try. Although the bigger question is, will Amy be willing?"

"I don't suppose we'll know unless we ask her." She could see him nod in the waning light. His profile cut a handsome silhouette, but it was his caring heart that appealed to her the most. If they'd met at a different time—before Henry had ruined her—perhaps they might have been attracted to one another. She closed her eyes, the pain in her chest so intense it took her breath away. Evan wouldn't want anything to do with a spoiled woman. She needed to go inside before she started weeping at the unfairness of Henry's actions.

She pushed up. "I should—"

A loud scream rent the quiet.

Evan bolted out of his chair. "That's Amy!"

Chapter 9

Evan charged through the parlor. Amy often acted out to get his attention, but that was a fearful scream.

"Evan!"

He raced to his sister's room, skidding around the corner into the hallway and then into her room. She sat up in bed, the covers over her head. Her wide eyes peered out the side, illuminated by the lantern he always left burning for her. She lowered the quilt, and her gaze shot to the window and back at him.

"A man was looking in my window."

He hurried over and peered out the opening. It was hard to see now that the sun had mostly set. Why would someone want to look in his sister's room, especially with him sitting so nearby on the porch?

"Close it. Please."

He did as requested and locked it. Then he made sure the window on the other side of the room was locked.

Zola rushed in and hurried to Amy's bed. "What happened? Are you hurt?"

Amy grasped Zola's hand. "A hairy man was looking in my room. At me."

Zola's gaze shot to Evan's.

"Stay here," he said. "I'm going to investigate."

A loud knock sounded out front. "Boss, y'all all right?"

Evan grabbed his rifle and met Smitty at the front door. He scowled at the man he'd worked with for years. The other hands were running toward the house. "Someone was looking in Amy's window."

"It weren't none of us. We was all in the bunkhouse playin' cards."

Evan's relief was palpable. He hated to think any of his men would peek in his sister's window. "Go around the house to the right, and I'll go this way. Be careful."

Dean and Ramon slid to a halt, both half-dressed but armed. Pete limped up to join them, one boot on and the other in his hand, along with his rifle.

"Spread out and look for a stranger." The men did as they were told. Evan went to the left side of the house. He slowed his steps as he reached the corner. It was unlikely the man was still nearby, but he wasn't going to risk it. He peered into the darkness, listening. All he heard was someone coming around the other way—Smitty, he hoped.

Zola must have turned up Amy's lantern, because a soft glow brightened the area just outside the window. He slipped around the corner and looked down. Boot prints—in the dirt beneath the window.

"What'd you find?" Smitty asked as he joined him.

"Footprints."

He rose and looked at his old friend in the shadows. "Why would anyone peep in my sister's window?"

"Could be a lonely drifter wantin' something to eat. Could be he didn't know whose room it was."

That made the most sense. But it still nagged at him that a man had scared his sister. Wouldn't any man be more interested in Zola, who was a beautiful, exotic-looking woman?

"Looks like he's gone, Boss."

"Maybe. I want a guard posted up in the barn loft. Tell him to make rounds every hour. Switch out men halfway through the night so the guard stays alert. I want to know who was here—and why."

Evan strode back inside. In the past, he had considered getting a cattle dog. If he'd had one now, it would have alerted him to a stranger's presence. Maybe it was time.

He slowed his steps as he entered his sister's room. Zola must have drawn the curtains. She sat on the side of the bed, still holding Amy's hand. Evan leaned down and kissed the top of his sister's head. "Don't worry, honey. I've got a guard posted. I even locked the front and back doors." Something he rarely did.

Zola looked up at him. "I can sleep in here tonight. That way Amy won't be afraid." She gently brushed back a strand of his sister's hair and tucked it behind Amy's ear, and his sister didn't jerk away.

Amy must have really been frightened to allow Zola's ministrations. He hated the thought of her scared and not able to flee her room. It was so unfair. Why had God allowed her to be injured?

"Perhaps *I* should stay tonight." Evan shuffled his feet, wishing Zola would get up so he could comfort his sister.

"No. I will be fine, especially since I know the men are on guard." Amy yawned.

Something twisted in Evan's gut. It felt as if his sister no longer needed him. He drew in a breath through his nose. *Toughen up, cowboy. She does too need you.*

Zola rose and patted Amy's shoulder. "I'll leave my door cracked, so if you need anything, please call me." She glanced at Evan as she walked by, and smiled.

He nodded to her then took the chair in the corner where he had slept the first few weeks after bringing his sister home. Sitting there for any amount of time was uncomfortable, but he would manage.

"I told you I'll be fine. I'm not a baby." Now that sounded more like his sister.

"Humor me. Once you fall asleep, I'll leave. But like Zola, I'll keep my door open." And his rifle handy.

While she dozed off, he struggled to figure out why anyone would be looking in the windows of his house. Smitty's suggestion that it was a drifter searching for a quick handout made the most sense. Still, come morning, he'd be tracking those footsteps to see where they led.

On Friday Zola walked into Amy's room, excited about finally starting school. If only the child would cooperate. Zola sat down and waited to be noticed.

After a moment, Amy looked up. "Did you need something?"

Zola wanted to cheer at the polite tone of her voice. "I thought we might start your studies today."

"You said we were going to wait until Monday."

"True, but I thought up something I think you will actually enjoy." She swatted at a fly buzzing around her face, and it flew to the nearest window. Windows that were still shut and locked despite the warming temperature.

Amy closed her book and laid it on the table beside her chair. "What is it?"

"Your spelling list for next week."

In typical fashion, she rolled her eyes. "Oh, that's wonderful." Though Amy's voice was laced with sarcasm, it was a more playful tone than in the past.

"Well, have a look. You might actually think so." She rose and handed the list to her.

Amy stared at the words, and after a moment, her eyes sparked with interest. "These are all horse words."

"Horse body parts to be exact."

Amy's brow wrinkled. "I know most of these, but what's a fetlock and withers? And a horse has a cannon? Does Evan know that?" Amy giggled.

"I imagine he does." Zola stepped behind Amy's chair. "I think since it's so warm in here, we'll go out on the porch for our lesson." She inwardly thrilled when Amy didn't object. Zola reached into her apron pocket and pulled out a carrot. "You'll also need this."

Amy wrinkled her nose. "Whatever for?"

"Your science class."

She curled her lip. "Why do I need to study science? I'll never have a use for it."

"I hear you have a fascination with insects and other critters." Zola smiled, inwardly delighted when Amy glanced over her shoulder, her cheeks blossoming in a pretty pink shade. "I think you will like this class."

Amy harrumphed but didn't object further.

Zola pushed her ward through the house and onto the porch, then situated the chair so that it was pushed up alongside the railing. Then Zola looked toward the barn.

Smitty must have been watching for them, because he walked out of the barn, leading a horse, and ambled toward them.

"Oh look! It's Smitty. I wonder where he's going." Amy reached across the railing and waved.

Smitty walked directly toward them and stopped in front of the porch, grinning wide. "It's good to see you outside, little missy."

"Nice to be out. Who is this?" She reached out to rub the horse's face.

"Her name is Bucket."

Amy giggled. "That's a funny name for a horse. How did she come by that?"

"She's always rummaging through any bucket she comes across, looking for a handout." He ran his fingers through the horse's black mane.

Zola walked down the steps and joined the ranch hand. "I actually asked Smitty to help us out today."

"You did?" Amy cocked her head.

"Yes. I'd like for you to read off your spelling words, one by one, and then Smitty will point to that particular part of the horse."

"Fun!" Amy clapped her hands then reached for her list. "Start with one I don't know. Withers. Where's that?"

Smitty patted the ridge at the base of the horse's shoulders.

Delight warmed Zola's insides at seeing Amy excited about learning. Perhaps next week when they studied about horse tack, she'd be equally as eager. The lesson went better than she could have hoped for, as Amy asked question after question.

Twenty minutes later, Smitty led Bucket to the pasture and turned her loose. Amy watched until the ranch hand disappeared into the barn, then she turned to Zola, a sweet smile on her face. "You know, none of those other ladies ever taught me anything fun. I really enjoyed this lesson." She ducked her head for a moment then looked up again. "Thank you."

"You're welcome, although I can't promise you'll enjoy every class as much as this one."

Amy stared in the direction of the barn. "You're a lot different than those other ladies."

Zola's heart leaped at the compliment. "How so? If you don't mind me asking."

She shrugged. "For one, you haven't lashed back at me for putting critters in your room."

"Yelling at people when you're upset rarely accomplishes anything positive." Henry sure had hollered a lot. It rarely made her want to do what he asked. Instead, it frightened her.

"Well, most of those ladies sure got riled at me and didn't mind saying so."

Zola understood that. At times Amy could try the patience of a saint.

"I'm really sorry for having, uh, for putting those crickets and that snake in your room."

"Think no more about it. I'm hoping we can move forward and be friends. I'd really like to help you, Amy. You're on the verge of becoming a woman, and there are many things you need to learn."

The girl leaned back and frowned. "What's the point, if I'm stuck in this chair?"

Zola pulled a rocker over, sat down, and took hold of Amy's hand. "Sweetheart, you don't know how long you'll be in that chair. Your body could heal itself, and medicine is growing by leaps and bounds. It's possible that doctors may learn how to help people with injuries like yours in the near future. The important thing is to not give up hope."

Amy looked as if she was going to say something but changed her mind. "I'll try."

"Good. Never give up." Zola squeezed Amy's hand and let go. "Think how long your brother works with a horse before it's tamed and trained enough that he can sell it. No matter how stubborn or mean the horse, he never gives up on it."

Amy grinned. "Like you didn't give up on me?"

Zola realized how the analogy must have sounded to Amy. "I didn't mean to compare you to a horse."

Amy laughed. "It's all right. I love horses."

Relaxing, Zola leaned back in her chair, thankful to God for helping her reach Amy. "How would you like to help me bake a treat for your brother?"

"Like what?"

"I was thinking about making apple pasties."

The child wrinkled her nose. "What's that?"

"A small circle of dough, filled with a meat blend, or in this case, apples with sugar and cinnamon. Then you fold over the dough, seal the edge, and bake it."

"Oh, like a small pie but without the dish?"

"Yes. I thought I could roll out the circles, then you could fill them and press the edges together."

Amy's expression took on a serious glint. "You're a brave woman to allow me to help in the kitchen. I've been known to sabotage the food."

"So I've heard. But I don't believe that will happen again. It hurts you and your brother as much as it does anyone."

"I know, but it was worth it to see the funny faces when those ladies and Evan tasted the tainted food."

Zola patted Amy's arm again. "Well, that's the behavior of a child, and we both know that you're a young lady. I would like you to help create things that taste delicious so that you'll be able to make them yourself one day when you have your own kitchen."

Amy sagged down in her chair. "That won't ever happen."

"You don't know that. Remember, don't give up. We will move forward with your lessons in hope that one day you'll walk again. Then you'll need to know how to cook, clean, and sew."

"If you say so."

Zola rose. "I believe that God can do anything."

"Mama used to say that."

"Your mother was a wise woman."

Zola pushed Amy to the kitchen, then with some wrestling and straining, she managed to help the girl get in her chair. She set a bowl, spoon, and measuring cup on the table. "I'll get the flour and sugar, then we can start."

She lit the lantern and carried it to the large pantry at the far end of the kitchen. With the door open, she set the lantern on a shelf and looked for the cans of apples. She gasped.

"What's wrong?" Amy hollered.

"Someone has been in the pantry and taken most of our cans of food."

Chapter 10

At the sound of the alarm bell ringing, Evan turned his horse toward the house and raced across the pasture. He skidded his mount to a halt, jumped off and opened the gate, rushed through, and closed it. He ran to the house. He pulled his gun as he reached the closest wall, unsure as to what—or where—the problem was.

Loud footsteps echoed across the front porch, and Smitty came into view. He wrapped his hands around his mouth and yelled, "Boss!"

Evan holstered his gun. "Here."

Smitty jumped and spun toward him, his rifle lifted. He quickly lowered it. "You scared five years off me."

Evan hurried toward him, less worried than he had been. "What's happened? Is Amy all right? Zola?" It dawned on him that he was as concerned about Zola as he was his sister. When had he started caring so much for her?

"The females are fine, although Miss Zola is spittin' mad. She discovered some yahoo stole a bunch of food."

Evan pursed his lips. He'd gone out the back door this morning and had forgotten to lock it. Now someone had the gall to come into his house and steal food? "You think it was the same man who peeked in Amy's window?"

Smitty shrugged. "No way to tell."

In his gut, Evan knew it was the same culprit. But what he didn't understand was why the man was still hanging around. What else had the thief taken? He stormed past Smitty and into the house.

"Evan! We've been robbed." Amy sounded more excited than fearful.

He patted her shoulder then crossed to Zola where she stood in the pantry doorway. He started to reach for her hand but decided not to since they had an audience. "Are you all right?"

"I'm fine. But it vexes me that someone just waltzed in here and helped himself to our food supplies."

He liked the way she used the word *our*, but he had more immediate things to dwell on. "I didn't think we'd need a guard during the day, but I'll post one." He didn't have a man to spare, especially since the men who guarded overnight needed to sleep some during the day, but he'd post one anyway. "I want you ladies to stay in the house."

"Can't we at least go out to the porch?" Amy whined.

"Not until I know who is hanging around here. And why. I want you both to be safe, and if you have to stay inside, so be it."

Zola's brow puckered, but she nodded at him. Knowing she would willingly suffer inconvenience to keep Amy and herself safe helped him relax a bit. "What was taken?"

She turned and looked in the pantry. "Canned goods and a small sack of cornmeal, from what I can tell."

"Did you check around the house?"

Zola frowned over her shoulder. "No. I was so upset over the missing food that I didn't think about anything else."

Evan spun around and strode into the parlor. There wasn't much of value here, other than the furniture. Most thieves weren't interested in books or knickknacks. He headed up the stairs to check his office. Though the room was a bit messy, due to his lack of organizing skills, everything looked to be in its place. He strode to the desk and sat, then tugged on the drawer where he stored the money box. Locked.

Relief flooded him that the two-hundred-some dollars he kept there was safe. Still, he pulled the key from his pocket, unlocked the drawer, and tugged out the box. He could tell by the weight that most of the money was still there. But it wasn't until he laid eyes on it that he knew for certain. He locked the box and returned it to the drawer, then took a careful scan of the office. As far as he could tell, nothing was missing.

As he left, he locked the office door to make it more difficult for the thief if he should make the unwise decision to return. Evan hoped the intruder was merely a hungry man down on his luck, but his gut told him otherwise. The fact that the thief was still hanging around these parts made Evan suspicious. If the man had just come to his door and asked for food, anyone from the household would have been glad to help.

He blew out a sigh as he went back down the stairs. Thank the good Lord the women hadn't been hurt.

"Smitty, round up the men. I'm staying here to watch over the ladies. I want everyone else out hunting for that thief."

"Even Ramon, Boss?"

"Yep. I know he was last on guard, but I need everyone on this. I want to know why that man is still on my land. See if Ramon can track him down."

Smitty nodded and headed out the door.

Evan returned to the kitchen. He could hear Zola banging around in the pantry. She'd handled the robbery like rain off an oiled slicker, and now she was back at work as if nothing had happened. He paused by his sister's chair. "You all right?"

"I'm fine. But I don't like the idea of not being able to go out on the porch. You do know it's hot in here? Especially when the stove is heated up."

"Sorry, but I want you to be safe."

"And hot."

He squeezed her shoulder, unwilling to argue, and crossed to the pantry. Zola was sweeping and looked up when he stepped inside the small room. He reached out and took the broom, then leaned it in the corner. He grasped her hand, causing her eyes to widen. "You sure you're all right?" he said quietly. "I'd hate for anything to happen to you."

She opened her mouth then closed it, looking surprised. He hoped she had some reciprocal feelings for him. They hadn't known one another long, but he knew in his gut that he wanted to get to know her better.

Zola seemed to have gathered her wits. She nodded. "I'm fine. We never saw the man. Amy and I were on the porch having a lesson about horses with Smitty. The thief must have come in the back door and exited there also. I don't think we were in any danger, but I do admit the timing seems odd, given the fact someone was peeking in Amy's window just a few days ago."

He squeezed her hand and let go. "I agree. I think it's the same man. For now, keep the doors and windows locked."

"Amy is right. When the house is closed up, it gets mighty warm in here."

Evan stared at the ceiling for a moment as an idea formed. "I'll cut some boards so you can open several windows enough to let in air but not so much that a person could climb in. We'll place the boards above the window so they can't be opened further by someone on the outside."

Zola touched his arm. "That's a brilliant idea."

He stared at her, warmed by her praise. She had the prettiest eyes he'd ever seen. The dim lighting of the lone lantern only enhanced their dark beauty. He wanted to kiss her. His heart pounded like it had when the alarm bell first rang, and his hand actually shook. This was loco. He barely knew her. He stepped back, wondering if that was disappointment or relief in her eyes.

"I. . .uh. . .should. . .uh. . . My horse. I left my horse saddled. . . in the pasture."

Zola cocked her head, her eyes warm. Was she enjoying his bumbling?

"Be right back." He turned and rushed out of the pantry, then bumped into a chair that wasn't fully pushed under the table, and took three stumbling steps before regaining his footing. *Great. Just great.*

Amy's mouth had cocked into a knowing smile.

He grabbed the handle and yanked the door open. He was trying to protect the women in his life, and they were both laughing at him.

That evening, after getting Amy settled in bed, Zola cast furtive glances at Evan as she stitched on her picture. He would read for five or ten minutes then jump up and make a tour of the house, checking the wood braces he'd cut for the windows and the doors and make sure they were locked. Then he would stand in the kitchen, where the room was dark, and stare out the window for a long while. She could barely see him from where she sat on the edge of the settee.

She relived the few minutes they'd had alone in the pantry, when Evan had taken her hand. She'd actually thought he might kiss her for a moment. Dare she hope that he had affections for her, as she did him?

They hadn't known one another long, but their partnering to care for Amy had quickly drawn them close. And those hours sitting on the porch together had been special. She missed that time, although sitting inside with him allowed her to study him.

He sat down again and blew out another loud sigh. The man was like a caged tiger she'd seen once as a child when a circus had come through town. "If you're so restless, why don't you go out and search and let Smitty stay with us?"

He shook his head. His dark hair was long, giving him a rugged edge, which she found appealing. "I couldn't live with myself if something happened to you two while I was gone."

Her heart thumped.

He picked up his book and started reading again.

After what she'd endured with Henry, she thought she wouldn't ever want to be with another man. Could never trust a man. But Evan was so different. He was kind, caring, a good provider, and most of all, he was protective.

She'd feared Henry. She dreaded the times he would come home. She might not have had much to eat when he was gone, but at least no one was yelling at her or beating her.

She glanced at Evan's handsome face. Most days he was clean-shaven, although by evening, he usually had a shadow on his jaw-line. Henry always had a mangy, smelly beard. It had turned her stomach to kiss him.

What would it be like to kiss Evan? Her hand drifted to her mouth, and she yanked it down.

He glanced up, stared at her for a long moment, then smiled and ducked his head. She dropped hers too, her heart galloping like a horse racing down the road. Perhaps it would be better if she did her sewing in her room. She folded the picture and picked up her tin. When she stood, he slammed his book shut and rose.

"You turning in already?"

"No. I thought I'd go to my room and do some stitching there."

He frowned. "All my pacing is distracting you."

No. *He* was distracting her.

He stepped closer, leaving only a few feet between them. "I, uh, hope I didn't upset you in the pantry this afternoon. The thought of a man in this house and how he could have harmed you or Amy, it made me worried for you and so angry." He lifted a hand and forked it through his hair.

Zola instantly ducked back. She would have fallen onto the sofa if Evan hadn't grabbed her upper arms to steady her. For a moment, she fought to get away, then stilled at his expression.

His eyes were filled with horror. "Did you think I was going to strike you?"

She hung her head. "No. It was. . .just a reaction."

He gently lifted her head so she could see his kind blue eyes. "I can promise you that I will never lay a hand on you in anger. I'm not like Henry. I don't hurt women."

"I know that. It was the combination of your anger and raised hand that frightened me."

He smiled, although his gaze still showed concern. "May I touch your cheek?"

She nodded, her mouth suddenly dry.

His lifted his hand and very gently rubbed his fingers along her jawline. Everything within her halted for a second before her senses went haywire.

"You're a kind, patient woman who deserves to know the love of a good man. You will never have to endure what Henry put you through again. You're safe here."

She closed her eyes, savoring his promise. That dreadful part of her life was truly over.

"Zola, would you please look at me?"

She did as requested, and his lovely eyes penetrated clear to her soul.

"After Amy moved in, I gave up any thought of finding a woman to love, not that I'd spent all that much time looking. And then you arrived. Though I suspected you had been treated badly, you didn't display any evidence. You were kind in the face of my sister's meanness. You even treated Amy with respect when she was cruel. No one else has been able to reach my sister like you have. I can't tell you how much it means to see her smiling again. I realize we haven't known one another long, but I hope you won't slam the door on love. I care for you, and I'm willing to take things as slow as you need them to go."

Tears filled her eyes. He truly cared for her. "It doesn't matter that I was with Henry? That we weren't married?"

"That wasn't your fault. You were tricked. What that man did was unconscionable." He looked away for a brief moment then turned back. "I'll confess that at first I did wonder how you couldn't have known Henry was an outlaw, but I believed you when you said you didn't. Men with underhanded motives can be very good actors. I've had a few who worked here for a short while who had schemes of their own, but they were found out and fired."

He rested his hands lightly on her shoulders, gave a gentle squeeze, then stepped back. "You have a home here for as long as you wish."

Tears burned Zola's eyes as his kindness overwhelmed her. "Thank you. I want you to know that I'm not opposed to seeing where things go between us. If you're sure that's what you want."

"I'm sure." His soft smile turned her insides to warm grits. He slowly leaned forward and placed a light kiss on her lips. Then he stepped back. "I should go outside and make sure no strangers are hanging around."

"Good night then." She smiled as he backed away, tipped his imaginary hat, and walked out the door.

She sagged down onto the settee, her wobbly legs no longer able to hold her. She pinched her arm to make sure this wasn't a dream. Evan cared for her. She glanced up at the ceiling. "Thank You, Lord."

~ Chapter 11 ~

$\mathcal{M}$onday morning, Zola smiled as she read over the list of spelling words that Amy had copied down. "Very nice. Your penmanship is lovely."

"Thank you." A smile danced on Amy's lips. "Mama always made me practice over and over until I wrote to her satisfaction. I soon learned to do my best penmanship so I didn't have to copy the words ten times."

"I knew you were a smart girl." She handed Amy a history book. "While you read the chapter about the Republic of Texas, I'm going to prepare lunch. Would you like water or milk to drink?"

"Milk, please."

Zola returned to the kitchen. She sliced the bread for ham sandwiches, then set the knife down as she remembered that she'd meant to show Amy the magazine she had with several floral patterns so she could pick one to start stitching this afternoon. She hurried to her bedroom, grabbed the magazine, then returned to her ward's room. She paused suddenly in the doorway and sucked in a sharp breath. Amy stood in front of the window, her chair a good three feet away. "You can walk?"

Amy jerked her head around, wobbled, then grabbed for the windowsill.

Zola hurried to her side and steadied her. "Careful now."

Amy clutched Zola's arm as Zola helped her back to the chair. The girl took several deep breaths before looking up. "I can just barely walk, and I'm very shaky. Only a few feet, if I'm holding on to something."

Zola knelt down beside the chair, tears in her eyes. "I have prayed for God to heal you since the day your brother told me about you."

"Truly?" Amy's voice held a measure of wonder.

"Yes. I'm so happy for you. Why didn't you tell me? Does Evan know?"

Amy shook her head. "I wanted to make sure I could actually walk before I got his hopes up. I've been practicing getting out of my chair by myself, and just last week, I felt strong enough to take a step."

"I will help you so you won't have to worry about falling. The more you use your legs, the stronger they will get. This afternoon we'll start. But I would prefer you stay in your chair when you're alone. All right?"

Amy stuck out her lower lip in a pout but nodded.

"Good." Zola rose and leaned over to hug the child. "I can't tell you how happy I am for you."

If she wasn't mistaken, Amy's eyes were damp too. Zola wanted so much to tell Evan, but she understood Amy's hesitation. How awful it would be to get his hopes up, only to find out his sister could never walk more than a few feet. If that book Zola had been reading was correct, exercise would make the girl's legs stronger. They would start small and work their way up.

Filled with excitement, she returned to the kitchen, pulled the leftover ham from the warmer, then reached for the knife she'd left on the counter. She searched the kitchen, but it wasn't there. Where could it have gone? Had she unknowingly carried it to her room?

She turned around and gasped. A bearded man in shabby clothes stood a few feet away, wielding her knife. Although six inches taller than she, he was thin as a broomstick. Was he the one who took their food? "What do you want?"

He looked her over for a long, unnerving moment. She stepped back, but with the counter behind her, there was nowhere to go.

"I knew you was her."

Well, that made a whole lot of sense. "Her?"

He rubbed the back of his hand across his mouth, the knife coming close to her face. "Henry's woman."

Her heart bucked. She looked at him more closely. "You were part of Henry's gang?"

He nodded.

She didn't remember him, but then only the same man had ever visited Henry. This man must have been the outlaw that got away when Henry was killed. "What do you want with me?"

He reached around her, coming so close she got a whiff of his dreadful scent, and speared a slice of bread. He wolfed it down in two bites. The man's gray eyes pierced hers. "I figure with you being Henry's woman and all, you'd know where he buried the money from the Denison bank robbery."

337

Zola's heart lurched. "I can assure you that I don't. I didn't even know Henry was an outlaw until after he was dead, when the marshal told me."

The man's mouth cocked up in a frightful sneer. "You expect me to believe that you was Henry's wife and he didn't tell you where the money was?"

She held up her hands. "It's true. Honestly." Her gaze latched onto the cord of the alarm bell across the room. If only she could edge her way to it. But what would the man do if she did?

He rubbed his thumb along the edge of the knife. "It'd be a shame for the little girl to get hurt."

Her whole body quivered. "Amy has nothing to do with this. She's just a child who is injured and stuck in a wheeled chair."

He shrugged. "She's a purdy little thang."

Zola's mind raced. She had to get him away from the house—away from Amy. She closed her eyes and drew in a steadying breath. "All right. I can show you where the money is."

His eyes lit up. "Well, that's more like it." He grabbed her arm and shoved her toward the back door.

Zola moved slowly. If she left with him, she would probably die, since she had no idea where any money was. But she couldn't let the man harm Amy. Or Evan. As they exited the back door, she muttered a quick prayer.

Help me, Lord.

Evan glanced at the front of the house as he rose after putting the final shoe on his horse. Something in his gut made him edgy. He started to turn back, when he saw movement at Amy's window.

Someone was trying to get in! He started running, pulling his gun as he did. But as he drew nearer, he realized that the person was Amy. She climbed out her window and fell to the porch floor. What in the world?

He holstered his gun, ran up the steps, and knelt beside her. "How—? What do you think you're doing?"

Amy looked up with fear-filled eyes. "A man took Zola. Out back."

Evan's heart bucked. He lifted his sister and carried her into the house.

His sister pushed at his arms. "Don't worry about me. Go save Zola."

Evan strode to Amy's room and put her in her chair. "Stay in the house until I get back."

"I will. But hurry!"

He rushed through the house, pausing long enough to grab his rifle and ammunition. Why would anyone want to take Zola? The ache in his chest at the thought of someone hurting her was profound. Painful. He paused at the rear door. In the distance, he could see two horses. Zola's skirts flapped in the breeze on one of them. He spun and raced to the alarm and rang it with gusto.

He jogged back to Amy's room and unholstered his gun. He handed it to his sister. Evan gave her some quick instructions then a stern stare. "Do not fiddle with this, and only use it if a stranger comes through that door."

She nodded. "Please bring Zola home."

He closed the door. How in the world had his sister managed to climb out the window? He shook his head. That was a topic for later. He had more pressing things to deal with now. As he exited the house, the men rode in.

"Someone has taken Zola," he shouted to them. "Smitty, stay here and guard Amy. And beware—I gave her my gun. You others ride with me."

At least the stranger would be outnumbered. He mounted and kicked his horse. "He-yah!"

The wind whipped his face, and behind him the sound of hoof-beats followed. He would find her. He *had* to find her. His heart felt shattered—scattered in pieces on the ground as he raced after the woman he loved. And he knew for sure that he did love her. He'd never expected that day he brought home a scorned and desperate woman that she'd change his life in such a short time. But she had.

Zola was kind and loving. Her patient but stern guidance had changed his sister faster than he'd thought possible.

But why would a stranger risk his life to kidnap her? A sudden thought hit him like a fist to his gut. Did she know more than she'd told him? Had she lied to him? Had she actually known Henry was an outlaw? Could she have been part of the gang?

He urged his horse up the hill where he'd seen Zola and the man riding.

No. He couldn't listen to those thoughts. He'd seen Zola's heart. In the way she took Amy's assault in stride. In how she read that medical book because of her desire to help his sister. He'd looked her in the eye when she told him she hadn't known about Henry's unlawful deeds. He believed her then. And he believed her now.

He had to save her. She was part of his future, and without her, both he and Amy would be lost.

Zola struggled to stay on the trotting horse. With her hands bound, she could barely hang onto the saddle horn. The bouncing assaulted her body.

Had Amy been the one to ring the alarm? Her hopes had soared when she heard it so soon after they'd left the house. Evan surely must know she was gone by now. He would come for her.

As they crested the next hill, she looked back, and joy filled her. Four men! Riding fast. Evan must be the one in the lead.

Her captor slowed their pace as they rode down the hill, but once they reached level ground again, he would surely want to gallop the horses. She needed to slow them down. But how?

At the bottom of the hill was a creek. They'd have to ride slower as they crossed it. An idea suddenly formed.

As she expected, the horses slowed when they stepped into the creek. Midway through, Zola wriggled her feet free of the stirrups, then pushed off the horse. Water sloshed through her clothes, and she landed hard on a rock, shooting pain through hip, back, and legs. She splashed as she struggled to sit up, but the weight of the water made it difficult.

The man cursed and drew his horse to a halt. He jumped down and splashed through the water, his eyes cold. "Get up, you dim-witted woman. Don't ya know how to ride a horse?"

Zola made her body go limp and moaned. Maybe if he thought she was hurt, he'd leave her. He stuck his arms under hers and dragged her backward through the water and mud. He struggled to hoist her to her feet. "Stand up, you fool."

"I can't. Hurt."

He shifted her weight, and she felt something hard press against her side. "Stand up or get shot."

Miraculously, her legs stiffened.

"Go! Now."

She struggled up the muddy embankment, and he followed. He dragged her toward the horse he'd been riding, but hers was farther away.

He cursed again.

The blessed sound of hoofbeats grew louder.

He muttered another foul word then tossed her over his shoulder. Zola kicked him in the knee just as Evan crested the hill.

Suddenly the man threw her to the ground, mounted his horse, and spurred the poor beast.

Evan crossed the creek and slipped from his horse. He bent down on his boot heels. "Are you all right? I was afraid I'd lost you."

The warmth in his sky-blue eyes drove away the fear of her harrowing escapade. "I am. Go get him. I don't want him coming back."

Evan pulled his horse out of the way as Pete, Dean, and Ramon crossed the creek. "Get him. Don't let that man get away."

The men charged after her captor, leaving behind a cloud of dust.

Zola coughed.

Evan tied his horse to a sapling then reached down. "Can you stand?"

"I think so."

"Did he hurt you?"

She shook her head, and her damp hair fell down around her shoulders. "No, but I hurt myself."

He lifted his brows, obviously curious.

She brushed the hair from her face and smoothed it back. "I jumped off the horse when we came to the creek."

Evan smiled. "And here I thought you fell off."

She lifted one shoulder. "I mostly did."

"Your hair is so pretty." He brushed it back at her temples, sending delicious shivers down her back. "I was afraid something awful would happen to you. I'm so thankful that neither you nor Amy were hurt."

"Me too. She is all right? Did she ring the alarm?"

His forehead wrinkled in a perplexed look. "No. I did. After I found Amy crawling out her window."

Zola felt her mouth drop open. Amy must have tried to go for help. "How did she manage that?"

"I aim to find out when we get home."

Home. She loved the sound of that.

"First, how badly are you injured?"

"Just bruises." She laid her hand on his chest, feeling his pounding heart. "Thank you for coming after me."

"Of course. I couldn't let that snake get away with the woman I love, could I?"

Zola's own heart stampeded as she shook her head.

Evan stepped closer and cupped her cheeks. "I've realized that I'm growing to love you more and more every day. We haven't known one another very long, so I won't pressure you, but I hope one day you'll feel the same."

She moved her hand up to his face. "I do care for you. I started the day you hired me, when no one else could stand to look at me. Your love for your sister first stirred my affections. You're a good man, Evan Clayborne." She ducked her head. "But how can you care for me after what Henry did? Doesn't it matter?"

He took hold of her arms. "I've been reading my Bible more lately, after you went to bed. I read in the book of Isaiah, 'Come now, and let us reason together, saith the Lord: though your sins be as scarlet, they shall be as white as snow; though they be red like crimson, they shall be as wool.' We've all sinned, but God washes us white like snow. I don't believe you sinned by living with Henry, because you thought you were married. But I know you feel shame for what happened. The way I see it, you're fresh as a blizzard." He shrugged. "Not sure what wool has to do with anything though."

She smiled, loving him for his bumbling analogy.

"I'm no poet, Zola, merely a cowboy. I just meant that what happened to you wasn't your fault. You had good intentions when you thought you were marrying Henry. He's the louse in my book."

She stepped closer. "Like I said, you're a good man, Evan. And I do love you."

His eyes sparked. "Does that mean I can kiss you whenever I want?"

She wrapped her hand around his neck. "I really wish you'd kiss me now."

"Happy to oblige, ma'am." He bent down, his arms slipping around her back as he closed the distance between them. His lips were soft and warm, and they stirred feelings within her she didn't know existed. The pressure on her lips deepened, and she found it hard to breathe, but she didn't care.

Through the wonderful fog of delight, she suddenly remembered her wet, muddy clothes and reluctantly pushed out of Evan's arms.

Alarm filled his eyes, and he searched their surroundings before looking at her again. "What's wrong?"

She waved a hand at her dress. "I'm getting you all wet."

He grinned. "Is that all? Come back here."

And she did.

❧ *Epilogue* ❧

Persimmon Hill, Texas
July 1, 1888

Zola walked down the church aisle, her heart racing like the roadrunner she'd seen on the drive to town this morning. Evan stood at the front in his Sunday suit, looking handsomer than she'd ever seen him. His joyful expression made her want to run toward him, but she remembered her mama's lessons in decorum.

Alice had agreed to stand up beside her, as Smitty had for Evan. Amy stood next to the piano, where she could lean if needed. In the past few weeks, the strength had begun returning to her legs with the exercises they'd been doing. Zola was so happy to see Amy standing and looking pretty in her new dress and shoes. Love for both Evan and his sister filled her heart.

How could things have been so awful less than two months ago and be so wonderful today? Soon she would be a true wife to a man she dearly loved. And her horrid past would be put to rest now that the last of Henry's gang was in prison.

She stepped up next to Evan. His blue eyes danced with excitement and promise. Perhaps soon she would be carrying his child, because now she knew that she'd never bear one of Henry's.

As she turned to face the minister with Evan, she thanked God for the wonderful changes and blessings in her life. Her sham of a marriage was over, and soon she would be truly wed.

 **Vickie McDonough** is an award-winning author of nearly fifty published books and novellas, with more than 1.5 million copies sold. A bestselling author, Vickie grew up wanting to marry a rancher, but instead she married a computer geek who is scared of horses. She now lives out her dreams penning romance stories about ranchers, cowboys, lawmen, and others living in the Old West. Her novels include *End of the Trail*, winner of the Oklahoma Writers' Federation Inc. 2013 Booksellers Best Fiction Novel Award. *Whispers on the Prairie* was a *Romantic Times* Recommended Inspirational Book for July 2013. *Song of the Prairie* won the 2015 Inspirational Readers' Choice Award. *Gabriel's Atonement*, book 1 in the Land Rush Dreams series, placed second in the 2016 Will Rogers Medallion Award. Vickie has recently stepped into independent publishing.

Vickie has been married for more than forty years to Robert. They have four grown sons, one daughter-in-law, and a precocious granddaughter. When she's not writing, Vickie enjoys reading, doing stained glass projects, watching movies, and traveling. To learn more about Vickie's books or to sign up for her newsletter, visit her website at www.vickiemcdonough.com.

The Galway Girl

by Erica Vetsch

Dedication

To Peter, as always.
All my love, Erica

Chapter 1

Boston, February 1875

The crack of Maeve O'Reilly's palm connecting with his face ricocheted through the scullery, sending a hot sting up her arm and a satisfying thrill through her heart—just before despair gripped her.

"Perhaps you don't understand your position in this household." Charles Kemper backed up a step, his icy gray eyes blowing a North Sea wind through the dank basement room. "You'd best reconsider, or you'll find yourself on the street without a character. Irish housemaids are plentiful in Boston, and I could have you replaced by noon."

Maeve clenched her fists, her right hand throbbing. "Sir, please. I just want to work. Nothin' more." Her brogue thickened as she fought to control her temper.

Her employer, or rather, her employer's son, raised his chin, narrowing his eyes and sneering down his long, straight nose. The slap mark stood out in angry red on his pale cheek. "I want you to work too, but as more than a scullery maid." Charles reached for her upper arm, and she swatted his hand aside.

How had she been so foolish to allow herself to be snuck up on? She knew better, and yet she'd let her guard down for a minute, and now she was trapped. The only way out of the scullery lay behind her tormenter.

"Mr. Kemper, please, leave me be." She backed up, feeling behind her for something, anything, with which to defend herself. Her hand closed around a metal shaft on the drain board. A ladle wouldn't be much of a threat. If only she had been washing knives or skewers. Still, anything was better than nothing, and she brandished the cooking utensil. "I won't be trifled with." A hank of her hair escaped her mobcap, partially obscuring her vision. She swiped it away, only to have more curls spring free.

"Ah, that hair." His eyes flashed. "It's a sure sign of the tigress who possesses it."

"Sir, you must leave me be. I neither want nor need your attentions." *And wouldn't have you if you came gift wrapped and guaranteed. You're a pig. No, that's insulting to pigs.*

"You'll do as you're told, or you'll be out on your sweet derriere." Charles advanced on her, and she tightened her grip on the ladle, feeling ridiculous and scared, but mostly angry.

No one should have to put up with this nonsense just because she was Irish, a domestic servant, and alone in the world. If Maeve was fired and sent away without a character, she'd find herself in dire straits. No one would hire a domestic without references from a previous employer. She'd had a hard enough time finding this position after her last employer, a sweet lady of eighty, passed away suddenly, leaving her entire staff scrambling for new placements. And Charles was right. Irish housemaids were thick on the ground in Boston. Competition for jobs was fierce. He'd have no trouble replacing her, perhaps with someone who wouldn't reject his advances, though Maeve pitied the poor girl who would submit to him.

"Miss O'Reilly, where have you gotten to? Those potatoes aren't going to peel themselves." Mrs. Hinchey's strident tone shot down the hall, and Maeve's throat loosened a tick. Though the housekeeper's voice usually set Maeve's teeth on edge, she'd never been so glad to hear it. Mrs. Hinchey's footfalls sounded in the passage from the kitchen, *tap, tap, tap.* The staff appreciated those hard wooden heels she wore, since they gave plenty of warning of her approach. The woman couldn't sneak up on a fence post.

"There you are." The housekeeper, who reigned supreme over the female staff, filled the doorway, her black bombazine dress rustling, the chatelaine at her waist jingling. She surveyed the scene, and Maeve knew she was noting Charles's cheek bearing lobster-red finger marks, Maeve clutching the ladle before her, pressed up against the sink, her hair escaping its bonds, and enough tension in the air to satisfy a Shakespearean actor.

"Mr. Kemper. Is there something you require?" Mrs. Hinchey's mouth pinched in a just-kissed-a-lemon pucker. "If you needed something from the scullery, you had only to ring and it would be brought to you."

Charles scowled, nodded curtly, and pushed past the housekeeper out of the room.

Maeve relaxed her grip on her "weapon" and sagged against the stoneware sink. "Thank you, Mrs. Hinchey. I'll go help Cook with those potatoes."

Mrs. Hinchey cleared her throat, and Maeve paused.

"Miss O'Reilly, I will not have my housemaids tempting, acting coy, and otherwise enticing men in this household. I will not have any disturbances with my staff." She folded her arms under her considerable bosom. "I was against hiring yet another loose-moraled Irish flirt. The last one wound up at St. Catherine's."

Outrage burned hot in Maeve's blood. A flirt, was she? When she'd been holding that lecher at bay with the only thing she could lay her hand to, and Mrs. Hinchey knew it? As for the previous girl to hold Maeve's job, the entire staff knew she'd been sent to St. Catherine's Home for Unwed Mothers as a result of Charles Kemper's attentions.

"Mrs. Hinchey—" Maeve began to defend herself, only to find herself cut off by the housekeeper's formidable glare.

"I do not wish to hear it. Keep yourself to yourself, and if there is another incident involving you and Mr. Kemper, I'll see you turned out, is that clear?"

Maeve clenched her teeth so hard she thought she might crack a molar. She breathed deeply through her nose, counting well past ten.

"I said, 'Is that clear'?"

Swallowing hard, she whispered, "Aye, mum."

"Now, get to work and let that be the end of it. And fix your hair. You look as if you've been dragged through a knothole backwards."

Maeve bobbed a quick curtsy and hurried toward the kitchen, stuffing her curls back under the safety of her cap while blinking back righteous tears.

Ah, Da, how did I come to this? How can I make our dreams come true when I have fewer rights and choices than a prisoner at Kilmainham Gaol?

That evening, after she'd washed the supper dishes not only for the Kempers and their guests, but also for all the staff, Maeve hung her drying cloths on the wall rack, banked the fire in the stove, and lit a candle to illuminate her way up the back stairs. She'd found that if she could get to the safety of the third floor while Charles Kemper was busy with guests in the parlor, she could relax in the small room she shared with the laundress without fear of being accosted.

"I thought you'd never get done. Is Hinchey still on the warpath?" Belinda sprawled in the chair beside the window, lanky and thin as a wading bird, her dark, straight hair escaping its pins and straggling over her shoulders. With a hookish nose and prominent teeth, no one could call her beautiful at first blush, but she'd been kindness itself to Maeve and in a short time had become her friend.

"There were sixteen for dinner tonight, four courses." Maeve blew out her candle and set it on the bureau. She closed the door and leaned against it, wishing it had a lock. "I thought I'd never get done either." Dragging her white mobcap off her head, she freed her riotous, fiery curls.

"So, what set Hinchey off this time? Was it the big dinner service?" Belinda frowned. "That makes no sense, since there are often more than sixteen at these dinner parties. What happened? Did she and Mr. Carson get into a snit again?"

"No, the butler had nothing to do with it. It was me." Maeve slung her cap across the room where it hit the wall with an unsatisfying *floof* and plopped to the floor. She hated the thing, hated having to hide her red hair lest it be a "temptation to the male members of the staff" as Mrs. Hinchey had stated when she'd applied for the job. None of the other maids had to stuff *all* their hair under a cloth cover as if they were ashamed of it. Even the cook only wore her cap well back on her head.

"What did you do? Break a dish?"

"No. I slapped Mr. Kemper across his lordly cheek." Maeve dropped onto the bed, its springs squeaking. How could she stay here if she had to be on her guard all the time? Yet where else could she go?

"You didn't." Belinda untangled her long legs and arms and sat up.

"Too right I did. He snuck up on me in the scullery and grabbed me from behind." She shuddered. "He spun me around and tried to kiss me." Bile rose in her throat, and fury stung her eyes. He hadn't *tried* to kiss her. He'd managed to get his nasty, narrow-yet-squishy lips on hers. She wanted to gag and to scrub her lips with soap until she could chase away the memory.

"Oh Maeve, what did he do when you hit him? I can't believe he didn't sack you on the spot."

"Mrs. Hinchey intervened before he could do anything more. He left, and then she started in on me like it was my fault, that I flirted with him and was no better than I should be." The impotent anger she'd toted all day swept over her again like a stiff sea breeze. If only she could stand beside the ocean, the pulsing, expansive, foaming Atlantic that touched her beloved Ireland, perhaps she could settle her soul and master her frustration. "What am I going to do?"

Belinda leaned over the side of her chair and dug in her mending basket. "Maybe you should do what I'm thinking of doing." She drew out a newspaper. "When I went to the store to pick up more starch and bluing, the shopkeeper put this in my parcel." With a sheepish grin, she handed it over. "I guess he thought I'd need the help to land a man."

Maeve took the newsprint, opening it to read the masthead. "The *Matrimonial News?*" She scanned the front page. Row after row of advertisements.

"Mail-order brides." Belinda eased onto the bed beside Maeve. "Look. Fellows who want a wife write in to the *Matrimonial News*, say what they're looking for, and see who answers." Her long, narrow finger slid down one column. "Every advertisement has a little number here in the corner. You write to the newspaper, give them the number you're interested in, and they pass along your letter or note or whatever. All the correspondence goes through their office in Kansas City until the couple is ready to meet up."

Maeve's heart sank. If Belinda found a husband through this newspaper, she, Maeve, would be without a friend in the Kemper household. For herself, she would never be a mail-order bride. She might currently be sitting between a rock and a very hard place, but she'd never be *that* desperate.

Lindsborg, Kansas

Kaspar Sandberg sat at his kitchen table, rolled his shoulders, and picked up the envelope. Postmarked Kansas City, he knew what it would hold. He turned it in his big, knobby hands, hearing the crinkle of the paper, feeling the seams. His neighbor had delivered it earlier that day, and it had sat propped up against the lamp in the middle of the table while Kaspar tried to ignore it.

"Go on." Grandmother's knitting needles clicked, and she slowly pulled another yard of yarn from the basket beside her rocker. Sleet pinged against the window, and the ceaseless Kansas wind scudded across the prairie, hitting the north side of the house and rushing over and around it on its way south. But this late in February, spring wasn't far away.

Warmer weather meant putting in crops, the birth of new animals, a fresh brace of young draft horses to train, and long days of hard work for him.

And long days for Grandmother too. Planting the garden, cleaning the house from top to bottom, washing all the winter clothes and bedding, preparing meals for himself and his hired man. Too much work for her to do alone, especially with her eyesight failing like it was. She needed help. It was a wonder she'd gotten along as well as she had for this long. But over the winter, she'd begun to fade some, letting things slip, either too tired or just not seeing the dust and clutter. And her cooking—that had gone right downhill. She either burned things or overseasoned them to the point of inedibility.

That was why he sat here staring at this letter, afraid to open it but resigned to the fact that he must.

He slid his knife from his pocket and opened the smallest blade. With barely a sound, because he kept the blade so sharp, he slit the envelope and drew out the single sheet of paper that was the only reply he'd received to the advertisement he'd placed more than two months ago. A bit of pasteboard fell to the table, facedown, but he ignored it in favor of the note. In a blocky scrawl, it read:

Dear Sir,

    I am Trudy Halvorg. I am thirty and Swedish. I would be interested to marry you. I am big, strong woman who work hard. I am enclose picture. Please reply. I am pleased to come soon.

Trudy

Short and to the point. He'd advertised for a Swedish girl who was healthy and willing to work a farm in Kansas. Beyond that, he hadn't stipulated an age, that she speak fluent English, or that she have fine handwriting.

Thirty. She'd be five years older than him. Did that matter? He wasn't sure.

Grandmother's needles stilled, a rare occurrence, though he marveled that she could knit by feel since she couldn't see the stitches very well these days. The clock sounded unnaturally loud to his ears, and his heart kept double time. He reached for the picture. Was he going to look into the eyes of his future wife?

Part of him was eager and part of him reluctant. As if by looking at the photograph he would cross some bridge that would immediately burn behind him. Grandmother's silence urged him to just get on with it. He'd promised her he would look for a bride, someone to help them both, so he should stop balking and get it done.

Don't be a coward.

With what he hoped was a nonchalant flip, he reversed the photograph and took a look.

Trudy Halvorg hadn't lied. She looked like a hard worker. Pale hair, pale eyes, plain features. The hair was scraped back into a knot on top of her head, so tight it seemed to pull her cheeks taut over her bones and narrow her eyes.

She wore a dark dress, buttoned up the front to the throat, and a shawl of some kind around her shoulders. Not petite, not large, just. . .solid.

He felt nothing.

What had he expected? A spark? A jolt? Some sort of connection?

That was ridiculous. He felt as though he was looking at a

photograph of a stranger because he *was* looking at a photograph of a stranger.

"Well?" Grandmother asked.

Without a word, he passed the note and photograph to her and then rose to stare out the kitchen window at the black night. He tucked his thumbs under his braces and rocked on his boots. The note was written in such a large scrawl, he thought Grandmother would be able to read it fine.

Why couldn't he just find someone from here? Why were all the girls he knew married or spoken for or not at all interested in staying in Lindsborg on a farm?

He knew he was no prize in the looks department. Too big, too broad, too plain, too ordinary. And he wasn't smooth like some of his friends, who could talk to any woman and sound smart and interesting.

Kaspar knew farming. He knew horses and sheep and cows. He knew his fields, every last acre of wheat and hay. He knew how to take care of barns and equipment. He knew how to watch the weather for signs of change.

But he was at a loss when it came to talking to women.

Hence the advertisement in the *Matrimonial News*. No one besides Grandmother knew he'd sent it. He'd not been able to tell his friends. Not that it was anyone's business but his own.

He tried to imagine meeting Trudy, bringing her into his house, introducing her at church. In some ways, she'd fit right in. She would know the culture, language, customs, food, and everything else in the Swedish community of Lindsborg. She could most likely cook and garden and clean and would be a companion for Grandmother, which was exactly what Grandmother needed.

But what about what he needed? When he'd thought about

getting married, it had always been to someone he would love and protect and cherish, someone who would be a friend and support, someone he could laugh with. Someone who would share his faith, his life, and. . .his bed.

Bleakness blew through his chest.

Maybe you're not giving her a chance. Maybe Trudy Halvorg could be all those things someday.

And maybe she couldn't. Truth be told, he needed a housekeeper more than he needed a wife right now. Maybe this Miss Halvorg would come on that basis. Maybe he needn't take such a drastic step as marriage.

"I think you should answer her." Grandmother lowered the picture and note to her lap, leaning her head on the back of the rocker and closing her eyes. "I can't tell you what a relief this is. I want to see you settled with a wife and family before I die. If I know this, I can die happy."

Kaspar sighed. A housekeeper wouldn't do if he was to please the woman who had raised him and meant more to him than anyone on earth. He needed a wife.

He'd have to answer the note and invite Miss Halvorg to Kansas.

❧ Chapter 2 ❧

*Y*ou spoke too soon, *cailín*." Maeve muttered her way up the back stairs carrying a can of hot water and a pitcher of cold for the mistress's morning wash. "Never be desperate enough to answer a mail-order bride advertisement, eh?" She tried to be quiet, since most of the household was still asleep.

Over the last month, Charles Kemper had become impossible. He contrived ways to "run into" her in the house, popping up around corners when she didn't expect him. In the ordinary course of things, the scullery maid, the lowest in the domestic pecking order, would have little or no cause to ever meet the son of the household, but at least once a day she found herself having to suffer his presence. After she'd found provocative notes to her left by him in the scullery cupboards, she asked Belinda to help her comb through the *Matrimonial News* for a likely match. She'd found one. Number 17197.

Mr. Sean Heaslip, Chicago, Illinois, grocery owner, Irish. His only drawback was that at thirty-six, he was not far off twice Maeve's age of nineteen. His family came from Dublin, and he'd been born in America. His picture showed a man who looked presentable enough, and she decided to consider sending a response, but when the next note from Charles was found under her pillow, she decided that even if Mr. Heaslip looked like the south end of a north-bound pit pony, she would prefer him to her current situation.

She'd written and received a reply quickly enough to wonder if she should be flattered or wary at his eagerness.

"I'll miss the sea, but at least I'll have that big lake to look on." Maeve had sealed the envelope containing the acceptance of his offer, resigned to the situation Charles Kemper had put her into. If she didn't leave soon, he would either compromise her virtue or she would be fired and on the street. Her meager savings would evaporate in less than a week.

"I can't believe you're leaving. I'll miss you." Belinda sniffed as she sewed lace onto a nightgown for their employer.

"You would anyway, since you've answered an advertisement yourself. Where is Birmingham, anyway?"

"Alabama. A long ways from here. Do you think I'll make a good preacher's wife?"

Maeve smiled. "Better than I would. My temper is too hot and my tongue too quick for a preacher. . .or for his congregation, I'm sure. You're going to make a lovely pastor's wife because you like taking care of people."

Belinda had accepted the proposal of one Reverend Malachi Davisson a week before. Tickets and travel expense money had arrived for the laundress, and within the month, Belinda would be gone.

A hard lump formed in Maeve's throat as she crept down the hall. In the weeks she'd been in the Kemper household, Belinda had become so dear to her, a friend and confidant. She'd taken to accompanying Maeve in the house whenever possible so Charles couldn't get Maeve alone, which was tricky, since the scullery maid and the laundress had different responsibilities and work areas.

Maeve tapped on the bedroom door of the mistress of the house and entered. At this early hour, the blinds were still drawn, and her employer was still abed in her massive tester. She tended to be a heavy and late sleeper, and in all the mornings Maeve had performed this duty, she'd never once awakened. Often Maeve had to bring a second can of hot water because the first had cooled to tepid by the time the lady of the house got out of her bed.

Quietly, Maeve set the pitcher on the washstand and placed the hot water on the hearth. She bent to start a fire to chase away the chill in the room, careful not to bang the poker on the andirons.

"You, girl." The mistress's voice snapped across the room like a bedsheet on a clothesline in a high wind.

Maeve jumped up, sending the poker clattering on the tile hearth. She winced at the noise. "Mum?" She bobbed her head, only then realizing she'd forgotten to put on her cap. A stray curl escaped the knot at the back of her head and grazed her cheek. Drawing the despised cap from her apron pocket, she clapped it over her hair, tucking the offending curl under the lace edge, hoping the darkness in the room would hide her hasty movements.

"Name?"

"Mum?"

"What is your name?" Mrs. Kemper spoke slowly, as if to an

idiot, which Maeve certainly felt at that moment.

"Maeve O'Reilly, mum." Maeve bobbed a curtsy.

"So, you're the one." She propped herself up on the mountain of pillows at the head of the bed. "Open the drapes a bit so I can get a proper look at you."

Puzzled, Maeve drew back the dark green velvet panels, the wooden curtain rings clacking softly on the curtain rod. Early morning sunlight filtered through the lace sheers, picking out some of the details of the sumptuous room. Maeve couldn't help but compare the ormolu furnishings, the massive mirror, the rich wallpaper and rugs to her own accommodations, where she and Belinda shared a metal bed, a washstand, a bureau, and a single rocking chair. Their looking glass was a four-inch square tacked beside the door, barely large enough for them to see to put up their hair, and the only warmth came from a stovepipe in the corner of the room.

"Where are you from, and how long have you worked here?"

"I come from Galway, mum, and I've been in your employ six weeks tomorrow."

Mrs. Kemper studied Maeve from her face to her feet, her disdain growing. "*Another* Irish maid? Your kind are becoming ubiquitous."

Lord, hold my tongue. Maeve swallowed, trying not to tense at the sneer on her employer's face.

"Hah, I suppose I shouldn't use such large words around a bog-Irish. Do you even know what ubiquitous means?"

"Aye, mum. I do." Her chin lifted a fraction, and she gripped her apron at her sides. She had been a good student, and her father had read aloud to her since before she could remember. "There are many things that appear to be ubiquitous in this household."

"Just what do you mean by that?" Mrs. Kemper was stung into asking.

"Just that the opinions and treatment regarding servants from Ireland seems to be in keeping with the rest of Boston society." The words came out before Maeve could stop them. "Your son can't keep his hands to himself, and you think I'm a simpleton because I have a brogue."

"You're impertinent." Mrs. Kemper's nostrils flared, and storm clouds gathered in her eyes. "As for my son, I imagine you're like all the rest, trailing your cloak before him, trying to get him to notice you. And when he responds, as any red-blooded male would, you cry foul. Just like a bog-Irish."

"Mum, I have never tried to get your son's attention. I can't think of anything I would desire less. He's the one making all the advances, and I wish he would stop. He's been a nuisance since the first day I came here." *Shut your trap, Maeve. You're going to get the sack right here if you don't stop.*

Mrs. Kemper's neck stiffened, and she sniffed. For a long moment, Maeve thought she'd really gone too far this time. Then Mrs. Kemper relaxed. "Good. Then we understand each other. Now get out of my room, and the next time I address you, there had better be a proper amount of civility and humility in your replies, or you'll find yourself on the other side of my front door. Do you understand?"

Maeve's knees felt like wet dishcloths as she descended the back stairs. Mrs. Kemper was as hateful as her son. The closer Maeve got to the scullery, the more her backbone firmed up and her temper rose. Sight of the sink full of dishes from the breakfast preparations made her grit her teeth.

"I speak two languages, can cipher, cook, and sew. What can

Mrs. Kemper do but host dinner parties that someone else does all the work for, and hand out judgments against people based upon where they're from? Oh, and dote on her obnoxious son." Maeve stormed about the scullery, kicking aside an innocent stool and clattering pots while getting hot water to wash the dishes.

"What's got you riled?" Belinda asked from the doorway. "Do I dare come in? Is it Charles again?"

"No, it's his impossible mother. She scolded me this morning, and you know why? For being Irish. Oh, and for trying to lure her beloved son. As if I would." The soap plopped into the washtub, and a gout of water spouted up and splashed Maeve's bodice. "Oh, that's just wonderful."

"Perhaps this will cheer you." Belinda held up an envelope. "It's stiffish, so maybe it has tickets in it." Her grin brightened Maeve's mood as she sponged her apron bib.

"So soon?" Hope exploded in Maeve's heart. Maybe she really could escape this awful house before it was too late.

"Mr. Heaslip must not believe in letting the grass grow under his feet. I wouldn't have thought your letter would've even made it to Chicago, much less that he could reply so fast." Belinda pulled a hairpin from her hair and handed it and the letter over. "Hurry. I can't stand it."

Slitting the letter, Maeve's fingers trembled. She tugged out the single sheet and opened it. A bank draft and a pasteboard ticket lay in the folded page, but she ignored those in favor of the note. She also ignored the greeting, going instead to the body of the letter.

Please find enclosed a ticket and money to cover your traveling expenses. I am pleased you have accepted my offer, and I look forward to meeting you. If you could cable me the date of your arrival, I will pick you up at the station. Please don't take too long. Spring work is starting up, and it is a busy time.

> *Sincerely,*
> *Kaspar Sandberg*

Kaspar? Maeve frowned and jumped up to the salutation.

Dear Miss Halvorg.

Miss Halvorg?
She turned over the train ticket. *Lindsborg, Kansas?*
What on earth?
The return address on the envelope was the newspaper from Kansas City. And in the corner, the number 17179.

She frowned. That wasn't Mr. Heaslip's advertisement number.

"What is it?" Belinda asked. "He sent you a ticket, right?"

"He did, but he's the wrong 'he.' " Maeve held out the bit of pasteboard. "This is from some man in Kansas. A Kaspar Sandberg writing to a Miss Halvorg." She wanted to ball up the letter, bitter disappointment pressing on her shoulders. "There's been some kind of mix-up. They sent the wrong reply. Look at the number. Mr. Heaslip's is 17197, not 17179."

"Oh no." Belinda's mouth twisted. "You'll want to reply right away and get this straightened out. Perhaps you can send a cable to the newspaper."

Maeve took back the train ticket and glanced at the bank draft. "Whoever this Mr. Sandberg is, he was certainly generous with the travel money. Miss Halvorg is a lucky woman." She folded everything back into the envelope and put it into her apron pocket. "I'll have to deal with this later. If I don't get these dishes washed, Mrs.

Hinchey will be down here scolding me. I've been scolded enough for one day, and it's not even nine o'clock yet."

Belinda nodded. "I've got plenty to do as well. There are overnight guests coming, and even though the beds are made up in the guest rooms, Mrs. Kemper wants all the linens changed anyway." She sighed. "Maybe when you're a rich grocer's wife in Chicago, you can take pity on all your domestics by not making unreasonable demands and extra work for them."

"Ha, more like I'll have to take in washing and sewing to help make ends meet. But I won't mind as long as I'm not here." Maeve waved to her friend and set about her chores. She wished she could run to the telegraph office right then, but it would have to wait. Perhaps at noon she could skip lunch and send her message.

By lunchtime, Maeve was ready to either throw a first-class tantrum or else dissolve into tears. Mrs. Hinchey gave her a tongue-lashing over the job she'd done polishing the silver, though there was nothing wrong with it that Maeve could see. The cook had burned her hand on the stove, and Maeve had stepped in to help with the luncheon. Though again there was nothing wrong with the salmon croquettes and asparagus tips, Mrs. Kemper had sent the food back twice, earning Maeve another scolding. And the boot boy, Liam, had broken a serving platter. Maeve had taken the blame, trying to shield the boy from Mrs. Hinchey's wrath, but the housekeeper ended up berating both of them for carelessness and lying.

On top of that, Mrs. Kemper had spoken to Mrs. Hinchey about Maeve, calling her impertinent and clumsy. Maeve was now on notice. If she crossed her employer one more time, she was fired.

"Mrs. Kemper? Mrs. *Temper* is more like it." Maeve hurried down the hallway to the parlor, the heavy coal hod bumping against her leg. "No doubt leaving coal dust on my apron, for which I will get another hiding. My tongue's practically bleeding from biting it all day." With her head down, muttering to herself, she crossed to the fireplace. "And I'll be glad when this chilly weather is over and I can stop carrying coal every blessed day. It's a footman's job, but they're too cheap to hire a footman."

"If you're cold, I can warm you up."

She whirled, banging the hod against the fireplace and scattering chunks of coal across the carpet.

Charles Kemper rose from his chair and moved to the side, cutting between her and the parlor door.

"I thought you were out of the house." She knelt and began gathering the coal before Mrs. Hinchey poked her nose into the room and saw the mess. Dark streaks of dust marred the rug. Maeve sighed, even while she kept an eye on Charles. At this rate, she'd wind up skipping lunch to scrub the carpet, not to send her telegram.

"I think we've played enough games, Maeve O'Reilly." Charles closed the pocket doors, shutting them into the parlor.

Maeve abandoned the coal, leaping to her feet. "Mr. Kemper, please open the doors. I've told you I am not interested. I must insist you leave me alone." Panic grabbed her windpipe, making it hard to force out the words. "If you don't, I shall be forced to scream for the butler."

"I've given Carson instructions to stay away." Charles advanced, and she darted to her right to put a marble-topped table between them. "Don't forget, if you scream, I'll say you are lying, and you'll be sacked. Mother will spread the word about town that you are untrustworthy, and nobody will hire you. What will you do then?"

"I'll go to the police."

"Ha, they won't take your word over mine, now will they?"

She edged behind a winged-back chair. "You forget, most of the coppers in this town are Irish. They might be inclined to take my word over yours."

Too late she realized her mistake. In taking the effort to reply to him, she'd boxed herself into a corner. A massive fern on a marble pedestal blocked her escape, and Charles had closed in from the other direction. Quick as a viper, his hand shot out and covered her mouth, even as he pressed her against the wall.

Squirming, with his breath hot on her cheek, she tried to push him away, but he was too strong. Hands scrabbling, she reached for anything she could find to defend herself. With a wild kick, she toppled the fern, but it fell to the carpet with a thud so dull, it wouldn't summon help. Her fingers closed over the top of a clock on the shelf beside her, and she gripped it, swinging it hard against Charles's head as he tore at her clothes.

The delicate wooden case shattered, and the glass over the dial exploded. Charles staggered backward, hissing a filthy slur. A cut on his temple cascaded claret-colored blood, and his eyes glowed with fury.

Maeve didn't hesitate. She bolted for the door. His hands scrabbled against her as she heaved the heavy oak door aside, and her sleeve tore as she jerked away from him.

Racing down the hall, she crashed into Mrs. Hinchey, shoving her aside in her haste. She didn't stop, bursting through the door that separated the servants' portion of the house, and pounded through the kitchen and up the back stairs to her room.

Chest heaving, she jerked open drawers and tugged out her few belongings, flinging them onto the bed.

The door burst open, and Maeve whirled. Somewhere along the way, she'd lost her cap, and her hair spilled over her shoulders. If he'd followed her up here, she was a goner.

But it was Belinda. Light-headed relief coursed through Maeve, and she sagged onto the bed, putting her head down.

"Oh Maeve, what did he do to you?" Belinda was on her knees at the bedside in a trice, running her hands over Maeve's shoulders, touching her torn sleeve, squeezing her hands, smoothing back her hair. "Did he hurt you?"

Maeve gulped, blinking back tears. "I'm all right." She wasn't, but she knew what Belinda meant. "He got the worst of it." As quickly as she could, she told Belinda what had happened. "I have to get out of here. I'm sacked anyway, but he's going to be in a towering rage. No telling what he might do."

"Where will you go? What will you do?" Belinda staggered to her feet, awkwardly dragging Maeve's battered valise from under the bed.

Maeve stood too, sweeping her Bible and hairbrush from the side table, gathering her nightgown and extra dress, stuffing them into the bag with chilly, clumsy fingers.

"I don't know." She had yet to be paid since coming to the Kempers, but she knew she would never collect the money owed her. Panic throttled her. What could she do? Where could she go? Tugging at her apron smeared with coal dust, dishwater, and the stink of being in contact with Charles Kemper, she heard a rustle.

"On second thought, I know exactly where I'll go."

❦ *Chapter 3* ❦

Late May

*K*aspar hated to be late, but in this case, it wasn't his fault. Why hadn't Miss Halvorg—he couldn't quite bring himself to call her Trudy yet—wired him sooner? He clucked to the horses. Lindsborg was twenty miles from Salina, a trip that took all day in the wagon.

Her telegram had arrived midmorning, announcing that she'd be on the afternoon train. The clerk must have edited the transmission, because it wasn't the disjointed communication he'd come to expect from Miss Halvorg. The grammar and vocabulary were easily readable.

Warm spring sunshine beat down on his back as he hunched over the reins. He should be in the fields sowing oats or checking on his winter wheat, which stood four inches high already and was a vibrant green. He should be close by before Dolly, his favorite mare, foaled. There were lambs coming, two cows recently calved with one more to go, and the repairs to be made to the barn and outbuildings after winter. He shouldn't be wasting two days going to Salina and back.

But this wasn't a job he could pass off to Edvin, his hired man.

Picking up a mail-order bride was something a man had to do for himself.

Kaspar took off his hat and wiped his brow on his forearm. Was it really hot, or was he sweating because he was going to meet her soon?

He wished he'd brought Grandmother along for company. The ride back to the farm was going to be awkward at best. Grandmother might have provided a good buffer. But the rattling of the wagon shook her up too much. If he had a buggy, he would've risked it, but better she stay at home.

Finally, Salina came into view. Bustling, busy, and several times larger than Lindsborg, the town held little appeal for Kaspar. Too many people made him uneasy. He preferred the silence and space of his farm, where he had his animals for companionship during the day and the restfulness of Grandmother in the evenings.

The town seemed more crowded than usual. As he drove north on Santa Fe, he passed under a banner being hung across the road. WELCOME, CATTLEMEN. Kaspar had read about the convention in the *Salina Journal* but, not being a cattleman himself, had taken little notice.

The wagon bounced over the rutted streets toward the depot, and Kaspar glanced down at his attire. He'd left home in such a hurry, he still had the mud of the barnyard on his boots and the dust of the haymow on his clothes. Perhaps he should've donned his Sunday suit. He looked like he was picking up a load of livestock feed, not a bride.

He shrugged it off. He was a farmer, and she knew it. If she wanted a city dandy, she shouldn't have answered his advertisement.

The train had been and gone two hours ago. He'd have to apologize first thing, which irritated him. Nothing about this situation had gone the way he had thought it would, and now he would be starting off on the back foot with his prospective bride. He wrapped the reins around the brake handle and leaped to the ground in front of the depot.

Clomping up the platform steps, he removed his hat and beat some of the dust off his clothes. His hair, stick straight, thick, and dark blond, resisted his efforts to smooth it down. He had a cowlick in front that defied attempts to get it to behave. As a result, his hair resembled the crest of a wave, and no pomade or wetting down would alter it.

Gathering his courage, he stepped through the open door into the waiting room, letting his eyes adjust from the blazing sun to the dimness of inside.

The place was empty. No stolid blond sat on a bench waiting for him. Had she missed the train? Had she grown impatient with his tardiness and set off to find accommodations for herself? Had she decided not to come after all? And was he disappointed or relieved?

"You Kaspar Sandberg?" A clerk appeared behind the metal grille at the ticket window.

"*Ja.*"

"Somebody waiting for you. I'll fetch her." He rounded the counter and headed for a door on the far side of the space.

Of course. She'd be in the ladies' waiting room. He should've known that. Kaspar gripped the brim of his hat, bracing his feet and taking a deep breath. His heart thudded against his flannel shirt.

This would either be a blessing or the biggest mistake of his life.

The clerk reappeared, followed by a bareheaded, tiny woman with fiery red hair. She kept her chin down, and he couldn't get a good look at her features, but this was nothing like the photograph Miss Halvorg had sent. Kaspar looked behind them toward the open door to the ladies' waiting room, but Miss Halvorg didn't emerge. A frown tugged at his face. What trickery was this?

"Here she is, one mail-order bride. She told me who she was and that she was waiting for ya to come pick her up." The clerk gave Kaspar a "lucky dog" grin and ducked back into his ticket cage, and Kaspar found himself looking down at the top of the woman's head.

Who was this? Where was Miss Halvorg? "Ma'am?"

"I know you weren't expecting me, but I was in a bit of a wee bind, and I had no choice but to come right away. I hope you don't mind." She spoke to his shirt front in a brogue so thick he could stir it with a spoon. Her knuckles showed white on the handles of her carpetbag, and a tremble went through her. She still didn't look up. Sunlight from the window streamed in, making her hair glow reds and oranges and golds. Beautiful, arresting even, but what woman traveled without a hat?

Kaspar could practically feel the clerk's quivering attention. Whatever the situation, he was reluctant to unravel it in front of a curious stranger. "Come." He took the bag in one hand—it was ridiculously light—and her elbow in the other, and guided her outside.

The moment they were outside, she drew a handkerchief from her sleeve, and he feared she might be going to cry. Instead of dabbing her eyes, she commenced to throttling the hanky. "Sir, please don't be angry. There was some mix-up at the newspaper, and the ticket you intended for a Miss Halvorg was sent to me instead. I meant to get it straightened out, but then I had to leave Boston in a hurry, and there wasn't time. I will reimburse you as soon as I am able, but that might take awhile because I have almost no money. . . ." The square of fabric took a mauling as the breeze teased a few curls from the knot at the back of her head.

He still hadn't gotten a good look at her face. Her hand came up, and with her little finger she hooked a curl and tucked it behind a perfectly formed ear in a purely feminine gesture that made his mouth go dry. Her bones were light and thin, delicate as a bird's.

"Who are you?" He felt as if he'd stepped off a forgotten stair in the dark. Because he had been expecting the sober-faced, rather plain Miss Halvorg, this woman with the vibrant hair and pale skin came as a complete shock.

"My name is Maeve. Maeve O'Reilly." She dug in her little purse and pulled out an envelope. "The *Matrimonial News* sent me your letter by mistake."

He took the paper and, glancing at it, recognized his handwriting. "If you knew it was a mistake, why did you come? Why not send the letter and ticket back?" He shook his head. "You know what, never mind. It can wait." He was going to have to undo this, and it would probably cost him more money. He'd have to pay for this woman to go back to where she came from, and he'd have to track down Miss Halvorg and pay for her to come here the way things should have happened in the first place. This is what he got for using that newspaper for his correspondence. Crumpling the envelope, he shoved it into his pocket and jammed his hat back on his head. What an anticlimax. He'd gotten himself all worked up to meet his bride, only to have an impostor show up instead. And now he'd have to do it all over again and waste even more time away from the farm. Women were more trouble than they were worth. Pleasing his grandmother was going to cost him a packet.

"Wait here." He pointed to the bench along the wall and dropped her valise onto the platform. She eased onto the bench, chin down, still hiding her face from him.

The clerk shot him an inquiring glance as he went back into the depot. "Yes?"

"When's the next train to"—he tried to recall where she said she'd come from—"Boston?"

The man's eyes widened. "It's a busy time here. Special trains coming in from the East full of cattlemen. There's a big convention in town, you know? Only thing heading the other way at the moment is freight. Won't be a passenger train east for a couple of days until we get all of the cattlemen through here."

Two more days? Wonderful.

"Where can I get a hotel room, then?" He needed to find somewhere to keep her for a while. He would get her a room, get her a ticket, and get her out of town.

"No rooms to be had, sir. Like I said, big convention in town. Anyway, don't you want to know where a preacher's house is first?" He waggled his eyebrows in a "nudge-nudge, wink-wink" way that set Kaspar's teeth on edge. Where was he going to park Miss O'Reilly until he could get her on a train if there were no hotel rooms?

The clerk clucked his tongue. "I'd want to make sure of a lady as pretty as that if she was my mail-order bride. I wouldn't want to chance her getting away."

Not only was she an impostor, but she'd blabbed to this clerk that she was his bride come to marry. That news would blow through town like a tumbleweed in a tornado, no doubt. He needed to send a telegram soon. Maybe, if he contacted the *Matrimonial News* and convinced them of their error, they would reimburse him for the train fare and get a message to Miss Halvorg quickly.

The clerk looked as if he wanted to say more, but Kaspar didn't give him the chance, nodding curtly and heading back outside. He shouldn't blame the man for being curious. If it was someone else in this predicament, Kaspar might be inclined to chuckle.

He didn't feel much like laughing now.

She sat on the bench, huddled and small, the picture of dejection.

Kaspar shoved down any feelings of sympathy. This quandary was of her own making. She should've sent the letter and ticket right back where they came from when she noticed the mistake. It wasn't his fault that she'd shown up unwanted. It would serve her right if he left her here. Though he wouldn't do that to any female, and not just because his grandmother would skin him for his hide and tallow. But the whole thing irritated him, the waste of time and money.

Then Miss O'Reilly looked up at him with enormous eyes bluer than the flag of Sweden. Freckles pattered her nose and cheeks, and her sweet bow of a mouth trembled. A jolt went through Kaspar akin to the one he'd gotten once when the clerk over at the telegraph office let him touch the electric wire that sent the messages. A little heat, a little pain, a little surprise.

The sort of response he'd hoped to have when he looked at the photograph of Miss Halvorg.

Hiding his reaction, he picked up her bag. "Come with me."

"Where are we going?"

This time when he took her elbow, the jolt hit him a bit harder. Pretty didn't begin to describe her, and he could understand the clerk's jibes.

"To send a telegram to the newspaper to see if I can get my

ticket and travel money back, and then I guess I have to take you home with me for a couple of days. There are no hotel rooms available in town right now and no trains back to Boston for a couple of days either. Some cattlemen's convention." He guided her to his wagon where his team of Belgians waited in the sun, heads down, resting, short tails flicking as they dozed.

She trotted at his side, and he realized his strides were too long for her to be comfortable. Her head didn't even reach his shoulder. He slowed and shortened his steps.

"I'm sorry to cause you so much trouble."

You should have thought of that before you used a train ticket you knew was meant for someone else. "Nothing we can do about it now. This is my wagon." Kaspar tossed her bag into the back and reached for her waist. He must have caught her by surprise, because she gave a little squeak as he lifted her up over the wheel to stand in the wagon box. Good thing she wasn't his real mail-order bride. One day of farmwork would wear a tiny thing like her right through. Light enough to blow away in an ordinary Kansas breeze, much less a high wind.

She settled on the seat and ducked her head. Her lips pressed together, and bless him, if a pair of tears didn't form on her lower lashes. And didn't that make him feel like a mean dog? Kaspar climbed into the wagon and took up the reins. Why was he feeling guilty? None of this was of his making.

She said nothing on the short drive to the telegraph office.

He pulled up in front of the small brick building. "Do you want to wait here, or do you need to send a wire to your folks, letting them know you're coming home?"

She shook her head. "I have no folks. I can't go back to Boston."

He wrapped the reins and pressed his palms into his thighs.

"Where will you go, then?"

She was silent for a moment, twisting her fingers together. Finally, in a voice so low he could barely hear it, she said, "Chicago, I suppose." She glanced up at him, the blue of her eyes startling him again. "I should send a wire to Mr. Heaslip. It was his advertisement I answered in the *Matrimonial News*. I sent a letter accepting his offer of marriage before I left Boston." She sighed. "He should have it by now. Perhaps he would wire the funds for me to go there from here."

Her tone held no joy, just resignation and perhaps a bit of weariness. She had traveled many hundreds of miles, so he supposed that was to be expected, but for the moment, he could only fasten onto her words with relief. Tension left his muscles. Someone else would take her off his hands. "Then let's get it done." He jumped from the wagon and reached up for her. She put her hands on his shoulders, and he swung her to the ground, light as thistledown. And he thought again that it was just as well she was destined for the city. She was too delicate for farm life. Trudy Halvorg would be better suited.

Maybe when he saw Trudy for the first time he'd feel that same zap of electricity he felt every time he met eyes with Maeve O'Reilly.

Maeve tried to tame her unruly hair, but the breeze seemed determined to have its way. She should've worn her hat, but in a fit of defiance, she'd tossed the thing away at the Boston railroad station. After weeks of being forced to keep her hair covered, she had rebelled. Now she felt exposed, and a bit foolish, as her hair uncoiled from its pins.

Mr. Sandberg might as well have been called Mr. Iceberg. He

was huge and frosty. Not that she could blame him. After all, he'd sent for one woman and gotten another one entirely, but still. Her need had been great, and he hadn't even let her explain it.

She followed him into the telegraph office. Wiring Mr. Heaslip should solve both of their problems. Mr. Heaslip would no doubt send the money for her to travel to Chicago, and perhaps the *Matrimonial News* would reimburse Mr. Sandberg, since it was their error that sent his letter to her rather than Miss Halvorg as he'd intended. Which would relieve her of the burden of trying to reimburse him out of funds she didn't have.

He stepped up to the window and took a sheet of yellow paper and a pencil, handed it to her, and took one for himself.

With quick slashes, he filled out his message, but Maeve dithered. What could she say in so few words? Then there was the matter of the cost of the telegram. She only had a few coins left of the travel money Mr. Sandberg had sent, and that rightfully belonged to him.

Mr. Sandberg finished and handed his paper to the man behind the counter, who scanned it quickly.

"Well, wouldn't you know it?" The telegraph operator's bushy brows rose. "Here I was just getting ready to send on this wire down to Lindsborg for someone at your farm, Mr. Sandberg. You're Miss O'Reilly?"

Mystified, Maeve nodded.

"This just arrived for you." He tore a sheet of paper off a tablet. It was from Belinda.

WIRE ARRIVED FROM MR. HEASLIP. QUOTED HERE:
"NO NEED TO COME. HAVE RECEIVED MULTIPLE
OFFERS THROUGH THE MATRIMONIAL NEWS AND

ACCEPTED THE HAND OF MISS O'BRIEN. WILL MARRY
WITHIN THE WEEK. ALL THE BEST.

SEAN HEASLIP"

WHAT ARE YOU GOING TO DO? SEND WORD YOU ARE
ALL RIGHT.

BELINDA

The return address was for the Kemper house in Boston, so
Belinda hadn't left yet for her soon-to-be husband's home in Alabama. But what was Maeve to tell her? She now had nowhere to
go and no money to get there. Mr. Heaslip had married someone
else while courting her via mail, and he would not be sending any
fare to bring her to Chicago. The room began to spin, and darkness
edged her vision.

"Miss?" A strong hand grabbed her elbow and tugged her
toward a chair.

Mr. Sandberg squatted before her, so tall his eyes were level
with hers as she sat. He took her hand and chafed it between his.
He had calluses that spoke of his hard work, but then again, so did
she. Dishwater, scrubbing brushes, and mops left their marks as
much as pitchforks and ax handles.

"Is it bad news?" he asked.

She shook her head. Mr. Heaslip was her problem, not his. "Just
a message from a friend. It must be all the travel that made me feel
faint."

He stared at her for a few long moments, and she wondered
if he knew she was keeping something from him. Finally, pushing
himself upright, he went to the counter. "Send my wire. If a response
comes, send it to Lindsborg. They'll get it to me at my farm."

Useless to send word to Mr. Heaslip now, the cad. With a slow hand, she filled out the telegram form on her lap, sending a wire to Belinda to let her know she had arrived safely and would write to her in Birmingham as soon as she found a place to settle. It was all Maeve could think to do, and she didn't want Belinda to worry. If Mr. Sandberg thought she was sending the telegram to Chicago, that was fine. He didn't need to worry about her either. She just needed a few days to figure out what to do and where to go.

Before Maeve knew what to think, they were back in his wagon, heading out of town. Everything that had seemed a good idea back in Boston now seemed incredibly brash as she set out for an unknown destination with an unknown man.

Almost immediately the houses gave way to open prairie that seemed to go on forever. Blue sky stretched from horizon to horizon in a manner she hadn't seen since her ocean voyage from Galway. The land was flat as a stove lid, and while some areas were clearly pasture, other great blocks of it were the bright green of some crop she didn't recognize.

"What is that growing there? It's green as a shamrock."

"Wheat. Winter wheat. Planted last year, wintered over, and just starting to head out. We'll harvest it in June." Mr. Sandberg slapped the reins against the horses' rumps.

She shaded her eyes with her hand, squinting against the glare of the sun. "How far is it to your farm?"

"Nearly twenty miles. It will be good and dark before we get there. Where's your bonnet?"

The question caught her off guard, and she blinked. "I don't have one. I don't like them."

With a swift motion, he removed his own wide-brimmed hat and dropped it onto her head. "Well, you need one out here. Your skin's so fair, you'll be the color of a rooster's comb without one."

The hat was large, but with all her hair, it actually fit quite nicely, and the shade it provided instantly cooled her face. She must look a perfect goose. And yet the gesture wasn't lost on her. He might be gruff and distant, but he was looking out for her.

By the time they reached his farm, well after dark, she was worn right through. All that train travel, on top of anxiety about both what she was fleeing from and what she was rushing toward had taken their toll. She felt as energetic as a used dishrag.

Mr. Sandberg drove straight toward a huge, square silhouette against the indigo sky. The barn was immense, nothing like the small stone structures of her native Ireland. Something moved beside the door, and Maeve realized it was another man.

"Evening, Boss. Thought I'd wait up for you. Evening, *Fru* Sandberg."

"She's not Mrs. Sandberg." He jumped down from the wagon seat. "Can you take care of the team, Edvin? It's been a long day. I'll see you for work in the morning."

Maeve, tired as she was, could tell Mr. Sandberg didn't want to have to explain her presence. Not that she blamed him. What a ridiculous position she'd put him in.

He guided her toward the house, where not so much as the light of a single candle showed. Was she supposed to stay here, with a strange man?

He halted when she tensed up.

"My grandmother lives here with me. Your virtue is safe."

She relaxed a fraction, grateful for the darkness that hid the red in her cheeks, and continued up the steps and into the house.

He scraped a match and lit a lamp. "Grandmother's long asleep, I hope. You can meet her tomorrow. I'll show you to one of the guest rooms." Leading the way up the stairs, he paused at the first door, opening it and putting the lamp on the bureau beside the doorway. "Good night, miss."

The door closed, and his footsteps sounded down the hall, followed by the sound of his own door closing.

Lamplight created shadows in the room, but she was too tired to inventory the furnishings.

She leaned back against the wall and realized she still had on Mr. Sandberg's hat. Dragging it off, she closed her eyes and let the tears fall.

Maeve rose with the sun, surprised to feel refreshed and more optimistic than she had the night before. What was it about the dark of night that made all your troubles seem twice as formidable?

Oh, she was still in a mess of her own making, but for some reason, the light growing on the horizon filled her with hope and possibilities. She'd heard it said that when God closes a door, somewhere He opens a window. She would put her faith in God, and she would do the next thing, whatever that was, that lay before her.

And for the moment, the next thing was to get up, dress, and see how she could make herself useful for the few days she was here.

She found her way downstairs, but the kitchen was empty and the stove cold. Had no one else gotten up yet? The porch door was open, and she looked out through the screen toward the barn.

Mr. Sandberg, sans hat, carried a pair of buckets out of the barn and disappeared around the corner. It must be his custom to do the morning chores and then return to the house to eat before digging into the day's work.

Maeve turned to survey the kitchen. While it wasn't filthy, it could use a good, deep cleaning. She could be of some use here. But breakfast first.

Soft footsteps sounded overhead. That must be the grandmother. Hopefully, she wouldn't be put out to find Maeve cooking in her kitchen. Maeve went into the small pantry to see what she could find. Pleased with the full larder, she gathered ingredients for a hearty breakfast.

Mr. Sandberg, his grandmother, and the hired man Maeve had met briefly the night before all arrived in the kitchen at the same time. Maeve gave them her brightest smile as she set a platter on the table. Mr. Sandberg had his sleeves rolled up, baring his muscular, suntanned forearms, and around his collar were damp patches where he'd washed at the pump outside. His hair rose and fell over his forehead in a wave.

"Morning."

"Who is this?" The tall, slender woman with snowy-white hair leaned on the back of a chair and peered at Maeve, blinking in an unfocused way that made Maeve wonder how good her eyesight was. "She looks nothing like her picture."

"Grandmother, this is Miss O'Reilly. There was a bit of a mix-up with the newspaper, and they sent her instead of Miss Halvorg." He sniffed the air. "And evidently, she can cook, if that tastes as good as it smells." His eyes met hers, and Maeve's cheeks warmed. She'd done the right thing by starting breakfast.

"Please, call me Maeve. It seems silly to stand on ceremony after last night." She had only been thinking about their encounter at the depot and the long ride to the farm, but the moment the words were out, she realized how they could be construed, and heat charged into her cheeks.

His grandmother's gaze sharpened, and she straightened her

bowed back, eyebrows raised.

Mr. Sandberg sighed, pulling back his chair and dropping into it. "Don't panic, Grandmother. We didn't do anything drastic like get married. There are no trains heading east for a couple of days and no hotel rooms in Salina, so I brought her home. I'll take her back the day after tomorrow, and she'll be on her way."

Maeve tucked a rogue curl behind her ear, swallowed, and picked up the skillet to slide the ham steaks she'd fried up onto a plate. On her way the day after tomorrow. But to where?

"I hope you don't mind, mum, that I made breakfast." Maeve waited until everyone was seated to see where she should sit at the table.

"I never complain when someone else does the cooking. And call me Svea, or even Grandmother." The white-haired woman smiled at her. "I can see you've got some of what around here they call 'gumption,' jumping right into the work. A good thing, I think." She had the same hint of a Scandinavian accent that her grandson had.

Mr. Sandberg said grace, and he and Edvin tucked into the food. After a couple of bites, the hired man said, "Boss, if you are not going to marry her, I tink I vill." Then he blushed to the roots of his hair, dropping his chin and staring at his plate as Mr. Sandberg's brows shot upward. "Vell, it is good food."

Svea laughed, her voice light as a girl's. "That it is. Better than mine has been of late."

Maeve noticed that Svea's hands were gnarled and bent, and that she held her fork and knife carefully. Age had left her skin wrinkled and tissue-thin, her back hunched, and her eyes the clouded blue of a stormy sky, but her smile was quick and her laugh easy. Maeve would have no problems with Svea over the next couple of days.

Mr. Sandberg reached for another biscuit, dousing it with ham gravy. He looked at her with a bit of puzzlement in his eyes, as if he didn't know what to do with her. She sensed she could have trouble with him. She studied him while trying not to appear to do so, peeking from beneath her lashes, inventorying his broad shoulders, large hands, blunt features. Everything about him was masculine and spoke of stability and hard work. Though his coloring was the same as Charles Kemper's, they were as alike as chalk and cheese.

Before they finished breakfast, a rider galloped into the yard and knocked on the door.

"Telegram for Kaspar Sandberg." The blond boy slid a yellow envelope out of his pocket. Kaspar rummaged in a jar on the sideboard for a coin, opened the door, and exchanged the money for the envelope.

As he read the paper, his shoulders slumped.

"What is it?" Svea asked.

"The newspaper won't refund my money. They say they'll send along a message to Miss Halvorg free of charge if I want, but that's all they can do."

Guilt swamped Maeve. She had cost him money that wouldn't be refunded. At the time, it had seemed like Providence, but what now? How was she going to repay him when she had no job, no home, and no prospects?

Svea tapped her chin with her finger. "What are you going to do?"

Kaspar folded the paper and tucked it into a drawer in the sideboard. "I'm going to move the cattle to the river pasture, and then I'm going to work with the colts. Edvin, you finish the repair to the mower. The way the hayfield is growing, we'll need it before long."

Edvin grabbed one last biscuit off the plate and nodded his

thanks to Maeve without meeting her eyes. "Ma'am."

When the farmworker had gone, Svea clicked her tongue. "That isn't what I meant, and you know it."

"I know." He picked up the hat Maeve had brought down from her room and hung on the rack beside the door. Dropping a kiss on his grandmother's head, he gave Maeve a small, two-fingered wave, and headed outside. "See you at dinner."

Maeve hurried after him with the idea that had sprung into her mind like a rocket. "Mr. Sandberg, wait."

He stopped on the bottom step and turned toward her. "Yes?"

With her standing on the top stair, they were eye to eye. He had hazel eyes that looked as if they might change color with whatever he was wearing. Today, with his light blue shirt, they looked gray. Yesterday, she had thought they were brown. He smelled of hay and sunshine, and he had fine lines beside his eyes as if he spent lots of time outdoors.

He shifted his weight, and she realized she had been staring. "Sir, about our situation. . . I'm sorry the newspaper won't give you a refund. I—I want to pay you back. Please. I'm a good housekeeper, and I can cook, as you saw. Let me work for you until I've paid the debt. Or until Miss Halvorg arrives." She knotted her fingers together, her heart beating fast. If she could just get a bit of breathing room to figure out where to go next, it would make all the difference. And if she could work off the ticket money she'd spent, and perhaps work a bit more to save up some money, she could find her way out of this mess.

When he didn't respond, her heart fell. "Mr. Sandberg?"

"Kaspar."

"Pardon?"

"My name is Kaspar. Call me that."

"Very well, Kaspar." She tasted his name on her tongue. It suited him. Strong, solid. "You are looking for someone to take care of your home and look after your grandmother. I can do that."

His brows came down. "I do not think that would be a good idea. Any woman who lives here needs to be able to work hard every day from sunup to sundown, and sometimes beyond. She needs to be strong and hardy, not a tiny little thing like you. Not to mention Lindsborg is a town of Swedish immigrants. You wouldn't know what to do with them, and they certainly wouldn't know what to do with an Irishwoman. And you are from the city. This farm is a long way from town. The closest neighbors don't even speak English. After about three days, you'd miss your city life, and you'd be miserable. That's why I advertised for a Swedish woman who knew how to work a farm."

Maeve clenched her fists, heat zipping along her skin. "So Kansas is no different than Massachusetts. Just because I'm Irish, no one will give me a chance." She stepped closer to him and poked him in the chest. "I'll have you know I might be small, but I can work any Swedish farmwife under the table."

He backed up a step, and his hand came up to cover the spot she'd jabbed.

Frustration and desperation fueled her anger. She stepped off the porch to stand in front of him, looking up—way up—into his startled eyes. "I left Boston hoping that the open prairie might mean open minds. My father, God rest his soul, thought America would be the land of opportunity, and apparently it is, as long as you're not from Ireland. We might as well have stayed in Galway if we only wanted to be mistreated by people who thought themselves our betters." This time she prodded him in the chest with both index fingers. Tears pricked her eyes, and she blinked hard, struggling to hold on to her anger, knowing that if she gave in to the hopelessness, she'd break right down and bawl.

His huge hands came up and covered hers, trapping them against the broad cotton front of his shirt. Warmth seeped through the fabric and into her palms. His heart thudded gently against her fingertips.

"Calm yourself. I meant no offense. My refusal has less to do with you being Irish than not being Swedish." He still held her hands captive in his, and this close, she could smell anew the scents of hay and biscuits. His size dwarfed her, but she felt no fear. Perhaps it was the patient kindness in those hazel eyes that looked down into hers. "Have you ever lived on a farm?"

"No." She shook her head. "My da dreamed of coming to America and having a place of his own, but ocean passage was so expensive, all his money was gone by the time we reached Boston. We both had to get jobs just to live, and then my da died. I've lived in Galway or Boston my whole life, but that doesn't mean I can't learn."

He tilted his head, his brows lowering and eyes narrowing. "Just to be clear, what is it you are asking of me?"

Heat flashed through her, and she swallowed, pulling away from him. "Not marriage." She shook her head. "Just a chance. Let me stay. . .for thirty days. If I work for you as a housekeeper for thirty days, I will have paid you back the passage money that brought me here, and I'll have had time to be sure of where I want to go next. I'll work hard, I promise, and you can write to your Miss Halvorg and get everything straightened out. When she comes, I'll go without a fuss."

Mr. Sandberg studied her, stroking his chin. "Thirty days as a housekeeper. Nothing more?"

Again warmth bloomed in her cheeks, and she crossed her arms. "Not a single thing more."

"You will stay until I can get Miss Halvorg here?"

Hope fluttered along her skin. "Yes. I'll cook, clean, wash laundry, whatever you need done."

Still he hesitated. "You don't look very strong. The work is hard."

Her spine stiffened, and she squared her shoulders. "I'm stronger than I look. I've been doing hard work since I was a child at my mother's knee."

His lips twitched. "We'll see. I think thirty days would be enough to pay what you owe. And your Mr. Heaslip can send you money for a ticket to Chicago. And thirty days should be long enough to make arrangements to bring Miss Halvorg here. If you last an entire month." He sighed. "We'll give it a try. Until we hear from Mr. Heaslip and Miss Halvorg, you're hired."

Touching his fingers to his hat brim, he turned and headed to the barn. Maeve didn't know whether to be more relieved or frustrated. He didn't think she was up to the work? Well, she'd show him.

❧ Chapter 4 ❧

*K*aspar hadn't meant to throw down a gauntlet, but that seemed to be the way Maeve took it. At the rate she was going, she wouldn't last a full week—she might not last the forty-eight hours he had thought she would be there in the first place.

First it was the kitchen. Yesterday she served lunch out on the porch, and he had to eat his meal leaning on the railing because she'd scrubbed every inch of the floor inside and wouldn't let farmyard boots in until it dried. And in the afternoon, she'd hauled bucket after bucket of water from the pump to the wash pots she'd set up in the backyard. Several baskets' worth of clothes decorated the clotheslines in the hot sunshine.

Between washings, she found time to help Grandmother wash her hair and to set her up near the washtubs with a basket of yarn to wind into balls.

Dinner last night had proven that Maeve O'Reilly's cooking skills went beyond the one breakfast. Kaspar had made rather a pig of himself, downing biscuit after biscuit so light they might float up into the air at any minute. Mr. Heaslip up in Chicago wasn't going to want for a good meal when he finally married Maeve.

Kaspar jabbed at the last pile of hay in the mow, driving the tines of the pitchfork deep into the mound and lifting it up to carry it to the door. The first cutting of the year would start soon, and he wanted all the old stuff out of the barn and the entire haymow swept and ready.

Tossing the old hay out into the wagon waiting below, he searched the landscape for Maeve, and sure enough, there she was, sunlight glinting off her red hair, bent over a scrub board in the backyard. As if washing every stitch of clothing in the house wasn't enough, today she'd started in on the sheets, towels, quilts, and even the curtains. Grandmother sat nearby, in the shade of the house, a bucket at her side and a bowl in her lap, shelling peas.

A feeling of contentment seeped into Kaspar. This was part of what he'd envisioned when he'd thought of taking a bride. Turning the house into a home, a companion for Grandmother, good meals, a friendly smile at the end of a long day.

When he contacted Trudy Halvorg and brought her here, would she make him feel the same way?

Maeve straightened from the washboard and pressed her hands against her lower back before swiping at her brow with her forearm. She still wore no hat or bonnet, though the sun was fierce today and her skin fair.

Leaning the pitchfork up against the wall, he stepped onto the ladder and climbed down. They could both use a break.

It was a matter of a minute's detour to hold a clean pail under the trickle of water coming from the windmill pump.

"Afternoon." Kaspar offered Grandmother the dipper first. "Thought you could use a cool drink."

"Thank you, my boy." She took a small sip, cradling the dipper with trembling hands. "Maeve, come rest for a moment. You're working too hard."

Maeve dried her hands on her apron and tossed her thick red braid over her shoulder. Curls had come lose and framed her face in a vibrant halo. Her cheeks were pink, whether from exertion or sun, he couldn't tell, but her skin seemed to glow.

"Ah, ye must be reading my mind. I was perishing for a cold drink." She took the dipper and tipped it up. Watching her slender throat made Kaspar's heart kick up like a spring colt, and he looked away, wiping his palms on his trousers.

"I thought you might like to see the barn and animals once you've had a rest." He didn't know what made him say that. He hadn't even been thinking it. Still, if she was going to be here for a few weeks, she might as well get the lay of the land.

She tilted her head, her blue eyes alight. "That will be a true adventure since I've always lived in the city. If I'm telling the truth, I'm a bit afraid of animals. Big ones, that is. I had a cat once, in Galway, but she was a bit of a snob and none too friendly. Would rather be out hunting than curled up by a fire."

Afraid of animals? Kaspar tamped down the unexpected disappointment. Animals were his life. Horses, cows, pigs, sheep, chickens. He couldn't imagine a life without daily contact with his animals. Yet another reason why she would be better off back in the city.

"You don't have to come see the barn if you don't want to."

When Trudy got here, no doubt she would be able to take over the feeding of the chickens and the milking. As a farm girl herself, she had probably never been afraid of an animal in her life.

"I'd love to see it." Maeve let the dipper plop back into the pail. "No time like the present. I'll let those sheets soak for a bit. It won't hurt them. Do you want to come, Svea?"

"No, child. I'll just finish these peas and maybe have a doze here in my chair. When you get back, we can start planning the garden. Peas is about all I got planted this spring, and though it's late, we can still grow a few things this year." She slit another fat pod, dumping the peas into the bowl and the pod into the bucket at her side. "It feels good to be of some use."

Kaspar remembered to shorten his steps as Maeve fell in beside him. He wasn't certain whether to offer his arm or not. He wouldn't mind, but now that they were partway there, it seemed awkward.

"I love how open it is here." She turned her face to the breeze. "You can see so much horizon. I missed that in Boston. In Galway I could stand on the shore and look out for miles and see the edge of the sky. On my half day off, I'd walk down to Ballyloughane Strand and listen to the cry of the seabirds, breathe the air fresh off the sea, and dream about coming to America with my da. When we got to Boston, it was buildings and people and trees and hills everywhere. The house where I worked was far from the harbor, and even there, there were ships and docks and warehouses. I couldn't get to a bit of open shore. No place to breathe and be alone. No open spaces."

"If you like open spaces, Kansas has plenty, but no seabirds or salt air. Grandmother used to say the open spaces here made her sad. She missed the forests and steep hills of Sweden."

"I suppose you always miss where you come from. But America was my da's dream. He wanted to move west, to have a place of his own. All his life he worked for someone else, paid rent, never owned much. We scrimped and saved until we had enough money to come to America, but when we got here, there wasn't anything left of our savings. We had to take jobs in Boston. He went right into a shoe factory there, and I went into domestic service. It was like we'd never left Ireland, except that Americans seemed to think we were worse than dirt for being Irish."

"America was your father's dream. Was it yours?" If she was homesick for Ireland, would she ever settle in America, even in a city?

"It was his at first. Now it's mine. When he died, I promised I would carry out his dream. To get out of Boston, to make something meaningful out of my life. To be a true American."

"And you think you can do that in Chicago with Mr. Heaslip?"

Her lips pressed together, and she shrugged. "Are all barns in Kansas this large?"

He frowned at the change in subject. Kaspar had noticed that she hadn't mentioned Mr. Heaslip at all over the past few days. Then again, he hadn't mentioned Trudy aloud either. "Not all. Depends on what you want the barn for. We have animals, crops, and hay on the farm, and there has to be a place to store them. Come, meet Röd. Her name means 'red.' She is inside today because she's due to calve soon. The rest of the animals are outside."

Kaspar breathed deeply of the scents he knew and loved. Hay and dust and animal. At the same time, he noticed Maeve wrinkling her nose at the earthy smells.

Röd stood in the box stall, placidly chewing her cud, her sides pleasingly round and her dark eyes liquid and languid. She came over to have her head scratched, and Maeve backed up a few paces. "Does she bite?"

He didn't laugh, though he wanted to. "She's very gentle and very friendly. You can pet her. She's never so much as kicked the milking stool." He scratched behind the cow's ears and along the top of her head where he knew she liked it. Röd practically leaned into him, her long lashes lowering slowly. "She's spoilt. I bottle-raised her, and she's more of a pet than anything. This will be her second calf."

In the shaft of light from the open barn door, he noted how the freckles stood out on Maeve's nose and cheeks. Tentatively, pulling back a couple of times, she reached out and touched the cow's cheek.

"She's warm."

Her palm flattened against Röd's furry neck, and she stroked her lightly. For a fleeting second, Kaspar wondered what it would be like if she should draw her fingers across his skin. He shifted his weight, fighting down a blush at such a thought.

"This side of the barn is for the cows. Horses are on the other side. Mostly they live out, but I bring them in during bad weather. And the cows come inside for milking of course." He jammed his hands into his pockets lest he do something foolish like twine one of those red corkscrew curls at her temple around his finger. "Come see the other animals."

He led her outside past the pigpen where the sow lay on her side, eight round little porkers nursing like they'd never been fed before. Maeve winced at the smell of the sty, and he didn't blame her. Pigs were especially pungent.

"The cow pasture gate is here. There are three milking cows, three yearlings, and this year's calves. The calves are in a pen on the other side of the barn."

"Not with their mothers?" She held her skirt hem up out of the dirt, and he caught sight of a trim ankle and a flash of petticoat lace.

"No. If we kept the calves with their mothers, the calves would drink all the milk and we'd have none to sell. We separate them and get them bucket feeding as quickly as we can."

Maeve stopped, her hem dropping. "That's terrible. Taking a calf from its mother so soon? The poor little things." Her brows came down, and her eyes accused him of cruelty as her hands went to her hips.

"It's not cruel. It's normal dairying practice." He shrugged. She really didn't know the first thing about farming. "Come see the calves."

Kaspar ducked into the barn and came out with a pail of bran he'd soaked overnight. The calves weren't due to eat this until their evening feed, but it wouldn't hurt them to have it now.

"See, they're happy enough, especially since they have each other." The three calves, each about a month old now, were bright-eyed and shiny-coated, and they possessed healthy appetites. In another couple of weeks, he'd turn them out with the sheep in the smaller pasture, close to the barn where he could keep an eye on them.

He took her hand, trying to ignore the swirl of sparks that spiraled up through his chest at the contact, and placed some of the bran mash on her upturned palm. Standing behind her, he guided her to bend and offer the food to the calves. When the oldest calf swiped it up with his rough tongue, she gasped, looking over her shoulder at him, her eyes colliding with his. The bright blue hit him, and his fingers tightened on hers. They stood so close, he could see her individual lashes and count the freckles across her nose. Her hair captured the sunlight and threw it back with interest, lines of fire racing along the strands. His hand came up to touch the wispy curl that lay against her cheek, and in that instant, he realized what he was doing and stepped back so quickly he dropped the bucket of bran.

The calves rushed forward, and Maeve shrieked at the sudden movement from the animals, edging away as they bumped her legs to get to the food. She toppled into him in her haste to get away. His arms came around her, and instinctively, he swung her away from the calves, though she was in no danger.

You should let her go. She's fine. She's regained her balance. You should let her go.

The words repeated in his head, but for some reason, his hands didn't move. She fit perfectly into his embrace, her forehead level with his chin, so that if she turned her head slightly, she could tuck her face into the crook of his neck. He could smell sunshine on her hair and skin. His mind was a complete blank as it whirled and spun.

And then he did a thing he'd never done before.

He kissed her. Slowly, advancing in increments, he lowered his lips to hers, brushing lightly. At the first touch, he felt as if a bolt of lightning had gone from his crown to his boot heels, nailing him in place. It felt so amazing, he kissed her again.

Her lips were warm, soft, tentative, as if she didn't have much experience at this either. Warmth from her hands seeped into his chest, and he was a heartbeat from pulling her close and deepening the kiss when those hands pressed hard, breaking both the kiss and his hold on her.

His eyes shot open, and he beheld the shock in hers, the tremble of her fingers as they came up to touch her mouth. And he remembered.

Guilt smote him on two fronts. She was spoken for. She would leave here in less than a month to marry a storekeeper in Chicago. And he was spoken for—sort of. As soon as he sent the letter to Trudy inviting her to come.

He had never poached on another man's preserve. Maeve didn't belong to him, and he had no right to kiss her, to put his arms around her, to think of her in that way at all. And he owed something to the woman he was intending to propose to.

Should he apologize? He had to say something.

She backed up another step, then turned on her heel, head down, skirting the calves still gobbling the spilled bran, and headed toward the house.

Go after her. Apologize.

But he didn't. He watched her run away, absorbing the pain, knowing that if he didn't protect himself, when she left for Chicago she might take his heart with him.

You've got boiled potatoes for brains. Maeve set the platter of pancakes on the table with more force than she'd intended. *It's been an entire week, and you're still thinking about that kiss.*

When it had happened, she'd been too stunned to know what to do. She hadn't been able to think at all. But in the days since, she'd done nothing but relive it in her mind. And she'd begun to dream some impossible dreams, think some impossible thoughts. Scrambled thoughts and emotions, especially at night before she fell asleep when she had no chores to distract her.

Kaspar must not have thought it too important, because he'd said nothing about it, acting as though the kiss had never happened. But Maeve couldn't put it away that neatly.

Why had he kissed her? Was he just taking advantage of the

opportunity? A matter of convenience when he found himself embracing her?

Perhaps he was shy. The entire thing had happened so quickly, so out of the blue. Had it taken him as much by surprise as it had her? It hadn't seemed that way at the time. He'd been deliberate about it—had even kissed her again.

Was he regretting it, or did he get a bit light-headed when he remembered it too?

Or. . . Anxiety crowded her chest. Did he think she'd only pretended to fall so he would have to catch her? That she'd somehow orchestrated the whole thing to entice him?

Mortification made her eyes water at the thought.

Clearly the kiss hadn't affected him as it had her. He wasn't losing sleep, fretting, vacillating between bursting with happiness and writhing with shame and guilt.

Was it that she was Irish, and he thought she'd be of easy virtue, just as Charles Kemper had? But Kaspar had done nothing, made no advances, suggested anything improper, tried to corner her like Charles had. Nothing in his behavior had put Maeve on her guard.

Oh for pity's sake, it was just a kiss. Stop it. Your brain is like a waterwheel, turning and turning and not going anywhere.

But she couldn't put it from her mind.

If you don't try, you're going to be late with the breakfast, so stop shilly-shallying. She cracked eggs into the skillet, hearing the satisfying sizzle as they hit the hot surface.

Boots sounded on the front porch, and the screen door banged open.

Her heart leaped at the sight of him, as it had taken to doing recently, and she forced herself to appear calm.

"Morning." Kaspar flipped his hat onto the rack beside the door.

Edvin followed, chin down, glancing at Maeve from the corner of his eye as was his habit. He rarely spoke a word around her, but he was always kind in his quiet way. And appreciative of everything she cooked.

"Ma'am." The hired hand slid into his seat, sniffing the scents of flapjacks and sausages.

Svea emerged from the staircase, cane in hand, her white hair falling down her back. She carried her comb and hairpins, and Maeve winced. How long had she been waiting in her room for Maeve to come up and fix her hair like she'd promised?

"Oh, I'm so sorry." Maeve wiped her hands on her apron. "I'm rattling about like a pebble in a tin can this morning. I got distracted and forgot to come help you." And all because Kaspar Sandberg had kissed her. She really needed to grow up. She hurried over to Svea's chair, pulling it away from the table, and took the brush, stroking the snowy tresses, gently plaiting them and admiring their smooth texture that never tried to escape confinement like her own riotous curls.

"Grandmother, I'll pull the wagon up to the door right after breakfast. I've already loaded the wheat. Do you have a shopping list ready?" Kaspar slid several sausage links on his plate.

"We put one together last night." Svea handed Maeve the pins one at a time, keeping her head still.

Maeve inserted the final hairpin, checked the results, and set the brush on the sideboard. "There, you look a picture."

"Thank you, dear. I can't tell you how nice it has been to have you here." Svea patted her hand, her expression kind. "I don't know when the house has looked as good, nor the garden. I'm glad we're all going to town today so you can have a rest from all the things you do. You work too hard." She stood, and Maeve helped her place her chair at the table.

"I don't work too hard. I just do the work that needs doing." But she was glad to be going to town today. She needed to get away from the farm, to remember that her time here was temporary, that she needed to make a plan.

Kaspar said the grace and then looked up. "When we get to town, you can go to the depot and wire Mr. Heaslip. I'm sure he's anxious to hear from you. Surprised you haven't written him any letters since you've been here. Edvin offered to take them into town for you." Was that a warning note in Kaspar's voice, a warning not to read too much into a simple kiss, because he thought she was going to marry another man?

"You haven't written any letters to Miss Halvorg that I've seen either." Svea buttered her pancakes. "Time's going to get away from you. Maeve will leave in a couple of weeks. Then what will we do?"

Kaspar shrugged. "I'll get to it. I plan to write to her in a few days."

Guilt at not telling the truth about Mr. Heaslip nudged Maeve's conscience. They all still thought she was heading to Chicago to become a mail-order bride. But how could she tell them that her intended had married another? That she had no place to go and no money to get there? No, the humiliation would be too much. She would figure out something soon. In the meantime, she had a place to stay, a way of working off her debt to Kaspar, and a bit of time to find a solution to her predicament.

She glanced around the tidy kitchen, a domain she had come to love. It hurt to think of another woman coming in and making the room her own, cooking at the stove, washing dishes at the counter, looking out the window toward the barn to see if Kaspar was in view.

Breakfast lost its taste, and she set her fork aside.

A half hour later, Maeve was hanging up the dish towels when the wagon rolled up to the front yard. Kaspar drove, and Edvin sat on a board affixed behind the high seat. Svea came out onto the porch, her face framed by a becoming bonnet. "I didn't know you were coming, Edvin. How nice." Svea let Kaspar help her climb aboard.

"Yes, ma'am. I have a few errands." Edvin touched his hat brim.

Maeve dashed inside to grab her reticule—not that she had anything to put in it besides her comb and a few pennies—and skipped down the porch stairs, her heart suddenly light. *You're being a goose. Just because you're going to spend all day with Kaspar away from the farm is no reason to feel like bursting into song.*

Kaspar waited beside the wagon, and his big hands spanned her waist, hoisting her up over the side for the ride into Lindsborg. His face was so close to hers for an instant, that she could've reached out and given him a kiss on the cheek, but then the moment passed, and red bloomed hot on her face as she sought to take a grip on herself.

Edvin edged over to make sure she had plenty of room, and they were off. As far as she could see, fields spread out around her to the horizon. In the distance, a strange, solitary hill jutted up.

"What's that?" She pointed, in spite of it not being very ladylike.

"That's the highest spot around for miles. Legend has it the Spanish explorer Coronado made it this far north and camped around here." Kaspar spoke over his shoulder, and Maeve took time to study him. His braces crisscrossed his back, pinning his white shirt to his broad shoulders. He rode with his elbows on his knees, his boots planted against the kickboard, the reins loose in his hands. Everything about him was masculine and capable. "Don't know if it's true, but it makes a nice story."

It was difficult not to be jealous of the absent Miss Halvorg who would arrive sometime soon and marry this man. He was a hard worker, a good provider, kind to his grandmother, and a very good kisser—though she didn't have much experience to compare his kissing to, just Charles Kemper's nasty, squashy, forceful attempts. Kissing one of the calves in the barnyard would have to be better than kissing Charles.

A laugh escaped Maeve's lips, and she clapped her hand over her mouth. Heads turned, brows raised, and she shrugged. "I'm just happy, I guess."

Svea gave her a smile, her eyes sparkling. "There is nothing wrong with being happy on a beautiful day like this."

Lindsborg was smaller than Salina, where Kaspar had met her train. Fewer houses, and a single high street. . . No, they called them main streets here. It was Saturday, and there were lots of people out and about. Heads turned as they drove between the wagons parked in front of the stores. Maeve could feel their stares. Did they not get visitors here very often? Or did people know who she was and why she had come?

"We'll go to the mill first and drop off the wheat to be ground. We can pick it up on the way out of town." Kaspar drove the team through town. As they approached a large stone building, Maeve could hear the sound of water. Trees lined a riverbank behind the mill, and Maeve longed to walk under their shade. She hadn't realized how much she missed trees out on the farm. Kaspar had planted cottonwoods around the farmhouse, but they were only a few years old, not yet shading much of the house or yard. The summer sun was merciless, the temperatures soared, and the hot breeze did nothing to cool things off.

The mill was the tallest building in town. A large waterwheel turned slowly, giving power to the rollers that ground the wheat to flour. Thumps and slaps and bangs came from inside, and wagons stood tied to hitching rails. Men mingled, talking and unloading bags of grain.

Maeve became aware that the men had stopped working as the Sandberg wagon rolled up. They stared, some benignly and some boldly. Kaspar drew even with a chute on the side of the mill and wrapped the reins around the brake handle before jumping down. Edvin hopped over the side of the wagon and went to the back.

"Morning, Kaspar. Who is dat vit you?" One large man stepped forward to shake Kaspar's hand, but he never took his eyes off Maeve—or rather her hair. He didn't exactly leer, but his stare made her uncomfortable. For the first time in a long while, she wished she had her white maid's cap, or a hat or bonnet to cover her red curls. "Is dis de bride ve haff been hearing about?"

"Nope. Temporary housekeeper. Miss O'Reilly." Kaspar joined Edvin at the back of the wagon and slid a bag of wheat off and onto his shoulder, straightening under the weight, his muscles bulging.

"Velcome to Lindsborg." Another man approached, a grin splitting his face. "It is very. . .nice. . .to meet you." His Swedish accent was strong, and she had to concentrate to decipher the words. Blue eyes sparkled, and a shock of white-blond hair fell over his forehead. His cheeks were red, but she didn't know if it was from heat, exertion, or something else. She bowed her head toward him but said nothing. "You are not going to marry Kaspar?"

She shook her head, gripping her hands in her lap.

"Before you get your hopes up, Nils, you should know she's engaged to a Chicago shopkeeper. She's just here for a couple more weeks." Kaspar spoke loud enough for everyone to hear, and guilt and sadness made Maeve's lips tremble.

A man in an apron emerged from the mill, a coating of white dust on his face and hair. He spoke to Kaspar in what she assumed was Swedish, and Kaspar held up four fingers. Four bags of wheat to be ground into flour. They negotiated, and Maeve kept her attention on them, trying to ignore the stares all around.

Svea gave her a conspiratorial look and beckoned Maeve to lean forward. The older woman whispered, "They have not seen a beauty like you before. If the word gets out that you can cook too, they will be beating a path to the farmhouse. It is too bad you are engaged to Mr. Heaslip. I wish it was you that Kaspar had written to in the beginning." She sighed and turned around again.

Maeve shook her head. She wished it too. There, she admitted it. She wished that it had been Kaspar's advertisement that she had answered from the start, that he had been expecting *her* at the train station in Salina, that they had gone to a preacher and gotten married.

"Ma'am, if it is not too bold of me, I would be pleased to escort you around town today. I could carry your packages." A tall, thin man who looked to be about forty stood beside the wagon looking up at her.

"She has an escort, Martin." Kaspar climbed aboard the wagon before Maeve could answer. "I'll take care of her. See you boys later." He slapped the reins, turning the wagon. "I'll be back for the flour this afternoon, Arvid."

Edvin sat in the back of the wagon, his boots hanging over the end. Soon they were on the main street, drawing up in front of a store.

Kaspar helped Svea down first, but when Maeve rose, there

were two men standing on her side of the wagon, hands held up to assist her.

Blushing, confused, she shook her head and stepped over to the other side where Kaspar waited. She put her hands on his shoulders as he reached for her waist, and in a trice, she was on the boardwalk. Kaspar offered his arm, and she latched onto it gratefully.

He leaned down to whisper. "There aren't a lot of unattached females around here. That's why I put an advertisement in the *Matrimonial News*. And there aren't many red-haired girls between here and Topeka, I shouldn't think. None like you anyways."

His breath was warm on her cheek, and a thrill went through her. *Keep a level head, girl. You've caused him enough trouble, and he thinks you're engaged.* But perhaps—just perhaps, if she told him about Mr. Heaslip, that she wasn't engaged to anyone, he might ask her to stay.

Her heart tripped at the thought.

Perhaps tonight, if her nerve didn't fail her, she'd tell him. Explain to him about her intended groom marrying someone else and that she was free. It wasn't as if he'd sent for Miss Halvorg yet. Well, he had, but the letter and tickets had gone to Maeve instead, so Miss Halvorg wouldn't know that he'd proposed. If he wanted Maeve to stay, he could send a polite note of regret to Miss Halvorg, couldn't he? Tell her that he didn't think things would work out between them and wish her all the best.

The bell over the door jangled as he opened it for her and Svea, and as she stepped inside, she breathed deeply the scents of leather, spices, and candle wax. Tonight she would talk to him and tell him everything. Before he wrote that letter to Miss Halvorg.

All around her, people spoke in Swedish to one another, glancing her way, not unfriendly, just curious. She understood a bit of

Kaspar's desire to have a Swedish girl for a wife. Some items on the shelves were labeled in Swedish, and some foodstuffs and goods she didn't recognize. Still, she could learn. Being from Ireland instead of Sweden shouldn't keep her from becoming part of the community.

"Svea, do you have the list?" Maeve asked. She realized she still held Kaspar's arm, but she was reluctant to let it go.

Before Svea could answer, a voice boomed through the store. "Ah, Kaspar, I hoped you would come in today. Someone here is looking for you."

A man Maeve assumed to be the storekeeper moved around the counter, his big voice belying his small frame. He had a bald head, a black broom of a mustache, and a gold tooth in the middle of his smile. "You have saved me a trip to your farm later this afternoon. Come, my dear. This is Kaspar Sandberg."

He motioned to a tall, buxom woman whose face was almost entirely hidden by a sunbonnet. As she stepped forward, she pushed the bonnet from her head, revealing tightly scraped-back blond hair and a pink-cheeked face.

Kaspar halted, his mouth opening.

Svea gripped Maeve's arm, sucking in a breath.

Who was this woman?

Kaspar found his voice. "Why are you here? I mean, how. . . ?"

She spoke rapidly in Swedish, her hands moving with every word. Maeve caught "Trudy Halvorg" and "the *Matrimonial News*" in there somewhere, and her heart sank.

Then Miss Halvorg turned her gaze to where Maeve's hand rested in the crook of Kaspar's arm, her brows raised, her expression challenging. Maeve was rooted to the spot, aware that all of this was playing out in front of a roomful of people. She let her fingers slip from Kaspar's arm.

Miss Halvorg asked a question in Swedish, then switched to halting English when Maeve shook her head. "What is this?"

Svea squeezed Maeve's arm, then let go and approached Trudy. "Hello, I am Kaspar's grandmother." She spoke in English, slowly, and Maeve was grateful. "Perhaps we could take this somewhere with more privacy?"

Chapter 5

Kaspar felt he was walking through someone else's nightmare—but he knew it was his. For twenty-five years, things had been simple. Faith, family, and the farm. Nothing complicated, nothing emotional, nothing that wasn't straightforward.

Until now.

Two truths that he had been avoiding now stood before him: one a blond Swede woman, one a red-headed Irish girl.

"Let's go outside." The walls of the store had started to close in on him. Grandmother took Maeve's arm, sending him a penetrating stare over her shoulder as they headed for the door. Miss Halvorg drew her bonnet back up on her head, her chin high, and marched ahead of him out into the sunshine.

To Kaspar's disgust, a handful of shoppers followed them

outside. Edvin had just emerged from the newspaper office next door and stopped on the boardwalk, his mouth opening as he let a newspaper dangle from his fingertips.

"Boss?"

Kaspar ignored the inquiry, looking up and down the street for a place where they could get away from his nosy neighbors and sort this out.

The church.

He started that way, and when he reached it, he ushered his grandmother, his housekeeper, and—his fiancée?—into the quiet building, shutting the door on the rest of the townsfolk who had trailed along.

Pastor Harvick came down the aisle. "Mrs. Sandberg. Kaspar. What can I do for you?"

"We need a place to talk in private." Kaspar ran his hands through his hair and laced his fingers at the nape of his neck. How had he gotten to this place in his life? What was he supposed to say?

"I'll be in my office then." Pastor Harvick looked from one face to another, then gave a small bow, headed toward the front of the church, and slipped through a door behind the pulpit.

Miss Halvorg began to speak in Swedish, but Kaspar held up his hand. "Speak in English, please." It wouldn't be fair to Maeve otherwise.

Maeve was so pale, every freckle stood out on her skin, and her blue eyes were clouded as she gripped her hands at her waist.

Trudy pressed her lips together, her brow bunched. "Ven I did not hear from you, I wrote to the newspaper. Dey explained how your letter vid the. . .asking to marry. . .vent to de wrong lady. Dey feel bad, and dey giff me vere you live, so I come." She spread her hands, giving a shrug. "You did write to ask for me to come, yes?"

Kaspar's gut clenched even tighter. "Yes, I did."

"Den dat is fine. Ve get married." Satisfaction smoothed Trudy's face.

Grandmother cleared her throat. "I don't believe you should rush into anything. A little time to get to know one another would be wise, don't you think?"

Kaspar grasped this suggestion like a lifeline in a tossing sea. "Yes, that would be best. We don't want to move too quickly. After all, marriage is a serious business." Just how serious, he was beginning to understand. When he looked at Trudy, he felt nothing. Not a spark, not a quickening of his breath, not a stirring of his imagination.

None of the things he felt when he looked at Maeve.

"Where are you staying, Miss Halvorg?" Grandmother asked.

"I stay no-vere. I come to get married. I stay vid Kaspar." She spread her hands again. "I haff no place to stay."

Maeve stepped forward. "Kaspar, Miss Halvorg should go home with you. She has had a long journey, and she must be tired. You can make plans just as well at the farm. I am sure that Svea can pack my bag for me, and Edvin can bring it to me here in town."

"What are you talking about?" Pack her bag?

"I was only staying until Miss Halvorg arrived. You won't need both of us."

The thought of her leaving pierced his chest like an arrow. It felt like dropping a precious stone down a well and walking away.

"You must stay." He crossed his arms. "You still have two weeks of work you owe me. To pay for the train ticket you used."

Was that a flicker of relief in her eyes? Or wishful thinking on his part?

Grandmother nodded. "No one should do anything too quickly. We will finish our shopping and go home. Things will become clear at the farm, I am sure."

The ride home was awkward, to say the least. Edvin rode in the back, with Trudy and Maeve on the bench behind the wagon seat. Grandmother kept sending Kaspar inquiring glances, and he could feel the women's eyes on his back.

Maeve didn't wait for him to help her down, jumping lightly to the ground and gathering parcels to carry into the house. She acted like she couldn't wait to get away from him. Trudy put her hands on her hips, surveying the house—square, white, clapboard—and the barn—large, red, sturdy. The cows stood at the gate, ready to come in for milking. The unbroken colts whickered to the team. She seemed to be satisfied that the farm was prosperous enough, because she nodded and narrowed her eyes.

"I'll unload the wagon, Boss." Edvin had his hands shoved into his pockets. He'd said nothing on the way home, and Kaspar felt foolish and embarrassed looking into his hired man's sensible face. He couldn't imagine Edvin getting himself into such a ridiculous situation.

"Thanks."

Inside the house, Maeve moved briskly, putting away the food-stuffs they'd purchased. Kaspar held Trudy's valise. Her trunk was still in the wagon.

"Grandmother, will you show Trudy upstairs?"

"Certainly. This way, Miss Halvorg."

Kaspar didn't miss that Grandmother had not used Trudy's first name.

"I'll start dinner?" Maeve asked. "Is that all right?"

"Of course." Why would she ask him such a thing? She'd been

416

cooking every meal for the past two weeks.

"I vill help. I am good cook." Trudy stopped at the base of the stairs. "I come back soon."

Edvin had most of the wagon unloaded, and together he and Kaspar carried Trudy's steamer trunk upstairs. Kaspar felt as if he was escaping as he went outside to take the horses to the barn.

He checked first on Röd, who still hadn't calved. She calmly chewed her cud, not a care in the world. Edvin came to lean over the stall door. "What are you going to do now, Boss?"

"I don't know. It all seemed so easy back in the winter, when I first placed an advertisement. Post what you want in a bride, get an answer, bring the girl here, get married. Now I've got a fiancée and a housekeeper who both answered the ad, and I don't know what to do with either of them." He took off his hat and smacked his thigh.

Edvin blinked. "I meant, what do you want to do first, feed the horses or milk the cows?"

Kaspar imagined that his picture could be used to teach people what foolish looked like. Edvin must think him without wits at all. "I'll milk. You feed." He grabbed a pail from a hook and went to let the cows in.

When he couldn't delay in the barn any longer, Kaspar followed Edvin to the house for supper. Trudy stood at the stove stirring a large pot, a snowy apron covering her dress. The heat had flushed her face.

Grandmother sat in her rocking chair, her knitting needles clicking rapidly, but her mouth was pinched, and her nostrils had narrowed in an expression that Kaspar knew meant she was unhappy.

Maeve was nowhere to be found.

"She went out to check on the garden." Grandmother looked

toward the back door. "Why don't you go fetch her for dinner?"

What could he say to Maeve? What did he owe to Trudy? What did he owe to Maeve? What did he owe to himself?

She stood in the garden, bent to examine a bean plant. She'd been so excited this week when the beans, carrots, lettuce, and tomato plants had sprouted, reporting at dinner on each new leaf and stem. Her enthusiasm had made Kaspar chuckle. Planting a garden was part of the fabric of Kaspar's life, but to her, it was all new, and she reveled in it.

Her joy in the simple things in life made her very appealing. So appealing that he'd succumbed to the temptation to kiss her.

And hadn't been able to think of much else since.

She straightened, shading her eyes, looking at the horizon. Sunlight ran riot in her curls, and he wanted to touch them. When she'd first come, he'd cautioned her to wear a hat, but he liked that most of the time she didn't, that her hair was allowed to show in all its glory.

She turned and caught him watching her. Her hand dropped to her side.

"Time for dinner." Kaspar kept his distance. "How does the garden look?"

"Good, but I suppose you would know better than me. I was just thinking that I won't get to harvest most of these vegetables. I'll be long gone when things ripen." She navigated the row, dusting her hands.

"I thought you were going to cook supper." They fell into step to head back to the house.

"Too many cooks spoil the stew. Trudy wanted to make the meal. She needs to feel needed, to find her place here. Might as well start as you mean to go on."

Start as you mean to go on. And just how was he supposed to do that?

Maeve longed for the days before Trudy came. The harmony of the house was totally disrupted, but Maeve knew it was her own fault. If she had kept her wits about her and not fallen in love with Kaspar, the arrival of Trudy Halvorg wouldn't have meant anything to her.

As it was, they seemed to clash over everything. Trudy turned up her nose at Maeve's Irish dishes, flattening her lips into a hard line, crossing her arms, and shaking her head. She let Maeve know in subtle and not-so-subtle ways that she was not wanted or needed in the kitchen.

Stolid, hearty, Swedish fare appeared on the table.

Laundry, housecleaning, gardening—Trudy had her own way of doing all those things, and she took them over.

The only aspect of Maeve's life that remained unchanged was her relationship and responsibilities toward Svea. Kaspar's grandmother insisted that Maeve be the one to help her bathe, dress, and do her hair.

And she requested special treats only Maeve knew how to make. Asked her opinion on a shawl pattern she was knitting, asked for stories of Maeve's childhood in Galway.

Maeve sat at her dressing table, brushing her red curls, staring into the mirror. She would miss this room. It was the nicest place she'd ever lived.

At least she didn't have to witness Kaspar and Trudy canoodling and sparking. Kaspar seemed to find no time to be in the house these days, working from dawn until dark, bolting his meals and then heading back to the barn or the fields. Trudy wore a puzzled expression most of the time, as if she couldn't understand why a man would request a mail-order bride and then avoid her.

Maeve couldn't blame her. Not really. Trudy had certain expectations, and none of them were being fulfilled. There was another woman living in the house she thought would be hers, and neither of them knew what to do about it.

"Maeve, are you awake?"

Kaspar tapped on her door. She grabbed her shawl off the end of the bed to cover her nightgown and opened the door a crack. "What is it?" He'd never knocked on her door before.

"Röd has finally decided to calve, and I thought you might want to see."

Happiness shivered up her arms. He had thought of her. "I'll just be a minute."

"Meet me at the barn." He disappeared.

Soft lantern light greeted her as she stepped into the cavernous barn. Kaspar stood at the door to Röd's stall, and Maeve joined him. She'd dressed in a hurry, stopping only long enough to quickly braid her unruly hair into a long rope down her back. She didn't think she was squeamish, but she'd never seen an animal born before. She gripped the rough wood and stood on tiptoe to peer over.

Röd lay on her side, her neck stretched out on the straw, her sides working like bellows. She tensed, her legs sticking out straight, and she gave a low grunt. Maeve tensed too.

"She is doing well. I won't step in unless she needs some help. I like to leave them alone as much as possible." Kaspar's shoulder touched hers as he bent to whisper in her ear. Her breath caught in her throat, and she became aware that it was nearly midnight, and they were alone.

The cow strained again, and Kasper's hand covered Maeve's on the door. "Look, hooves."

From that moment, things moved quickly, and soon a red, wet, bewildered calf lay on the straw, legs splayed, eyes wide.

The new mama lurched to her feet, turning to nose her new calf. Maeve laughed when the baby shook its head, its ears flapping.

"It's so sweet. And smaller than I thought it would be." Maeve breathed in a deep breath at the wonder of a new life. "Is it a boy or a girl?"

"I'll check." Kaspar lifted the latch and opened the stall. "Come meet him or her."

Maeve followed a few steps into the deep straw, but before she could bend to greet the baby, Röd bellowed, stamped her hoof, and charged. Kaspar took the blow in the midsection, cannoning back into Maeve and sending them both sprawling into the barn aisle. Maeve hit her head on the hard-packed dirt, and all the air whooshed out of her lungs as Kaspar landed on top of her.

Quick as a match flare, he was on his feet, putting himself between Maeve and the angry cow. He shouted, waving his hands at Röd, and in the split second of the cow's confusion before she charged again, he slammed the stall door shut. Röd bellowed again, then was quiet.

"Maeve, are you all right?" He knelt beside her, and his face swam in her vision. She blinked against the pain in her head, her shoulder, and her hip. But more urgent was the lack of air. She opened her mouth, but no breath rushed in. She gulped, clutching at his arms, panic rising.

Then Kaspar did the unimaginable. He hit her.

He smacked her in the stomach, right under her ribs, and as if she'd just broken the surface after being underwater too long, her lungs sucked in fresh air, and she whooped.

"Easy, just relax. Breathe a bit." He pressed his hands to her shoulders, forcing her to be still. She took deep breaths, but her head still whirled with stars.

"What happened?" she croaked.

"I'm so sorry. I should've been more careful. Röd's always been so friendly, I never thought she would turn like that. Some cows do when they have a calf. They get very protective. She thought we were going to harm her baby."

Maeve struggled to sit, and his arm came around her to help her up. She closed her eyes, feeling wobbly, and found her head tucked into the crook of his neck. He stroked her shoulder. "Are you all right?"

She hurt all over, and her stomach was doing swoopy things, but none of that seemed to matter in the shelter of his arms. "I'm fine."

Remembrances of the last time he had held her came rushing back but were superimposed with the thought of Trudy. She pushed out of his embrace, scrambling ungracefully to her feet, her head protesting. Pressing her fingers against her temples, she fought to gain her equilibrium.

"Maeve?"

"I should go. Thank you for letting me see the baby born. Good night." She headed out into the dark, half afraid he would follow her, half afraid he wouldn't.

He didn't.

She made her way back into the house, body aching, head ringing. The clock was ticking, counting down the days until she would be free to leave here. Wherever she was heading, she knew she would leave her heart behind.

❧ Chapter 6 ❧

I should stay ho—here." Maeve caught herself just in time. "It's supposed to be a party for church members. I'll only be here another week." She drew a tea towel around the Irish soda bread she'd made that morning, much to the pinch-lipped disapproval of Trudy, who fashioned meatballs and stirred gravy as if her life depended on it.

"Nonsense." Svea tucked a dishcloth around the crock of corned beef and cabbage Maeve had cooked in a big stew pot overnight. "For the time being, you are part of the fellowship. Now go get yourself prettied up for the party."

Full of doubts, Maeve went to her room. She had nothing with which to really pretty herself up for the party. Her best dress was the black sateen she'd worn as a maid, an outfit she hadn't donned once since leaving the Kemper household almost a month ago.

Still, she could do something with her hair. Though it took ages, and her arms ached by the time she was finished, she was pleased with the results. Her red curls were piled and pinned into an attractive knot at the back of her head, threaded through with a blue ribbon that she thought matched her eyes rather well.

Her dress was a plain blue with dark blue buttons, collar, and cuffs, but it was clean, and she'd pressed it that morning.

With a shrug, she put down her hairbrush and picked up her gloves. If she had to go to this function, she would go with a smile on her face. Nobody would know her heart wasn't in it.

Trudy wore a beautiful dress the color of ripe grapes and a bonnet festooned with flowers. With her apron over her arm and a prim expression on her face, she marched ahead of Maeve out to where Edvin had pulled the wagon up before the house.

Kaspar clattered down the steps, and Maeve's breath caught high in her lungs. He wore a black, broadcloth suit, snowy shirt, and shiny black boots. He looked wonderful.

And off-limits. He was promised to someone else.

If only she had answered his advertisement first.

But she hadn't, and she firmly believed that God put fences around things for a good reason. Kaspar had to honor his promise to Trudy, and she wouldn't want him to renege on his word.

Still, it hurt.

On the ride to town, Trudy spoke only Swedish, and mostly to Edvin, who rode in the back with her and Maeve. Svea looked back over her shoulder often, a frown creasing her brow, but Maeve just smiled. If Maeve had found someone to speak her native tongue to, she'd probably talk nonstop for a week.

Wagons clogged the churchyard, and people greeted one

another, setting up tables beneath the cottonwood trees beside the river. Children ran and shouted, enjoying the hot summer day and the chance to be with friends. Svea and Kaspar were greeted again and again as he drove to a spot where he could park the wagon in the shade.

Several young men came to the wagon and crowded around, offering to help carry the foodstuffs and escort the ladies. Maeve found herself being led to the picnic area by a tall, thin man who stammered that his name was Hans, and he was pleased to meet her.

Maeve glanced back, surprised to find that Edvin was escorting Trudy, while Kaspar had Svea on his arm.

"Hello, Miss O'Reilly." Pastor Harvick greeted her. "I was hoping you would be able to come. I wasn't sure when you would be leaving us."

"Pastor. I'm here for another week." She nodded her thanks to Hans and let her hand drop from his arm.

"Then where will you be going?" the pastor asked.

Thankfully, Maeve was saved from answering by the arrival of Svea and Kaspar. "We should set out our food," Svea said. "The picnic will start soon."

Trudy was uncovering her dishes and sticking serving spoons into them. Maeve had to admit, they smelled good. She made quick work of unwrapping her bread and setting out her corned beef and cabbage, aware that her food looked nothing like the rest of the dishes on the long table.

"A nice feast, isn't it?" Svea set out her plate of cinnamon buns that she called *kanelbullar*. Maeve had helped her make them last night, and they'd had such fun together, Svea sharing stories of making the delicious buns with her grandmother in Västerås in

Sweden. When asked, Trudy just said that her family had lived on a farm outside of Stockholm, and that they had boarded a ship for America for a better life, but she didn't elaborate on either her family or the journey.

Svea had asked about Maeve's own ocean crossing, and a wave of homesickness for Galway hit her. "I miss the sea. I miss the salt air and the waves and the sunsets over the water."

She'd looked up, and Kaspar stood in the porch doorway, his eyes somber.

Maeve was jolted from her memories of the previous evening when Nils and Martin, whom she had met the previous Saturday, arrived at her elbows.

"We'd be pleased if you'd save the first two dances for us, Miss O'Reilly." Martin spoke for the pair of them.

"Dancing?"

Svea nodded. "After the meal and testimony time, there will be a dance."

Maeve loved to dance. What would it be like to dance with Kaspar? Did he dance? Would he ask her? She shouldn't expect it, or even desire it. Still, the prospect made her heart thump faster.

"That would be very nice. Thank you."

They bowed to her, grinning, and nodded to Svea and Trudy before heading over to a cluster of men under one of the trees.

"Miss O'Reilly?" Another man tipped his cap toward her. Why, why couldn't they leave her alone?

"Yes." She forced a smile.

"A letter arrived for you. Thought I'd bring it over." He handed her a fat envelope, and she remembered that he worked at the general store where the mail was delivered.

"Thank you." She glanced at the address, and her heart warmed.

It was postmarked Alabama, and the handwriting was Belinda's. "Excuse me."

She took the letter over toward the riverbank to read in privacy.

Dearest Maeve,

I hope this finds you well. This letter was sent by the Matrimonial News *to the Kemper home, and Mrs. Hinchey sent it on to me, since no one there knows where you went. I'm sending it on to the last address I had for you, in the hopes that it will reach you. Please write to me and let me know you got it and what Mr. Sandberg's reaction to your arrival was.*

Yours,
Belinda Davisson

Maeve took the letter Belinda had enclosed and opened it, her stomach tight. Her supposition was correct. It was from Mr. Heaslip.

Dear Miss O'Reilly,

The other mail-order bride didn't work out. Turns out she was only after my money, and I sent her packing before the wedding. If you're still interested, I'm ready to meet you. Will wire ticket money whenever you say. If you're not still willing to marry me, I will understand.

Sincerely,
Sean Heaslip

A weight lifted off her heart. She could tell Kaspar that Mr. Heaslip had released her from their engagement—sort of. He'd said if she didn't still want to marry him, he would understand. She was under no obligation, though Mr. Heaslip was still a single man.

But that didn't solve the issue of Trudy Halvorg. What a mess.

Maeve searched the crowd for Kaspar, and his eyes met hers. They held for a long time before Maeve looked away.

She was the most beautiful woman there.

Kaspar took a sip of his lemonade, wincing as the tartness hit his tongue.

"She said it would be nice to dance with me." Martin stuck out his chest.

"She vill dance vid me also." Nils blushed to the roots of his white hair. He was barely dry behind the ears, unlike Martin, who was nearly forty.

"You two do remember that she is engaged to someone in Chicago, right?" Kaspar set his lemonade on the table. The acid burned in his stomach. "And, she is a guest in my house." He sent a pointed look at the two of them.

"What is the old saying?" Martin asked. "Many times the cup slips between the cup and the lip?"

"Something like that, but not in this case. I'll be taking her to Salina and the train station a week from today." Kaspar crossed his arms and tried to appear as if his heart wasn't involved.

"And you will marry Miss Halvorg soon?" Martin asked. "She seems to be fitting in already."

Trudy did seem at ease. She spoke Swedish with the church ladies, sitting under a tree on a blanket and holding one of the Olsen babies, probably swapping recipes and housekeeping tricks. Just as Kaspar had imagined his wife would do when he placed his advertisement in the *Matrimonial News*.

Maeve stood off to the side, leaning against a tree, her plate forgotten in her hand, watching the water flow by, a wistful expression on her face. She'd done something different with her hair. It was all bound up on her head, and he found himself missing the less formal style she usually wore, the one that tempted him to thread his fingers through her curls and let them slip across his skin.

He took a grip on his thoughts. *Stop mooning and go get some food.* He went to the table, and as he arrived, Trudy was there to greet him.

"Have some meatballs." She held out a spoonful. "You vill like them. I am good cook."

"That you are, Trudy. Thank you." He took the meatballs. When he tore off a piece of the Irish soda bread though, her expression darkened. His chest felt heavy. He didn't know how those fellows in the Bible did it, having more than one wife. He couldn't even have a housekeeper and a mail-order fiancée in the same house without offending one or the other of them.

Not to mention his grandmother. She wasn't happy about the situation any more than he was. But what could he do? He'd asked Trudy to marry him via a letter that had gone astray, and here she was.

The music started, and people gathered around the area that had been smoothed and pounded for dancing. Martin took the plate from Maeve's hands and led her over. The dance was a *hambo*, and couples began the fast-paced pattern. Maeve, clearly unfamiliar with the steps, stumbled and stopped, started again, and faltered.

Shaking her head with laughter, she held up her hands in protest. "I will just watch for a while."

Martin looked downcast, but he shrugged and led her out of the way of the other couples. Kaspar's chest muscles loosened.

To his surprise, Trudy was dancing the lively hambo with, of all people, Edvin. Kaspar hadn't even known Edvin enjoyed dancing, but he was very good. Trudy's face was alight with pleasure, and for the first time, Kaspar thought she was a bit pretty.

The next dance was a *snoa*, and again, Maeve shook her head when Nils came calling. Nils nodded his understanding. Whatever she said to him must have placated him as it had Martin. The two men stood one on either side as she clapped along to the tune, and Kaspar couldn't help but admire her lively eyes and sweet smile.

Martin stepped up to the band leader and spoke into his ear, and with a nod, he began a waltz. Maeve went into Martin's embrace and swung into the dance, light on her feet. And when that dance ended, she performed a reel with Nils.

Trudy came to stand beside Kaspar, and he knew he should ask her to dance. It was the expected thing. The right thing. As he turned to her, however, when a polka began, Edvin arrived and got in first.

"Miss Trudy?" He held out his hand, and with a bemused look, Trudy took it, looking back over her shoulder at Kaspar before disappearing into the throng of dancers.

Maeve turned up at his elbow, her face flushed and her hair beginning to escape its pins and cluster in little curls around her face.

"Enjoying yourself?" he asked, just for something to say.

"It's more fun than I thought it would be. After people got over the horror of trying Irish food." She laughed. "I thought I would have to sit out all the dances at first, but thankfully, I do know how to waltz."

"The first two were traditional Swedish dances." Edvin stomped by with Trudy on his arm, his feet keeping time to the music. "I had no idea Edvin could dance like that."

"Or Trudy either. They make a nice pair out there." Maeve slipped a handkerchief from her sleeve and dabbed at her temples.

When the dance ended, Edvin delivered Trudy back to Kaspar's side and offered his arm to Maeve for the next song. "Ma'am?"

Kaspar fetched Trudy some lemonade. "You dance well."

"Thank you. Why are you not dancing?" She took the cup. "Do you not dance?"

He raised one shoulder. "Sometimes." He actually liked dancing, but the situation was too complicated today. If he didn't ask anyone to dance, he couldn't be accused of asking the wrong person.

Just as the sun was beginning to cast long shadows and Kaspar was thinking of rounding up his party and heading home, the band struck up a new tune: "The Irish Washerwoman." To his surprise, Maeve moved to the center of the now-cleared dance area and, raising her skirts a few inches, began a dance like he'd never seen before. The crowd clapped and cheered, and her feet flew, her cheeks pinked, and her eyes sparkled. The music went faster and faster, and finally, she threw up her hands with laughter.

"There you have it, an Irish jig. Thank you for indulging me."

Kaspar couldn't take his eyes off her.

But on the way to fetch the team, his friend Arvid, the mill owner, caught his arm. "A good day, ja?"

"Yes," Kaspar agreed. "Good weather, good food, good company."

"I am thinking that it is a good thing that you are to marry Miss Halvorg. She is like us. Good Swedish. She will fit in here with no trouble."

Yes, most likely she would. She knew the culture, the language, the food, the customs. She was exactly what he had advertised for.

And yet his heart yearned for the redhead who had shown up

unexpectedly and turned his life upside down.

Hours later, Kaspar couldn't sleep. He sat at the kitchen table in the dark, drinking coffee and brooding.

Lord, what should I do? Is it right to marry one woman when I am in love with another? Is it right to be in love with a woman who is pledged to another? I thought I was following Your will when I sent off for a bride to help Grandmother. Now I don't know what to do.

A creak sounded on the stairs, and he glanced up to see Grandmother, wrapped in her shawl, slowly descending. "You should be asleep," he said.

"So should you." She crept across the room and eased down into the chair beside him. "What is on your mind that is keeping you awake?" Her wrinkled hand came out to cover his, and he was comforted.

He shook his head.

"I think I already know. Maeve and Trudy." She tilted her head, her braid lying over her shoulder, and her eyes clouded. "What are you going to do?"

"I don't know. I know what I want to do, and I know what I think I should do, but they aren't the same thing." He turned his coffee cup in a slow circle. "I've been thinking of the pros and cons, weighing things up."

Grandmother shook her head. "I feel guilty. I know you only advertised for a bride because of me. And you took such a calculated, rational approach. But that's not how the heart works."

He had been rational. Lining out what he should want in a wife, what the farm needed, what Grandmother needed.

But what about what he needed?

"She's different. Not like anyone I ever met before. Not like any of the women in town or at church. You saw how people reacted to the food she made and the fact that she didn't know any of the traditional dances. She couldn't even speak to half the people there because she doesn't know any Swedish."

"And yet she made some new friends, shared her culture, and seemed to enjoy herself. It is not wrong to be different."

"Trudy fit right in without any problems. She is a help in the barn with the milking and the chickens. She already knows everything she will need to know. Maeve's last encounter with a cow might permanently put her off going into the barn, she can't drive a wagon, she has no experience with caring for a garden or the chickens. She's a city girl from Ireland."

"And you are in love with her." Grandmother's eyes were kind as she said aloud what Kaspar hadn't even whispered.

"And she's engaged to someone else. A man who will be expecting her on the train in a week. You saw the letter she got at the picnic. She wandered away and read it, and got all quiet. It must have been some letter. She's probably already got her bags packed." He shook his head, frustrated by the jealousy that welled up in his chest. He had no right to feel jealous. "And I've got Trudy to consider. What kind of man invites a woman to be his wife and then says he's changed his mind? That he prefers someone else?"

"Kaspar, this is the rest of your lives you're talking about. How fair is it to Trudy for you to marry her when you love someone else? Talk to her. Better a broken engagement than a broken marriage."

Grandmother put her hand to her head, her eyes closing.

"Are you all right?" Kaspar leaned forward.

"I just have a bit of a headache. No doubt it was too much sunshine and fresh air." She smiled, but her eyes looked tired. "I will go to bed, but you must go as well. No more brooding. Things will look better in the morning light. They always do."

❧ Chapter 7 ❧

It wasn't just too much sun, as Svea protested when she woke with the same headache that had sent her to bed the previous night. Maeve dipped a cloth in cold water and put it on Svea's feverish forehead.

"You're going to stay in bed, young lassie," she admonished Svea. "Give me a chance to pamper you."

"You have enough work without that. And you already pamper me." Svea's gnarled hand covered the cloth and moved it down over her eyes. "I will be better in a while and come down and help with candling the eggs."

Maeve frowned when she knew Svea wasn't looking. The older woman's fever was no trifle, and as for candling the eggs, Trudy had made it plain that she needed no help with the task. Trudy had made it plain that she had no need of help with *any* task.

"Rest, and I'll bring you some tea in a bit."

She left as quietly as she could, a niggle of worry settling behind her breastbone. Svea was spry enough for her age, but she wasn't strong. Any illness at this point in her life was serious. Maeve hoped she'd be on the mend before the weekend when Maeve's time here would be up.

Trudy looked up from washing the breakfast dishes, then bent her head again when she saw who it was. Maeve sighed. "Svea has a fever this morning. I'm going to brew her some tea."

Trudy's eyes shot up again, this time wide. "Is it bad?" She clutched the dishrag in her hands, making the soap plop into the water. "Ve get a doctor?"

Maeve paused. "I don't think she needs a doctor. So far it's a headache and a bit of a fever. I'll try some tea and see how she feels after a rest."

The Swedish woman sat in the closest chair, her face pale. "I do not like. . .sickness. My family. . .they die of sickness on boat to America. My *mor* and *far* and *bror*. . .brother?" Tears filled her eyes, and Maeve's heart went out to her. She'd lost her entire family. No wonder she hadn't said much about it at the picnic. "I get. . .afraid. . .when there is sickness now." She tangled her fingers together, still wet from the wash water.

"Are you all alone here in America?" *Just like me?*

Trudy nodded. "I vork in restaurant in New York and then hotel in Pitts-borg. Hotel is where I find marrying newspaper and Kaspar's vords. I quit and come when marrying newspaper send me Kaspar's town. I use all my money to come. Hotel vas bad place to vork."

In her own way, she was as desperate as Maeve. She had nowhere else to go. And it was the most she had shared about herself. Maeve nodded to her and set the kettle on the stove. "I am sorry about your family. My father passed away not long after we got to America. As for Svea, I am sure she just needs some rest. If she's not feeling better by tomorrow, perhaps we can send for the doctor."

Lord, please forgive me. I've been so centered on my own situation, I never gave a thought to Trudy's. I've been jealous of her position here as Kaspar's fiancée. She has no other place to go, and though I don't really want it, I do. Mr. Heaslip will send money for me if I let him know I want to come to Chicago. Maeve prayed silently, her heart heavy. Trudy had no other option but to stay here. Maeve should do the right thing and just go in a few days' time.

She went into the pantry and found the small tin of ginger. That would help with Svea's headache.

"Trudy, would you please brew up some tea and add a teaspoon of this. I'll come back with something for the fever." Maeve found the gardening shears in the drawer of the sideboard. Grabbing a shawl from the peg by the door, she tossed it over her head and stepped outside. It had been raining since before breakfast, a steady drizzle, a welcome break in the heat.

In the garden, she walked down the row nearest the fence, where Svea's perennial herbs grew. Svea had told Maeve what each one was and what it was for when they had planted the peas and beans almost a month ago.

Yarrow. There it was. Maeve snipped a few stems, even though the yellow flowers were barely open. A pungent aroma filled her nose. Her mother had used yarrow back in Ireland whenever Maeve had gotten sick with a fever. It didn't taste too good, but it worked.

A low moo from the barn caught her ear. Röd was in the corral, dark red from the rain. Kaspar had not separated the cow from her calf, saying they had enough milk from the three other cows to provide for the calves and the house. Maeve suspected it was because of the affection he had for the cow, since he'd mentioned raising Röd from the time she was a baby. Her calf, a little heifer, lay in a small hollow under the eave of the roof. Maeve shook her head. It would be a long time before she trusted that cow again. Motherhood had made Röd cranky and protective.

Kasper stood in the barn doorway, his hat brim shielding his face. He raised his hand, holding a piece of cloth and a strap of leather, in a wave.

They needed to talk.

Tonight. No excuses. You'll tell him you need to send a wire to Chicago so Mr. Heaslip can send tickets and travel money. You'll do the right thing for Kaspar and Trudy. You never should've come here in the first place, and you need to leave the minute your debt is paid.

She headed back into the house without waving back.

It was the longest day Maeve could remember. Svea slept, her fever reduced by the tea and quiet. Maeve sat by her bed, hemming new tea towels, trying to keep her mind on her stitches but unable to keep reviewing the upcoming conversation in her head.

Kaspar would most likely be relieved. He could get his life back on the rails. She would go to Chicago and meet Mr. Heaslip.

But, she also resolved, if she didn't fancy him as a husband, she would walk away. Surely somewhere in Chicago there would be another domestic position for her, perhaps somewhere that didn't look down on the Irish. She would find a way to save money, and someday she would fulfill her da's dream of owning a bit of American earth. No longer willing to be a victim or afraid of the future, she admitted that leaving Boston and coming to a farm in Kansas had forever changed her.

She was stronger than she thought, braver, smarter. The experience had given her a new perspective and an appreciation for the vastness of her new country. She had fallen in love with a good man. She knew love was possible, and that giving someone your heart meant they had the power to break it.

And she had learned anew that the right thing to do was often the hardest.

Tears blurred her eyes, and she blinked them away. A month ago, she would have acted impulsively, blurting out to Kaspar that she loved him and putting him in a terrible position. She would have grasped at her happiness, not even considering what that might mean to Trudy.

Anyway, Kaspar was probably looking forward to seeing her leave and settling down. And Trudy would welcome her departure too. The only one who would probably miss her was Svea. . .and she could still write to this kind old woman, no matter where Maeve's path took her.

"I will miss you." Svea opened her eyes. "My grandson is a man of honor, but I think it will cost him a heavy price."

Maeve nodded. "I have to go. It's the right thing to do. Trudy needs to stay more than I do. She will fit in here well, and I know that once I'm away, you and she will grow closer. I will wire Mr. Heaslip tomorrow. Edvin will take the message to town for me, I am sure."

Svea sighed. "God bless you, child. I will pray for you, that He will make His way plain and will bless you."

Please, Lord, answer her prayers.

Kaspar scowled at the rain that kept him inside with too much time to think. The weather must be affecting Edvin too, because the normally easygoing hired man had been sullen and snappish all day.

The tack room had gotten too small for the two of them, so Kaspar had led one of the colts into the aisle of the barn, cross-tied him, and begun grooming him from nose to tail. He'd gotten behind on training, so today would be a good day to handle him, maybe even put a harness on him to let him get used to it.

Long strokes with the brush soothed Kaspar's temper a bit. He didn't even know why he was mad, except that nothing had gone the way he'd planned, not since the minute he'd looked into the eyes of an Irish beauty at the train station.

The colt tucked one hind foot up and closed his eyes.

Edvin stomped out of the tack room where he'd been repairing a halter, glared at Kaspar, turned on his heel, and headed outside toward the house. Kaspar frowned but shrugged. Everyone was entitled to a bad day now and again. He had enough to think about without worrying about his hired man's moods.

Rain drummed harder on the barn roof, and Kaspar's arm began to burn. Deciding he couldn't take another minute of the indecision and procrastination, he threw the brush into the grooming box and returned the colt to his stall. Training could wait for a better day and a better frame of mind.

He splashed through the puddles in the farmyard and shoved aside the picket gate. Rain pattered on his hat brim, wetting his shirt, chilling his skin, but he didn't care. He didn't care about much of anything right now.

When he opened the kitchen door, Edvin and Trudy were there—and they sprang apart with a guilty start.

Kaspar stood with his hand on the doorknob, his mind blank. Trudy had tears tracking down her cheeks, and Edvin's face was red as an apple.

"What's going on here?"

Edvin's hands fisted, and he stepped in front of Trudy. "Boss, I've been telling Trudy we need to come clean. You deserve the truth."

"Which is?" Kaspar's voice seemed to come from a long distance.

Edvin swallowed, and he took a deep breath. Trudy's hand came to rest on his shoulder, and before he could speak, she blurted out in Swedish, "I am so sorry, Kaspar. I did not mean for this to happen. *We* didn't mean for this to happen. I have fallen in love with Edvin."

The hired man covered her hand with his, drawing it down and lacing their fingers so they stood side by side. "Boss, I love Trudy, and I know you don't. I know you two have an understanding, but I don't care. I fell in love the minute I saw her, and I mean to have her for my wife. If that means I can't work for you anymore, I understand, but you need to know the truth. If you marry her, I can't work here anymore anyway."

Kaspar looked from one to the other. Trudy had eyes only for Edvin, her expression soft, maybe a little fearful, but full of love. How had he missed that? He'd been so caught up in his own misery that he'd missed his sort-of fiancée falling in love with his employee? He rubbed his palm on the back of his neck, knocking his hat so that a stream of water fell over the front brim. He took off the hat and dropped it onto a peg without even looking.

"You two are in love, and you want to get married?"

"Yes." Edvin's chin went up, but he looked at Trudy with pride and love.

Kaspar felt as if he'd missed a stair in the dark. This explained Edvin's mood and Trudy's unwillingness to warm up to Kaspar. If they had fallen in love when they first met, they must have been as miserable as he was at the situation.

"We don't mean to upset you, but I know you only sent for a bride to help with your grandmother. Trudy will still do that, at least for a while, until we start having little ones of our own." Edvin's blush deepened. "That will give you time to figure something out."

Trudy nudged his arm and shook her head, whispering something in his ear that Kaspar couldn't make out. All he knew was that he felt as if a ton weight had been shoved off his shoulders.

Edvin and Trudy. In love. Married.

Which meant he was a free man.

His heart soared right up to the sky—and came crashing down again when he realized that though he might be free, Maeve was not. She was engaged.

"You both have my blessing. I'll not hold you back."

Trudy gave a squeak, and Edvin's arms came around her, lifting her and twirling her in a small circle, bumping into a chair and the table in their exuberance. "Thank you, Boss."

Kaspar turned away, and his eyes locked with Maeve's. She stood on the bottom stair, a pitcher in her hand and bewilderment on her face. He realized that he and Edvin and Trudy had all been speaking Swedish, and she'd understood nothing.

The pitcher lowered, and he was afraid it might slip from her fingers, so he stepped close and took the porcelain vessel and set it on the step.

"What's going on?" Her red brows tucked toward one another.

"Let's go outside. We need to talk." He took her hand, thrilling to how small and dainty it felt in his, and tugged her toward the door.

"It's raining," she protested.

"We'll stay on the porch." He didn't miss the grins on Edvin's and Trudy's faces as he closed the door, but it was too soon to celebrate anything.

He might still find himself putting Maeve on a train in five days' time.

"What is going on?" she asked again when they stood alone on the front porch. Water streamed off the roof, creating a curtain that closed them in.

"Edvin and Trudy are going to get married." He shoved his hands into his pockets to stop himself from grabbing her up. "They've fallen in love, and I've given them my blessing."

She looked so adorably puzzled, he couldn't resist. He took her hands in his.

"Maeve, I know I've no right to ask, but Edvin and Trudy have given me the idea that some plain speaking might work out best for all of us. I know you answered that fellow up in Chicago's advertisement, and that he's expecting you to show up there, and you have every right to go, but you can't leave without knowing that. . ." A lump had formed in his throat as all his feelings clogged there, trying to get out.

"What?" She squeezed his hands. "Without knowing what?"

"That I love you. That I want you to stay. That I want to marry you." He shook his head. "I shouldn't even be asking, when I know you're spoken for, but I would regret it my whole life if I didn't say something."

She stared so hard at him, he felt as if she could see right down into the deepest parts of his heart. But she said nothing, and doubts began to grow. Had he read her wrong? Was she counting the days until she could leave, to head to a sophisticated city, with a successful businessman waiting to marry her, someone from her own country?

At last she spoke. "I have been gathering my courage to speak to you all day." She blinked, and for a moment, he couldn't breathe. "When I first showed up, and I got that telegram from Mr. Heaslip. . ." Her tongue came out to touch her lips. "He told me not to come, that he had found another woman he wanted to marry. I was so ashamed, so afraid of being destitute, that I didn't tell you." She looked down but then seemed to take hold of herself to be brave. "I talked you into letting me come here to work off the train fare I had used, but really, I just needed a bit of time to decide what to do next."

"So you're not engaged to Mr. Heaslip?" The shocks just kept on coming. "He married someone else?"

She shook her head. "No, he didn't marry her after all. And he wrote again, inviting me to come if I was still interested, but said that if I wasn't, he would understand."

All around him water splashed and puddled, ran and collected, and he couldn't find a drop of moisture for his own mouth. His entire future hung on the answer to his next question.

"And are you? Interested?"

Without hesitation, she shook her head. "Not in the least."

Then his arms were around her, and he was kissing her, and he wasn't sure if the vibrations under his feet were from thunder or the love that crashed through him.

When he needed to breathe, he broke the kiss and trailed his lips along her temple, relishing the texture of her red curls against his lips. "Maeve, I thought I would have to let you go."

She tightened her hold on him, pressing into his chest. "I thought I would have to leave." She pulled back to look into his eyes. "Tell me that you're sure. I'm not anything that you advertised for. I don't know Swedish, and I'm afraid of cows and horses, and I don't know how to can or preserve. I've never lived on a farm. I don't know that I'll make a good farmer's wife."

He laughed, hugging her, his joy overflowing. "Ah, *älskling*—there, a Swedish word for you to learn. It means 'darling,' and I'm going to be using it constantly." He threaded his fingers into her hair, not caring that he was messing up her braid. "I think you'll make a wonderful farmer's wife." His lips came down on hers again.

Eventually, he led her over to Svea's big rocking chair beside the door and pulled her down into his lap. She rested her head on his shoulder, and he thought he would never be as content as he was at that moment.

"I was coming downstairs to tell you that Svea's fever has broken, and that she is feeling much better." Her hand rested over his heart as she spoke against his collar. "I told her she had to stay in bed the rest of the day, but that she could be up and around a bit tomorrow. I do love your grandmother. It won't be a burden at all to care for her."

"You can cook, clean, and do laundry. You are learning to garden, you can dance a jig, and you already love my grandmother." He kissed her cheek, marveling in the freedom to do so, inhaling the scent of ginger and herbs and whatever it was that was uniquely Maeve. "If word gets out about you, all the single men I know will be booking a passage to Galway to get an Irish lass for themselves."

"Wouldn't it be easier to just advertise in the *Matrimonial News*?" She giggled, nuzzling his neck and sending a shiver down his spine.

"Ah, that paper. I would've sold it for a dollar when you first stepped off the train, but now I bless the person who made the mistake of sending you my letter."

"I think I will scare up a copy of your advertisement and cut it out as a keepsake. We can tell our grandchildren the story."

He hugged her tight. Grandchildren.

Someday.

But for now he was content to have his Galway girl.

Erica Vetsch is a transplanted Kansan now residing in Minnesota. She loves books and history, and is blessed to be able to combine the two by writing historical romances. Whenever she's not following flights of fancy in her fictional world, she's the company bookkeeper for the family lumber business, mother of two, an avid museum patron, and wife to a man who is her total opposite and soul mate. Erica loves to hear from readers. You can sign up for her quarterly newsletter at www.ericavetsch.com.

You can email her at ericavetsch@gmail.com or contact her on her author Facebook page.